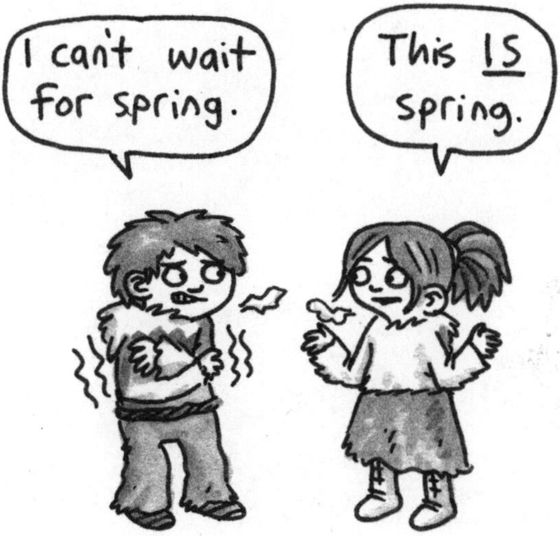
I can't wait for spring.
This IS spring.

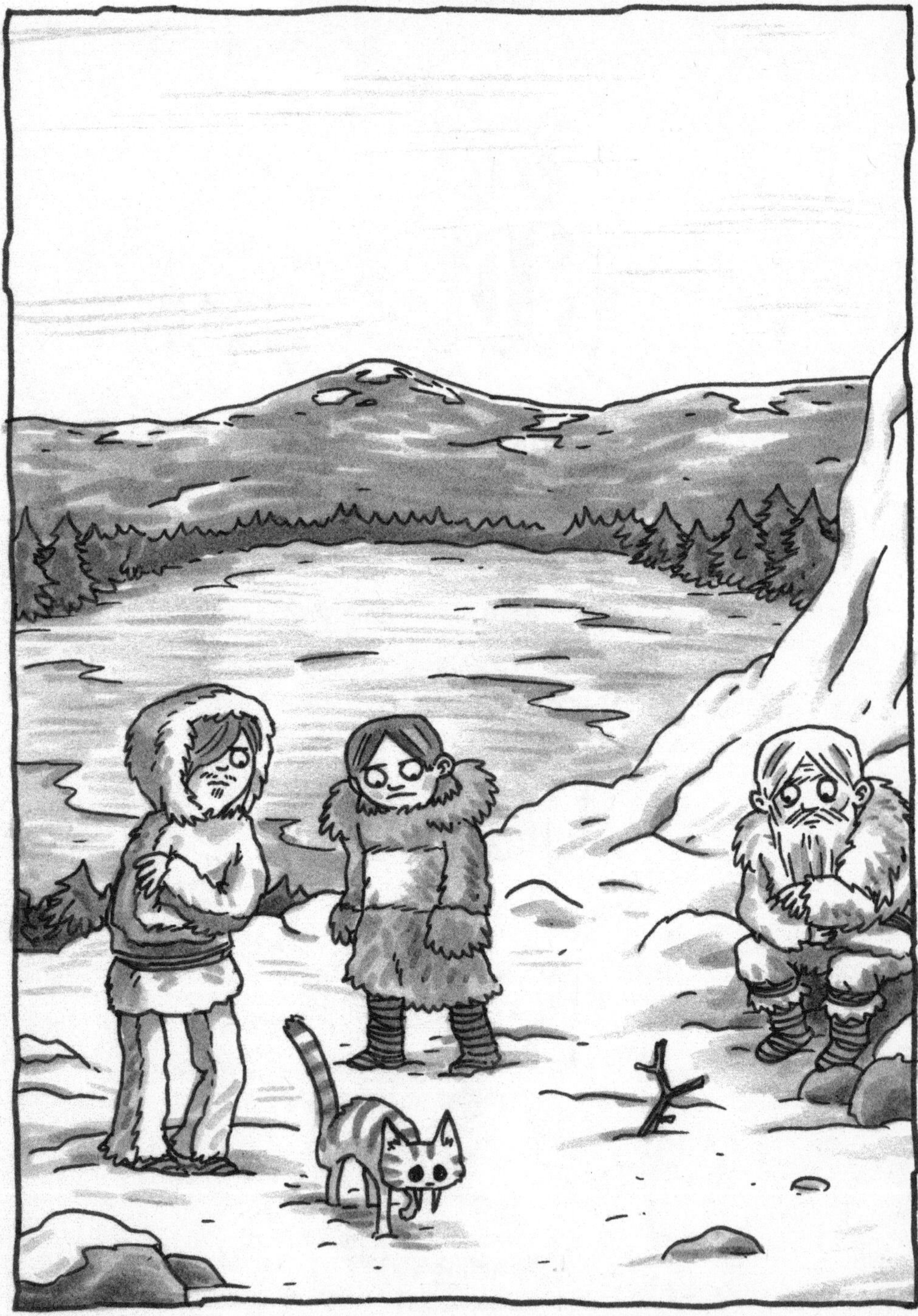

LUCY & ANDY NEANDERTHAL

THE STONE COLD AGE

Jeffrey Brown

A Yearling Book

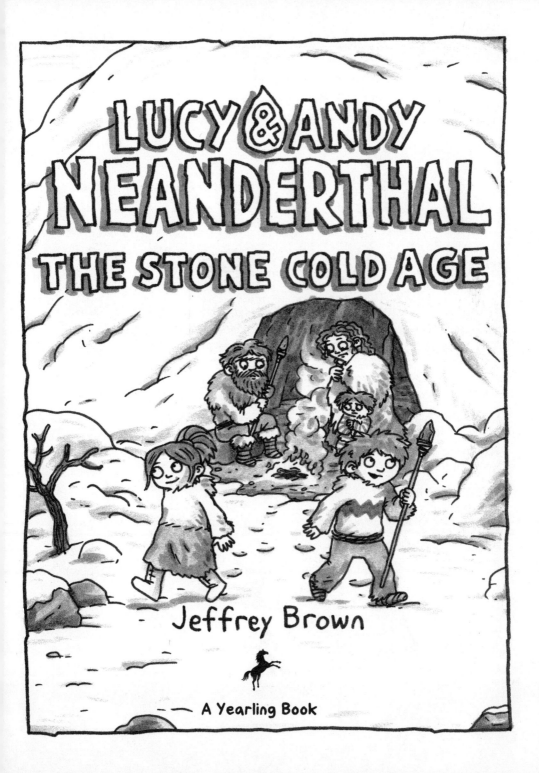

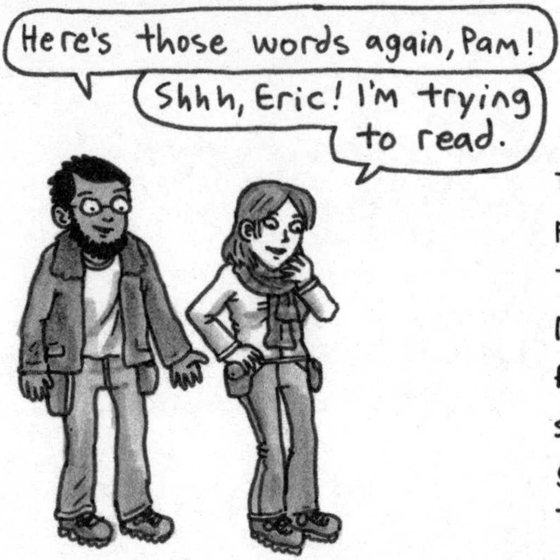
Here's those words again, Pam!
Shhh, Eric! I'm trying to read.

Thank you to my family, friends, publishers, and readers for all of their support. Thanks also to Marc, Phoebe, and everyone at RH for making this book happen. And special thanks to Kevin Lee for giving me the nudge that led to the idea for this series.

For his expert assistance, grateful acknowledgment to Jonathan S. Mitchell, PhD, Evolutionary Biology, and member of the Geological Society of America, Sociaty of Vertebrate Paleontology, and Society for the Study of Evolution.

This is a work of fiction. Names, characters, places, and incidents either are the product of the author's imagination or are used fictitiously. Any resemblance to actual persons, living or dead, events, or locales is entirely coincidental.

Visit us on the Web! rhcbooks.com
Educators and librarians, for a variety of teaching tools, visit us at RHTeachersLibrarians.com

Library of Congress Cataloging-in-Publication Data is available upon request.
ISBN 978-0-385-38838-2 (trade) — ISBN 978-0-385-38840-5 (lib. bdg.) — ISBN 978-0-385-38839-9 (ebook) — ISBN 978-0-525-64398-2 (pbk.)

Printed in the United States of America
10 9 8 7 6 5 4 3 2
First Yearling Edition 2018

Random House Children's Books supports the First Amendment and celebrates the right to read.

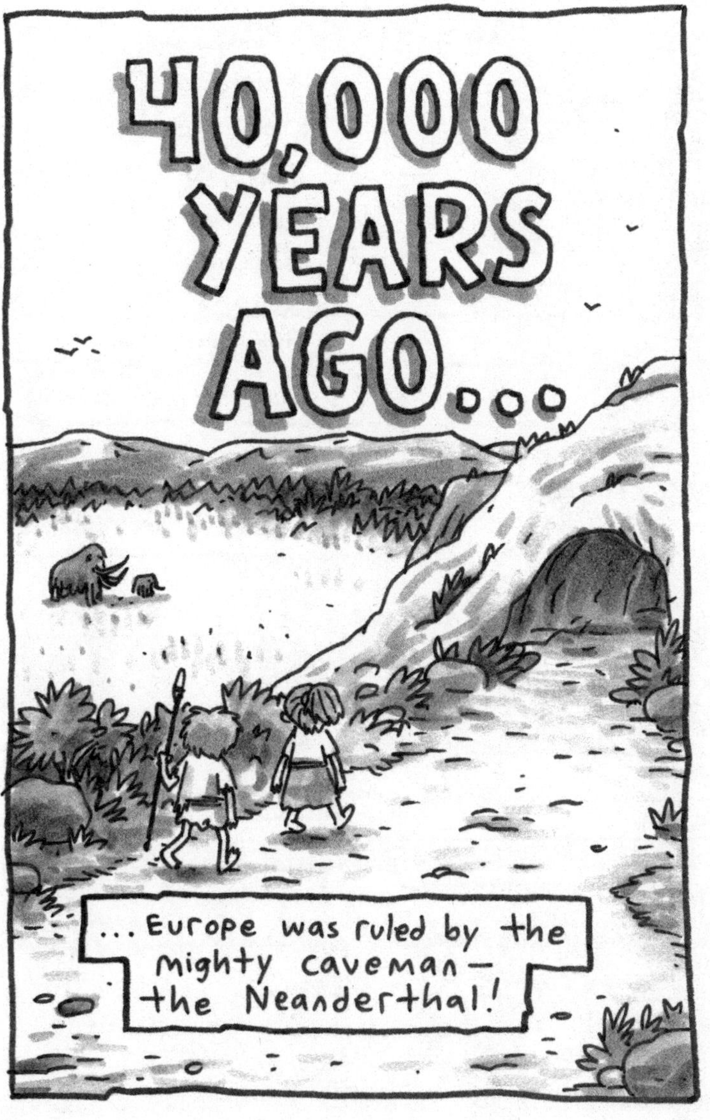
40,000 YEARS AGO...
...Europe was ruled by the mighty caveman— the Neanderthal!

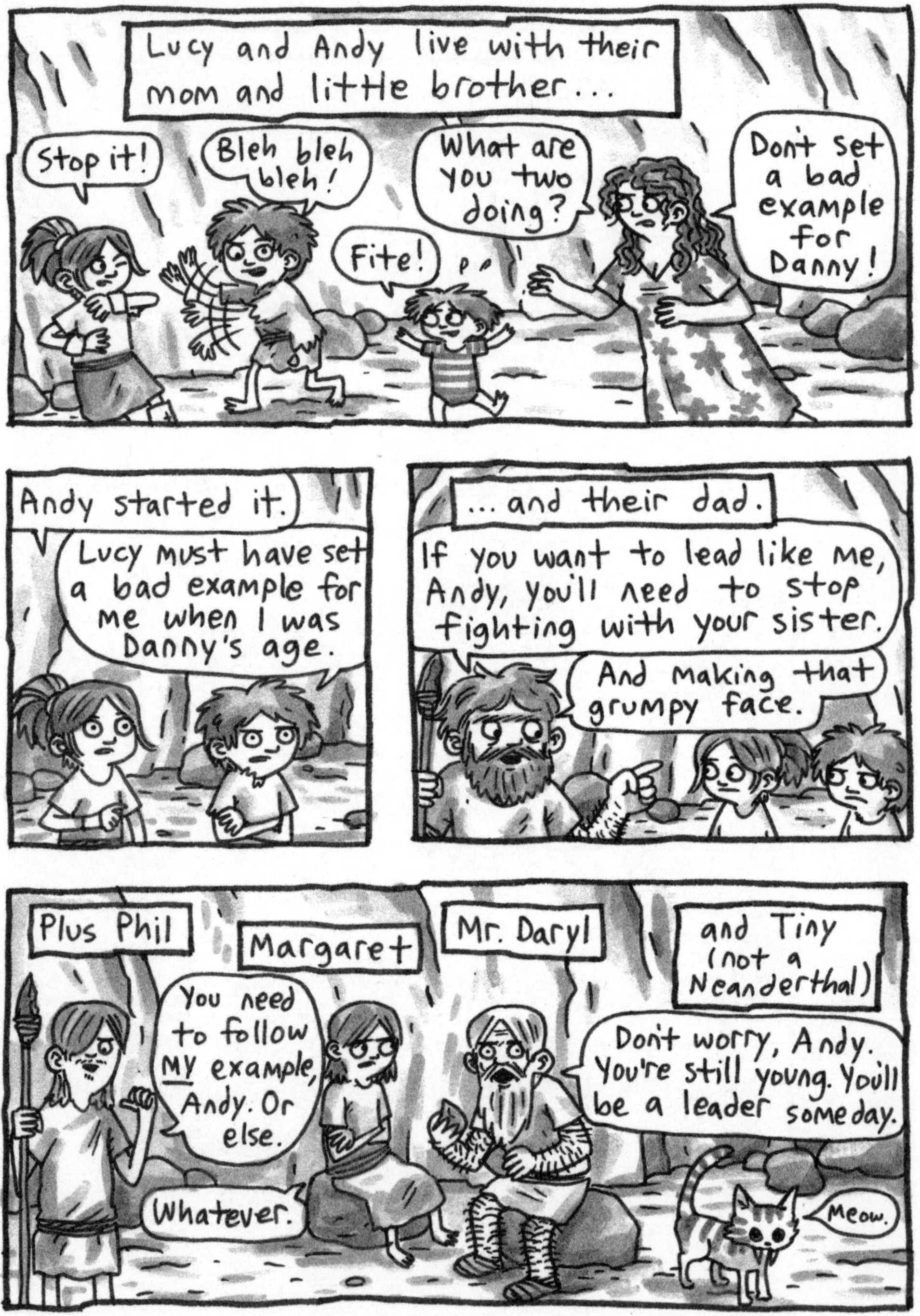
Lucy and Andy live with their mom and little brother...
Stop it!
Bleh bleh bleh!
What are you two doing?
Fite!
Don't set a bad example for Danny!
Andy started it.
Lucy must have set a bad example for me when I was Danny's age.
...and their dad.
If you want to lead like me, Andy, you'll need to stop fighting with your sister.
And making that grumpy face.
Plus Phil
Margaret
Mr. Daryl
and Tiny (not a Neanderthal)
You need to follow MY example, Andy. Or else.
Whatever.
Don't worry, Andy. You're still young. You'll be a leader someday.
Meow.

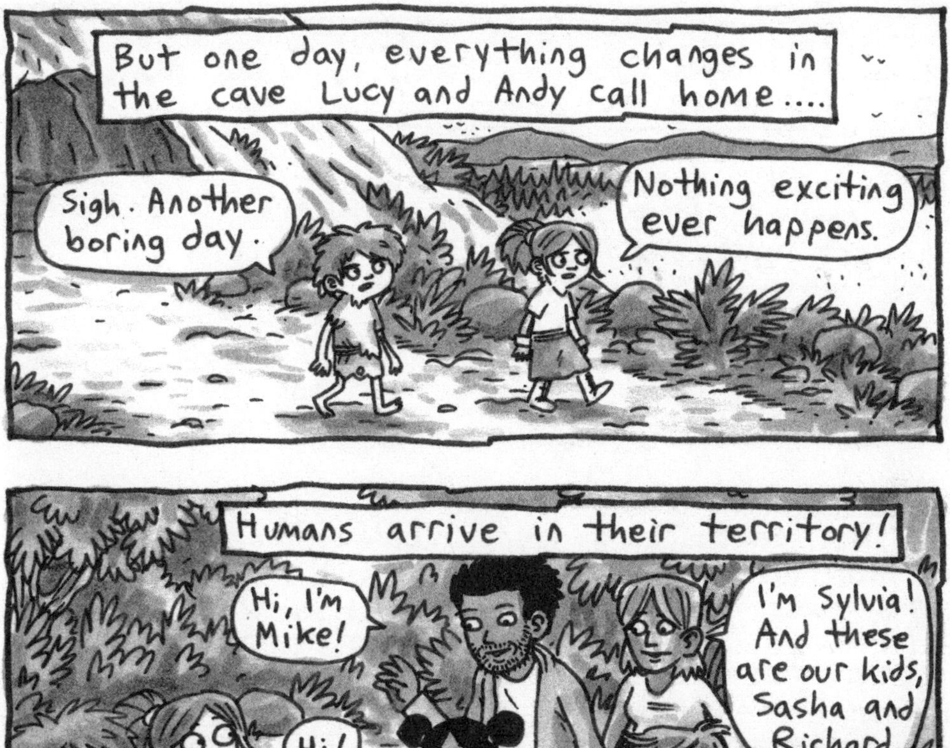
But one day, everything changes in the cave Lucy and Andy call home....
Sigh. Another boring day.
Nothing exciting ever happens.
Humans arrive in their territory!
Hi, I'm Mike!
I'm Sylvia! And these are our kids, Sasha and Richard.
Hi!
'Sup.
Joe
A whole clan of humans!
Wendy
Chris
Gerald
Gina
Claire
Bones (not a human)
Tommy
Jamie
Kathy
Chuck

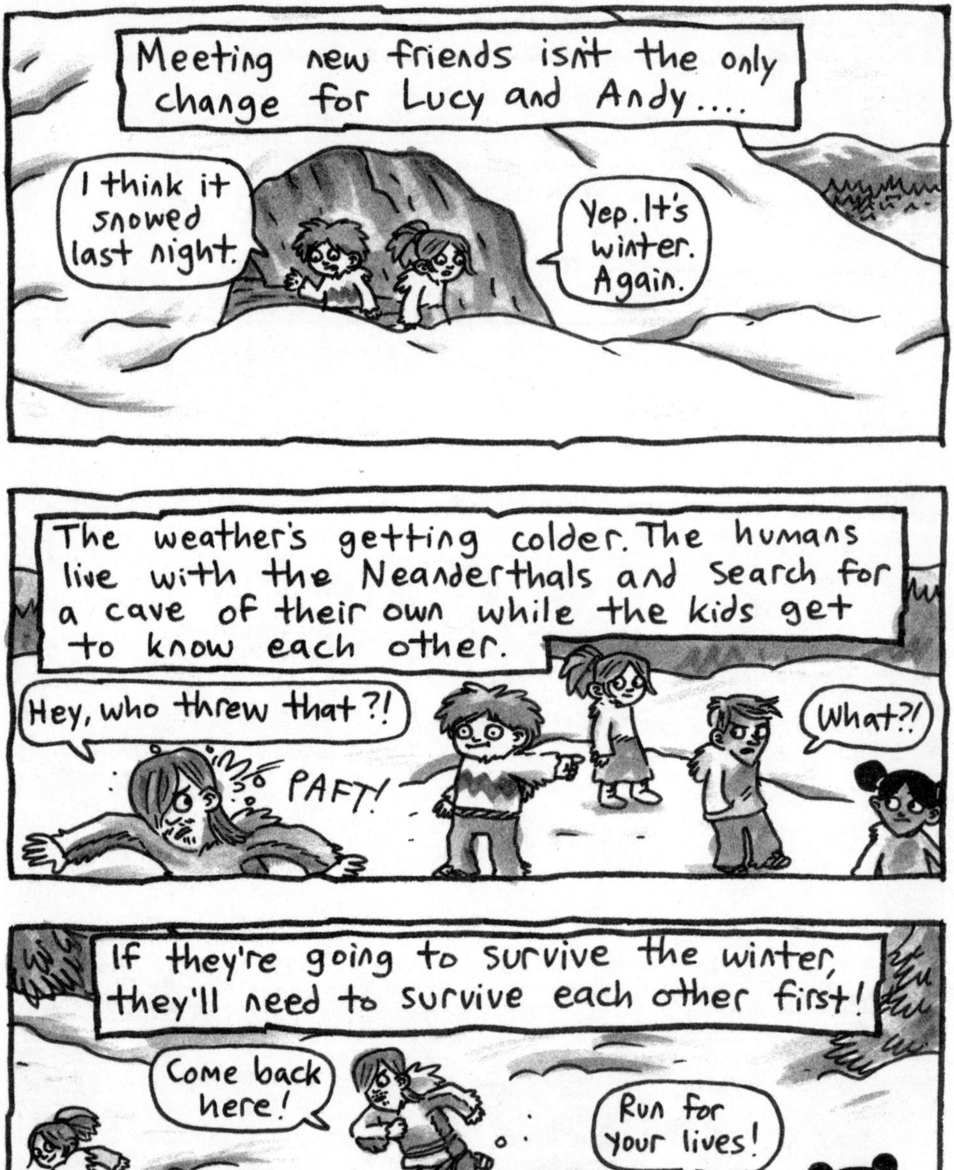
Meeting new friends isn't the only change for Lucy and Andy....
I think it snowed last night.
Yep. It's winter. Again.
The weather's getting colder. The humans live with the Neanderthals and search for a cave of their own while the kids get to know each other.
Hey, who threw that?!
PAFT!
What?!
If they're going to survive the winter, they'll need to survive each other first!
Come back here!
Run for your lives!

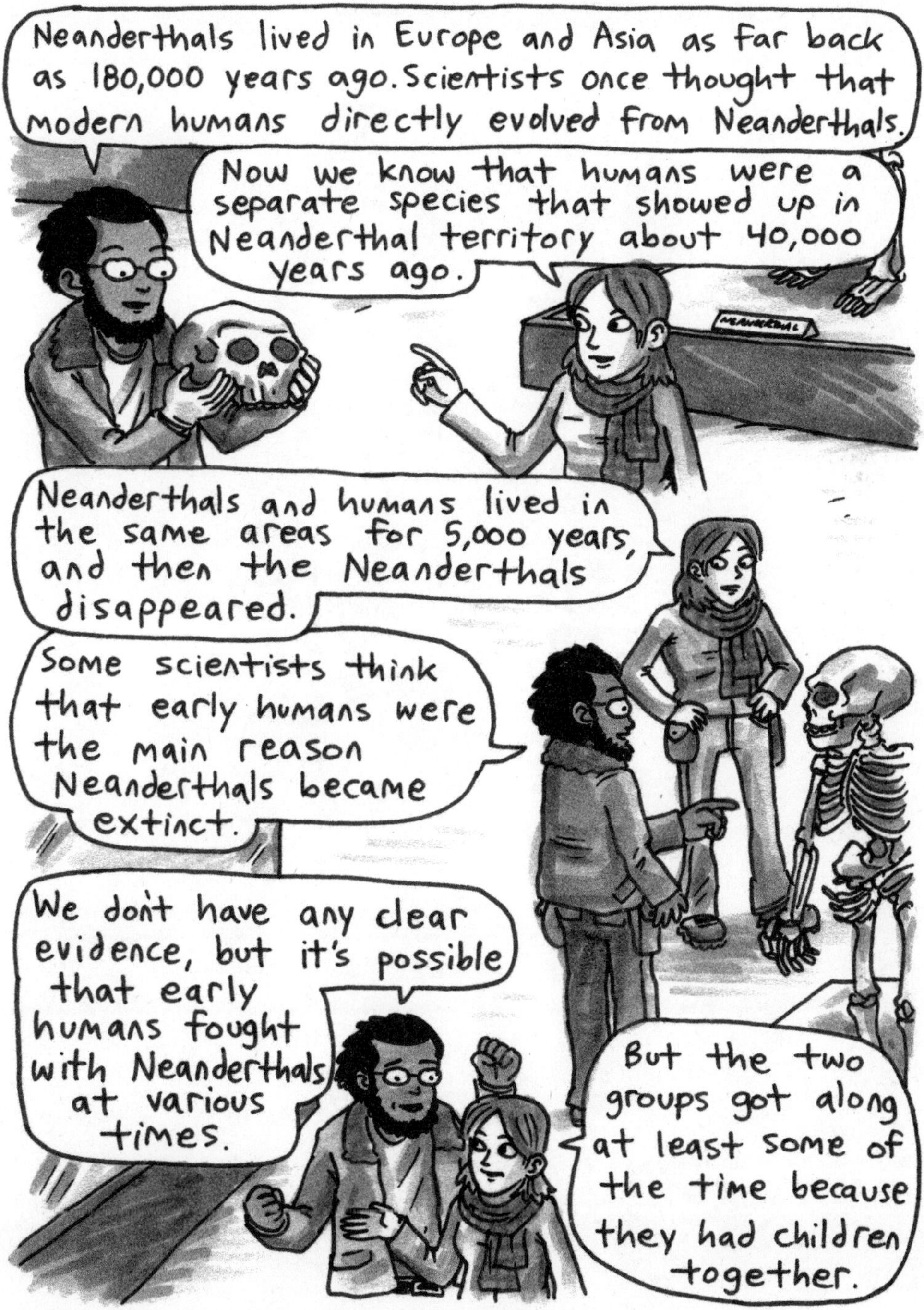
Neanderthals lived in Europe and Asia as far back as 180,000 years ago. Scientists once thought that modern humans directly evolved from Neanderthals.
Now we know that humans were a separate species that showed up in Neanderthal territory about 40,000 years ago.
Neanderthals and humans lived in the same areas for 5,000 years, and then the Neanderthals disappeared.
Some scientists think that early humans were the main reason Neanderthals became extinct.
We don't have any clear evidence, but it's possible that early humans fought with Neanderthals at various times.
But the two groups got along at least some of the time because they had children together.

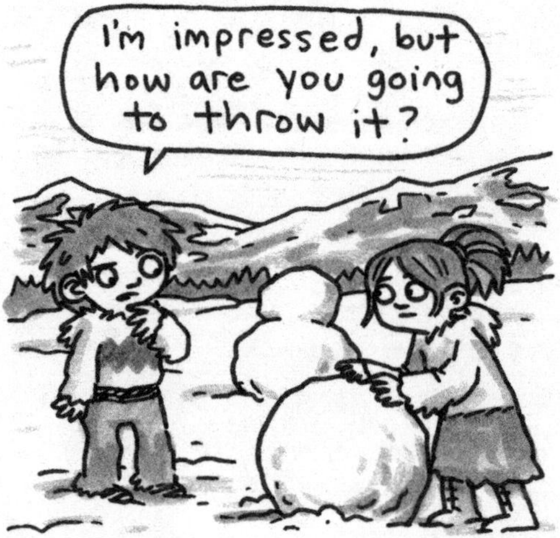
I'm impressed, but how are you going to throw it?

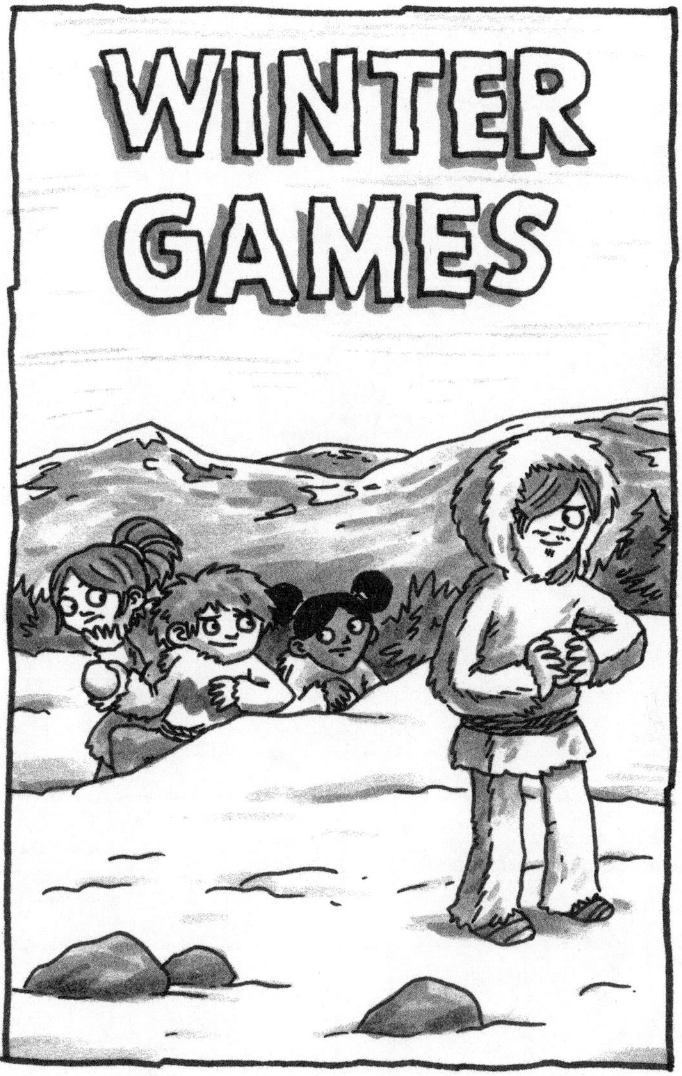
WINTER
GAMES

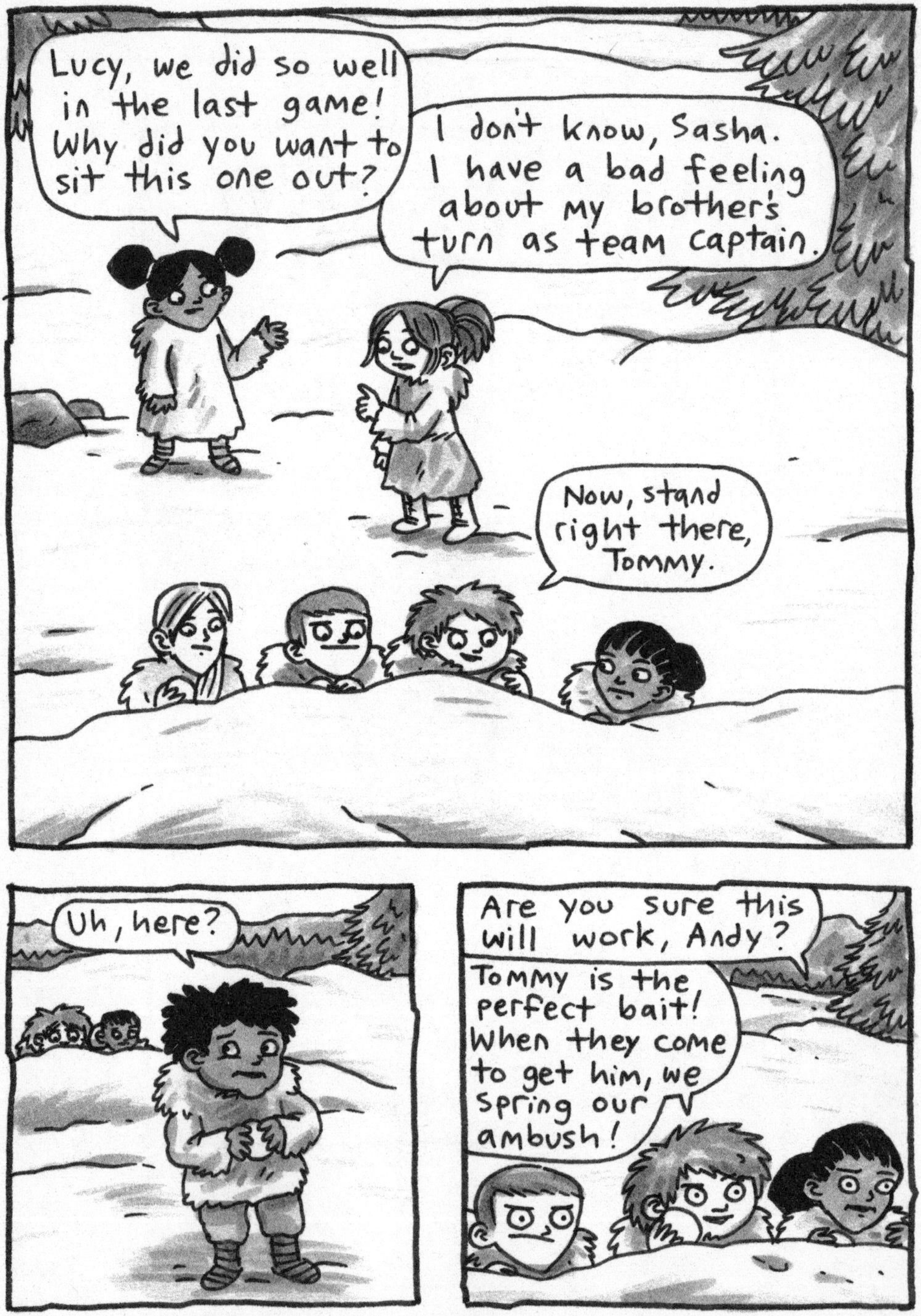
Lucy, we did so well in the last game! Why did you want to sit this one out?
I don't know, Sasha. I have a bad feeling about my brother's turn as team captain.
Now, stand right there, Tommy.
Uh, here?
Are you sure this will work, Andy?
Tommy is the perfect bait! When they come to get him, we spring our ambush!

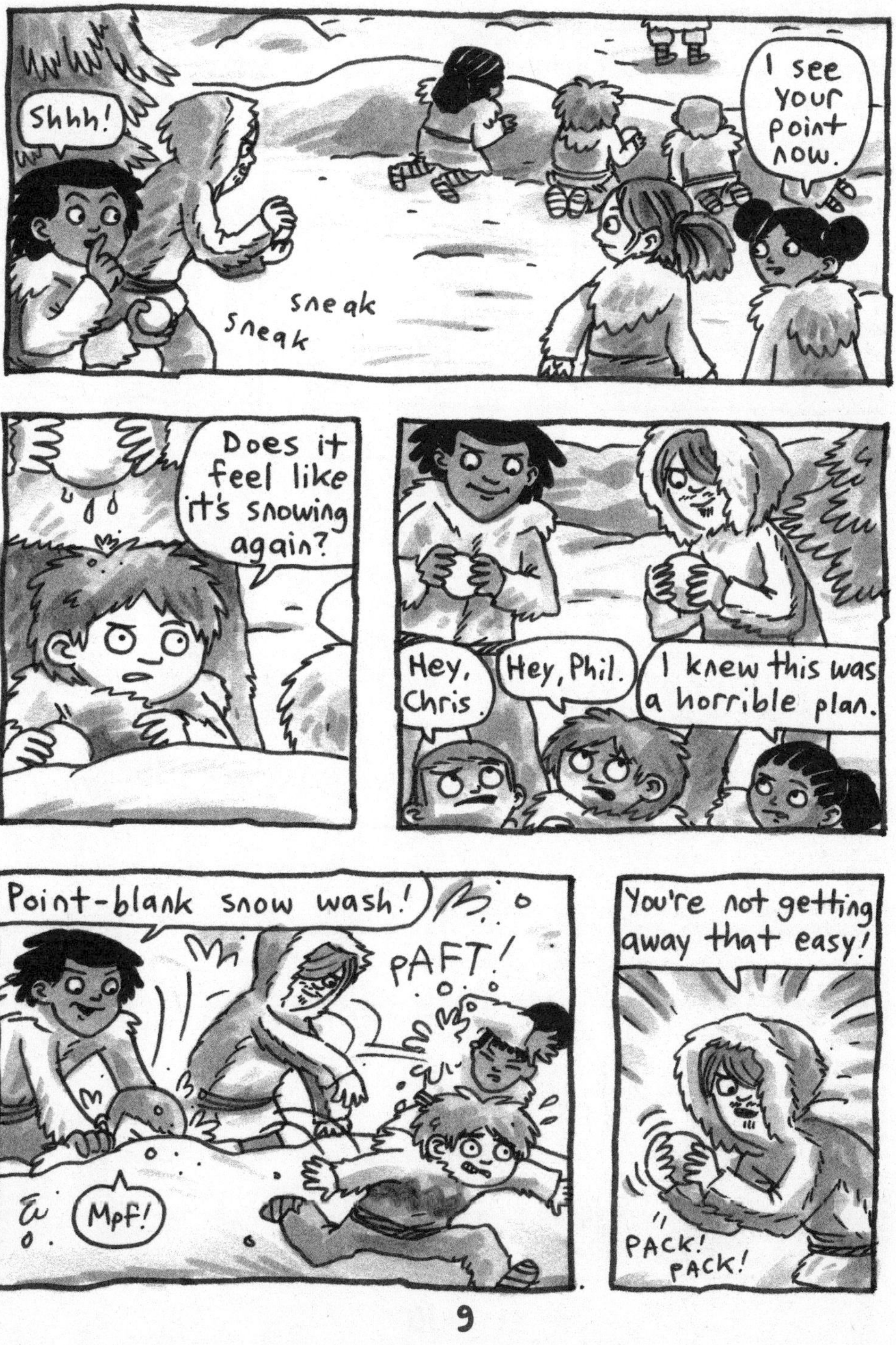

Shhh!
sneak
Sneak
I see your point now.
Does it feel like it's snowing again?
Hey, Chris.
Hey, Phil.
I knew this was a horrible plan.
Point-blank snow wash!
PAFT!
Mpf!
You're not getting away that easy!
PACK!
PACK!

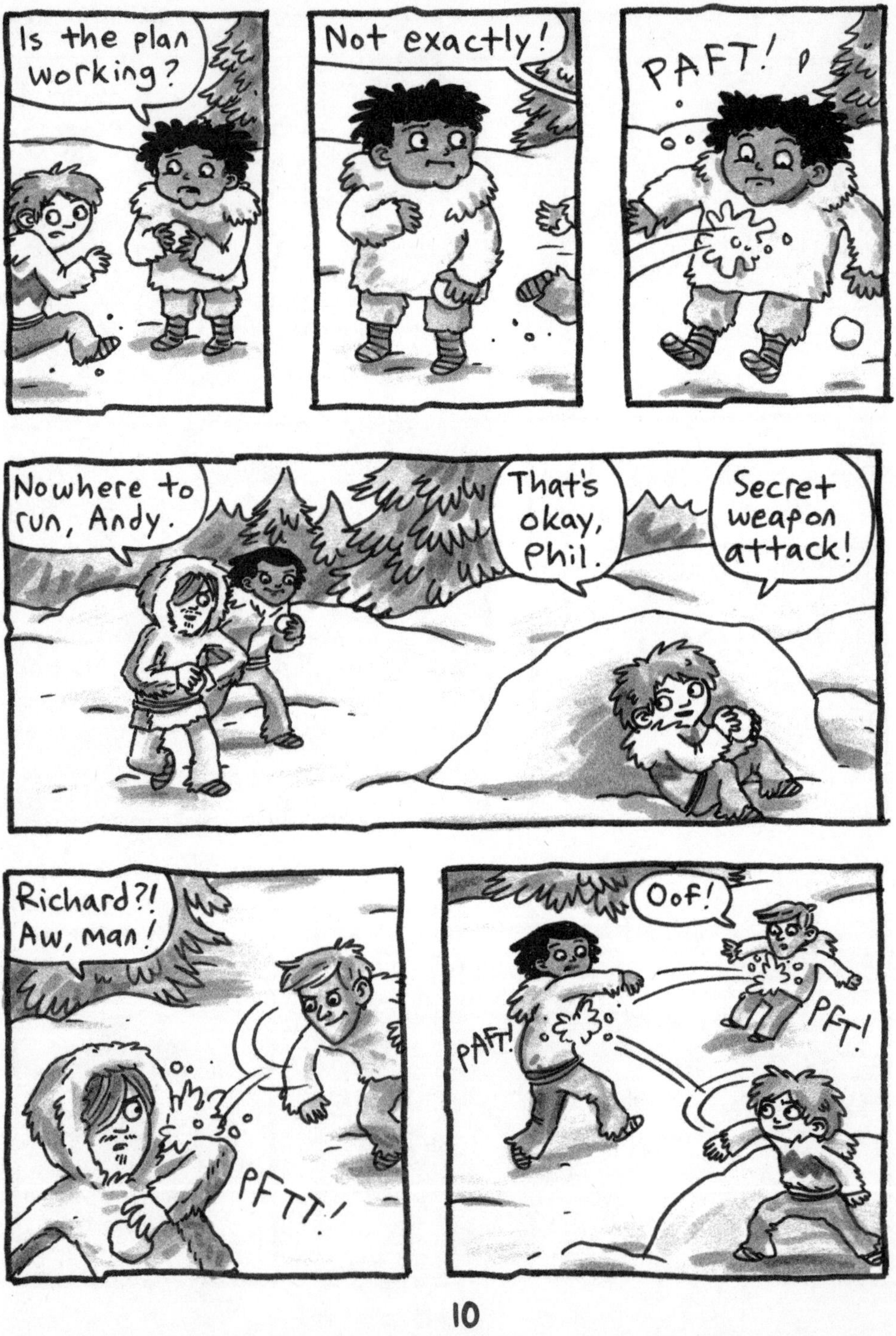
Is the plan working?
Not exactly!
PAFT!
Nowhere to run, Andy.
That's okay, Phil.
Secret weapon attack!
Richard?! Aw, man!
PFTT!
Oof!
PAFT!
PFT!

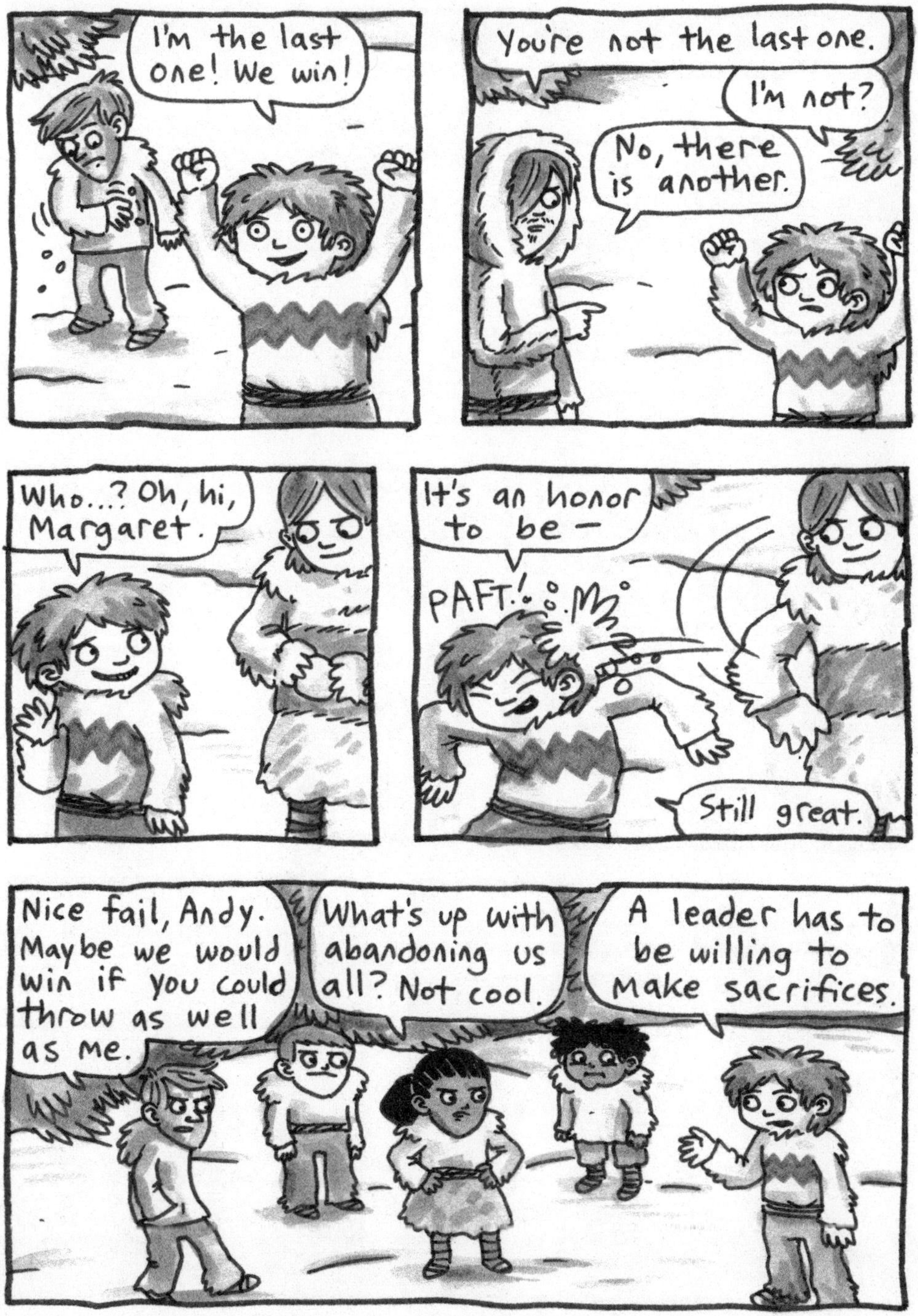
I'm the last one! We win!
You're not the last one.
I'm not?
No, there is another.
Who...? Oh, hi, Margaret.
It's an honor to be—
PAFT!
Still great.
Nice fail, Andy. Maybe we would win if you could throw as well as me.
What's up with abandoning us all? Not cool.
A leader has to be willing to make sacrifices.

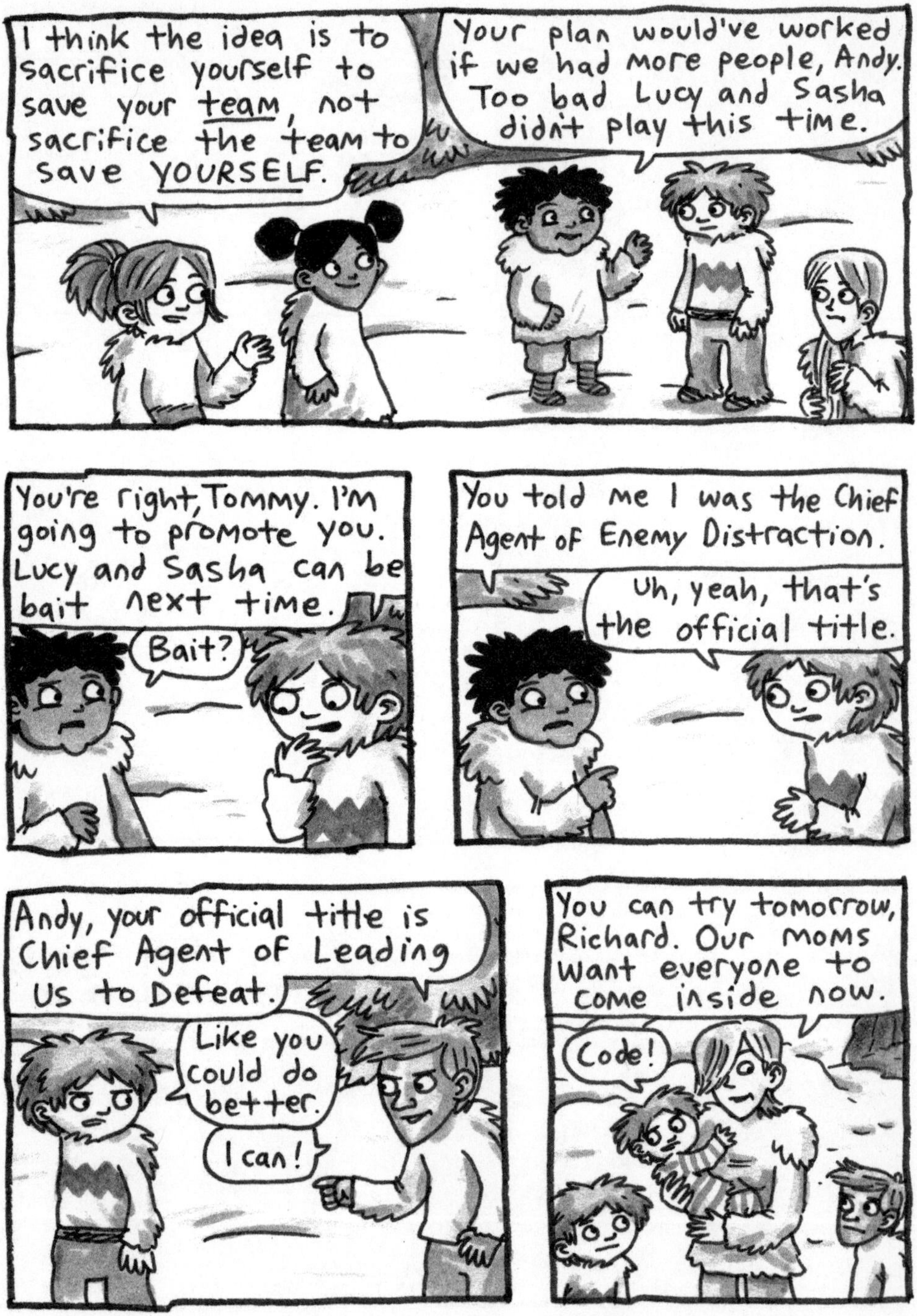
I think the idea is to sacrifice yourself to save your team, not sacrifice the team to save YOURSELF.
Your plan would've worked if we had more people, Andy. Too bad Lucy and Sasha didn't play this time.
You're right, Tommy. I'm going to promote you. Lucy and Sasha can be bait next time.
Bait?
You told me I was the Chief Agent of Enemy Distraction.
Uh, yeah, that's the official title.
Andy, your official title is Chief Agent of Leading Us to Defeat.
Like you could do better.
I can!
You can try tomorrow, Richard. Our moms want everyone to come inside now.
Code!

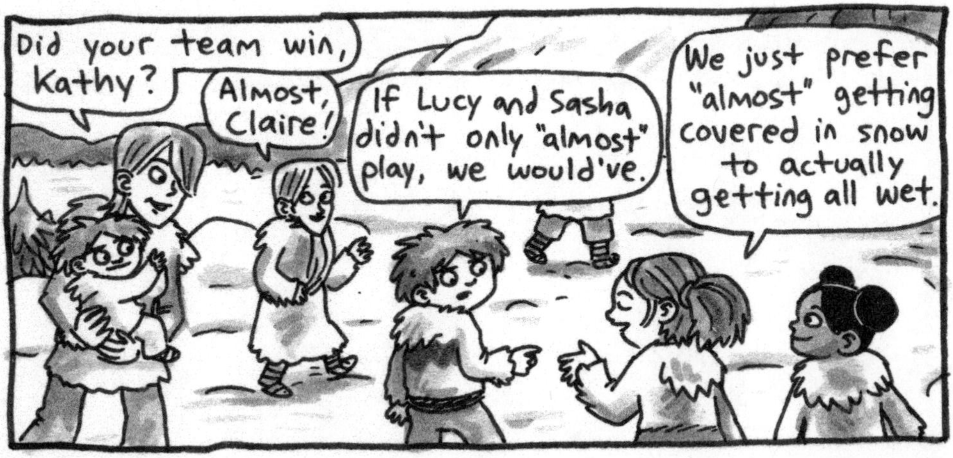
Did your team win, Kathy?
Almost, Claire!
If Lucy and Sasha didn't only "almost" play, we would've.
We just prefer "almost" getting covered in snow to actually getting all wet.

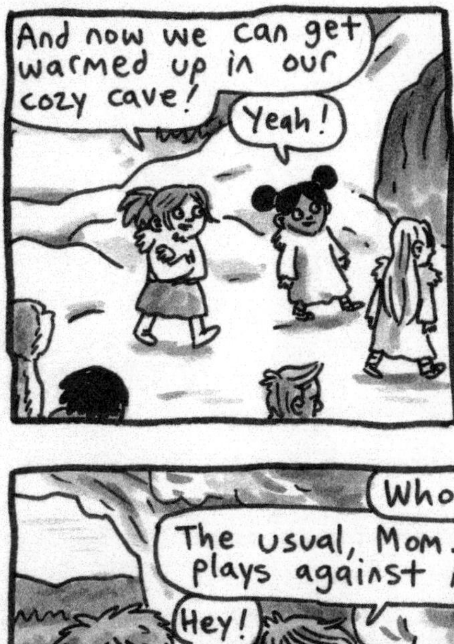
And now we can get warmed up in our cozy cave!
Yeah!

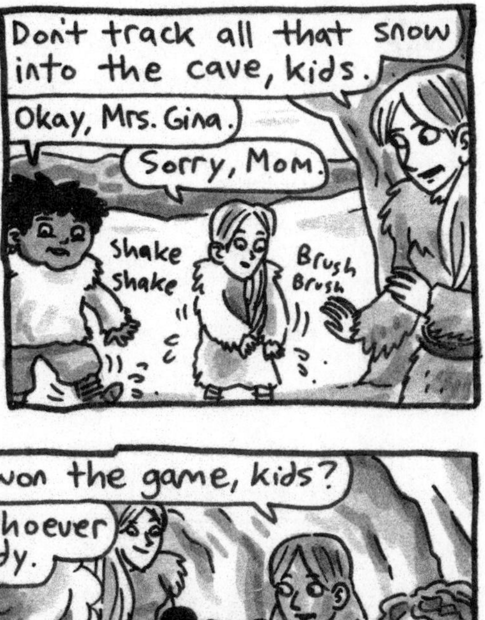
Don't track all that snow into the cave, kids.
Okay, Mrs. Gina.
Sorry, Mom.
Shake Shake
Brush Brush

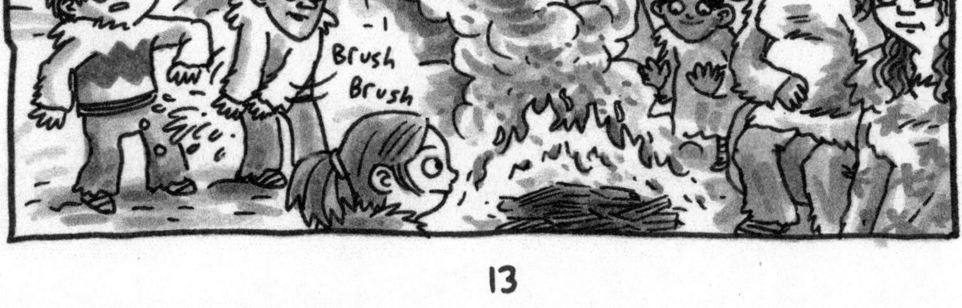
Who won the game, kids?
The usual, Mom. Whoever plays against Andy.
Hey!
Brush Brush

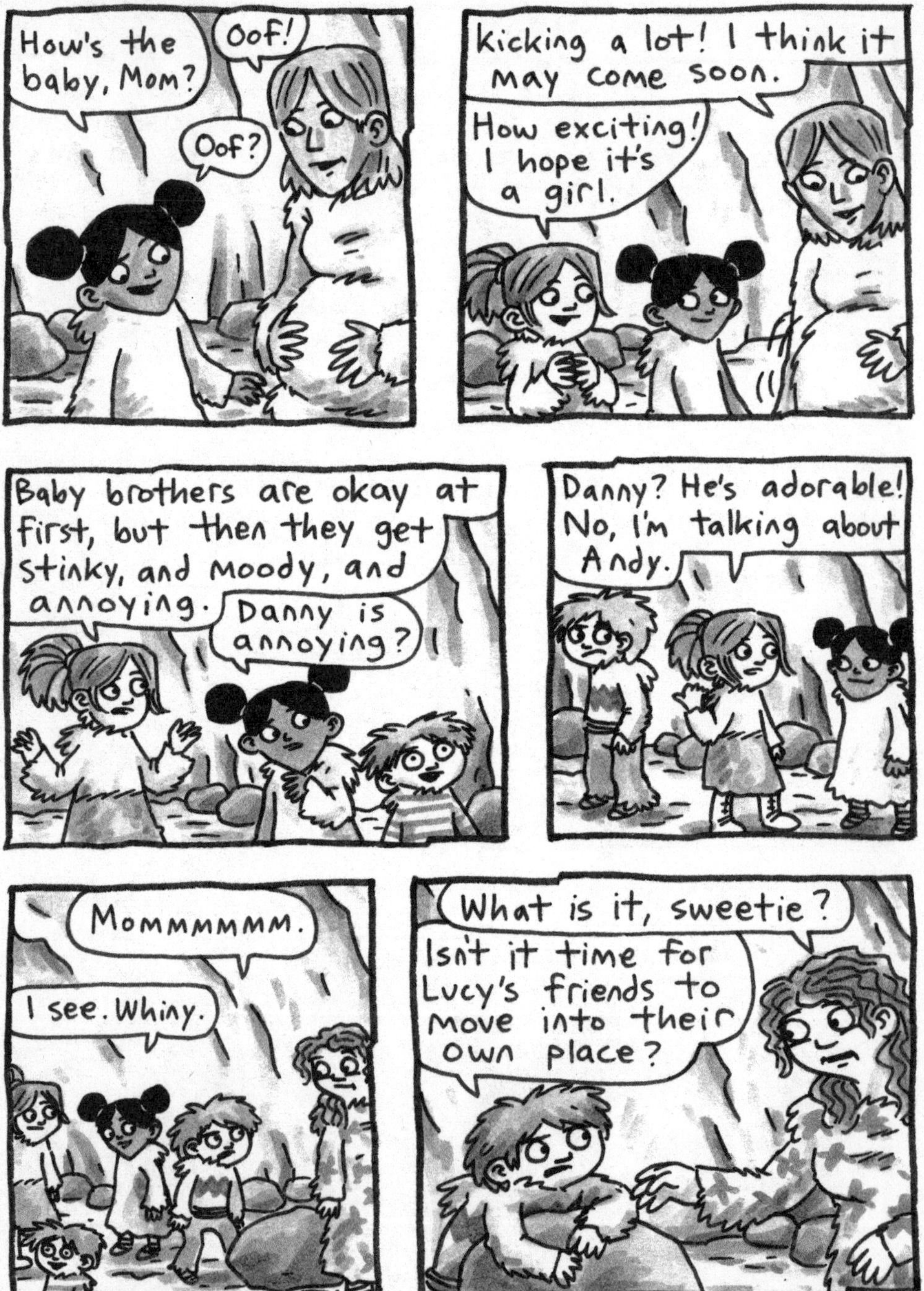
How's the baby, Mom?
Oof!
Oof?
Kicking a lot! I think it may come soon.
How exciting! I hope it's a girl.
Baby brothers are okay at first, but then they get stinky, and moody, and annoying.
Danny is annoying?
Danny? He's adorable! No, I'm talking about Andy.
Mommmmmm.
I see. Whiny.
What is it, sweetie?
Isn't it time for Lucy's friends to move into their own place?

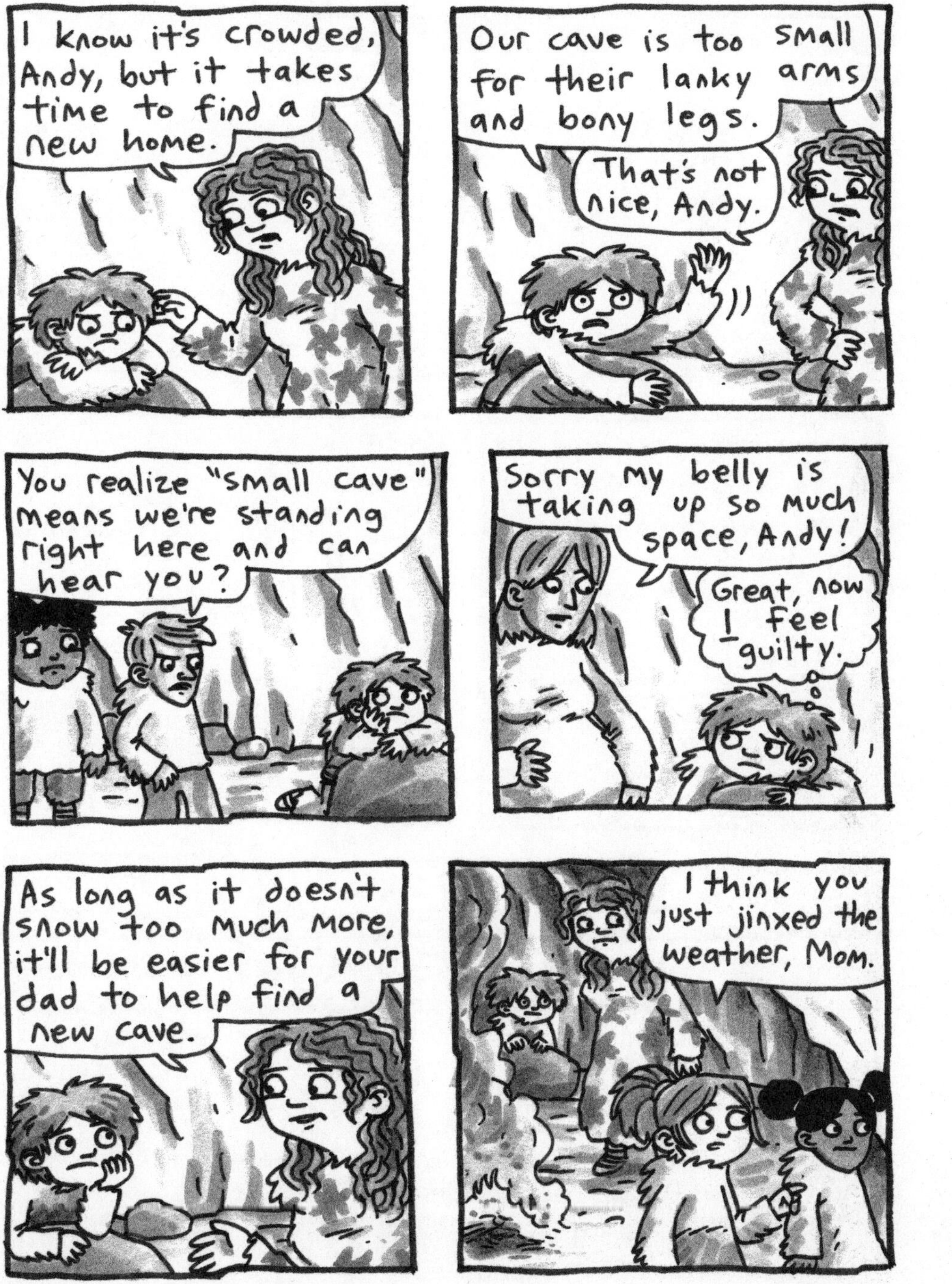
I know it's crowded, Andy, but it takes time to find a new home.
Our cave is too small for their lanky arms and bony legs.
That's not nice, Andy.
You realize "small cave" means we're standing right here and can hear you?
Sorry my belly is taking up so much space, Andy!
Great, now I feel guilty.
As long as it doesn't snow too much more, it'll be easier for your dad to help find a new cave.
I think you just jinxed the weather, Mom.

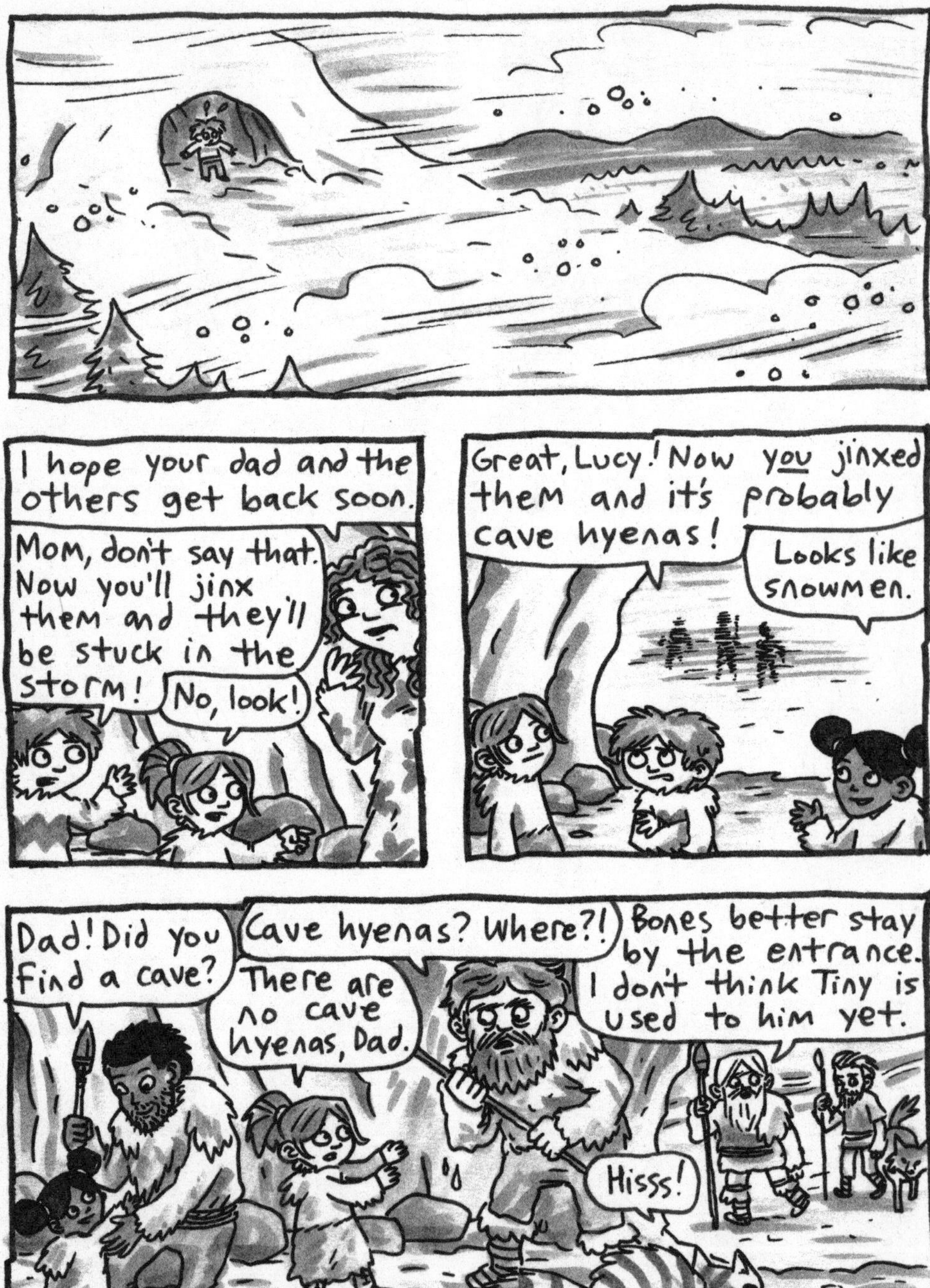
I hope your dad and the others get back soon.
Mom, don't say that. Now you'll jinx them and they'll be stuck in the storm!
No, look!
Great, Lucy! Now you jinxed them and it's probably cave hyenas!
Looks like snowmen.
Dad! Did you find a cave?
Cave hyenas? Where?!
There are no cave hyenas, Dad.
Bones better stay by the entrance. I don't think Tiny is used to him yet.
Hisss!

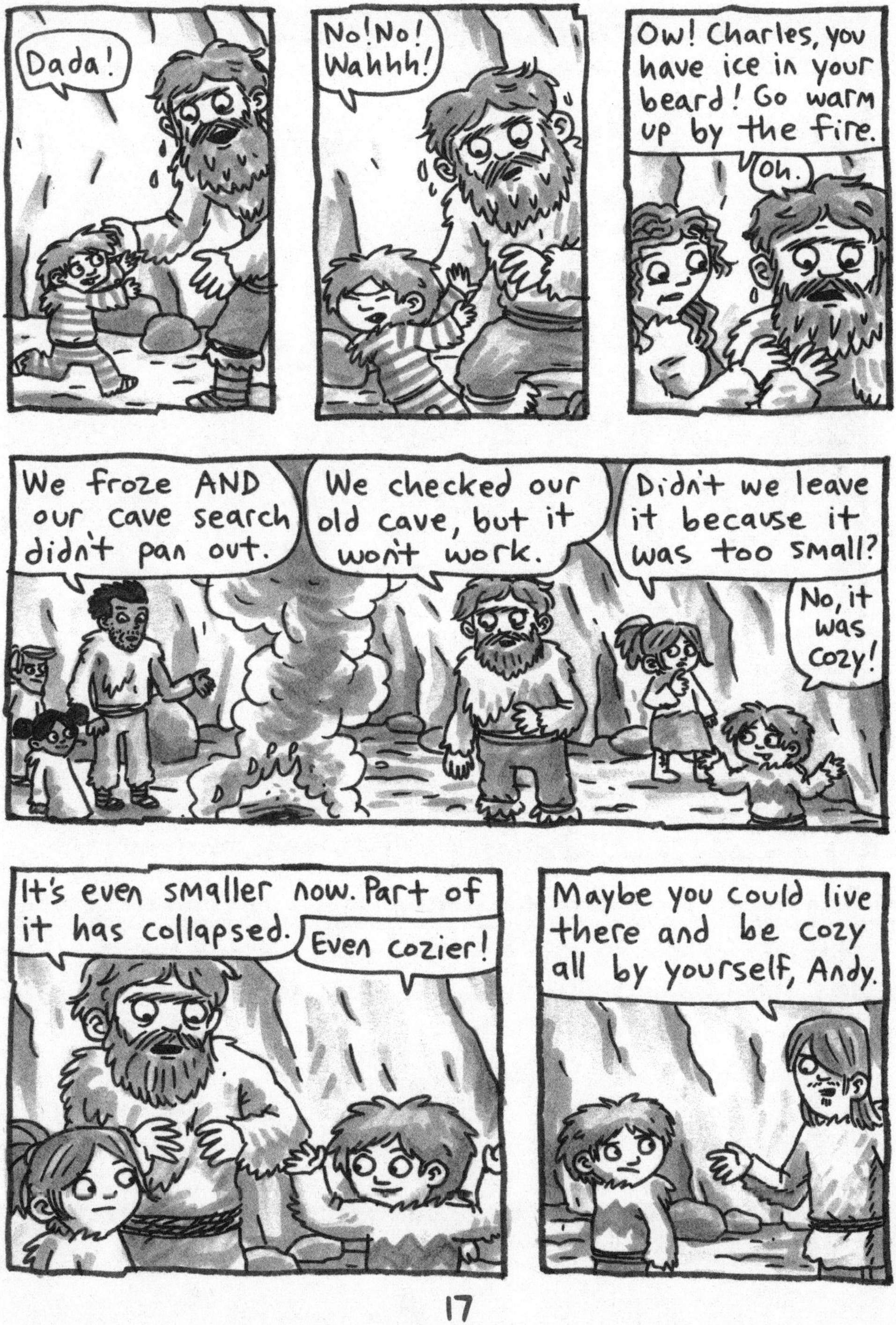
Dada!
No! No! Wahhh!
Ow! Charles, you have ice in your beard! Go warm up by the fire.
Oh.
We froze AND our cave search didn't pan out.
We checked our old cave, but it won't work.
Didn't we leave it because it was too small?
No, it was cozy!
It's even smaller now. Part of it has collapsed.
Even cozier!
Maybe you could live there and be cozy all by yourself, Andy.

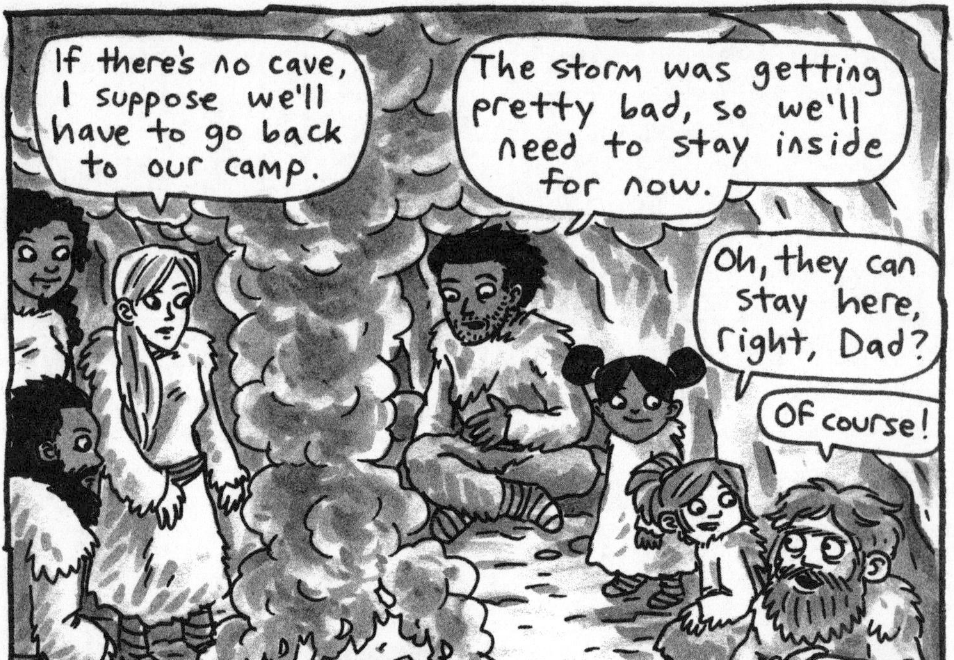
If there's no cave, I suppose we'll have to go back to our camp.
The storm was getting pretty bad, so we'll need to stay inside for now.
Oh, they can stay here, right, Dad?
Of course!
Groan.
It's only temporary, Andy.

Scientists have studied the soil of caves to learn that the smoke and residue from Neanderthal fires was the first man-made pollution!

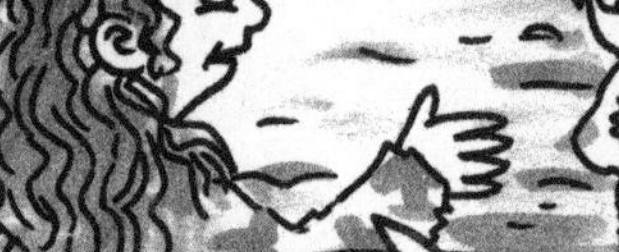

Needing to stay warm while living in a small, enclosed space made exposure to this pollution inevitable.

No warnings about the danger of secondhand smoke have been found in Neanderthal caves.

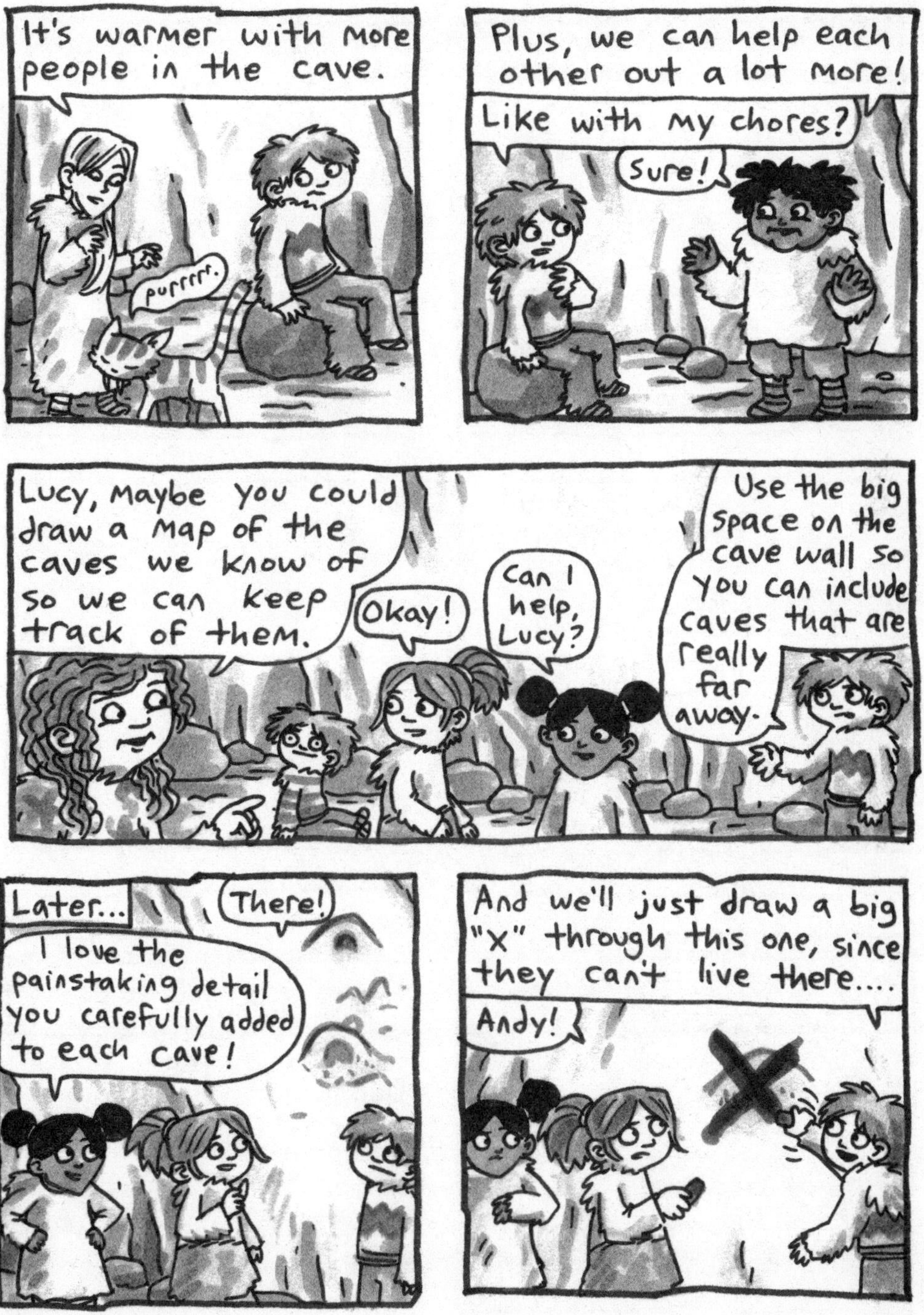
It's warmer with more people in the cave.
purrrrr.
Plus, we can help each other out a lot more!
Like with my chores?
Sure!
Lucy, maybe you could draw a map of the caves we know of so we can keep track of them.
Okay!
Can I help, Lucy?
Use the big space on the cave wall so you can include caves that are really far away.
Later...
There!
I love the painstaking detail you carefully added to each cave!
And we'll just draw a big "X" through this one, since they can't live there....
Andy!

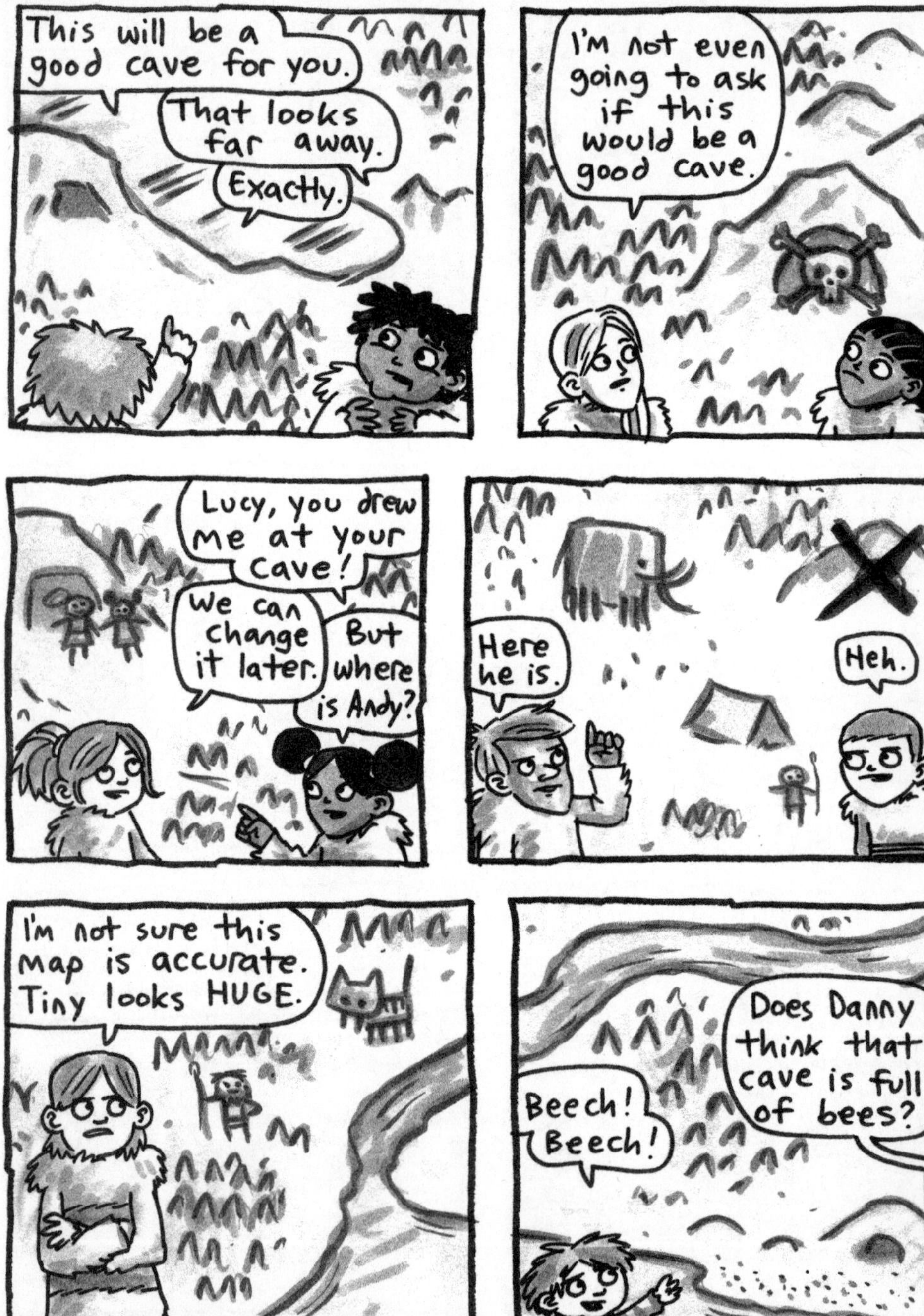
This will be a good cave for you.
That looks far away.
Exactly.
I'm not even going to ask if this would be a good cave.
Lucy, you drew me at your cave!
We can change it later.
But where is Andy?
Here he is.
Heh.
I'm not sure this map is accurate. Tiny looks HUGE.
Does Danny think that cave is full of bees?
Beech! Beech!

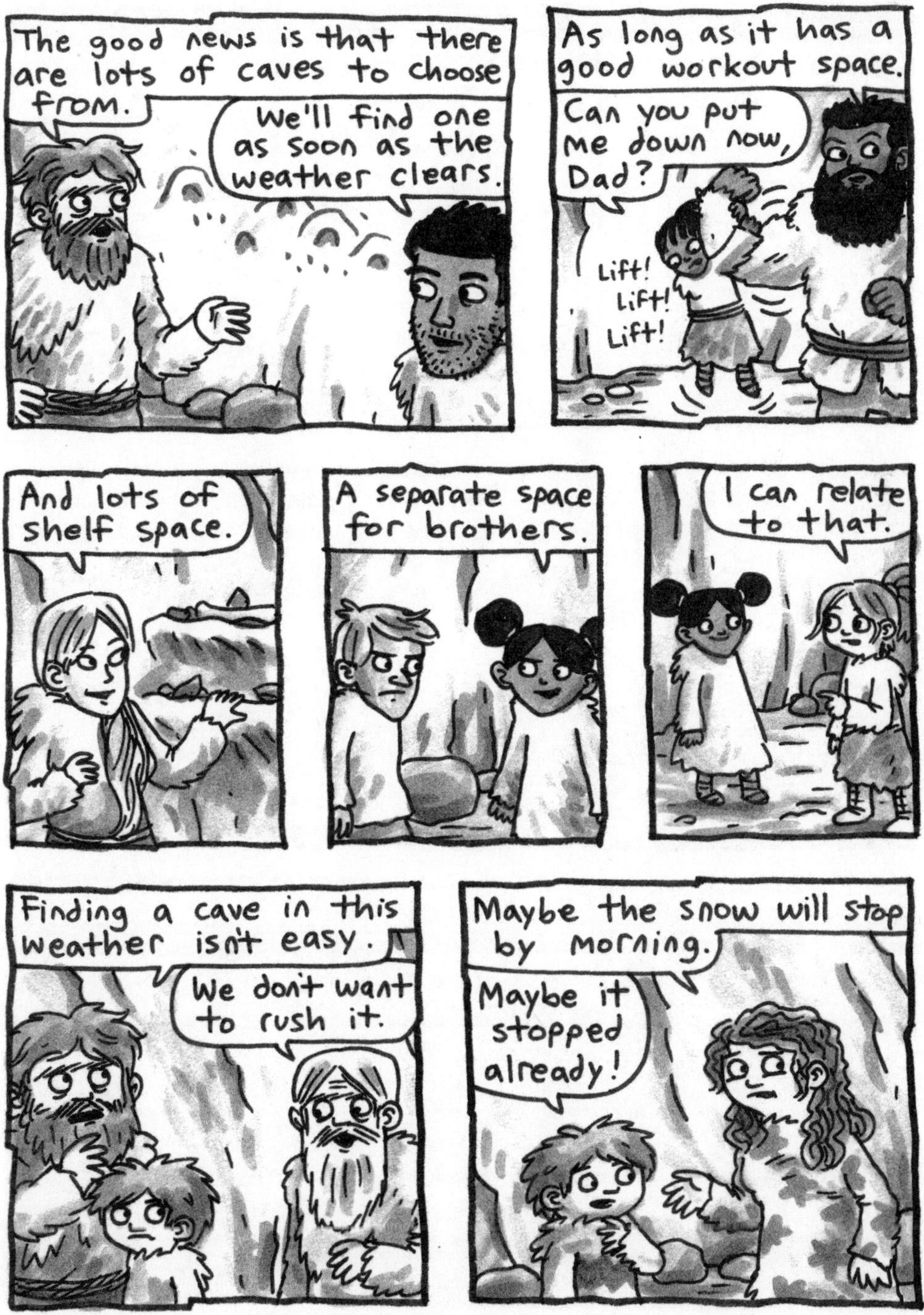
The good news is that there are lots of caves to choose from.
We'll find one as soon as the weather clears.
As long as it has a good workout space.
Can you put me down now, Dad?
Lift! Lift! Lift!
And lots of shelf space.
A separate space for brothers.
I can relate to that.
Finding a cave in this weather isn't easy.
We don't want to rush it.
Maybe the snow will stop by morning.
Maybe it stopped already!

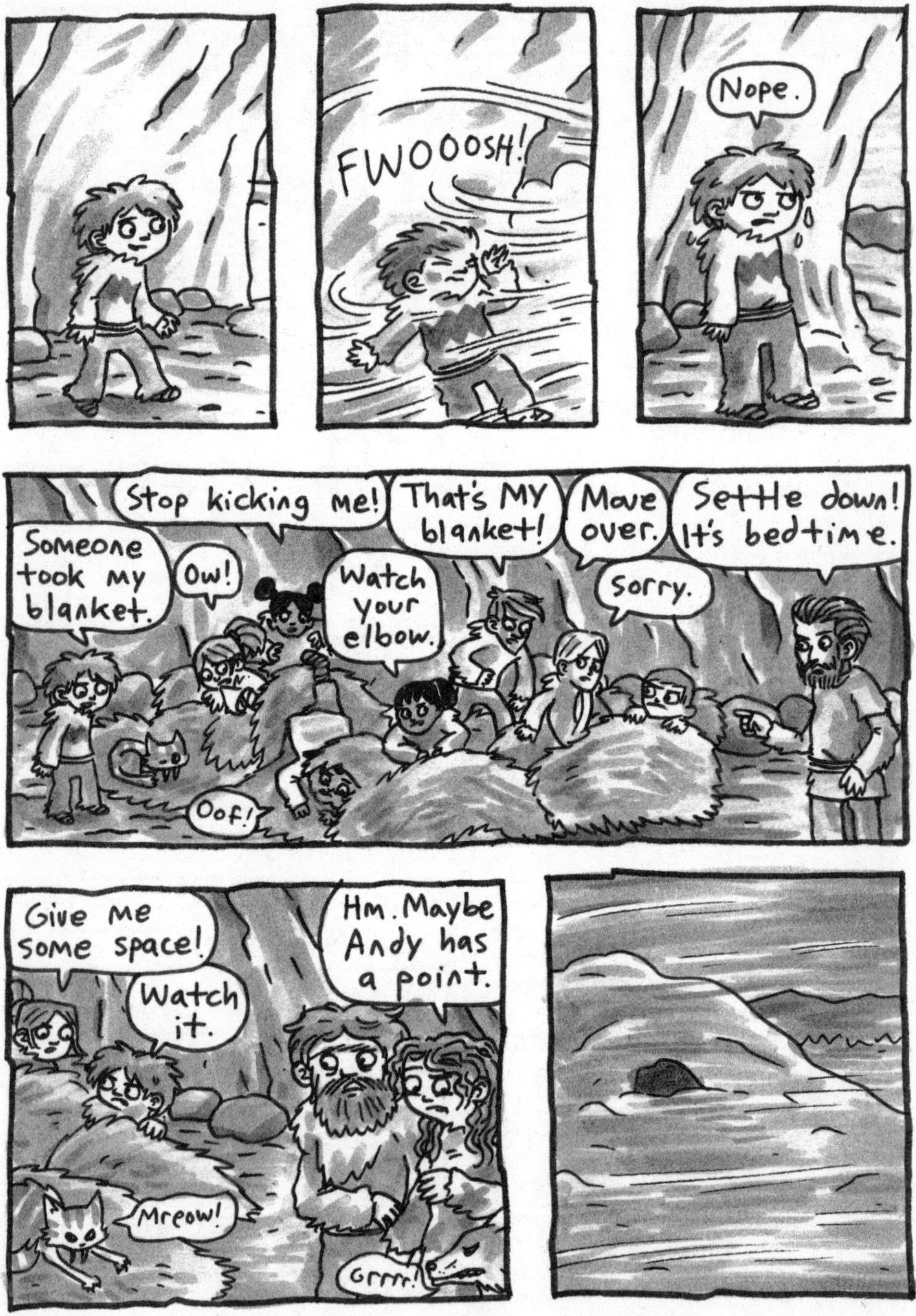
FWOOOSH!
Nope.
Someone took my blanket.
Stop kicking me!
Ow!
Watch your elbow.
That's MY blanket!
Move over.
Sorry.
Settle down! It's bedtime.
Oof!
Give me some space!
Watch it.
Hm. Maybe Andy has a point.
Mreow!
Grrrr!

Brrr! It's getting colder. We'll have to wait until next summer to dig up more of the cave.
At least we're not living in the Ice Age. Then we'd be really cold!
Actually, aren't we living in an ice age now?
An ice age is a period of time on Earth when glacial ice sheets cover extensive areas of land. Today, ice covers the Arctic, Antarctica, and Greenland. So you're right, we're living in an ice age.
"Ice age" sounds like it would be cold and snowy everywhere, but it's not.
Some parts of the Earth still have warm weather.

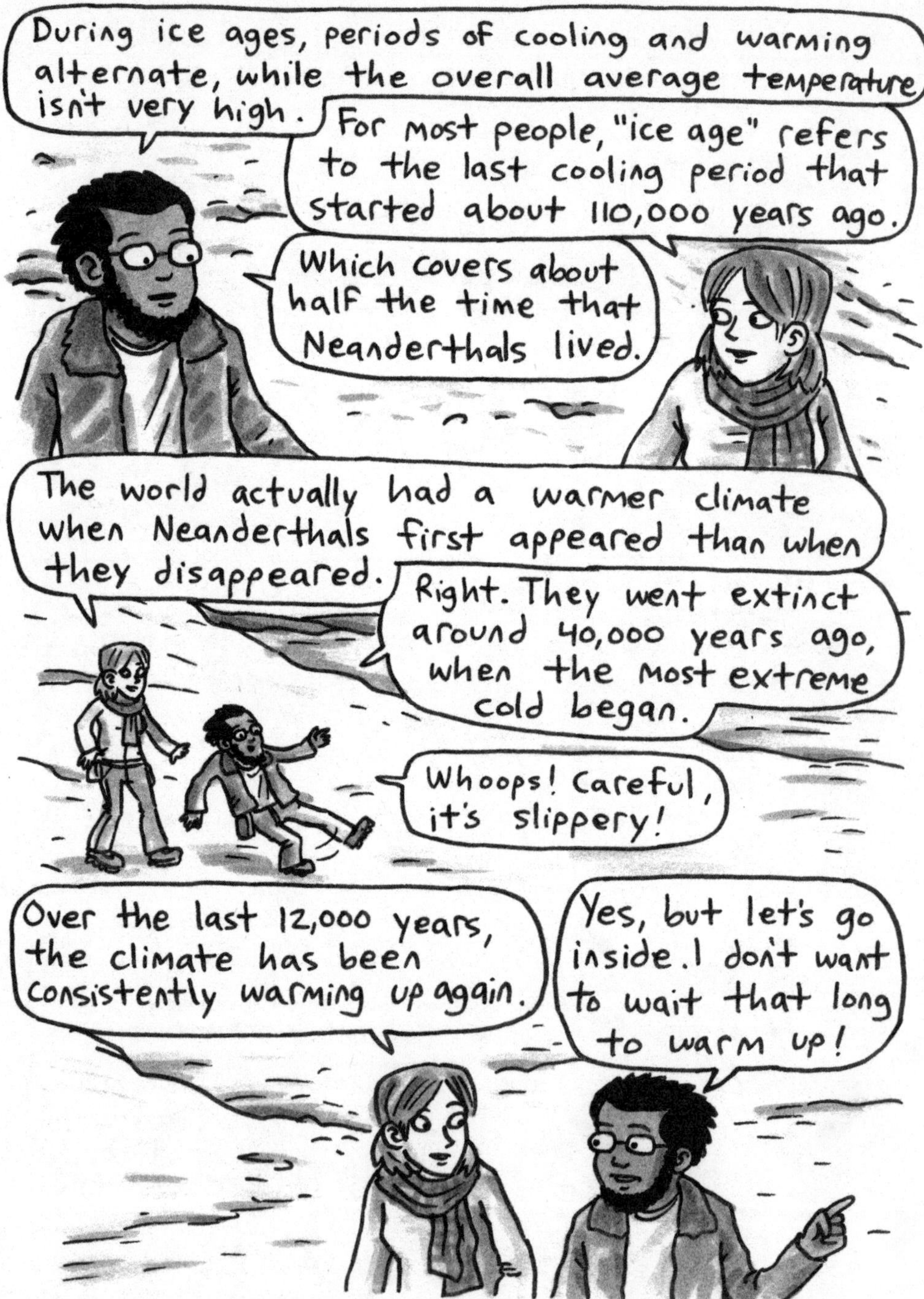

During ice ages, periods of cooling and warming alternate, while the overall average temperature isn't very high.
For most people, "ice age" refers to the last cooling period that started about 110,000 years ago.
Which covers about half the time that Neanderthals lived.
The world actually had a warmer climate when Neanderthals first appeared than when they disappeared.
Right. They went extinct around 40,000 years ago, when the most extreme cold began.
Whoops! Careful, it's slippery!
Over the last 12,000 years, the climate has been consistently warming up again.
Yes, but let's go inside. I don't want to wait that long to warm up!

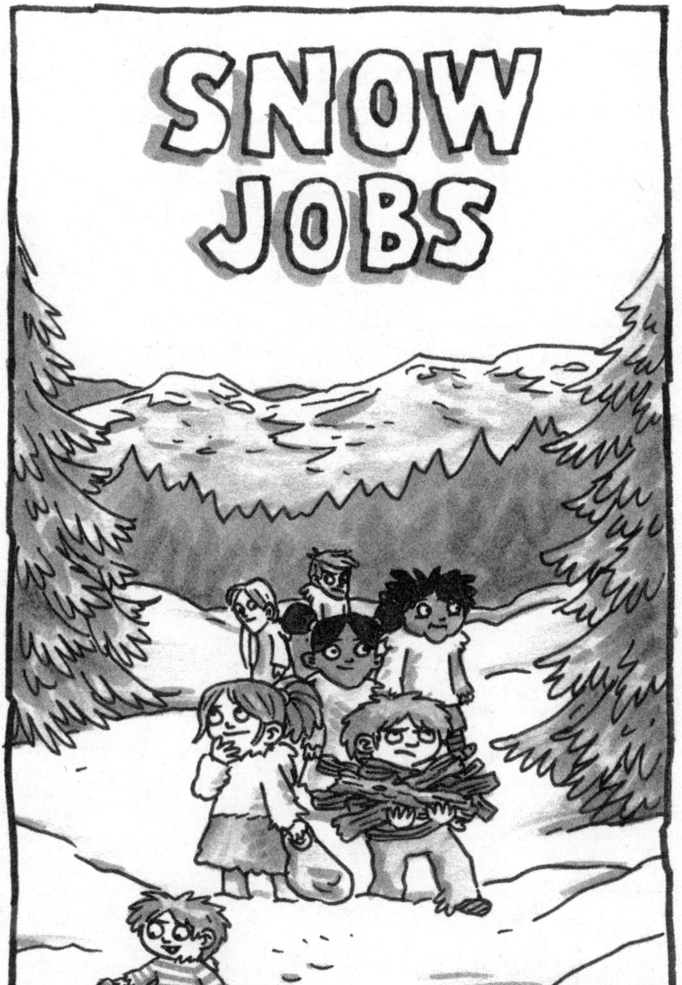
SNOW
JOBS

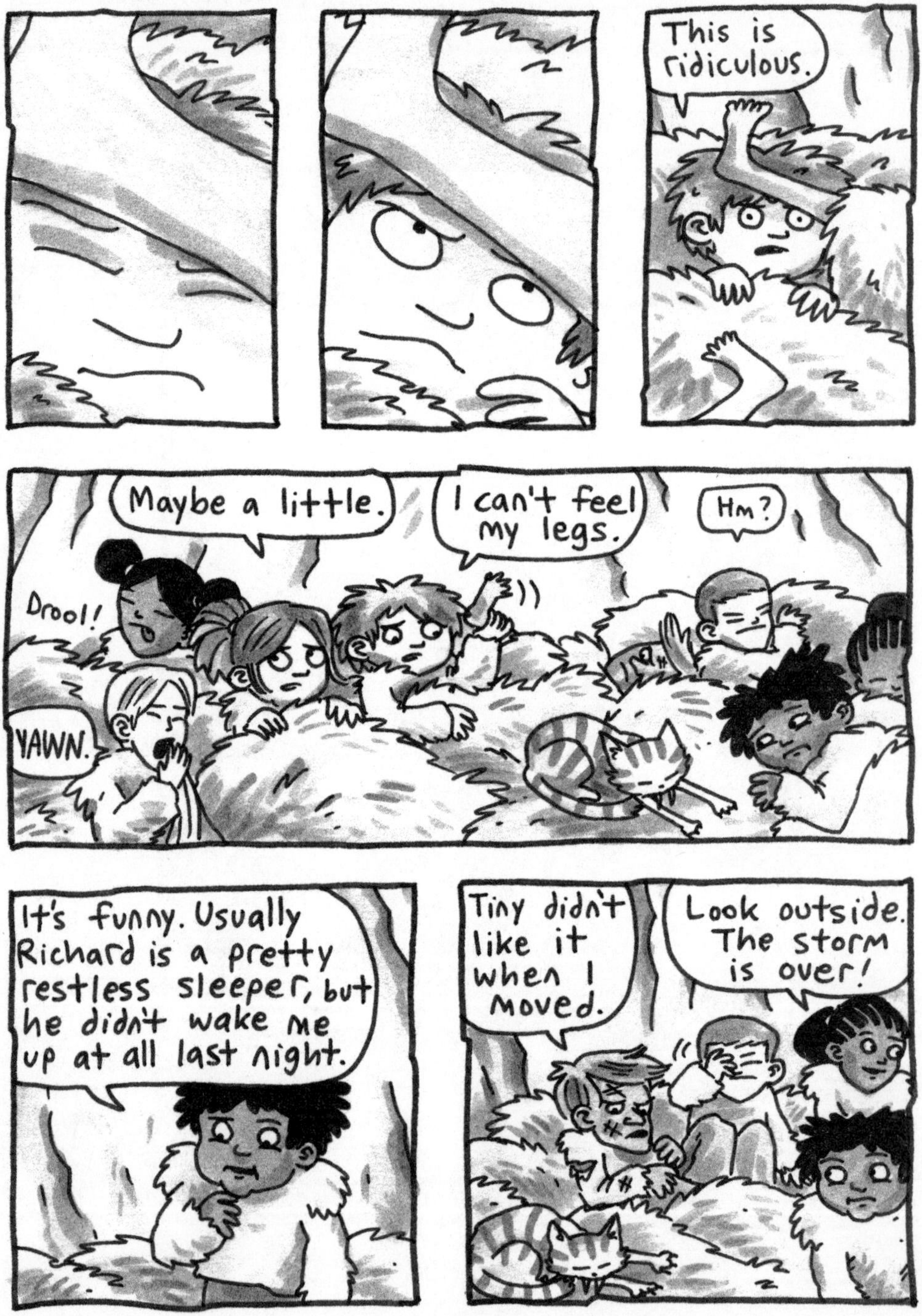

This is ridiculous.
Maybe a little.
I can't feel my legs.
Hm?
Drool!
YAWN.
It's funny. Usually Richard is a pretty restless sleeper, but he didn't wake me up at all last night.
Tiny didn't like it when I moved.
Look outside. The storm is over!

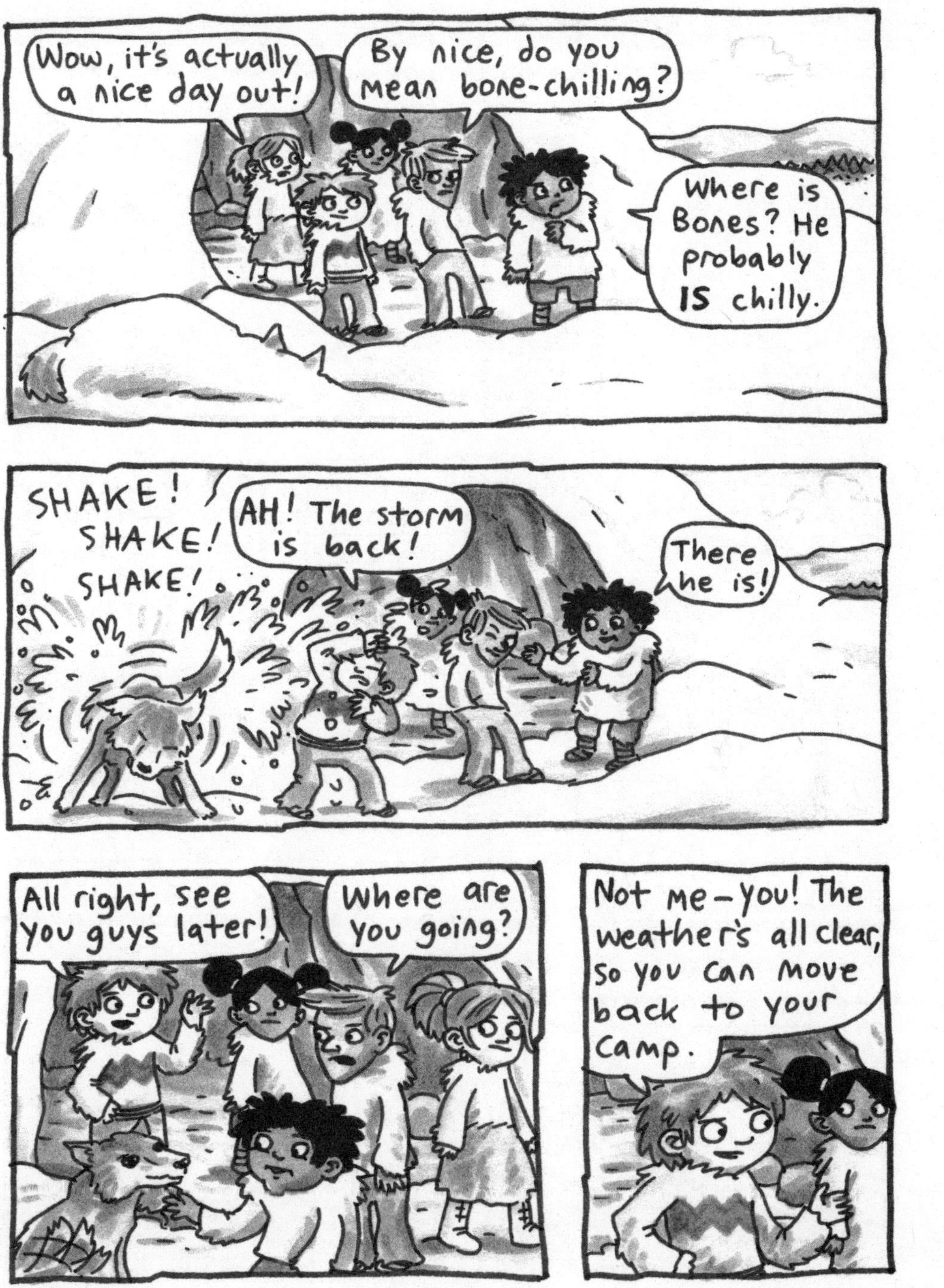
Wow, it's actually a nice day out!
By nice, do you mean bone-chilling?
Where is Bones? He probably IS chilly.
SHAKE! SHAKE! SHAKE!
AH! The storm is back!
There he is!
All right, see you guys later!
Where are you going?
Not me—you! The weather's all clear, so you can move back to your camp.

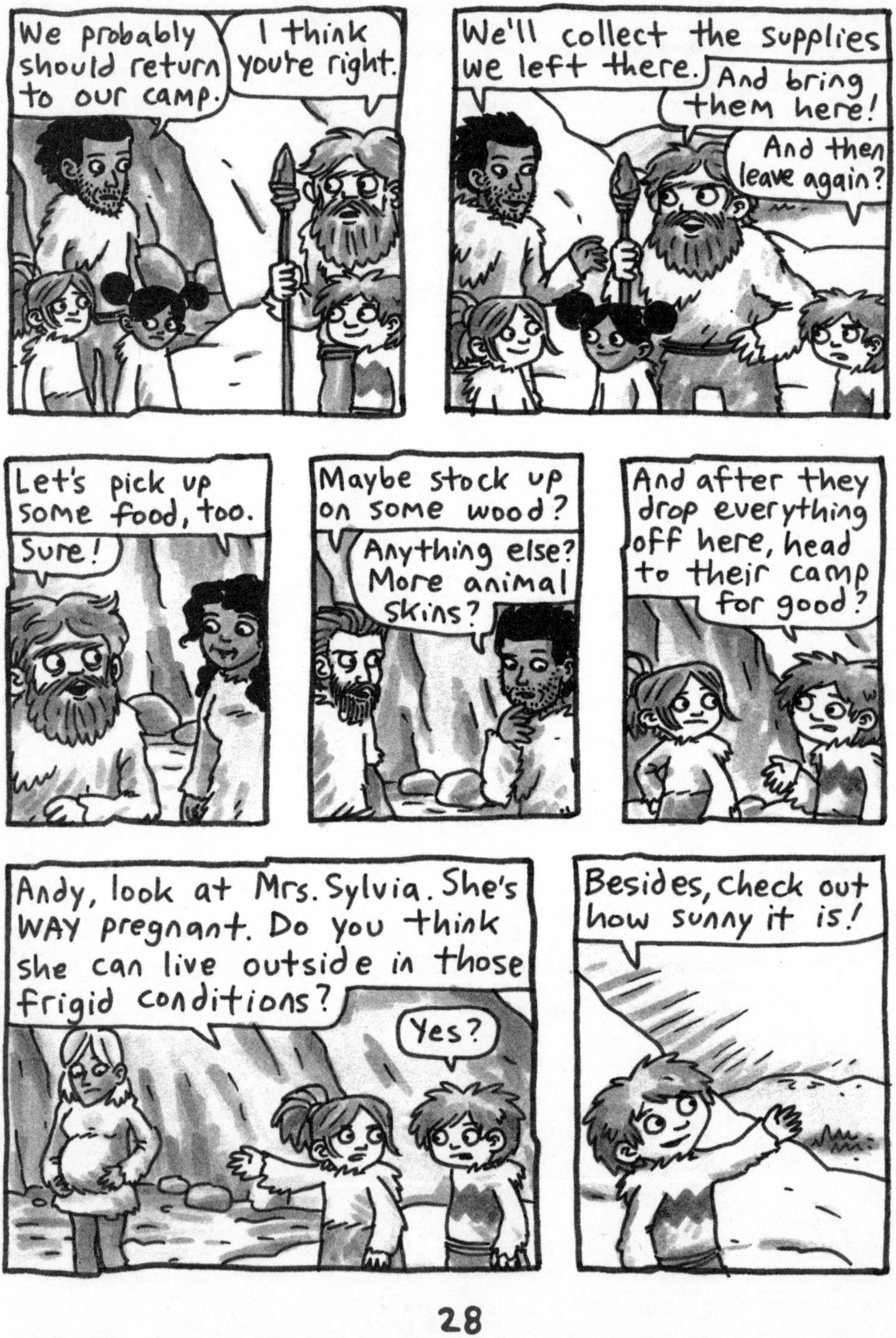
We probably should return to our camp.
I think you're right.
We'll collect the supplies we left there.
And bring them here!
And then leave again?
Let's pick up some food, too.
Sure!
Maybe stock up on some wood?
Anything else? More animal skins?
And after they drop everything off here, head to their camp for good?
Andy, look at Mrs. Sylvia. She's WAY pregnant. Do you think she can live outside in those frigid conditions?
Yes?
Besides, check out how sunny it is!

Yeah, don't mind those ominous clouds moving this way.
Good eye, Lucy. We should go before there's more snow.
What?
I know.
I can't come.
Again.
Andy, why won't your dad let you hunt with him? Did something bad happen the last time you went?
He's actually never gone on a hunt. He's a little accident-prone.
The reason they won't let me go is because they think I'm just a kid.
They don't appreciate my skills!

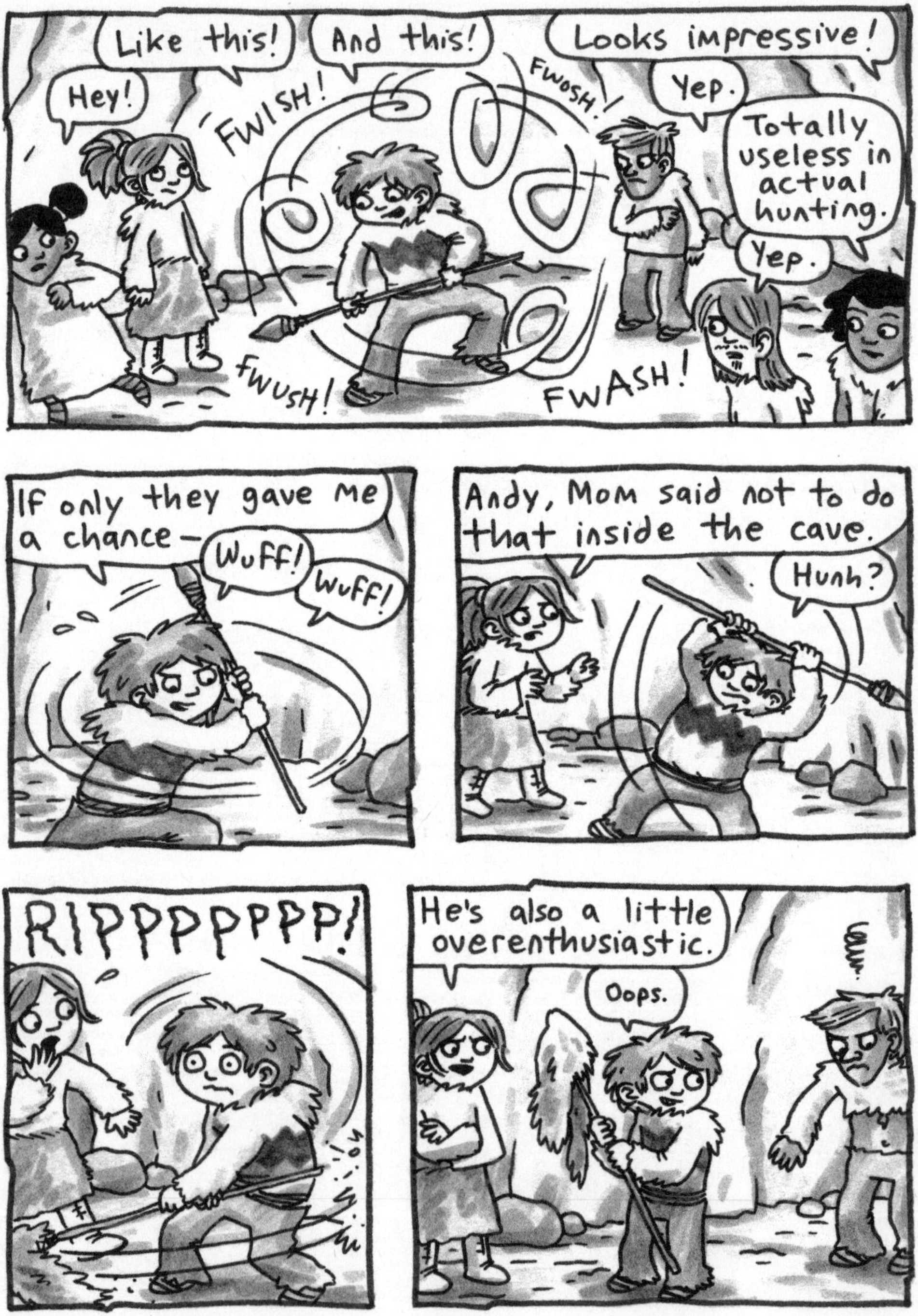

Hey!
Like this!
And this!
FWISH!
FWOSH!
FWUSH!
FWASH!
Looks impressive!
Yep.
Totally useless in actual hunting.
Yep.
If only they gave me a chance—
Wuff!
Wuff!
Andy, Mom said not to do that inside the cave.
Hunh?
RIPPPPPPP!
He's also a little overenthusiastic.
Oops.

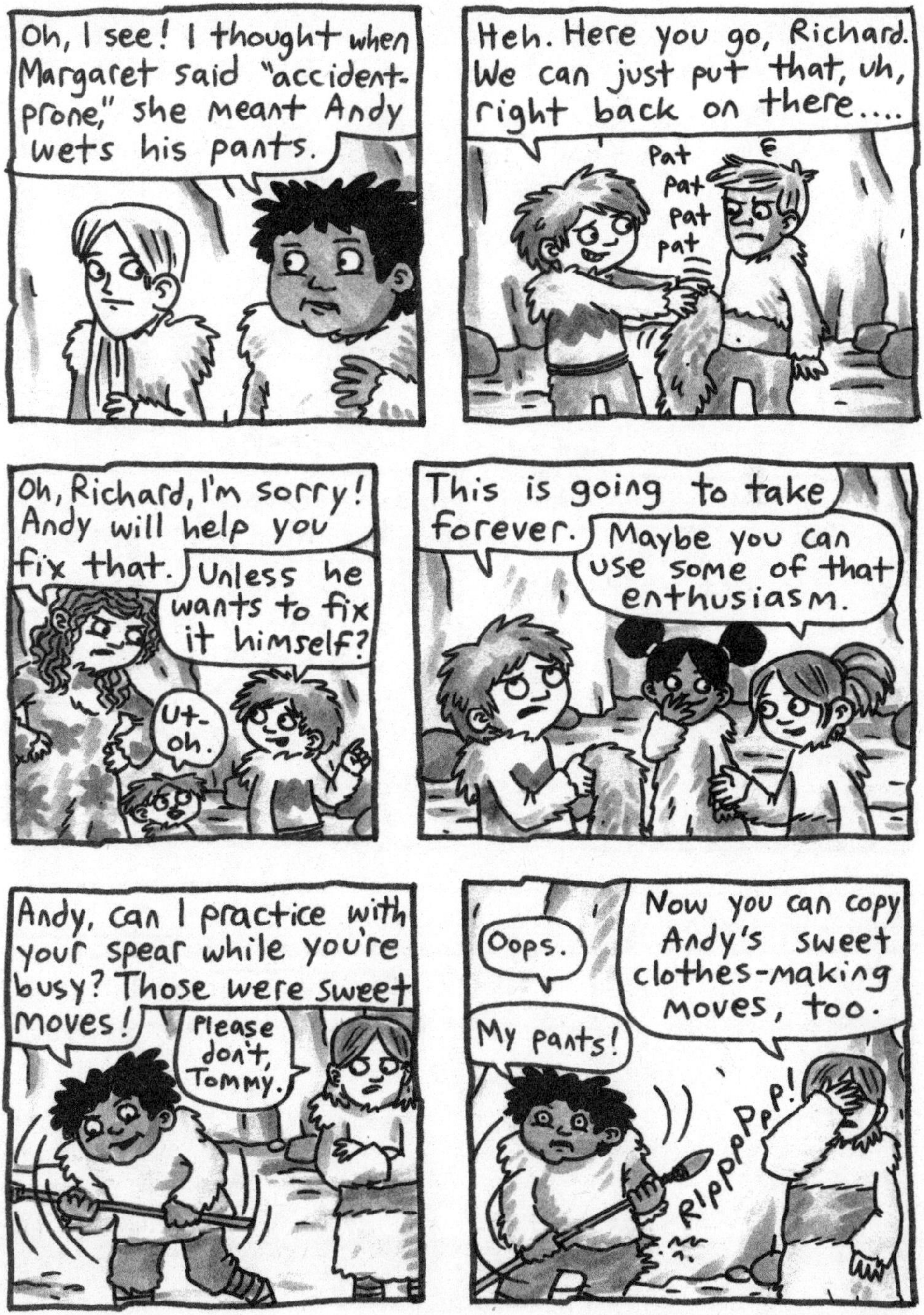

Oh, I see! I thought when Margaret said "accident-prone," she meant Andy wets his pants.
Heh. Here you go, Richard. We can just put that, uh, right back on there....
Pat pat pat pat
Oh, Richard, I'm sorry! Andy will help you fix that.
Unless he wants to fix it himself?
Ut-oh.
This is going to take forever.
Maybe you can use some of that enthusiasm.
Andy, can I practice with your spear while you're busy? Those were sweet moves!
Please don't, Tommy.
Oops.
Now you can copy Andy's sweet clothes-making moves, too.
My pants!
RIPPPPPPP!

Neanderthals needed a new outfit every year.

It took the skins of 6 to 8 large deer to make a new outfit, and each skin needed at least 8 hours of scraping.

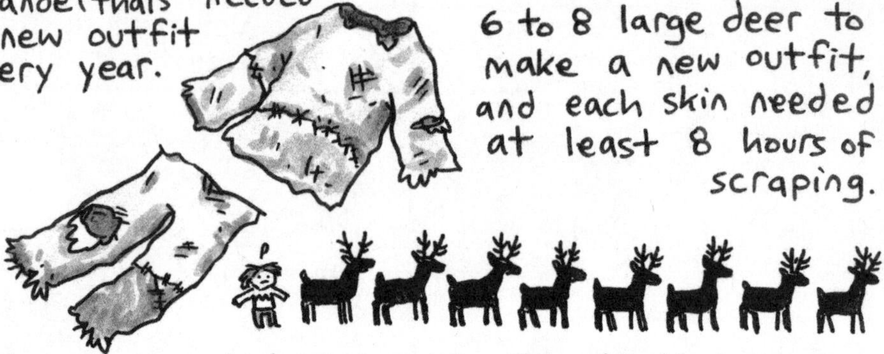

Scientists don't know if Neanderthal kids wore their clothes out faster.

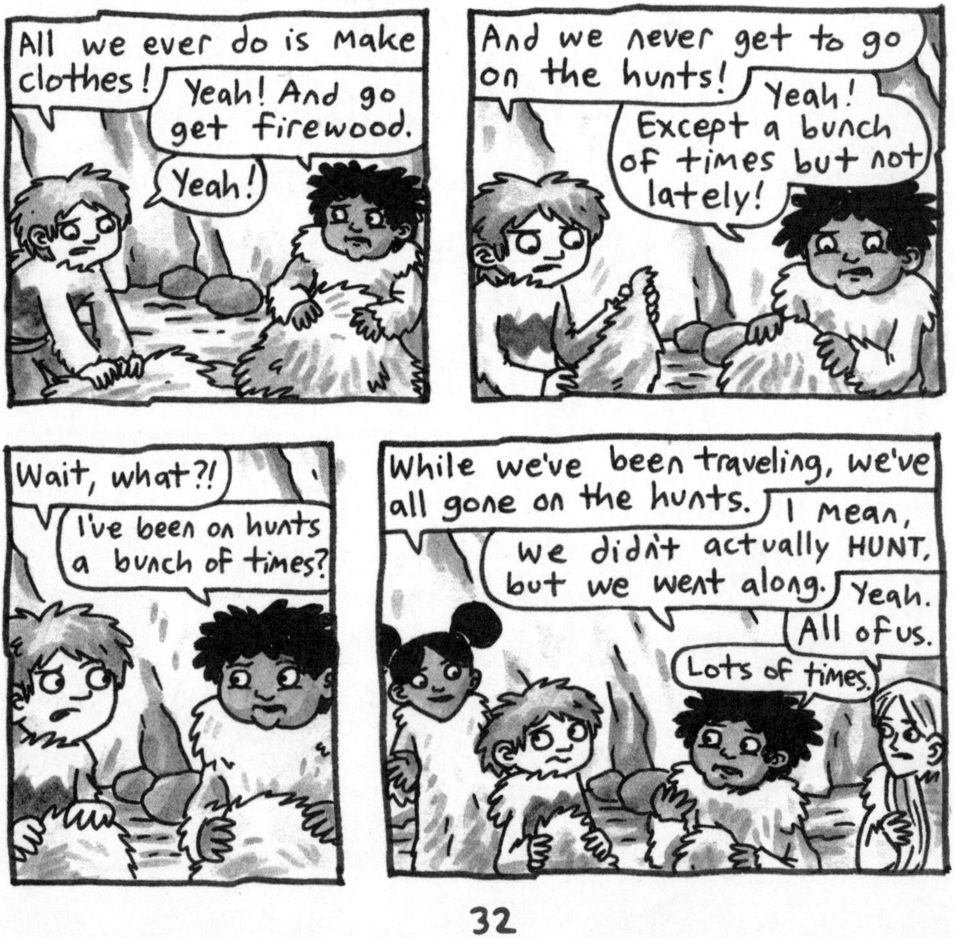

All we ever do is make clothes!
Yeah! And go get firewood.
Yeah!
And we never get to go on the hunts!
Yeah! Except a bunch of times but not lately!
Wait, what?!
I've been on hunts a bunch of times?
While we've been traveling, we've all gone on the hunts.
I mean, we didn't actually HUNT, but we went along.
Yeah. All of us.
Lots of times.

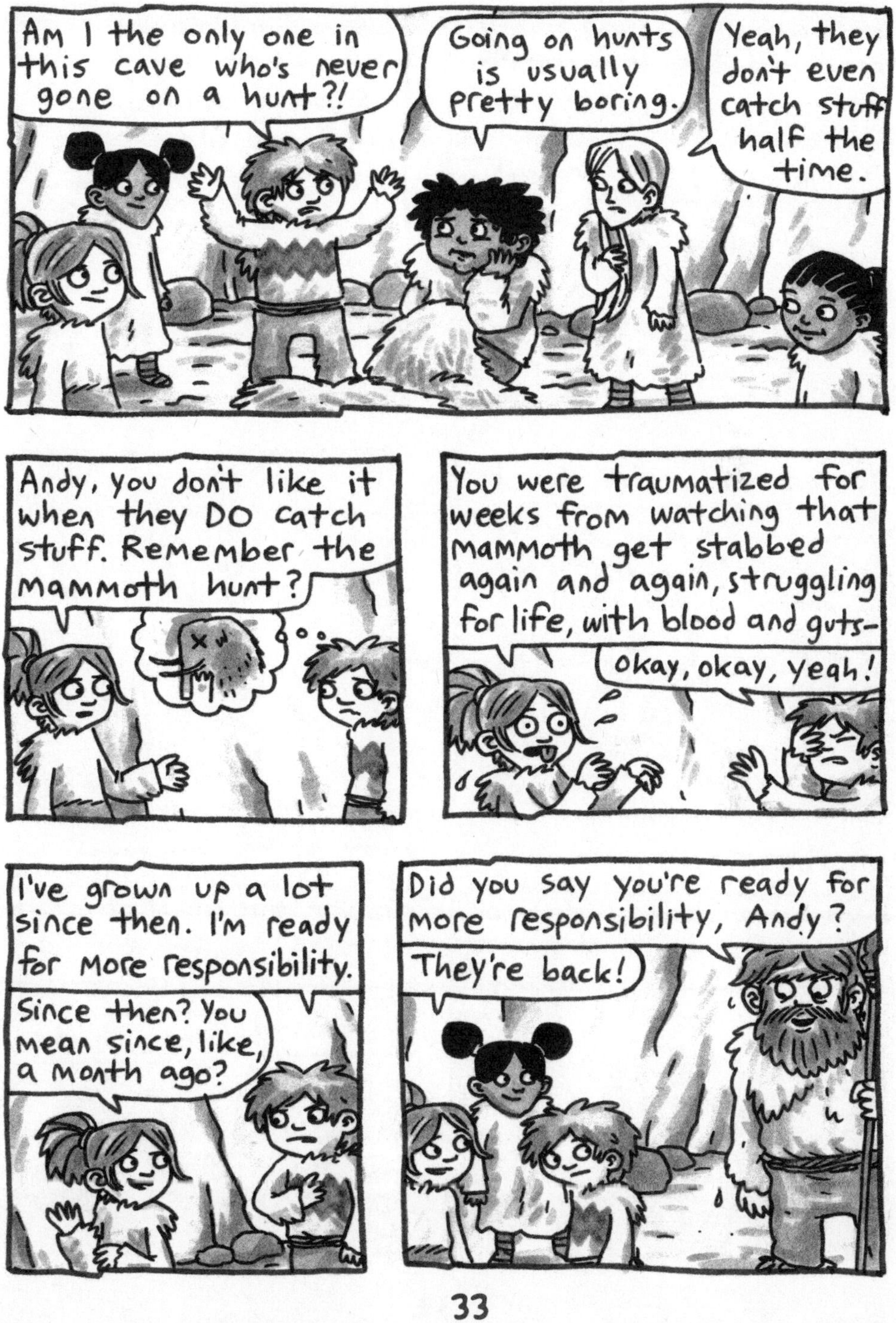
Am I the only one in this cave who's never gone on a hunt?!
Going on hunts is usually pretty boring.
Yeah, they don't even catch stuff half the time.
Andy, you don't like it when they DO catch stuff. Remember the mammoth hunt?
You were traumatized for weeks from watching that mammoth get stabbed again and again, struggling for life, with blood and guts-
Okay, okay, yeah!
I've grown up a lot since then. I'm ready for more responsibility.
Since then? You mean since, like, a month ago?
Did you say you're ready for more responsibility, Andy?
They're back!

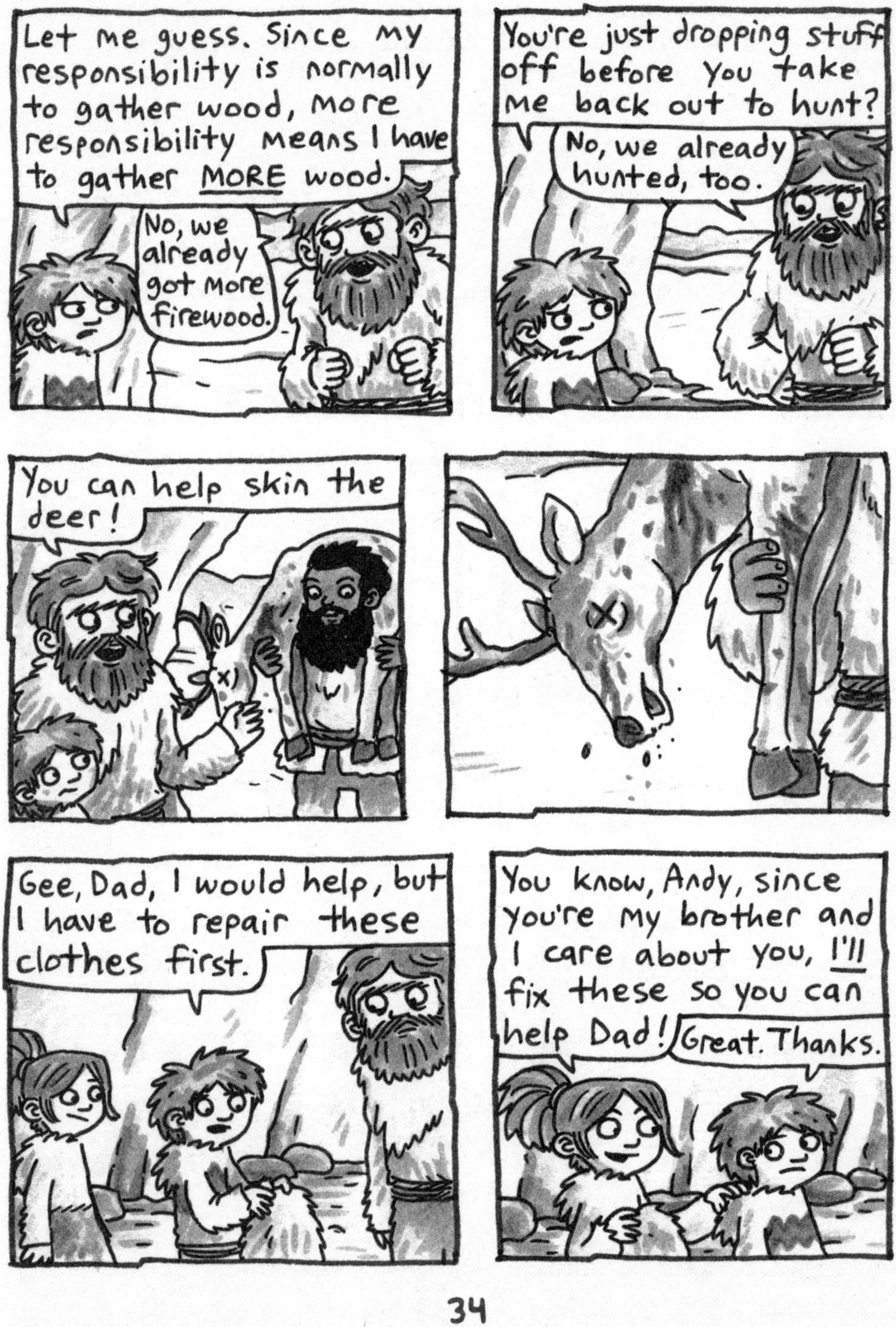

Let me guess. Since my responsibility is normally to gather wood, more responsibility means I have to gather MORE wood.
No, we already got more firewood.
You're just dropping stuff off before you take me back out to hunt?
No, we already hunted, too.
You can help skin the deer!
Gee, Dad, I would help, but I have to repair these clothes first.
You know, Andy, since you're my brother and I care about you, I'LL fix these so you can help Dad!
Great. Thanks.

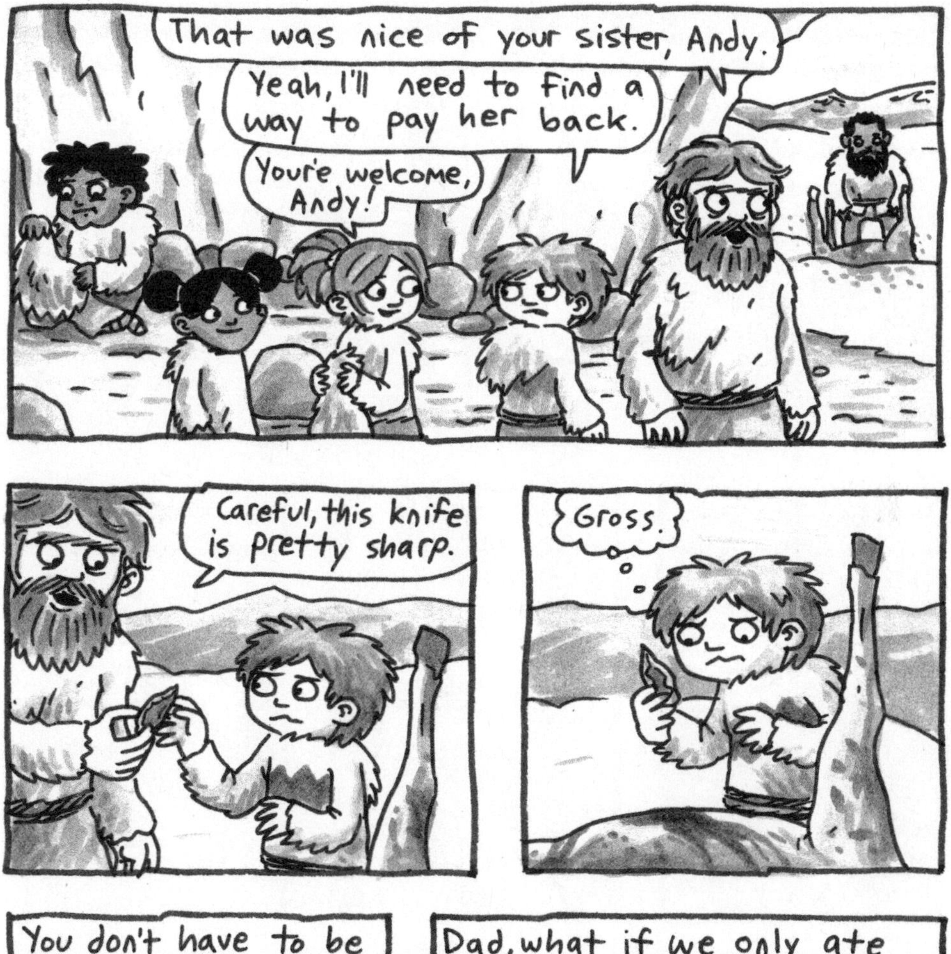
That was nice of your sister, Andy.
Yeah, I'll need to find a way to pay her back.
You're welcome, Andy!
Careful, this knife is pretty sharp.
Gross.
You don't have to be THAT careful, Andy. Use some muscle. Go for it!
Ooh, stringy tendons there.
Ew.
Dad, what if we only ate fruits and vegetables? Then we wouldn't have to hunt.
Ha ha! Good luck finding plants this time of year!

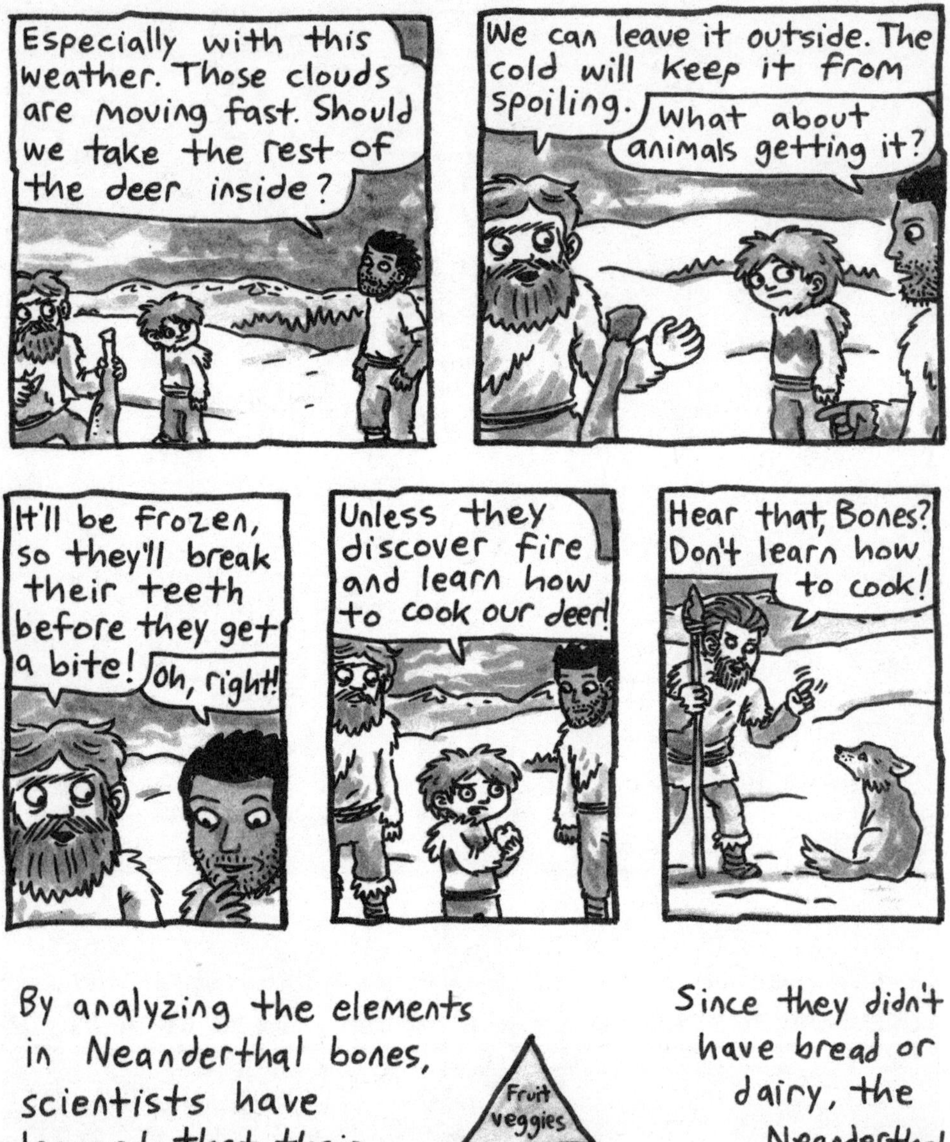
Especially with this weather. Those clouds are moving fast. Should we take the rest of the deer inside?
We can leave it outside. The cold will keep it from spoiling.
What about animals getting it?
It'll be frozen, so they'll break their teeth before they get a bite!
Oh, right!
Unless they discover fire and learn how to cook our deer!
Hear that, Bones? Don't learn how to cook!

By analyzing the elements in Neanderthal bones, scientists have learned that their diet was about 80% meat and 20% vegetables and fruit.

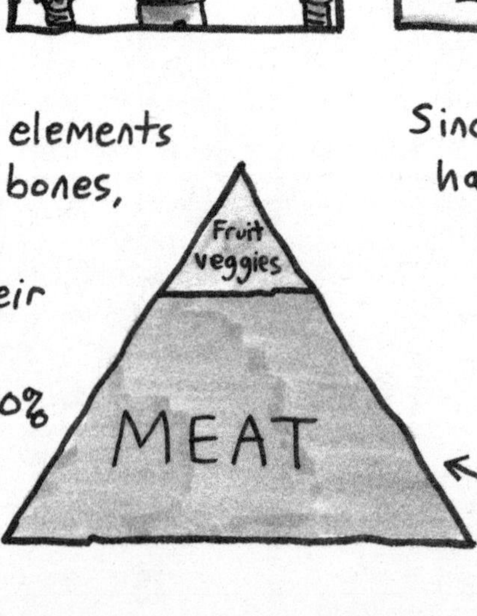
Fruit
veggies
MEAT

Since they didn't have bread or dairy, the Neanderthal food pyramid looked like this!

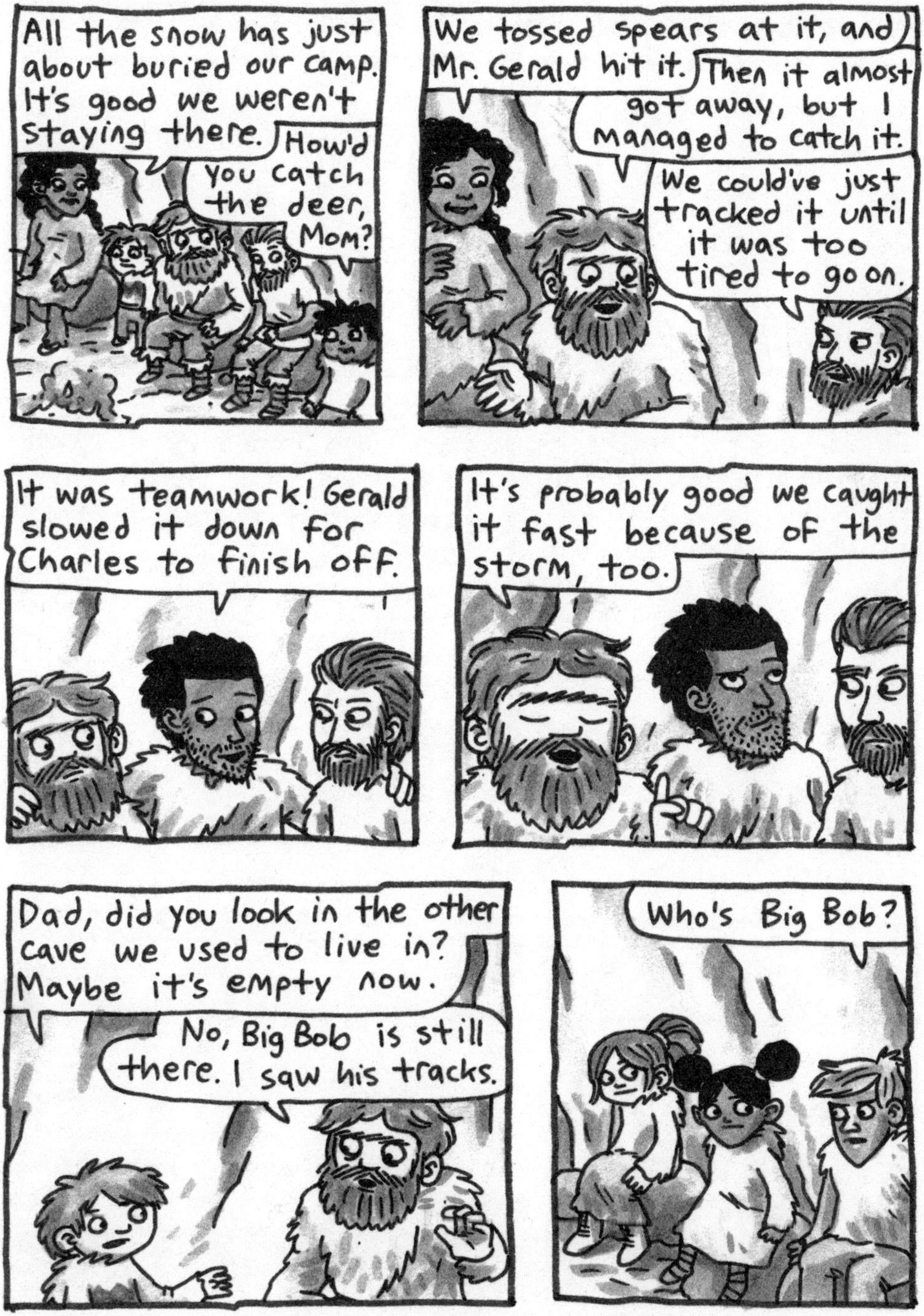
All the snow has just about buried our camp. It's good we weren't staying there.
How'd you catch the deer, Mom?
We tossed spears at it, and Mr. Gerald hit it.
Then it almost got away, but I managed to catch it.
We could've just tracked it until it was too tired to go on.
It was teamwork! Gerald slowed it down for Charles to finish off.
It's probably good we caught it fast because of the storm, too.
Dad, did you look in the other cave we used to live in? Maybe it's empty now.
No, Big Bob is still there. I saw his tracks.
Who's Big Bob?

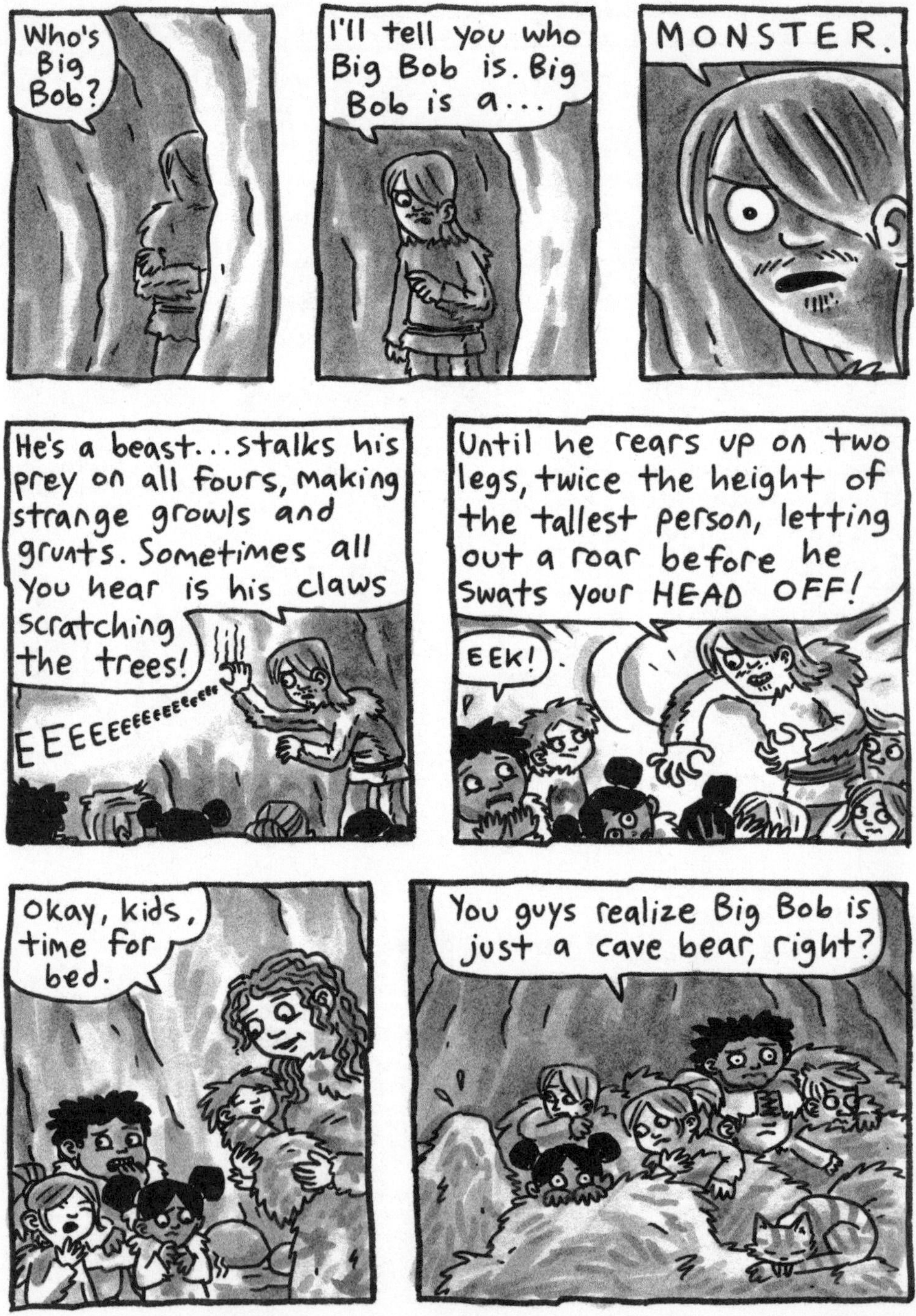
Who's Big Bob?
I'll tell you who Big Bob is. Big Bob is a...
MONSTER.
He's a beast...stalks his prey on all fours, making strange growls and grunts. Sometimes all you hear is his claws scratching the trees!
EEEEEEEEEEEEEEEEE
Until he rears up on two legs, twice the height of the tallest person, letting out a roar before he swats your HEAD OFF!
EEK!
Okay, kids, time for bed.
You guys realize Big Bob is just a cave bear, right?

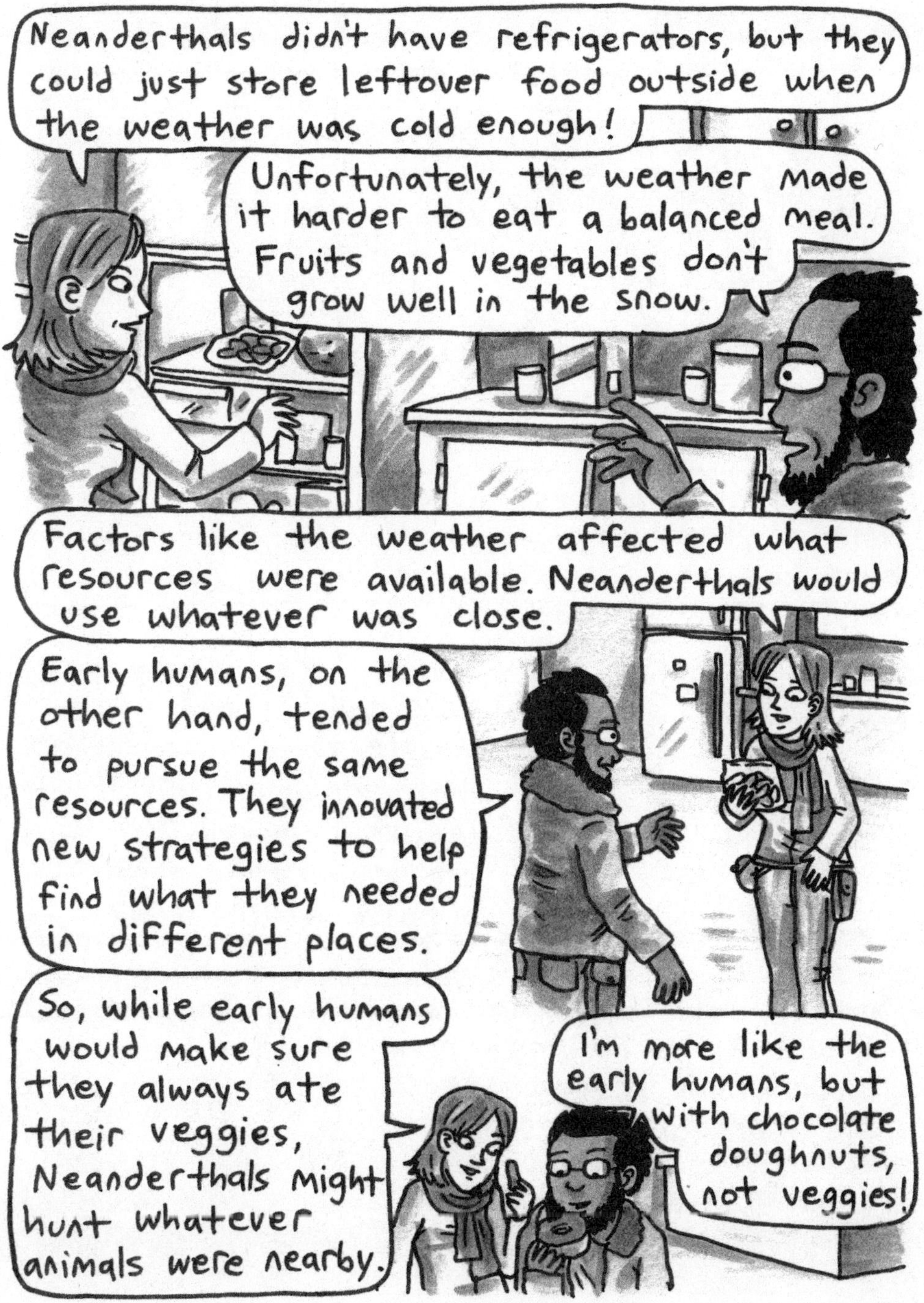

Neanderthals didn't have refrigerators, but they could just store leftover food outside when the weather was cold enough!
Unfortunately, the weather made it harder to eat a balanced meal. Fruits and vegetables don't grow well in the snow.
Factors like the weather affected what resources were available. Neanderthals would use whatever was close.
Early humans, on the other hand, tended to pursue the same resources. They innovated new strategies to help find what they needed in different places.
So, while early humans would make sure they always ate their veggies, Neanderthals might hunt whatever animals were nearby.
I'm more like the early humans, but with chocolate doughnuts, not veggies!

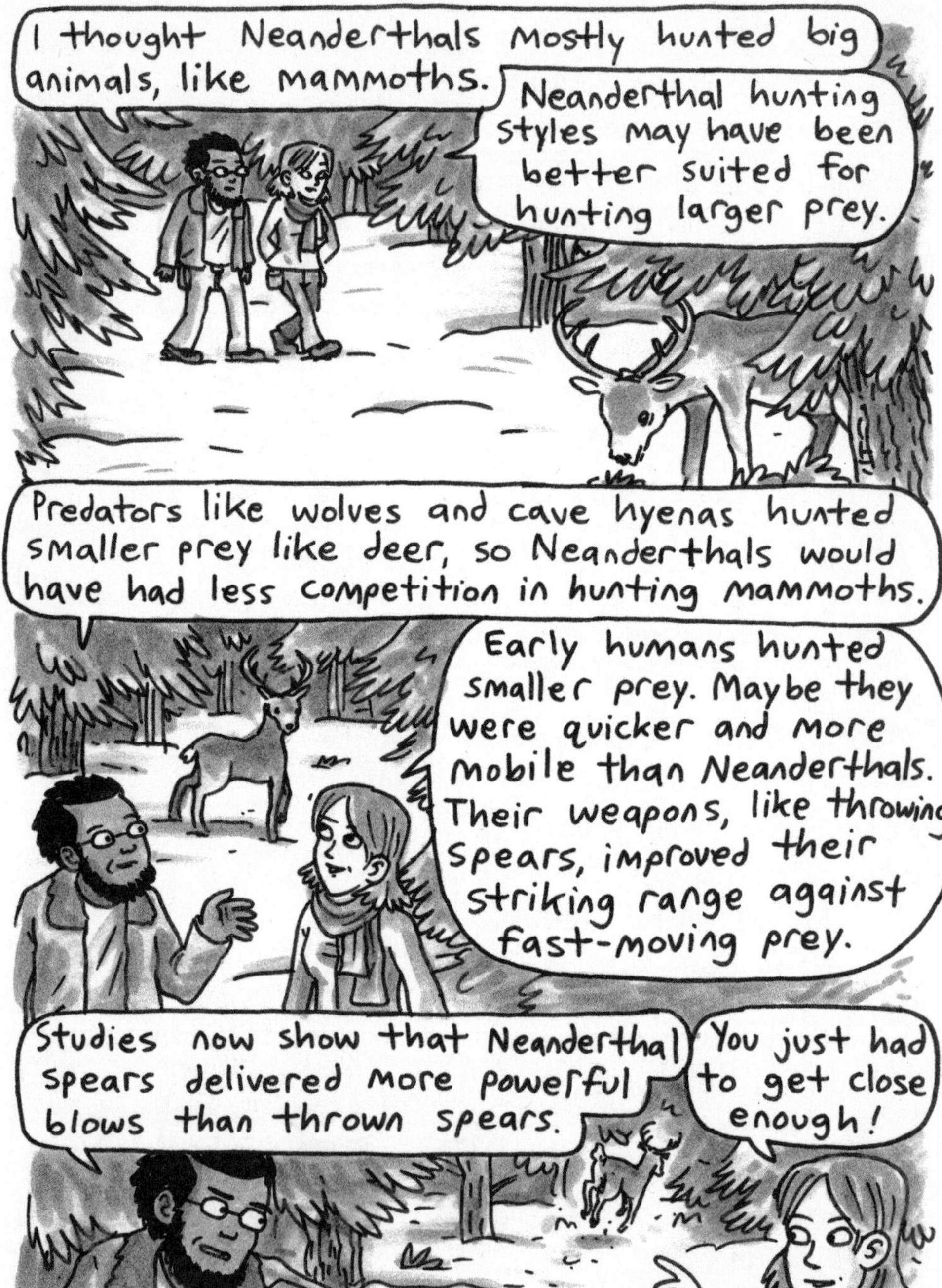
I thought Neanderthals mostly hunted big animals, like mammoths.
Neanderthal hunting styles may have been better suited for hunting larger prey.
Predators like wolves and cave hyenas hunted smaller prey like deer, so Neanderthals would have had less competition in hunting mammoths.
Early humans hunted smaller prey. Maybe they were quicker and more mobile than Neanderthals. Their weapons, like throwing spears, improved their striking range against fast-moving prey.
Studies now show that Neanderthal spears delivered more powerful blows than thrown spears.
You just had to get close enough!

CAVE BEARS 101

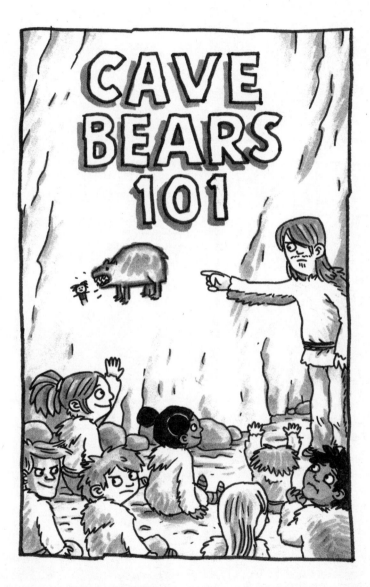

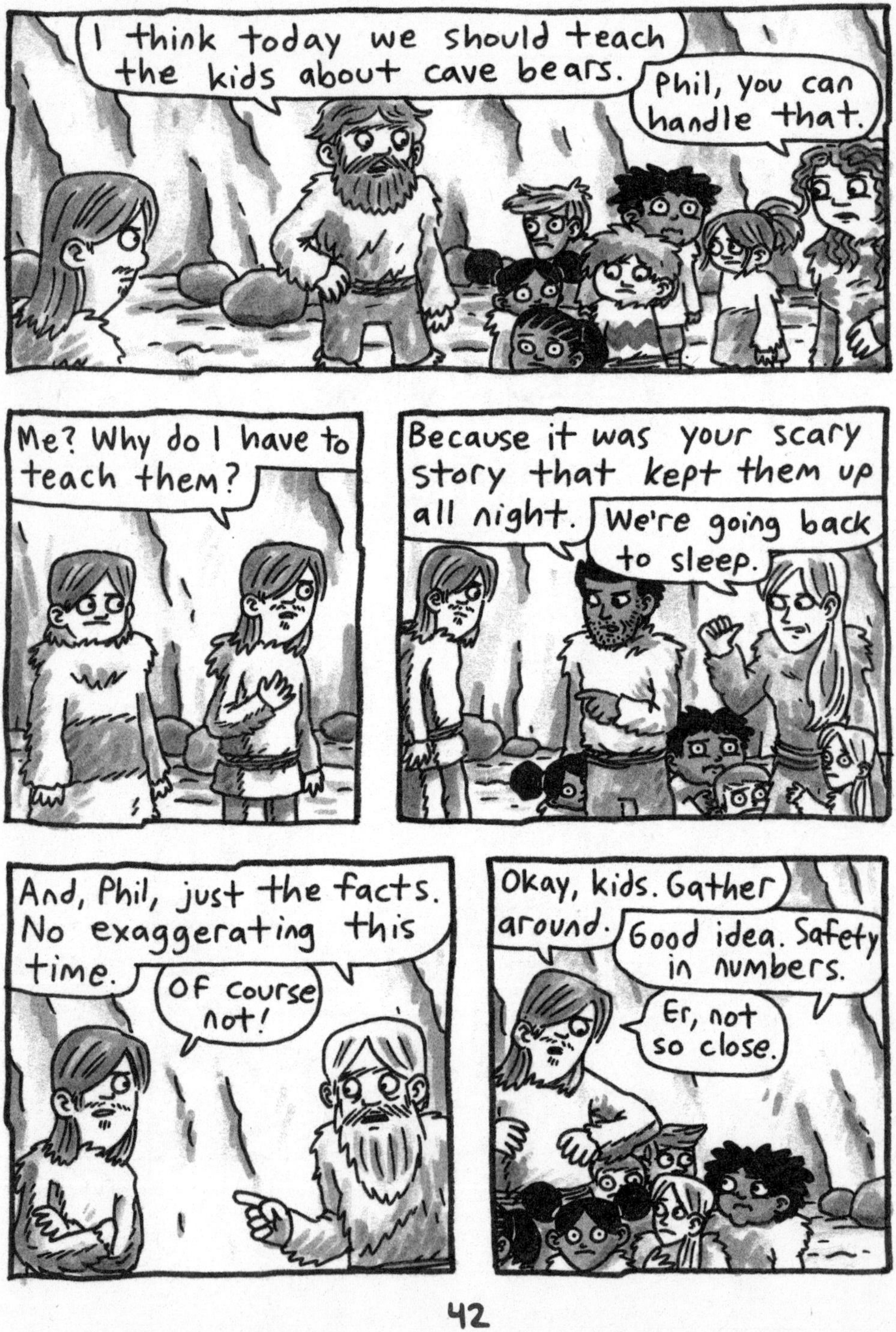
I think today we should teach the kids about cave bears.
Phil, you can handle that.
Me? Why do I have to teach them?
Because it was your scary story that kept them up all night.
We're going back to sleep.
And, Phil, just the facts. No exaggerating this time.
Of course not!
Okay, kids. Gather around.
Good idea. Safety in numbers.
Er, not so close.

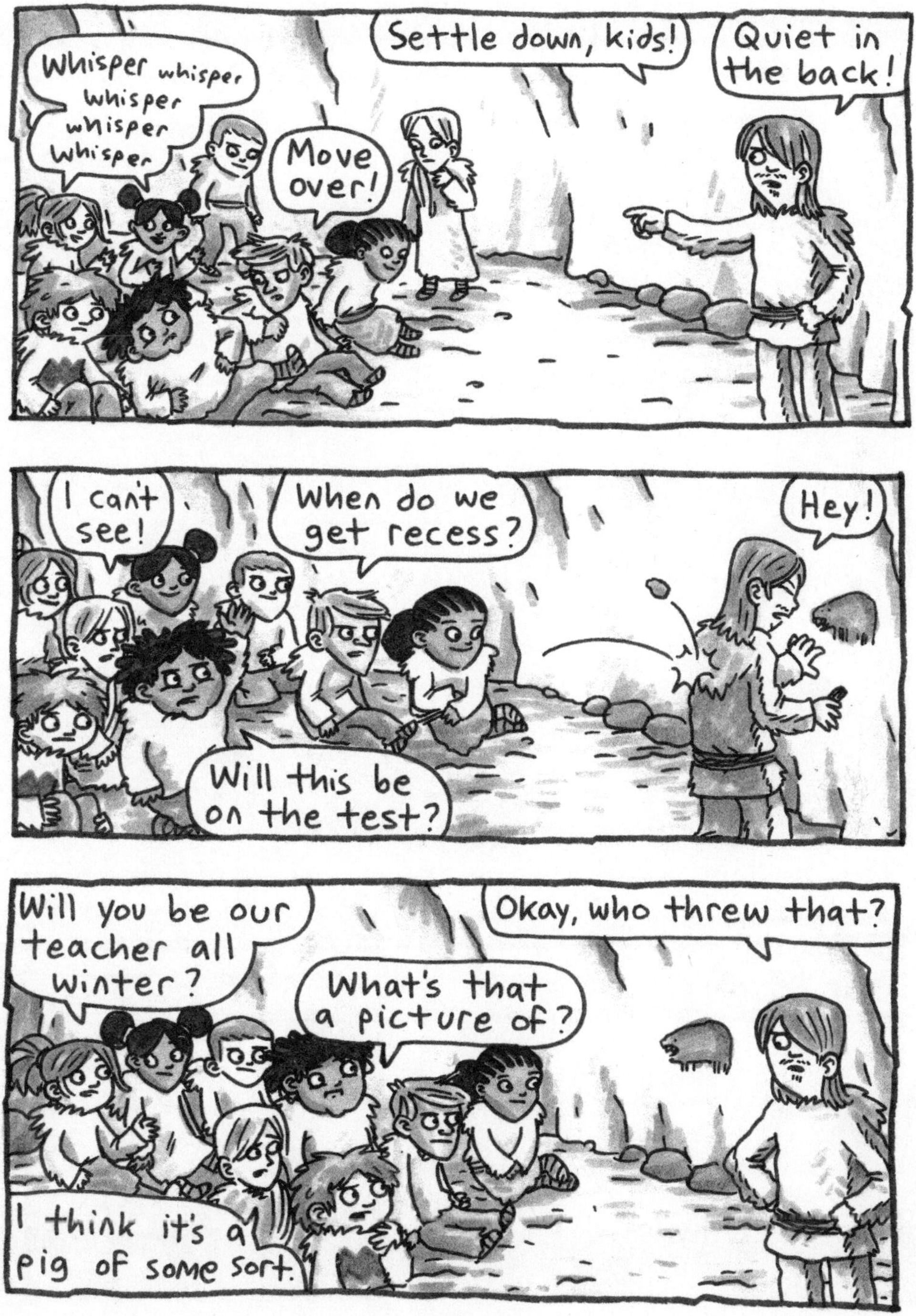
Whisper whisper whisper whisper whisper
Move over!
Settle down, kids!
Quiet in the back!
I can't see!
When do we get recess?
Will this be on the test?
Hey!
Will you be our teacher all winter?
What's that a picture of?
Okay, who threw that?
I think it's a pig of some sort.

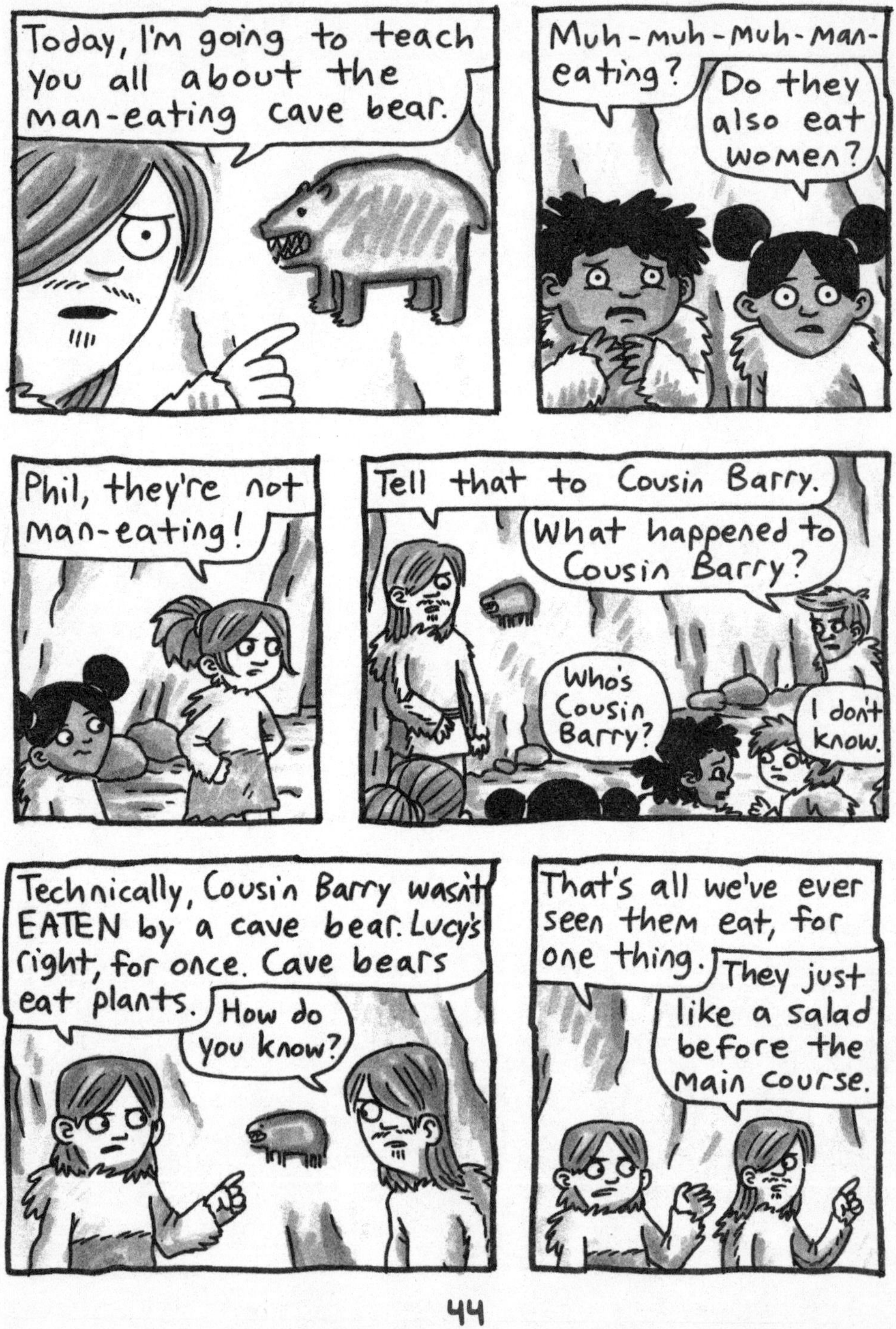
Today, I'm going to teach you all about the man-eating cave bear.
Muh-muh-Muh-Man-eating?
Do they also eat women?
Phil, they're not man-eating!
Tell that to Cousin Barry.
What happened to Cousin Barry?
Who's Cousin Barry?
I don't know.
Technically, Cousin Barry wasn't EATEN by a cave bear. Lucy's right, for once. Cave bears eat plants.
How do you know?
That's all we've ever seen them eat, for one thing.
They just like a salad before the main course.

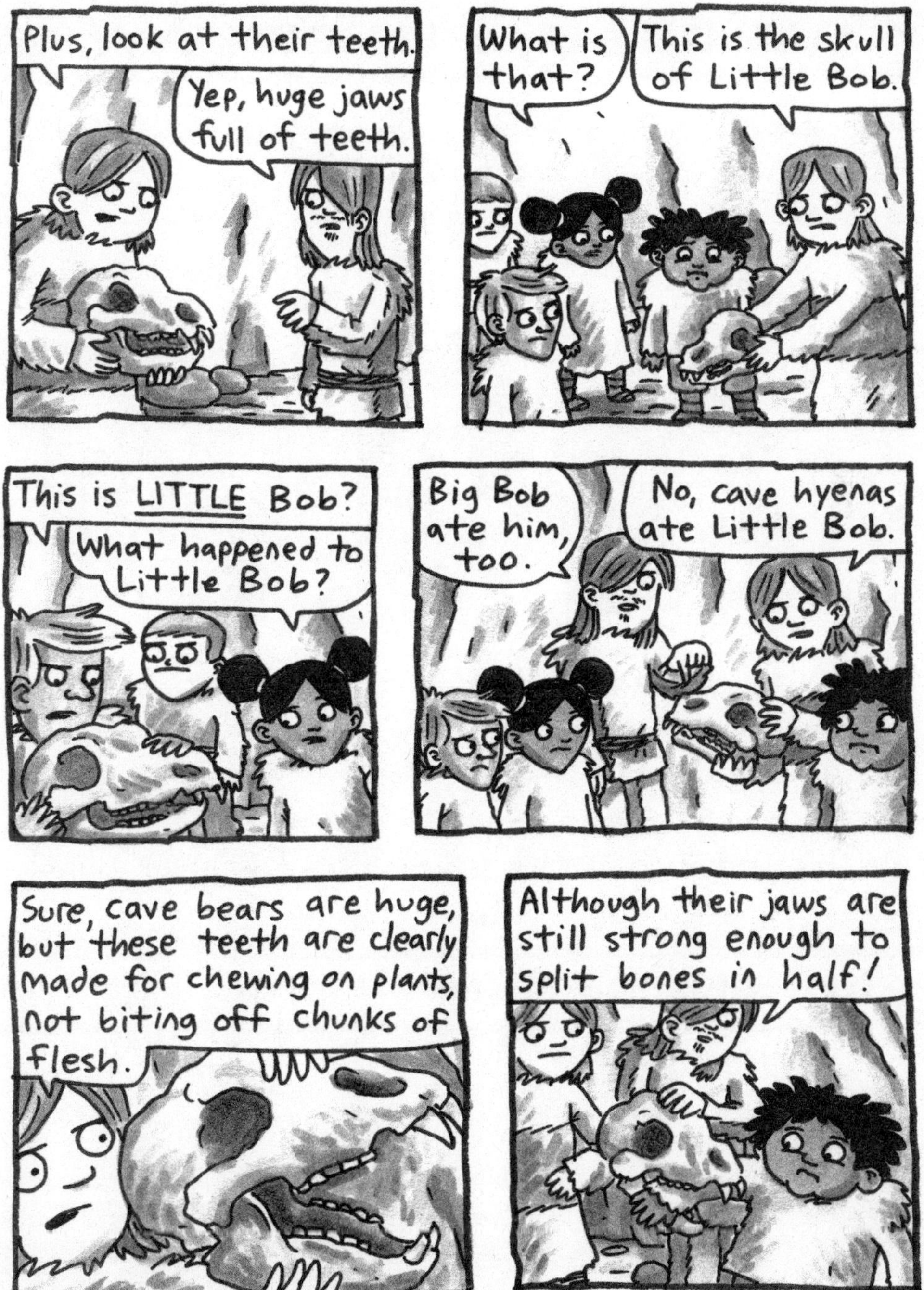
Plus, look at their teeth.
Yep, huge jaws full of teeth.
What is that?
This is the skull of Little Bob.
This is LITTLE Bob?
What happened to Little Bob?
Big Bob ate him, too.
No, cave hyenas ate Little Bob.
Sure, cave bears are huge, but these teeth are clearly made for chewing on plants, not biting off chunks of flesh.
Although their jaws are still strong enough to split bones in half!

CAVE BEAR CLASS NOTES!

The cave bear lived in Europe and western Asia from about 300,000 years ago until around 28,000 years ago.

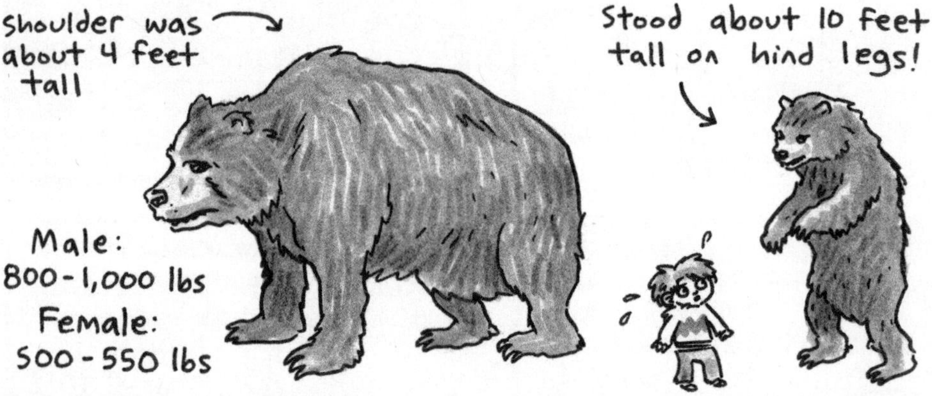
Shoulder was about 4 feet tall
Stood about 10 feet tall on hind legs!
Male: 800-1,000 lbs
Female: 500-550 lbs

Were polar bears the dominant bear during the Ice Age? No! During the time of the Neanderthals, cave bears and the smaller brown bear were the most common bears found in Europe and Asia. The biggest bear, the short-faced bear, occupied North America until about 12,000 years ago.

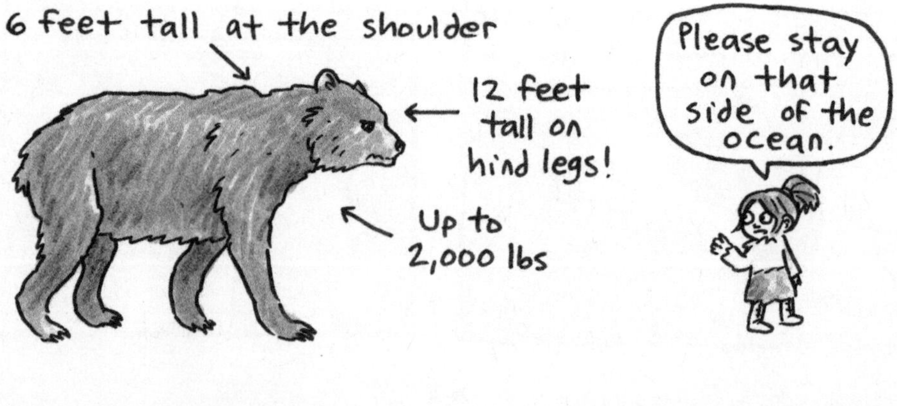
6 feet tall at the shoulder
12 feet tall on hind legs!
Up to 2,000 lbs
Please stay on that side of the ocean.

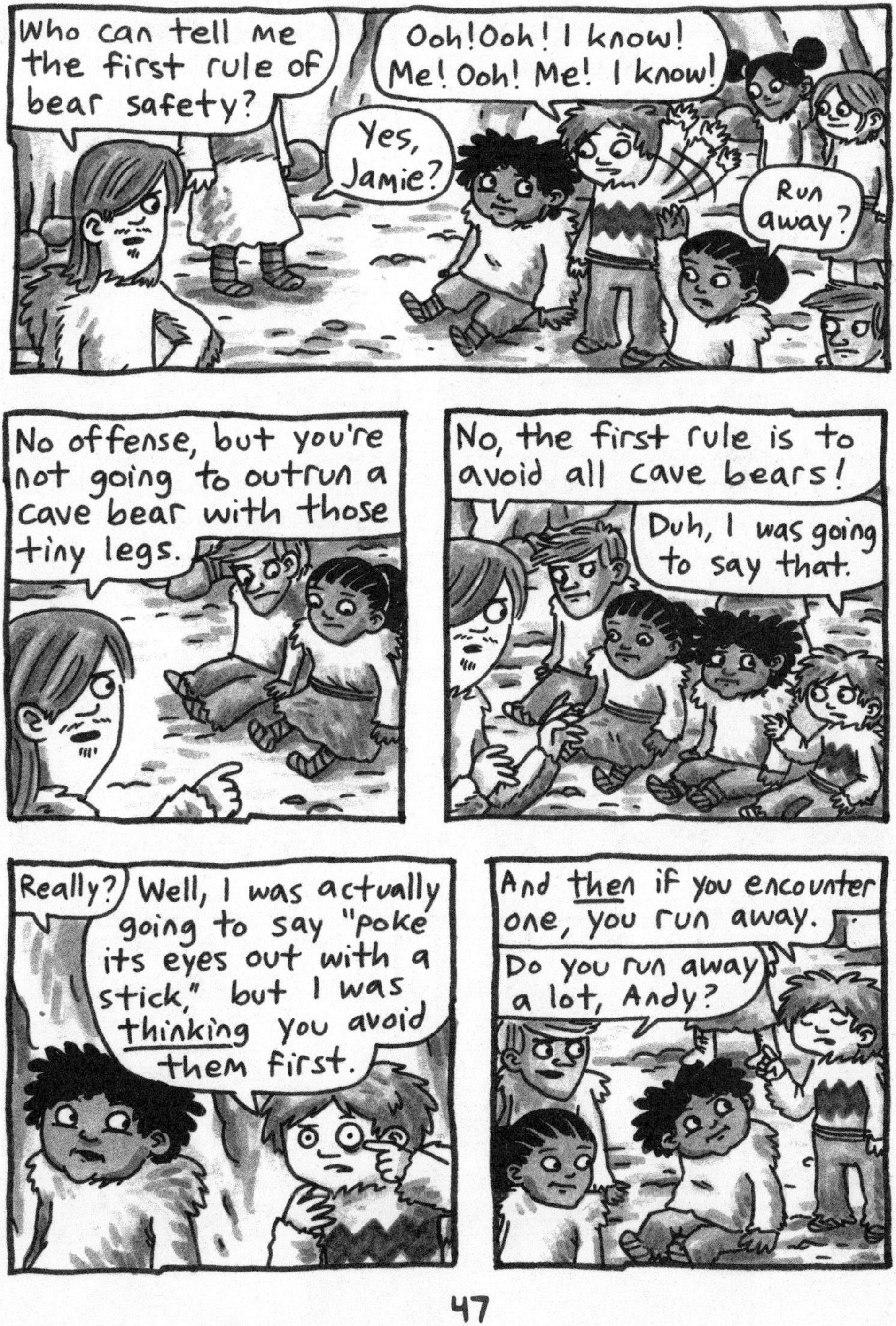
Who can tell me the first rule of bear safety?
Ooh! Ooh! I know! Me! Ooh! Me! I know!
Yes, Jamie?
Run away?
No offense, but you're not going to outrun a cave bear with those tiny legs.
No, the first rule is to avoid all cave bears!
Duh, I was going to say that.
Really?
Well, I was actually going to say "poke its eyes out with a stick," but I was thinking you avoid them first.
And then if you encounter one, you run away.
Do you run away a lot, Andy?

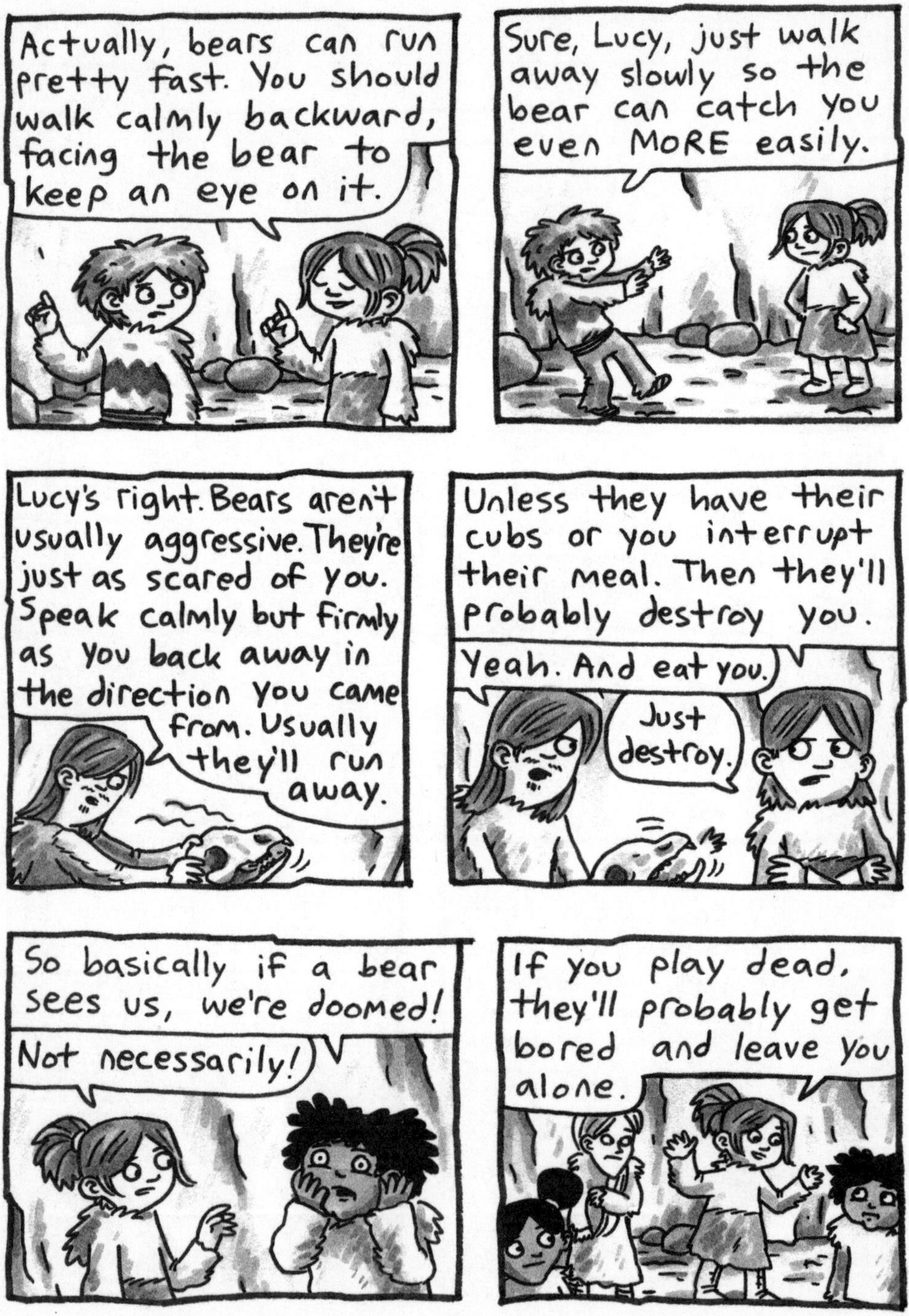
Actually, bears can run pretty fast. You should walk calmly backward, facing the bear to keep an eye on it.
Sure, Lucy, just walk away slowly so the bear can catch you even MORE easily.
Lucy's right. Bears aren't usually aggressive. They're just as scared of you. Speak calmly but firmly as you back away in the direction you came from. Usually they'll run away.
Unless they have their cubs or you interrupt their meal. Then they'll probably destroy you.
Yeah. And eat you.
Just destroy.
So basically if a bear sees us, we're doomed!
Not necessarily!
If you play dead, they'll probably get bored and leave you alone.

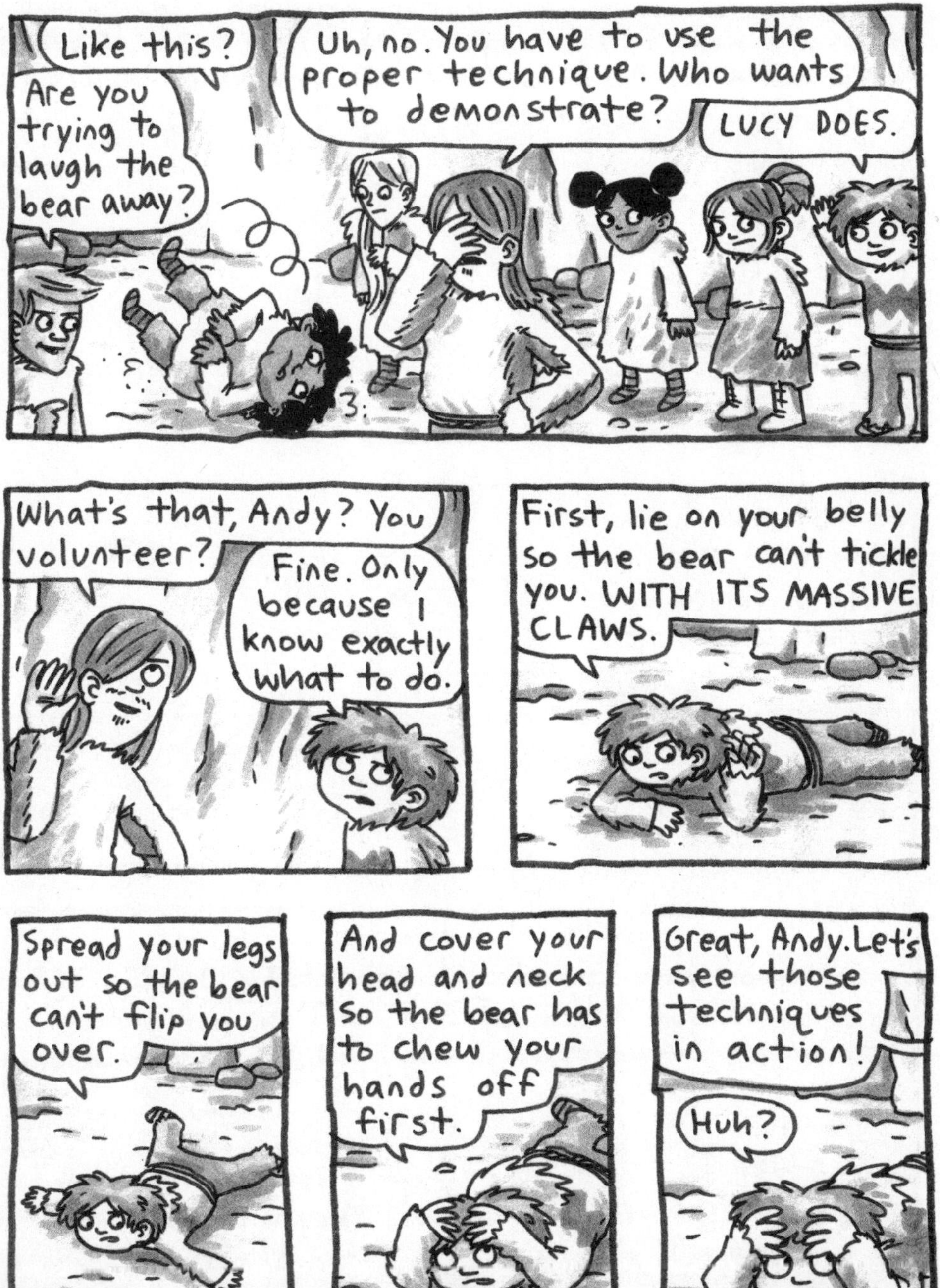
Like this?
Are you trying to laugh the bear away?
Uh, no. You have to use the proper technique. Who wants to demonstrate?
LUCY DOES.
What's that, Andy? You volunteer?
Fine. Only because I know exactly what to do.
First, lie on your belly so the bear can't tickle you. WITH ITS MASSIVE CLAWS.
Spread your legs out so the bear can't flip you over.
And cover your head and neck so the bear has to chew your hands off first.
Great, Andy. Let's see those techniques in action!
Huh?

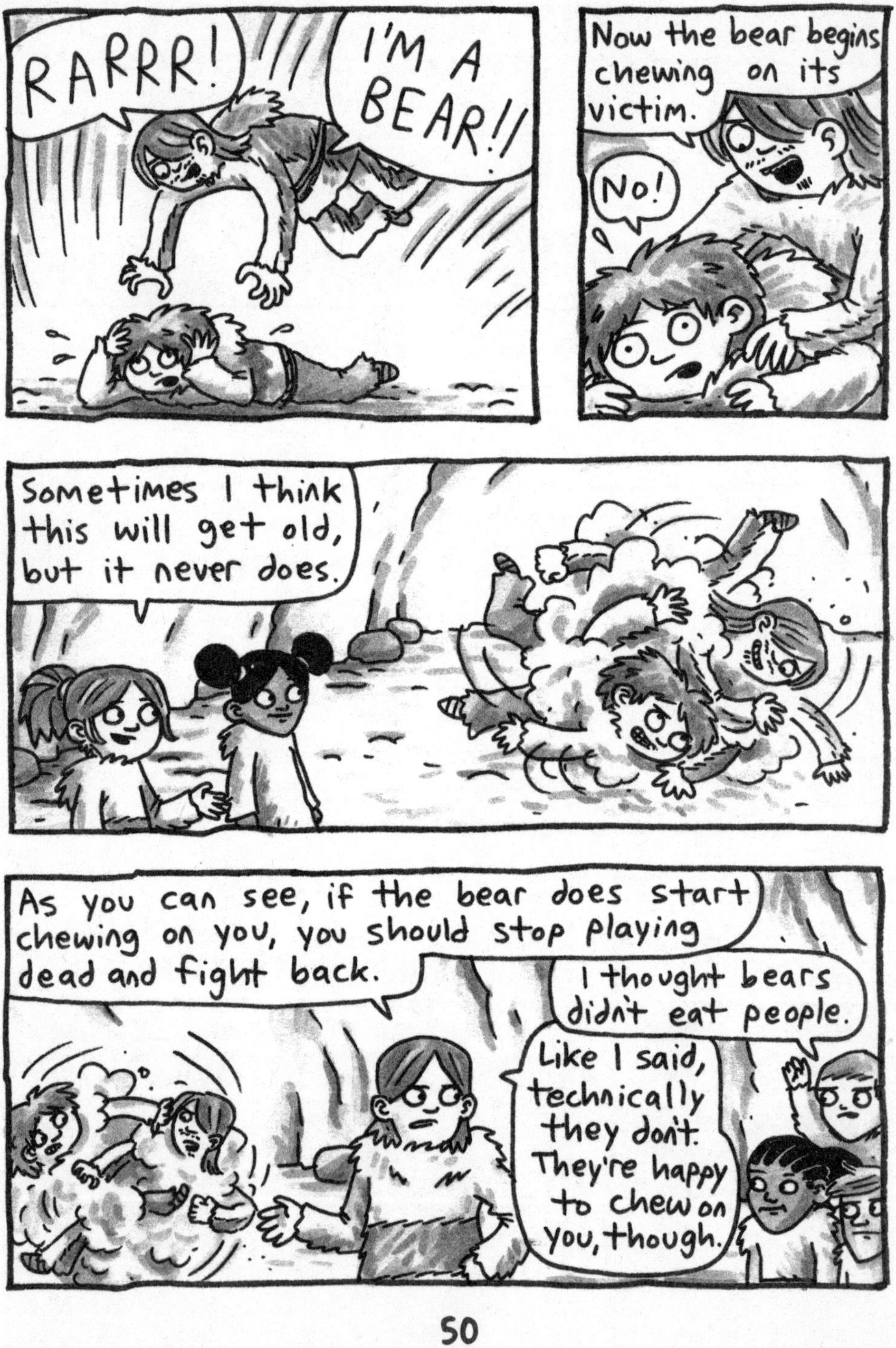
RARRR!
I'M A BEAR!!
Now the bear begins chewing on its victim.
No!
Sometimes I think this will get old, but it never does.
As you can see, if the bear does start chewing on you, you should stop playing dead and fight back.
I thought bears didn't eat people.
Like I said, technically they don't. They're happy to chew on you, though.

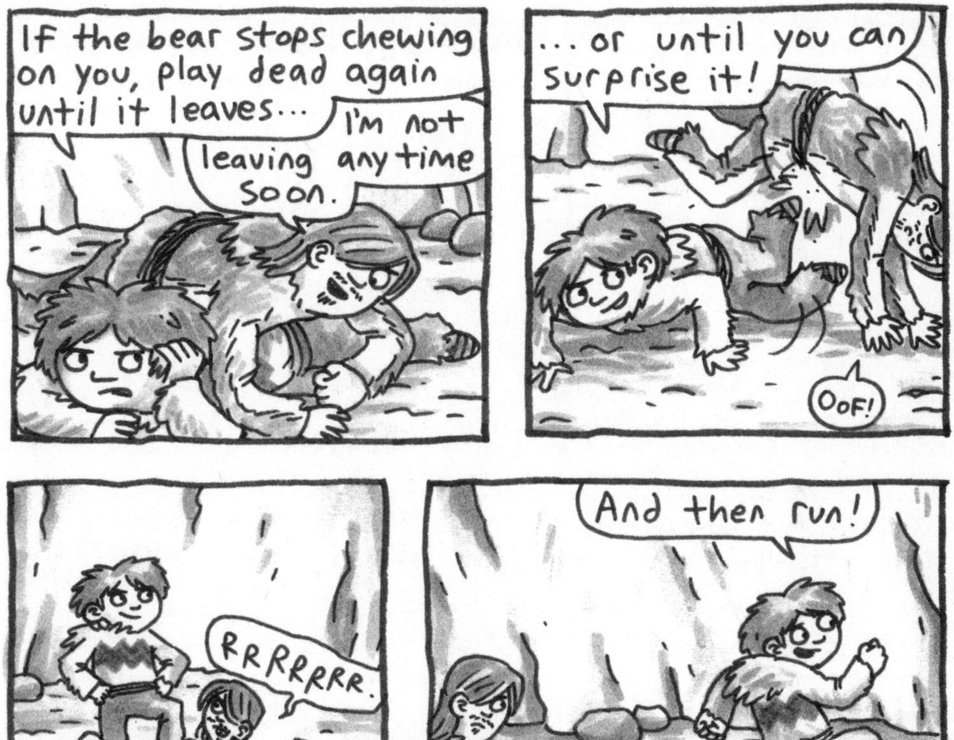
If the bear stops chewing on you, play dead again until it leaves...
I'm not leaving any time soon.
...or until you can surprise it!
OoF!
RRRRRRR.
And then run!
That was rad, Andy! Have you ever done that with a real bear?
I've never gotten that close.
No, I meant the running. I want to be that fast!

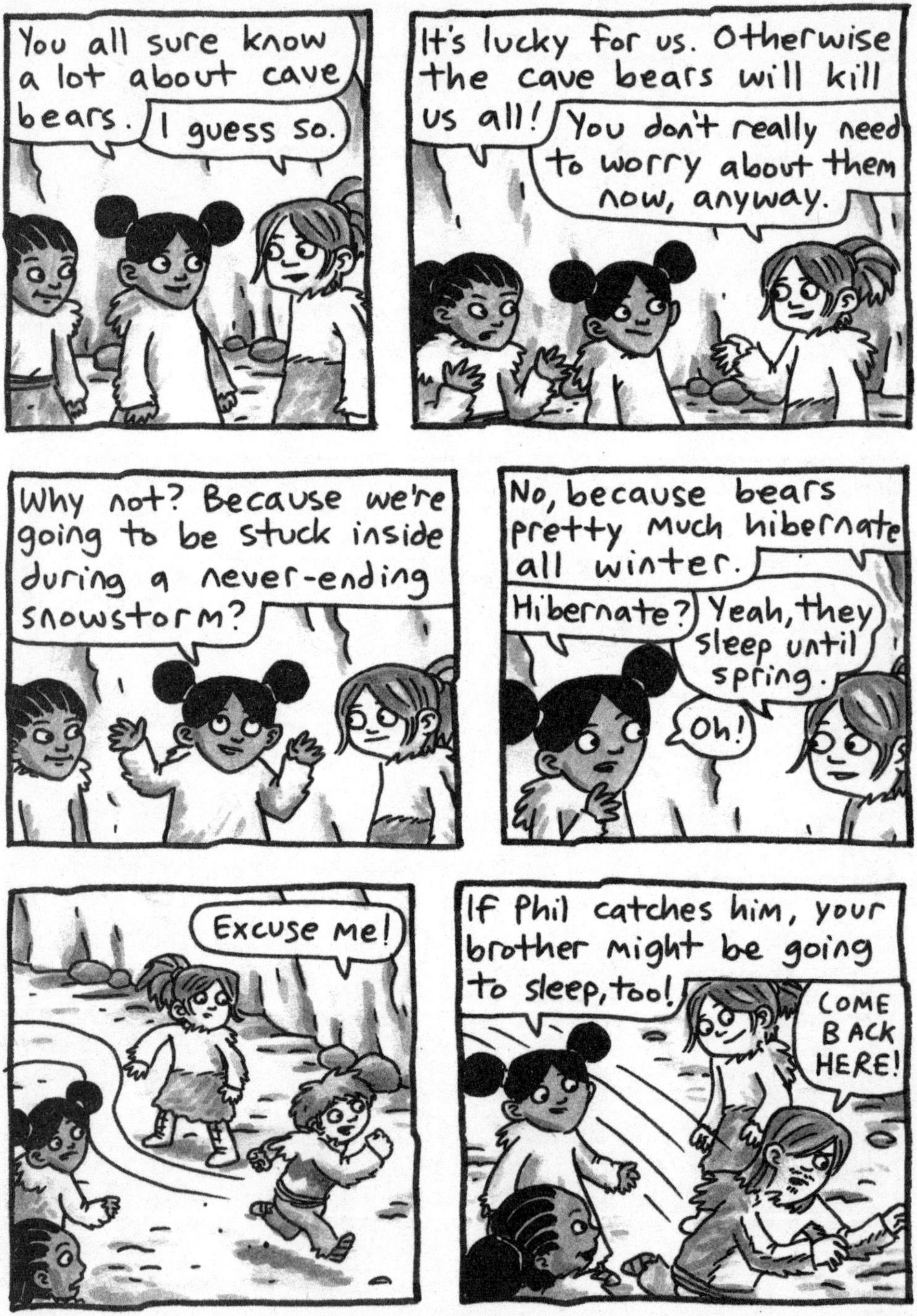
You all sure know a lot about cave bears.
I guess so.
It's lucky for us. Otherwise the cave bears will kill us all!
You don't really need to worry about them now, anyway.
Why not? Because we're going to be stuck inside during a never-ending snowstorm?
No, because bears pretty much hibernate all winter.
Hibernate?
Yeah, they sleep until spring.
Oh!
Excuse me!
If Phil catches him, your brother might be going to sleep, too!
COME BACK HERE!

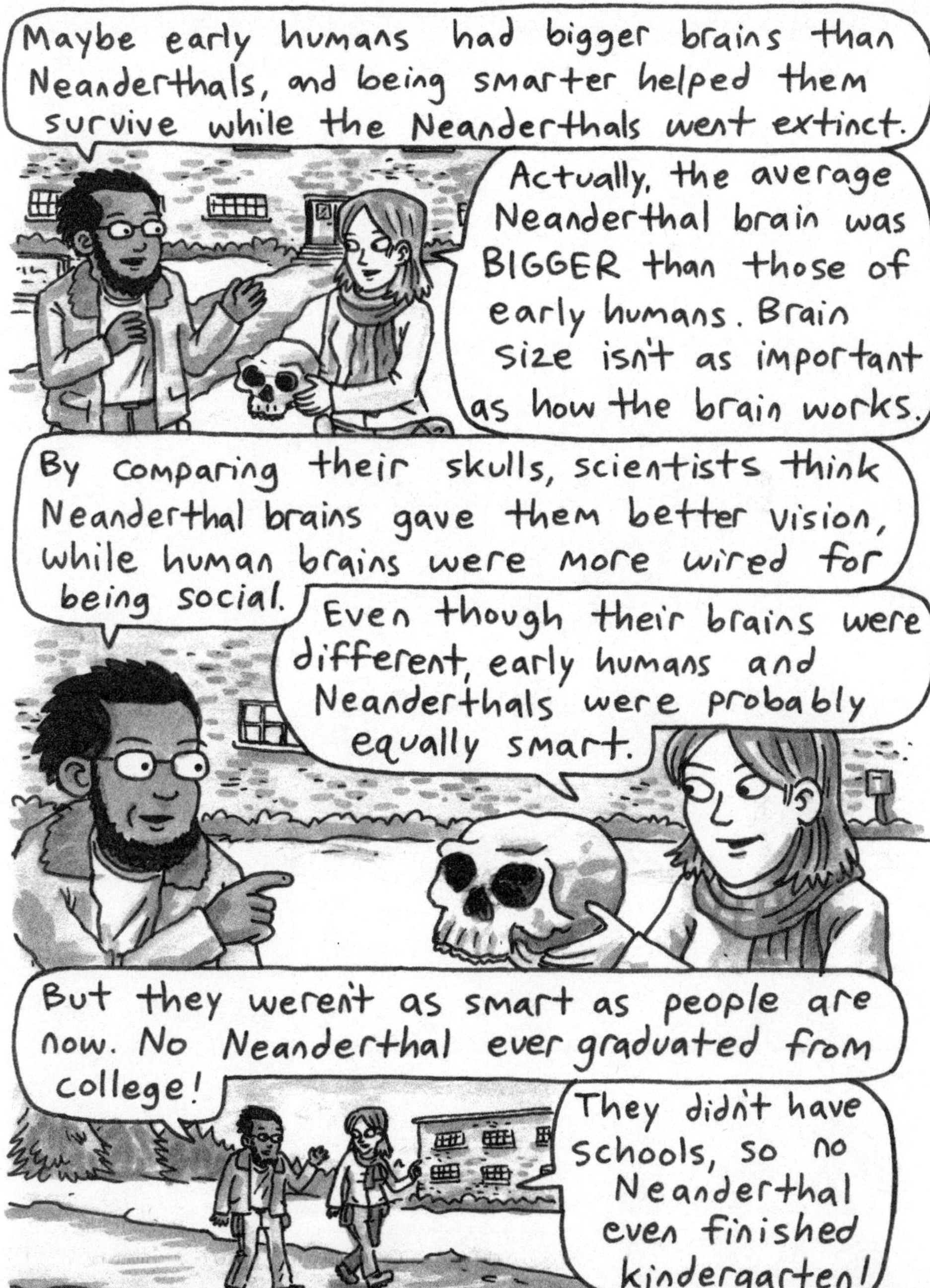
Maybe early humans had bigger brains than Neanderthals, and being smarter helped them survive while the Neanderthals went extinct.
Actually, the average Neanderthal brain was BIGGER than those of early humans. Brain size isn't as important as how the brain works.
By comparing their skulls, scientists think Neanderthal brains gave them better vision, while human brains were more wired for being social.
Even though their brains were different, early humans and Neanderthals were probably equally smart.
But they weren't as smart as people are now. No Neanderthal ever graduated from college!
They didn't have schools, so no Neanderthal even finished kindergarten!

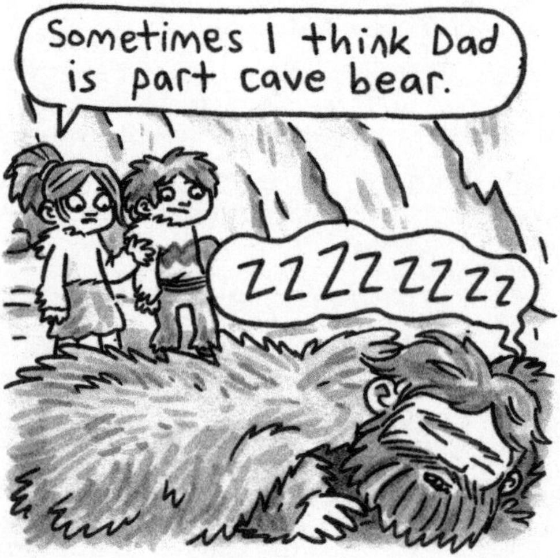
Sometimes I think Dad is part cave bear.
ZZZZZZZZz

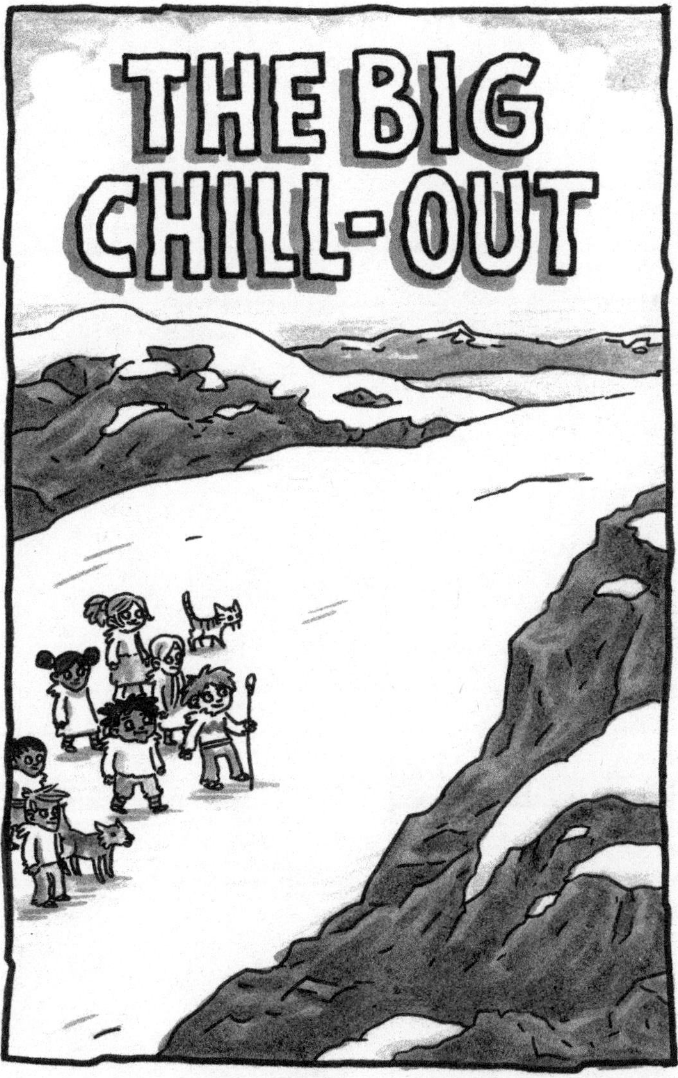
THE BIG CHILL-OUT

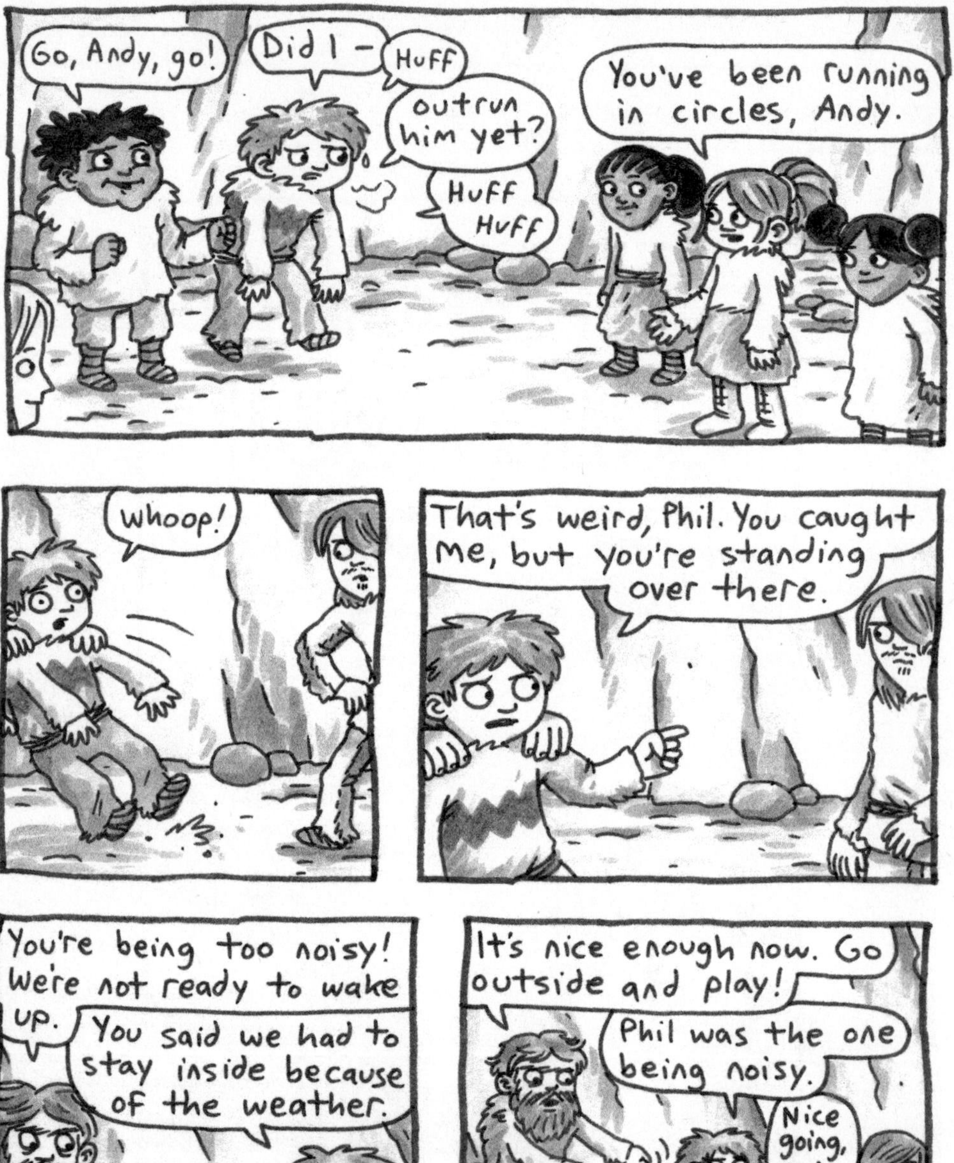
Go, Andy, go!
Did I -
Huff
outrun him yet?
Huff Huff
You've been running in circles, Andy.
Whoop!
That's weird, Phil. You caught me, but you're standing over there.
You're being too noisy! We're not ready to wake up.
You said we had to stay inside because of the weather.
It's nice enough now. Go outside and play!
Phil was the one being noisy.
Nice going, Andy.

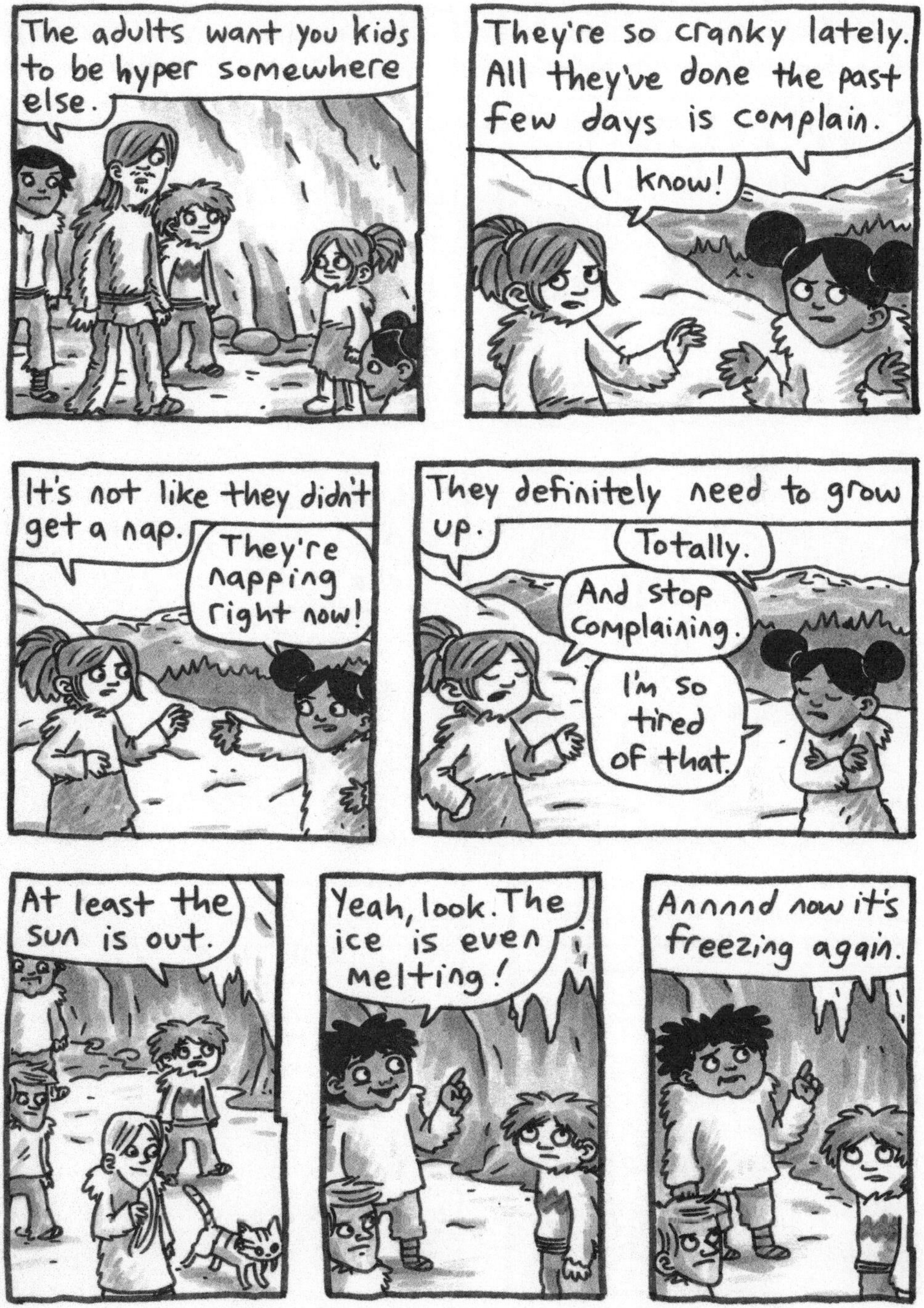
The adults want you kids to be hyper somewhere else.
They're so cranky lately. All they've done the past few days is complain.
I know!
It's not like they didn't get a nap.
They're napping right now!
They definitely need to grow up.
Totally.
And stop complaining.
I'm so tired of that.
At least the sun is out.
Yeah, look. The ice is even melting!
Annnnd now it's freezing again.

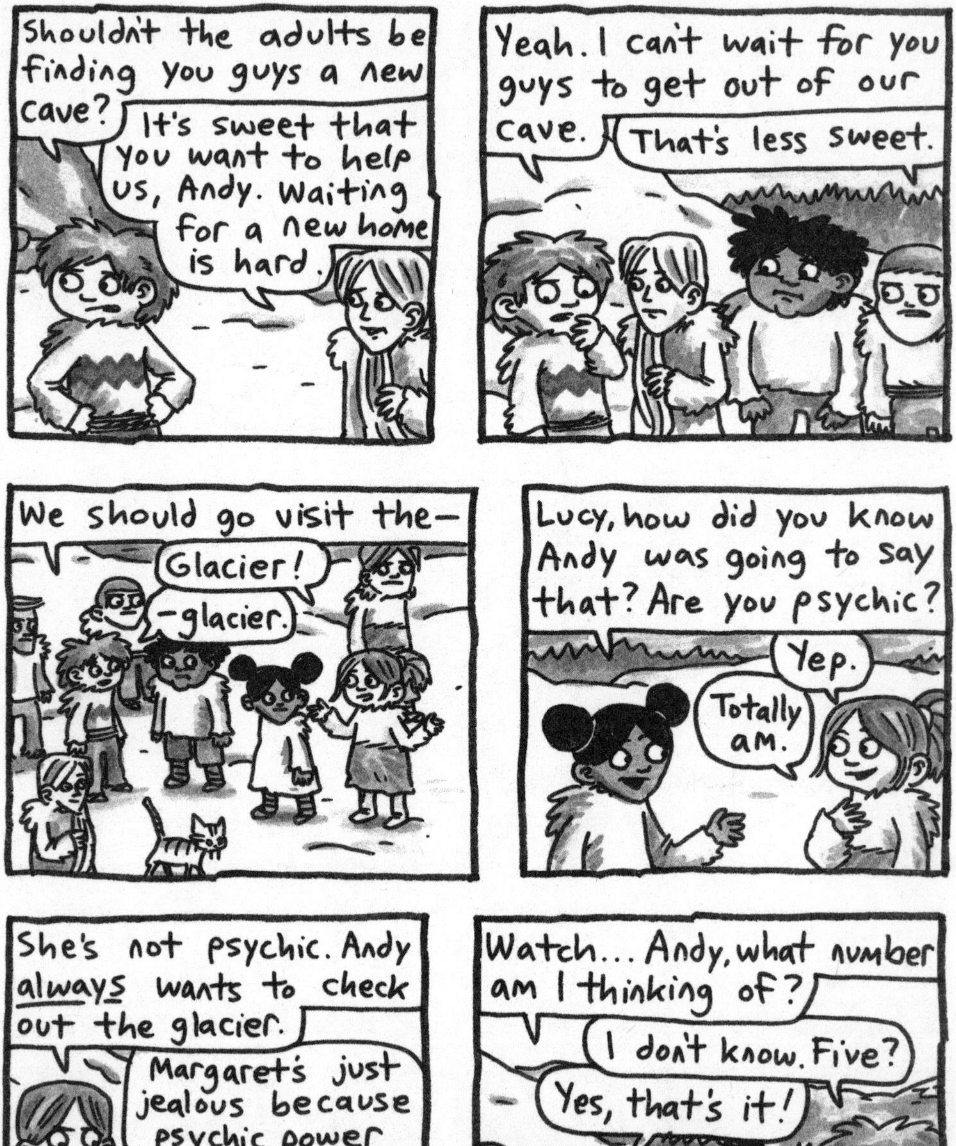
Shouldn't the adults be finding you guys a new cave?
It's sweet that you want to help us, Andy. Waiting for a new home is hard.
Yeah. I can't wait for you guys to get out of our cave.
That's less sweet.
We should go visit the—
Glacier!
—glacier.
Lucy, how did you know Andy was going to say that? Are you psychic?
Yep.
Totally am.
She's not psychic. Andy always wants to check out the glacier.
Margaret's just jealous because psychic power runs in my family.
Watch... Andy, what number am I thinking of?
I don't know. Five?
Yes, that's it!

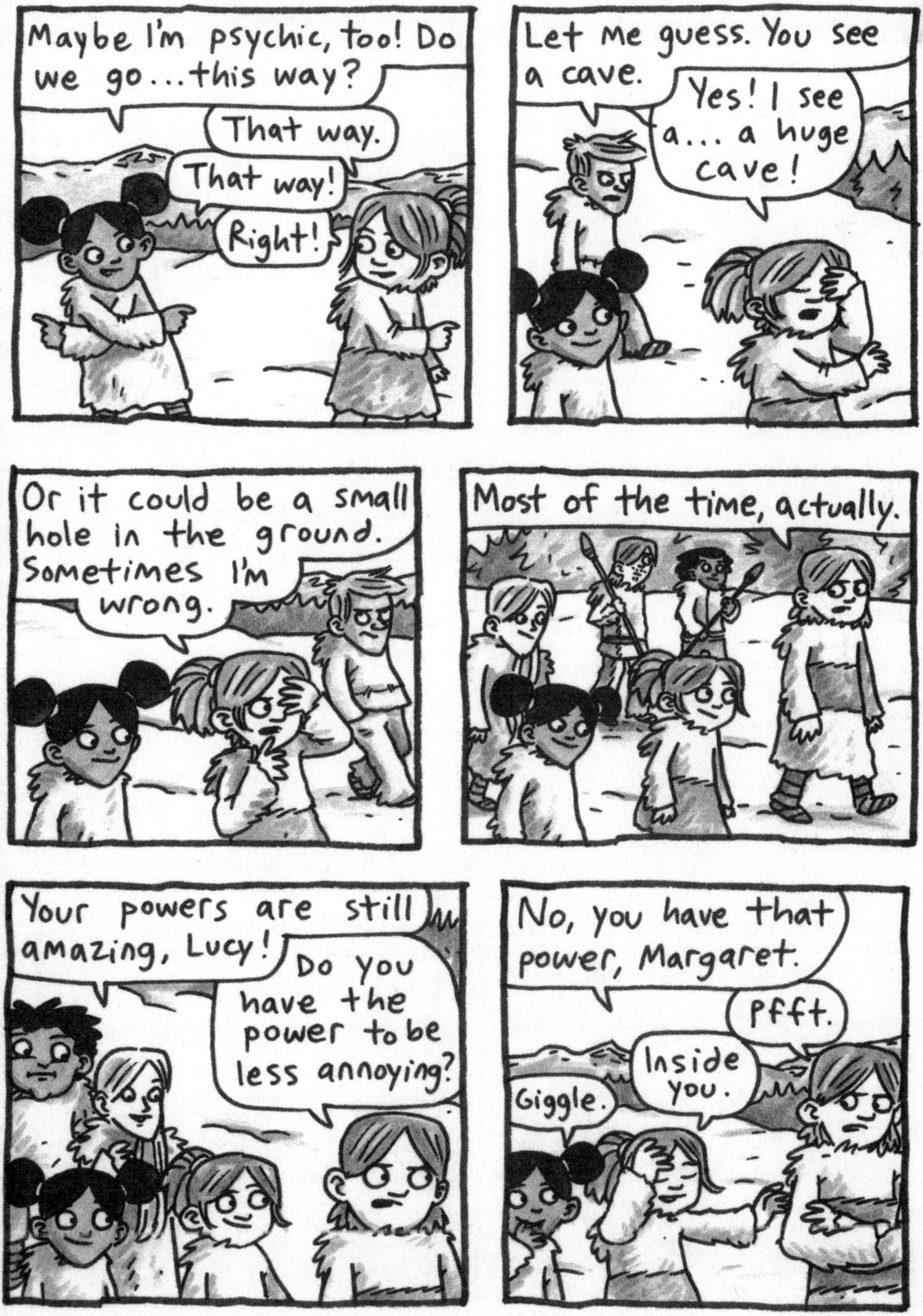
Maybe I'm psychic, too! Do we go... this way?
That way.
That way!
Right!
Let me guess. You see a cave.
Yes! I see a... a huge cave!
Or it could be a small hole in the ground. Sometimes I'm wrong.
Most of the time, actually.
Your powers are still amazing, Lucy!
Do you have the power to be less annoying?
No, you have that power, Margaret.
Pfft.
Inside you.
Giggle.

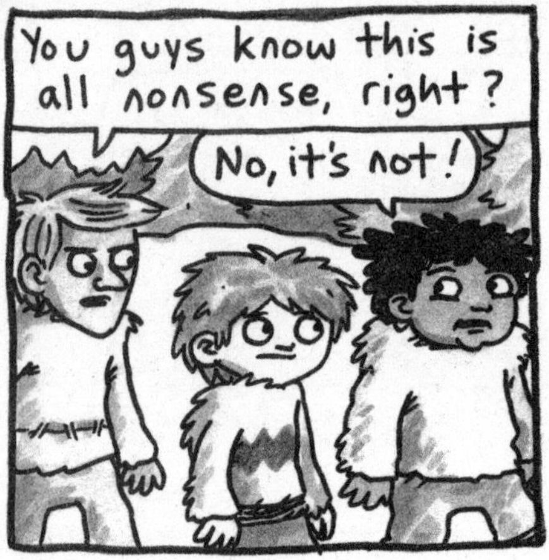
You guys know this is all nonsense, right?
No, it's not!

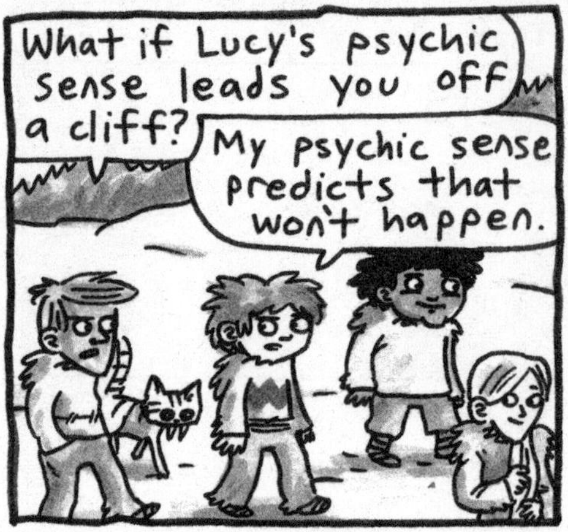
What if Lucy's psychic sense leads you off a cliff?
My psychic sense predicts that won't happen.

If psychic powers were real, paleontologists would have an easier time finding fossils. People who claim to be psychic are correct about as often as random guessing!

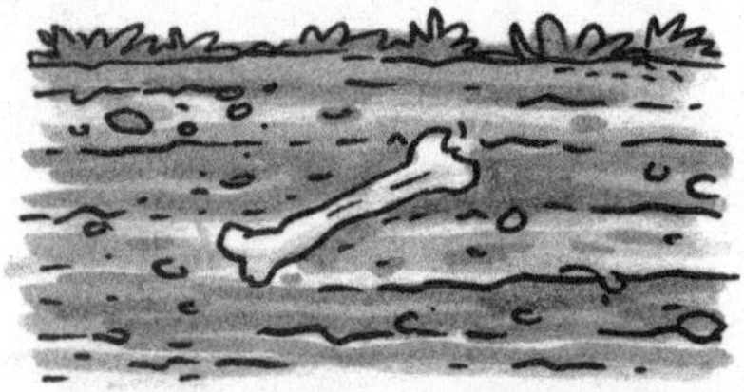

Instead, paleontologists rely on knowing where to look based on previous discoveries, help from locals who know that area, experience, and practice.

And sometimes a little luck!

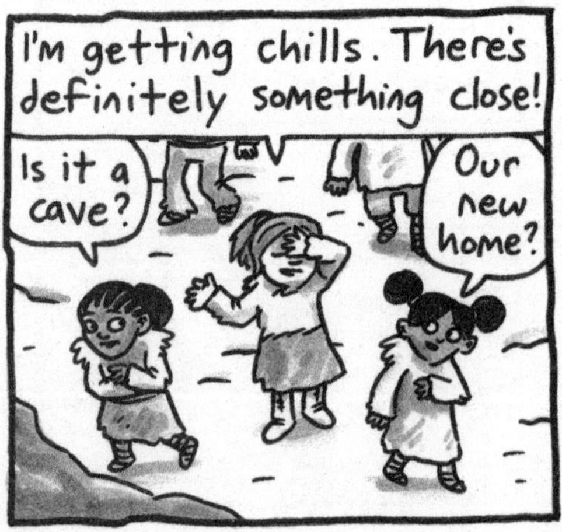
I'm getting chills. There's definitely something close!
Is it a cave?
Our new home?

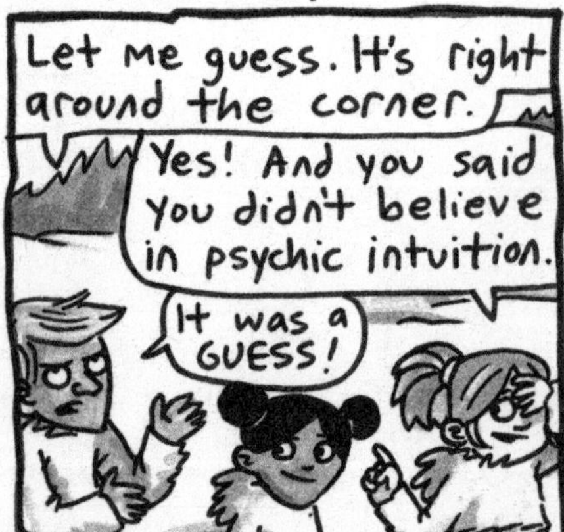
Let me guess. It's right around the corner.
Yes! And you said you didn't believe in psychic intuition.
It was a GUESS!

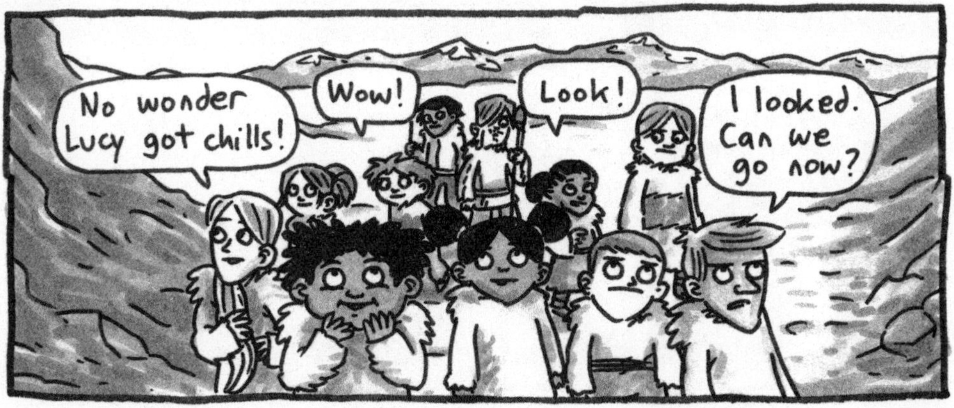
No wonder Lucy got chills!
Wow!
Look!
I looked. Can we go now?

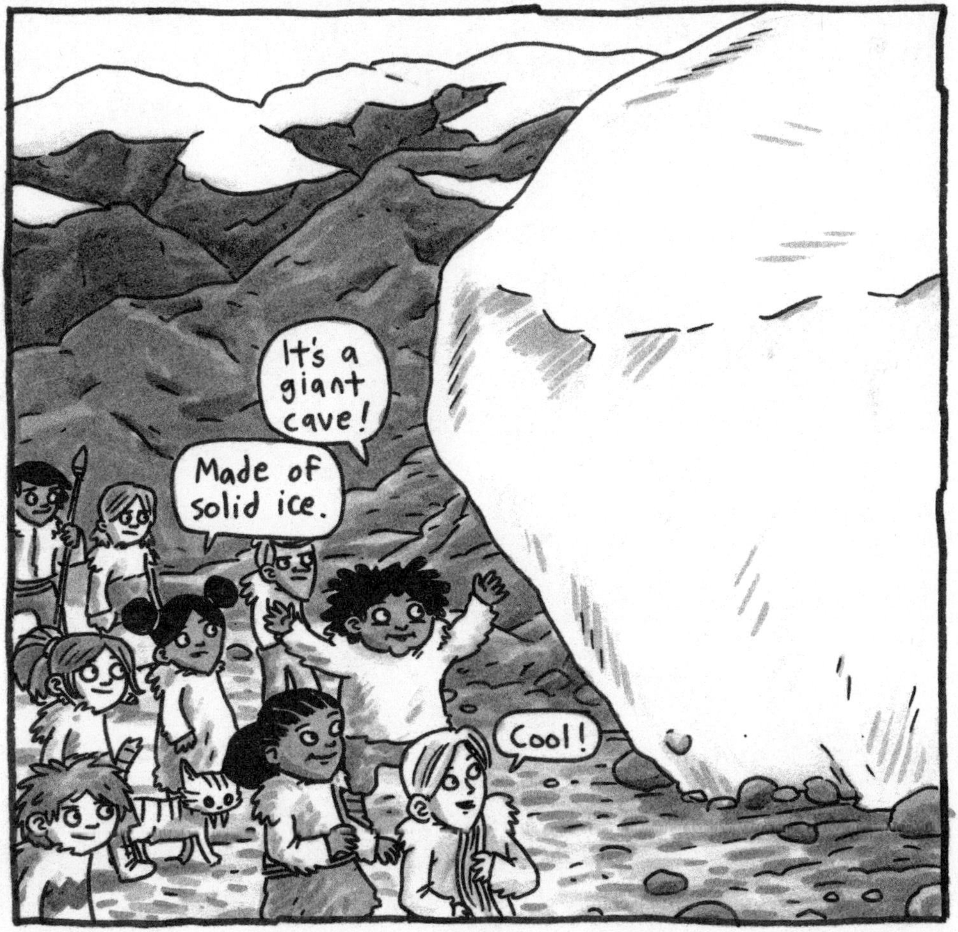
It's a giant cave!
Made of solid ice.
Cool!

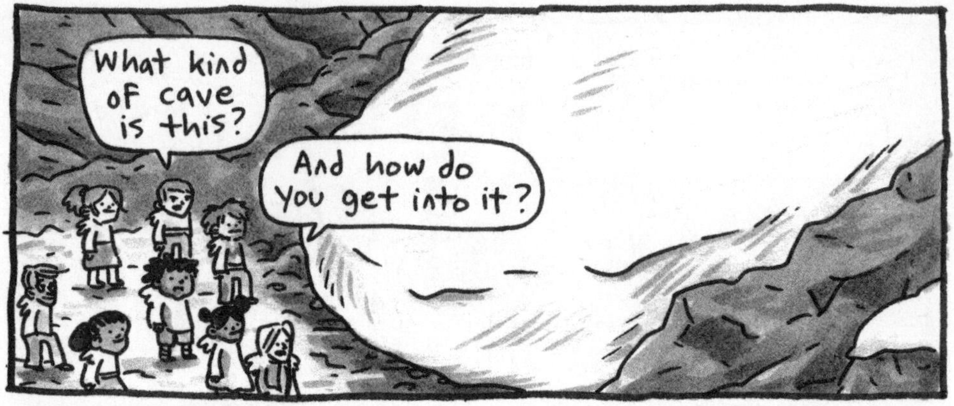
What kind of cave is this?
And how do you get into it?

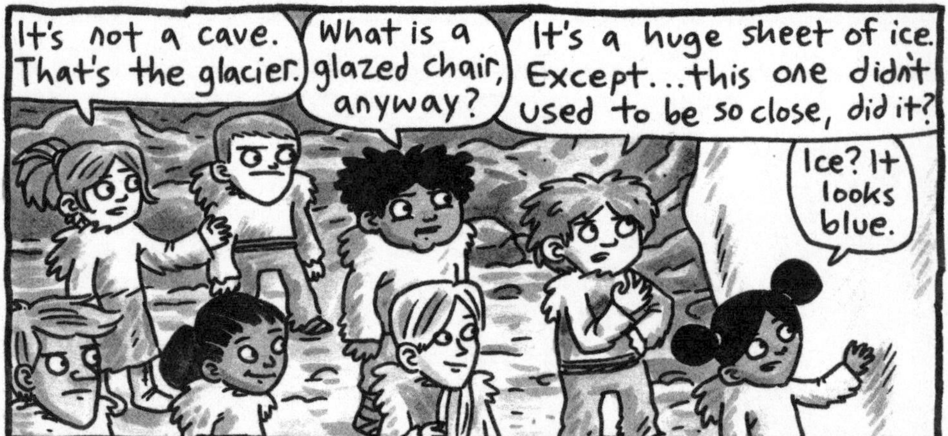
It's not a cave. That's the glacier.
What is a glazed chair, anyway?
It's a huge sheet of ice. Except...this one didn't used to be so close, did it?
Ice? It looks blue.

A glacier forms when enough snow and ice gather creating an ice sheet—almost like a river of ice!

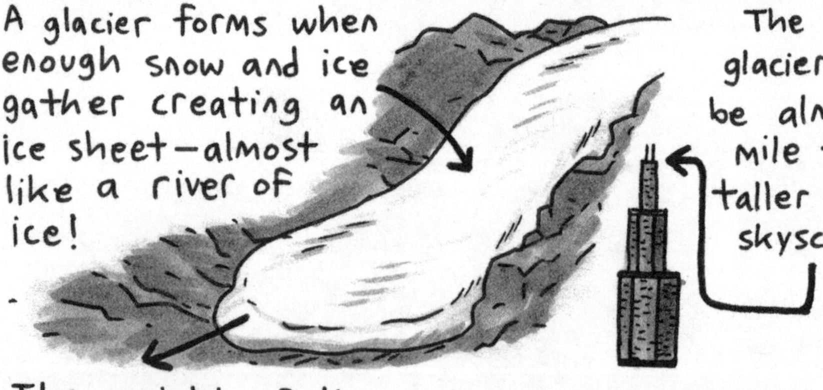

The thickest glaciers can be almost a mile thick—taller than a skyscraper!

The weight of the ice causes a glacier to move downhill—usually slowly, but sometimes 100 feet a day!

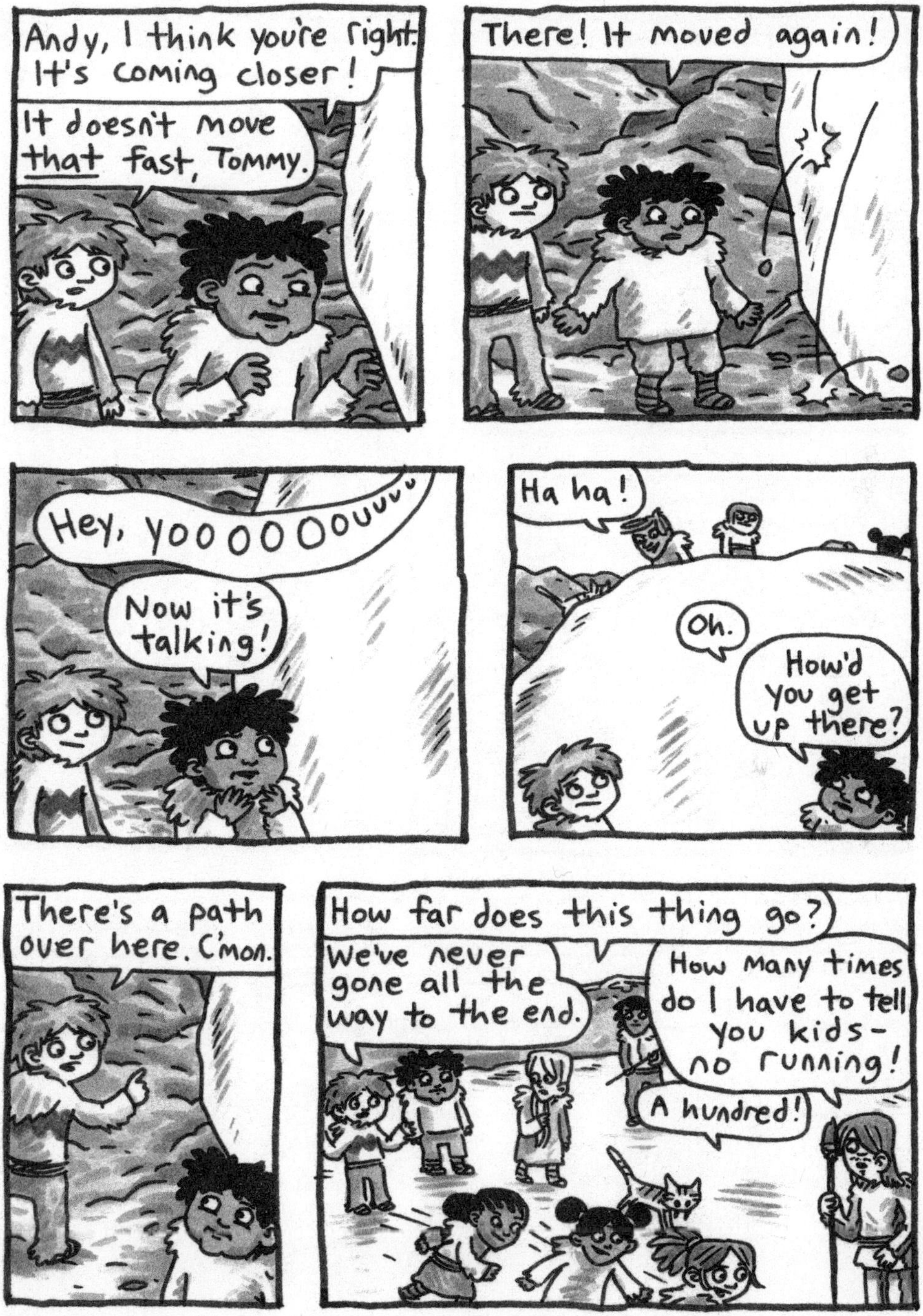
Andy, I think you're right. It's coming closer!
It doesn't move that fast, Tommy.
There! It moved again!
Hey, yooOOOOouuuu
Now it's talking!
Ha ha!
Oh.
How'd you get up there?
There's a path over here. C'mon.
How far does this thing go?
We've never gone all the way to the end.
How many times do I have to tell you kids - no running!
A hundred!

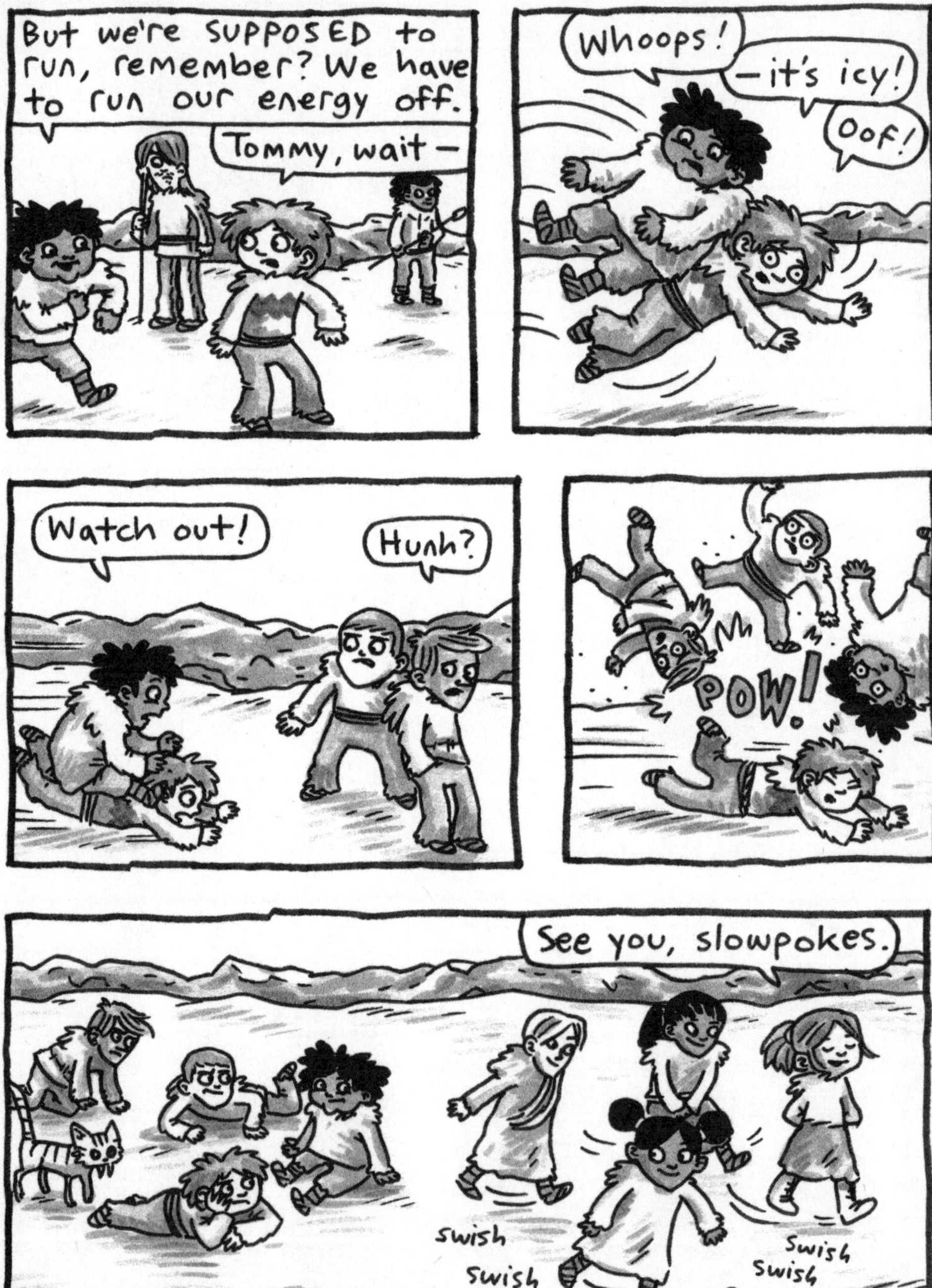
But we're SUPPOSED to run, remember? We have to run our energy off.
Tommy, wait—
Whoops!
—it's icy!
Oof!
Watch out!
Hunh?
POW!
See you, slowpokes.
swish
swish
swish
swish
swish
swish
swish

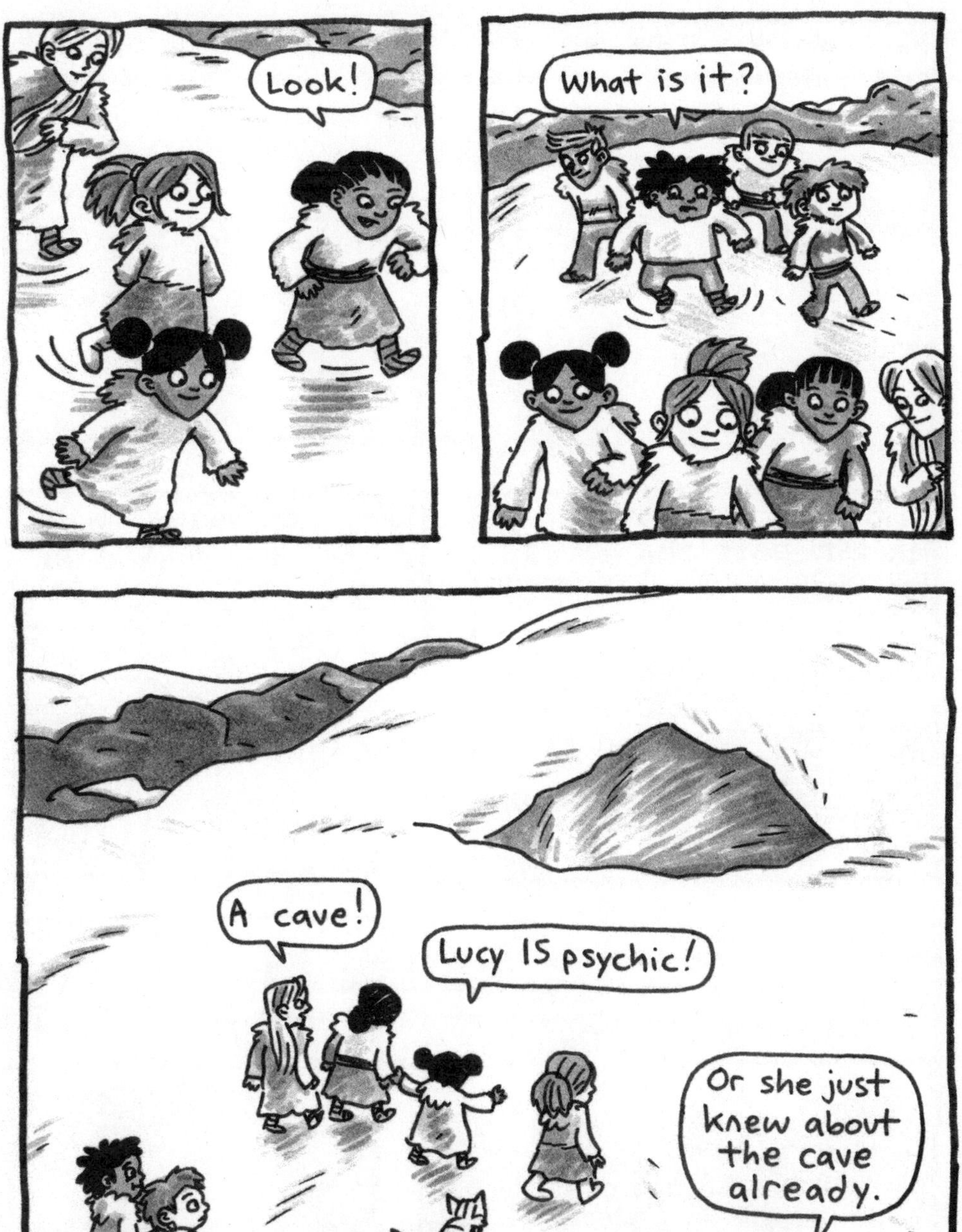

Look!
What is it?
A cave!
Lucy IS psychic!
Or she just knew about the cave already.

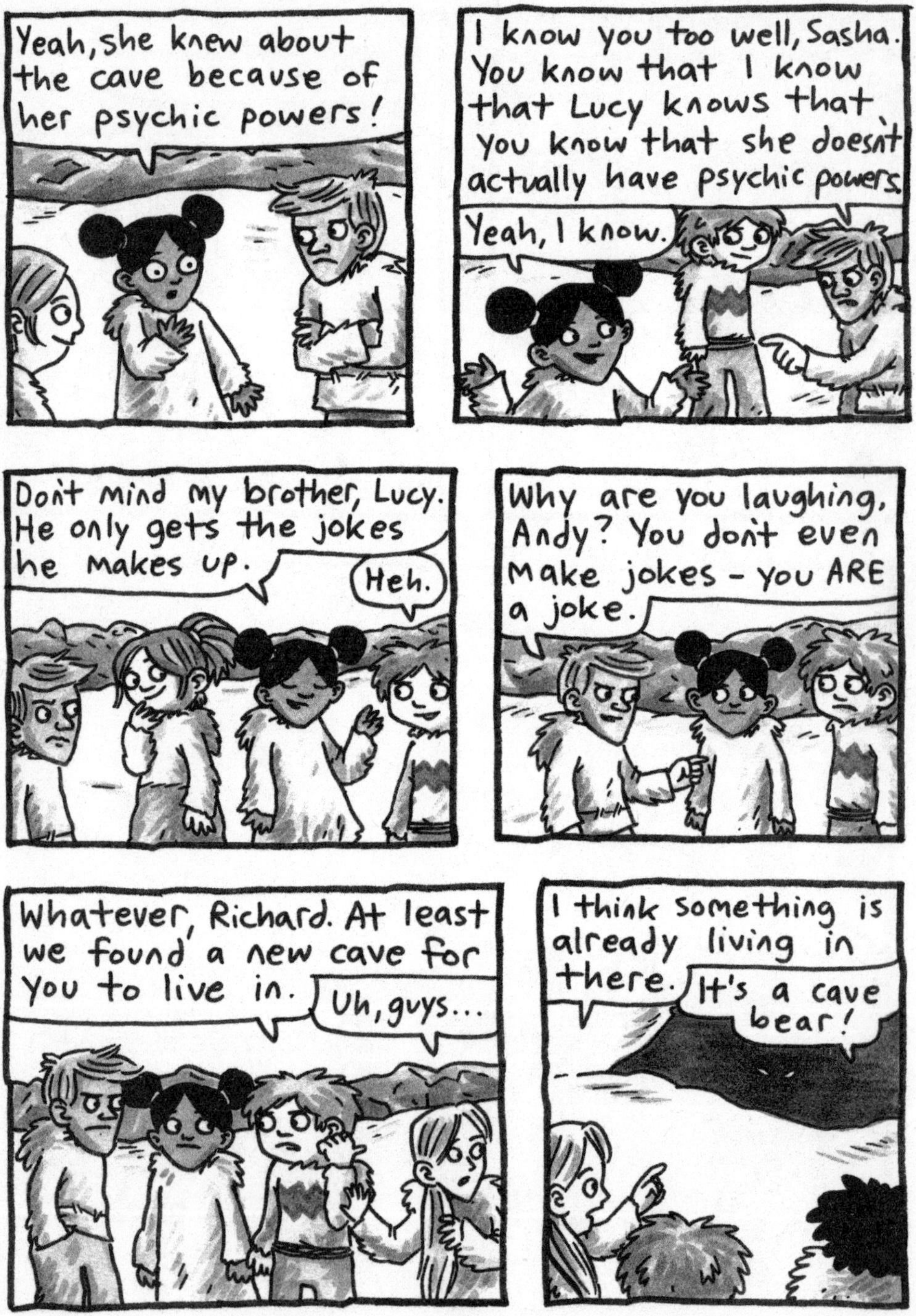
Yeah, she knew about the cave because of her psychic powers!
I know you too well, Sasha. You know that I know that Lucy knows that you know that she doesn't actually have psychic powers.
Yeah, I know.
Don't mind my brother, Lucy. He only gets the jokes he makes up.
Heh.
Why are you laughing, Andy? You don't even make jokes - you ARE a joke.
Whatever, Richard. At least we found a new cave for you to live in.
Uh, guys...
I think something is already living in there.
It's a cave bear!

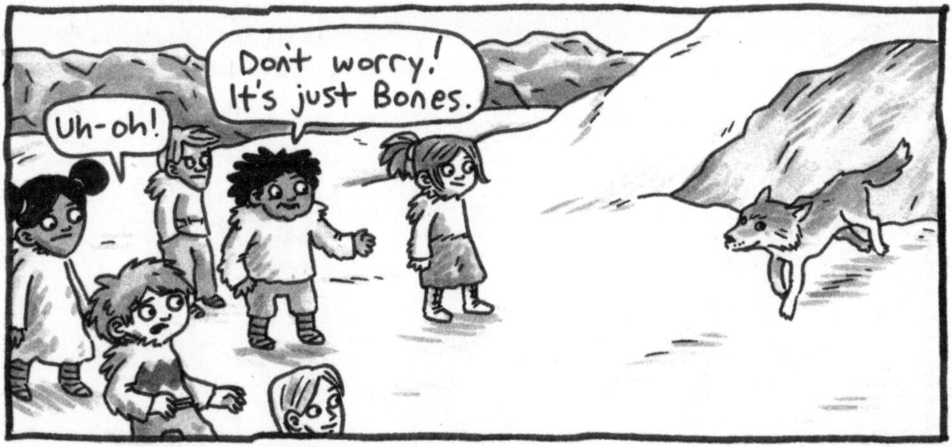
Uh-oh!
Don't worry! It's just Bones.

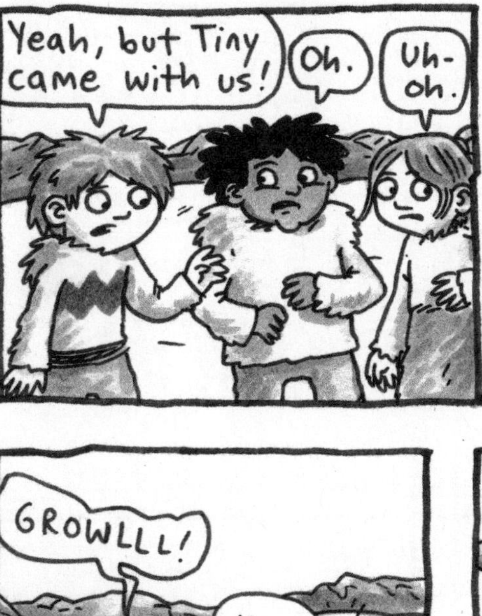
Yeah, but Tiny came with us!
Oh.
Uh-oh.

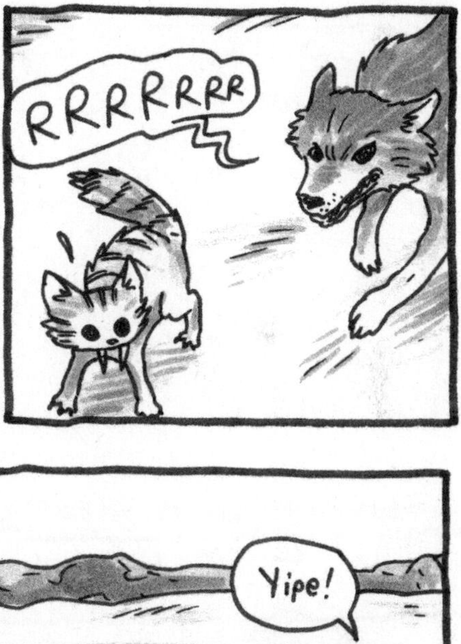
RRRRRRR

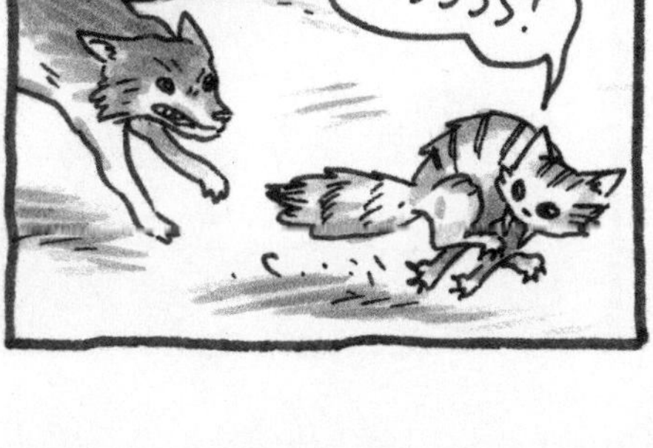
GROWLLL!
HISSSS!

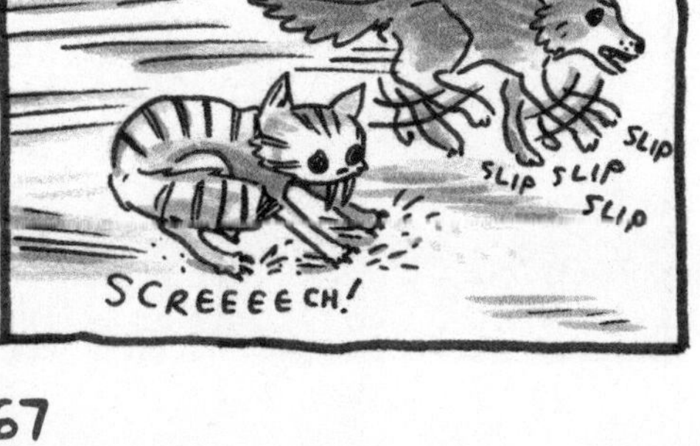
Yipe!
SLIP
SLIP SLIP
SLIP
SCREEEECH!

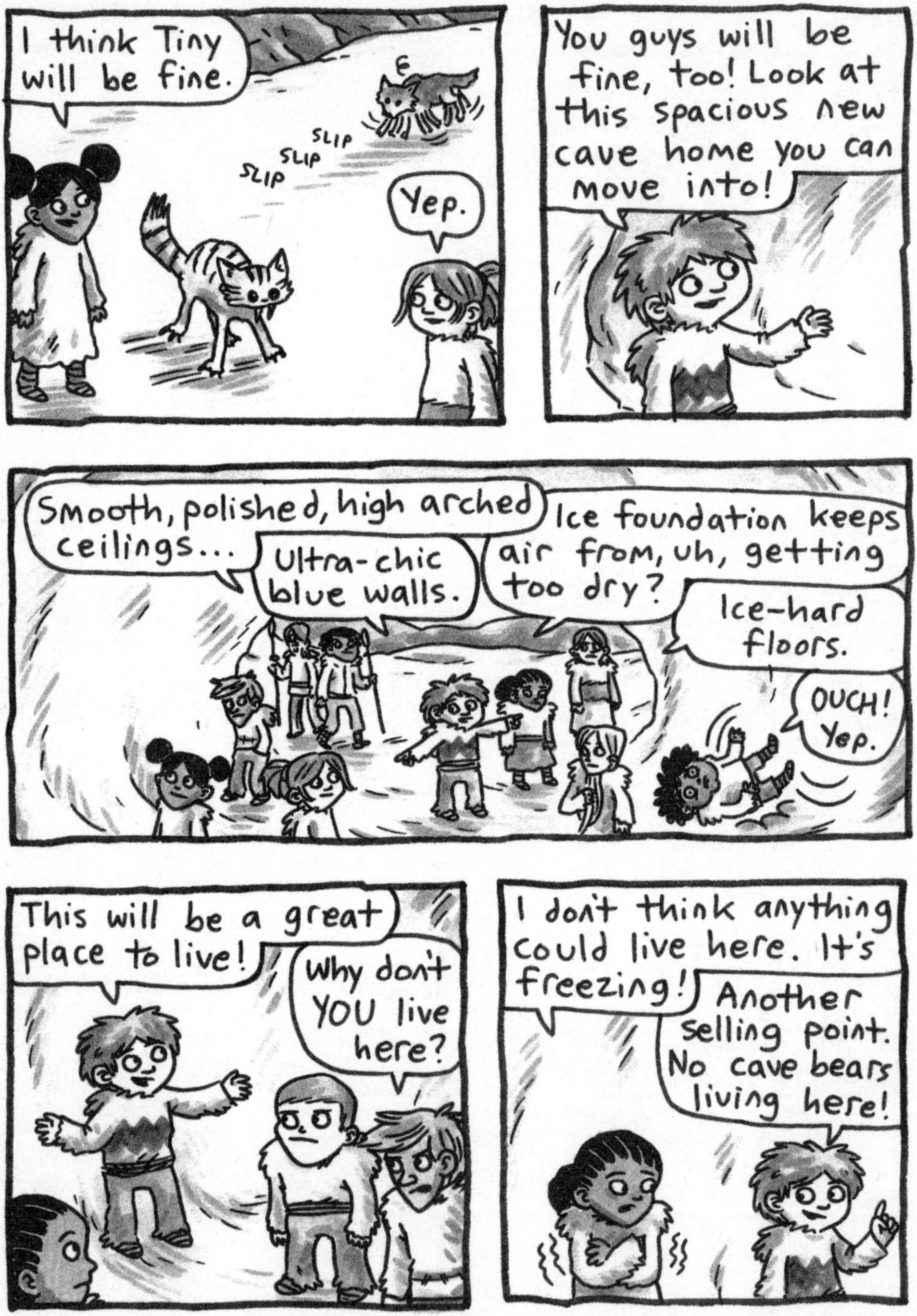

I think Tiny will be fine.
SLIP SLIP SLIP
Yep.
You guys will be fine, too! Look at this spacious new cave home you can move into!
Smooth, polished, high arched ceilings...
Ultra-chic blue walls.
Ice foundation keeps air from, uh, getting too dry?
Ice-hard floors.
OUCH! Yep.
This will be a great place to live!
Why don't YOU live here?
I don't think anything could live here. It's freezing!
Another selling point. No cave bears living here!

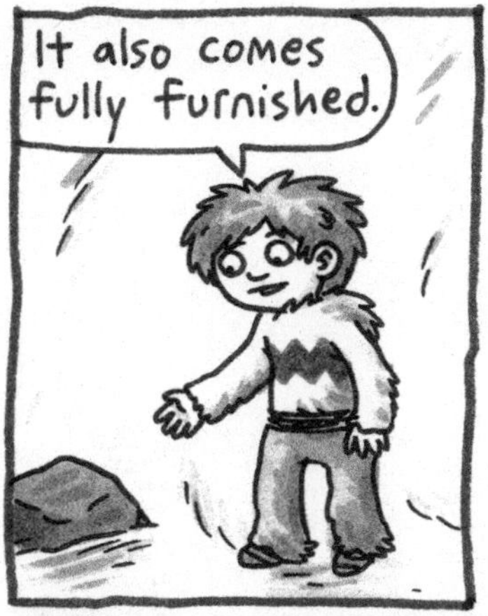
It also comes fully furnished.

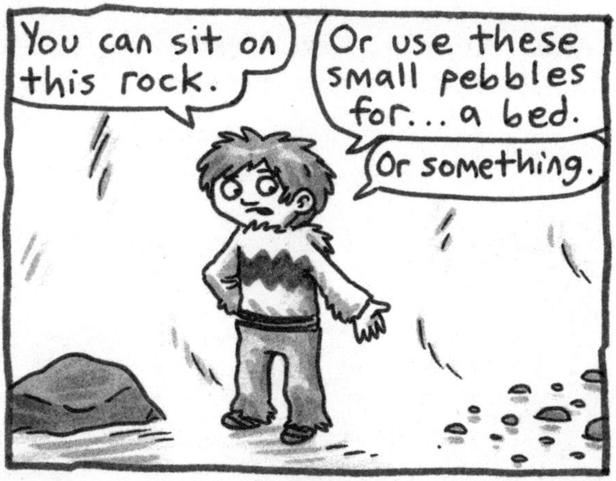
You can sit on this rock.
Or use these small pebbles for... a bed.
Or something.

Before scientists studied glaciers, people wondered how large boulders could end up far away from where that type of rock is found.

Glaciers can carry everything from soil and dirt to heavy rocks over long distances.

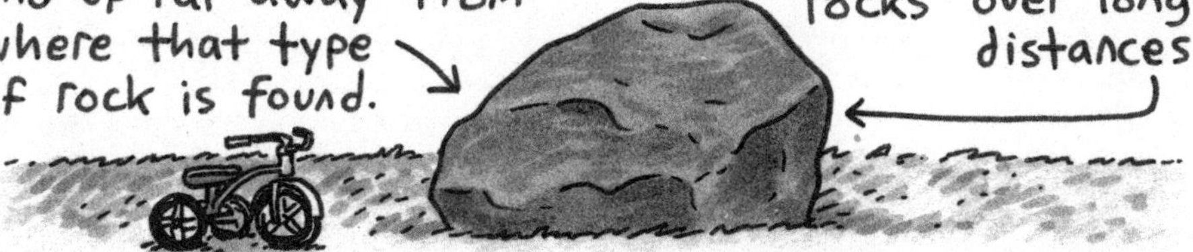

If you leave something out in your yard, your parents may not believe you when you tell them it was carried there by a glacier.

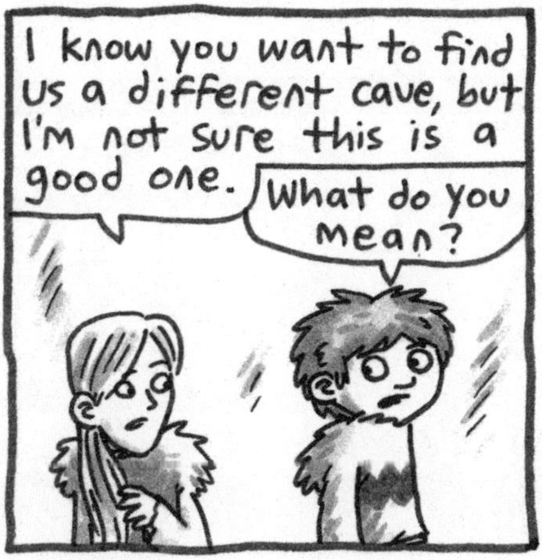
I know you want to find us a different cave, but I'm not sure this is a good one.
What do you mean?

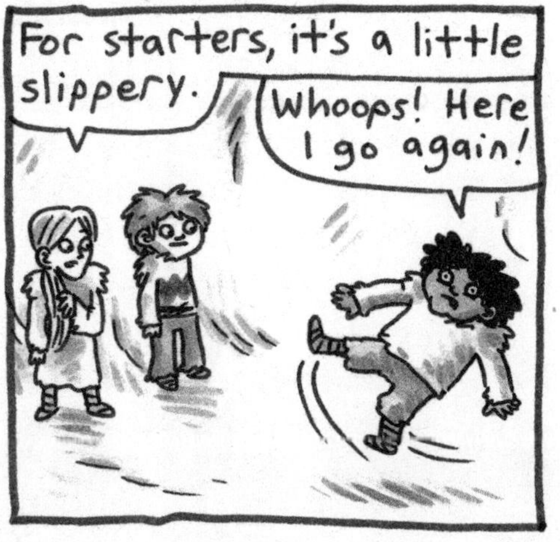
For starters, it's a little slippery.
Whoops! Here I go again!

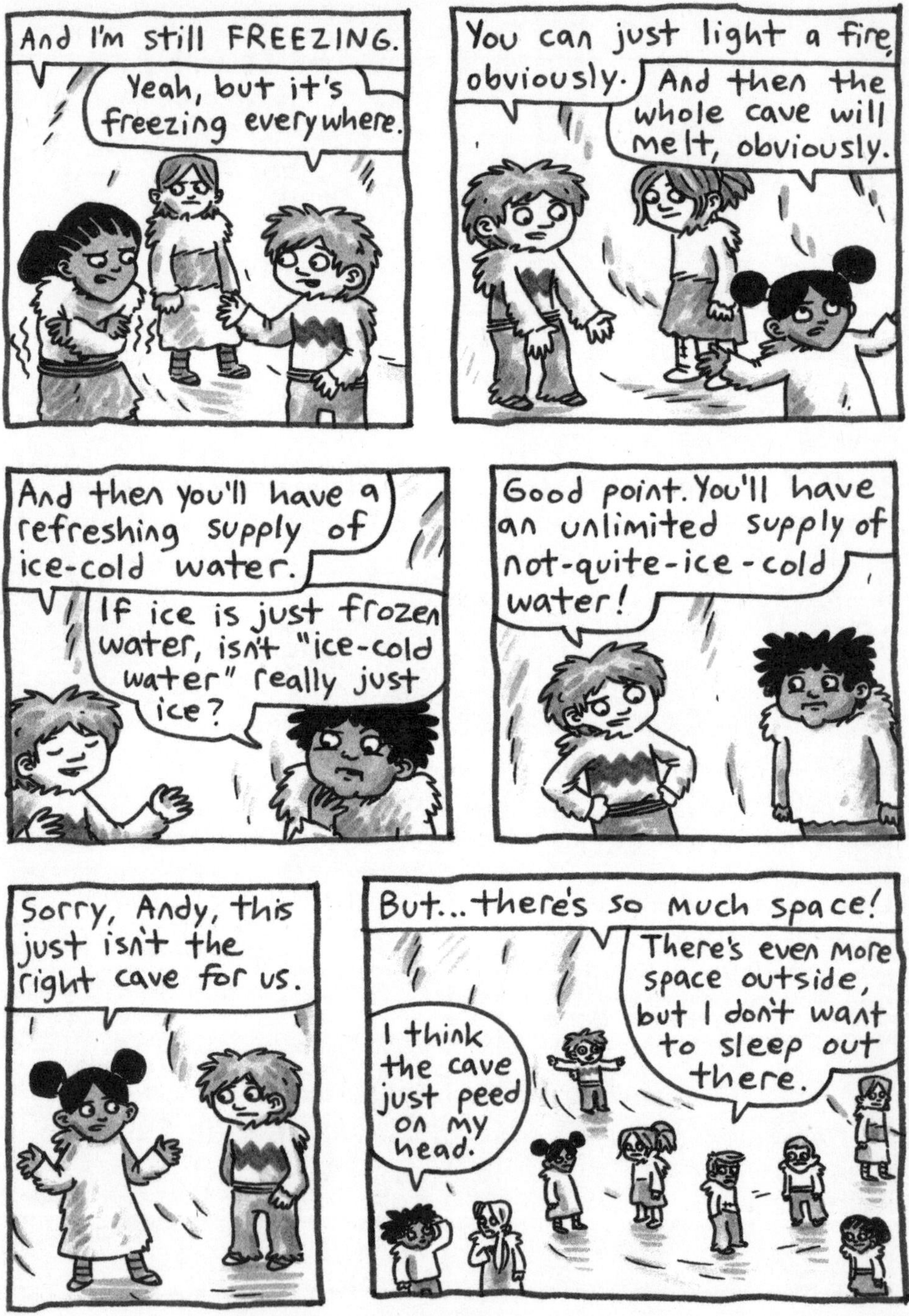
And I'm still FREEZING.
Yeah, but it's freezing everywhere.
You can just light a fire, obviously.
And then the whole cave will melt, obviously.
And then you'll have a refreshing supply of ice-cold water.
If ice is just frozen water, isn't "ice-cold water" really just ice?
Good point. You'll have an unlimited supply of not-quite-ice-cold water!
Sorry, Andy, this just isn't the right cave for us.
But... there's so much space!
There's even more space outside, but I don't want to sleep out there.
I think the cave just peed on my head.

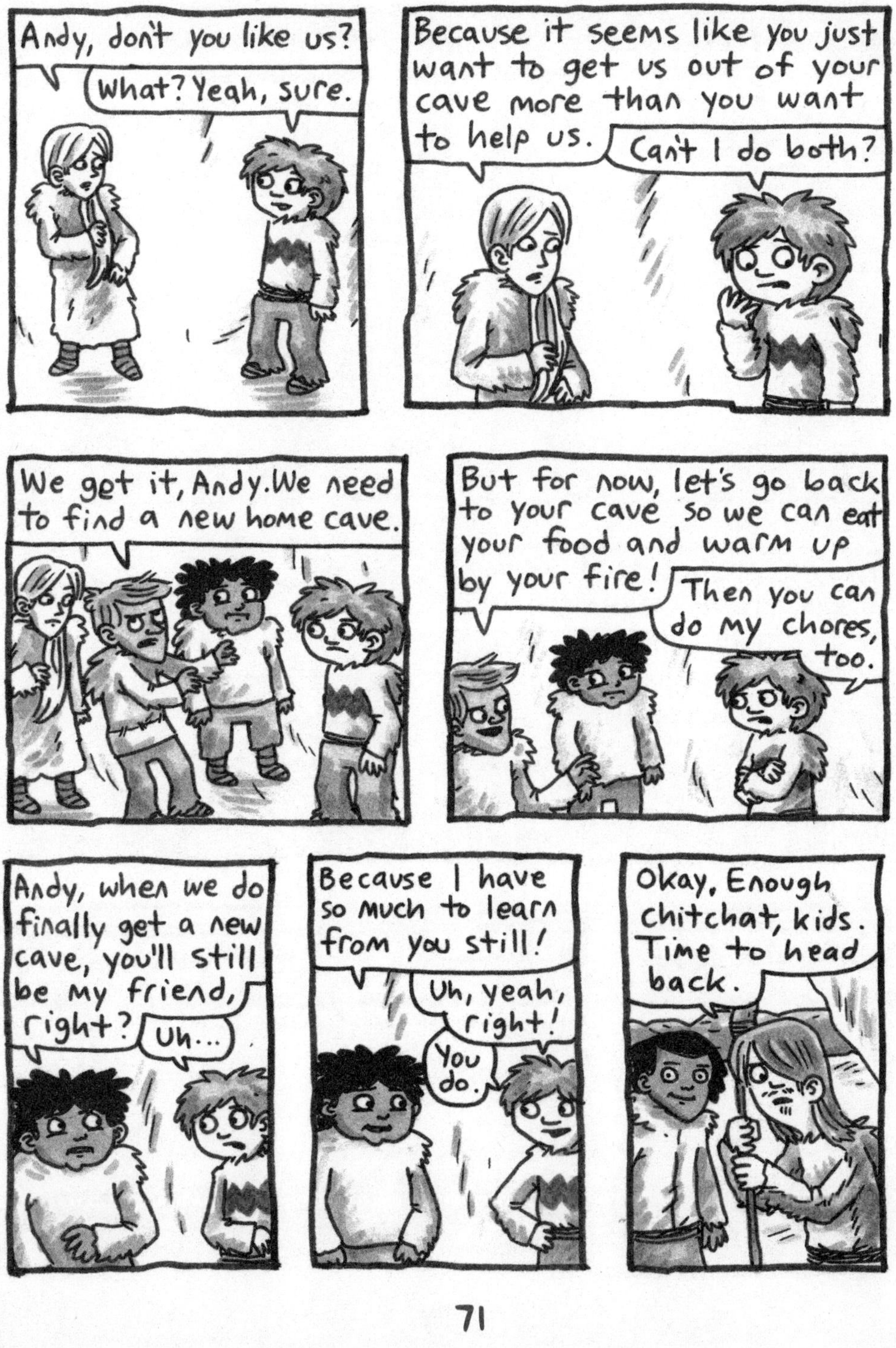
Andy, don't you like us?
What? Yeah, sure.
Because it seems like you just want to get us out of your cave more than you want to help us.
Can't I do both?
We get it, Andy. We need to find a new home cave.
But for now, let's go back to your cave so we can eat your food and warm up by your fire!
Then you can do my chores, too.
Andy, when we do finally get a new cave, you'll still be my friend, right?
Uh...
Because I have so much to learn from you still!
Uh, yeah, right!
You do.
Okay. Enough chitchat, kids. Time to head back.

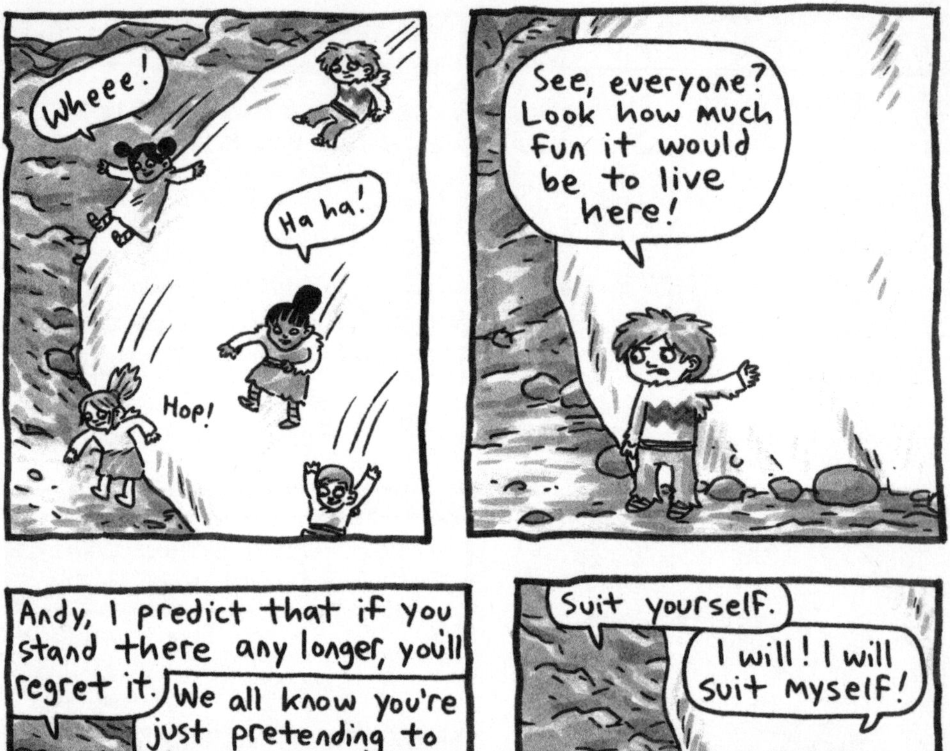
Wheee!
Ha ha!
Hop!
See, everyone? Look how much fun it would be to live here!
Andy, I predict that if you stand there any longer, you'll regret it.
We all know you're just pretending to be psychic, Lucy.
Suit yourself.
I will! I will suit myself!
MREOWRRR!
Yip!
Okay, I'm coming!
Wait up!
Mew.
WHUMP!

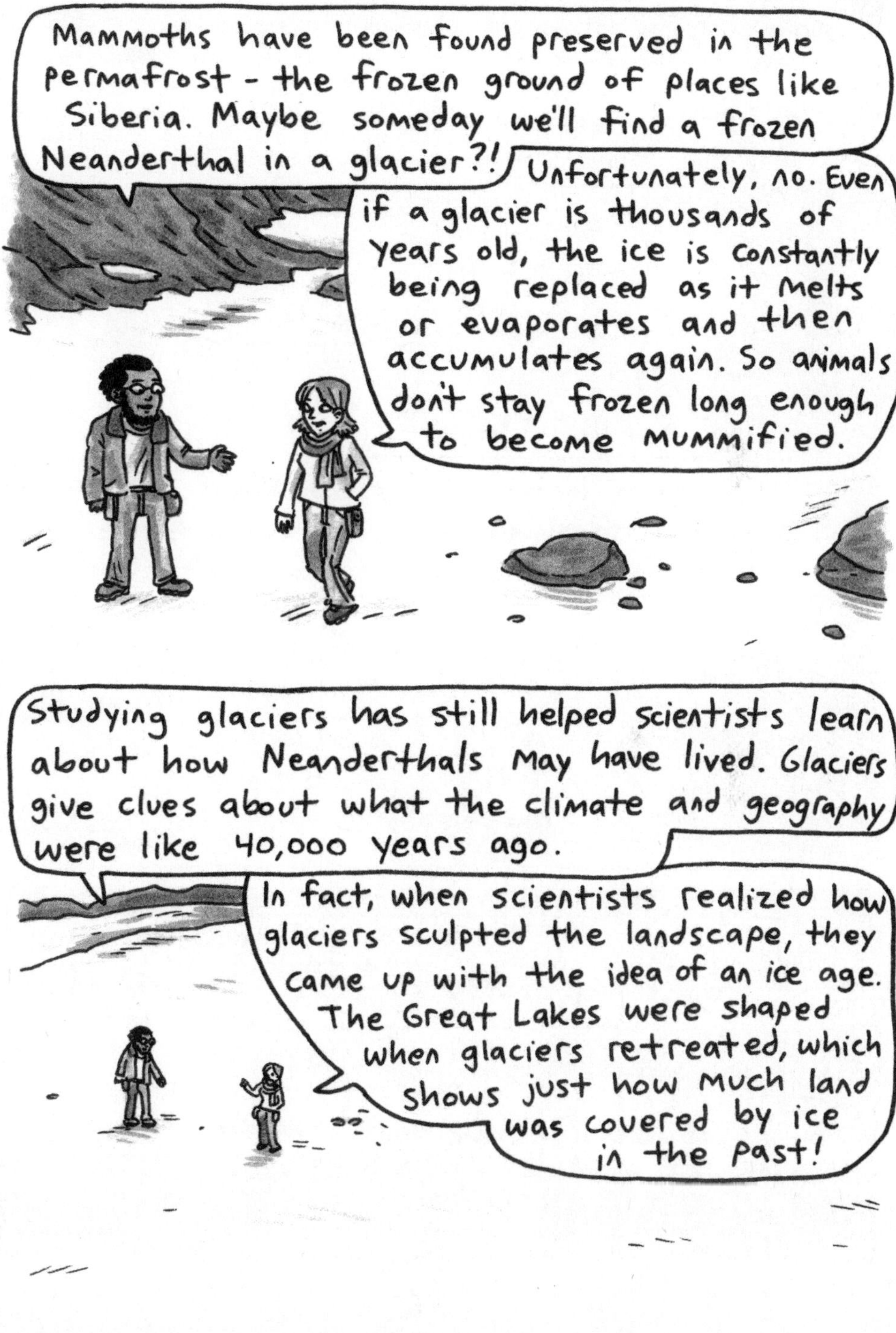
Mammoths have been found preserved in the permafrost - the frozen ground of places like Siberia. Maybe someday we'll find a frozen Neanderthal in a glacier?!
Unfortunately, no. Even if a glacier is thousands of years old, the ice is constantly being replaced as it melts or evaporates and then accumulates again. So animals don't stay frozen long enough to become mummified.
Studying glaciers has still helped scientists learn about how Neanderthals may have lived. Glaciers give clues about what the climate and geography were like 40,000 years ago.
In fact, when scientists realized how glaciers sculpted the landscape, they came up with the idea of an ice age. The Great Lakes were shaped when glaciers retreated, which shows just how much land was covered by ice in the past!

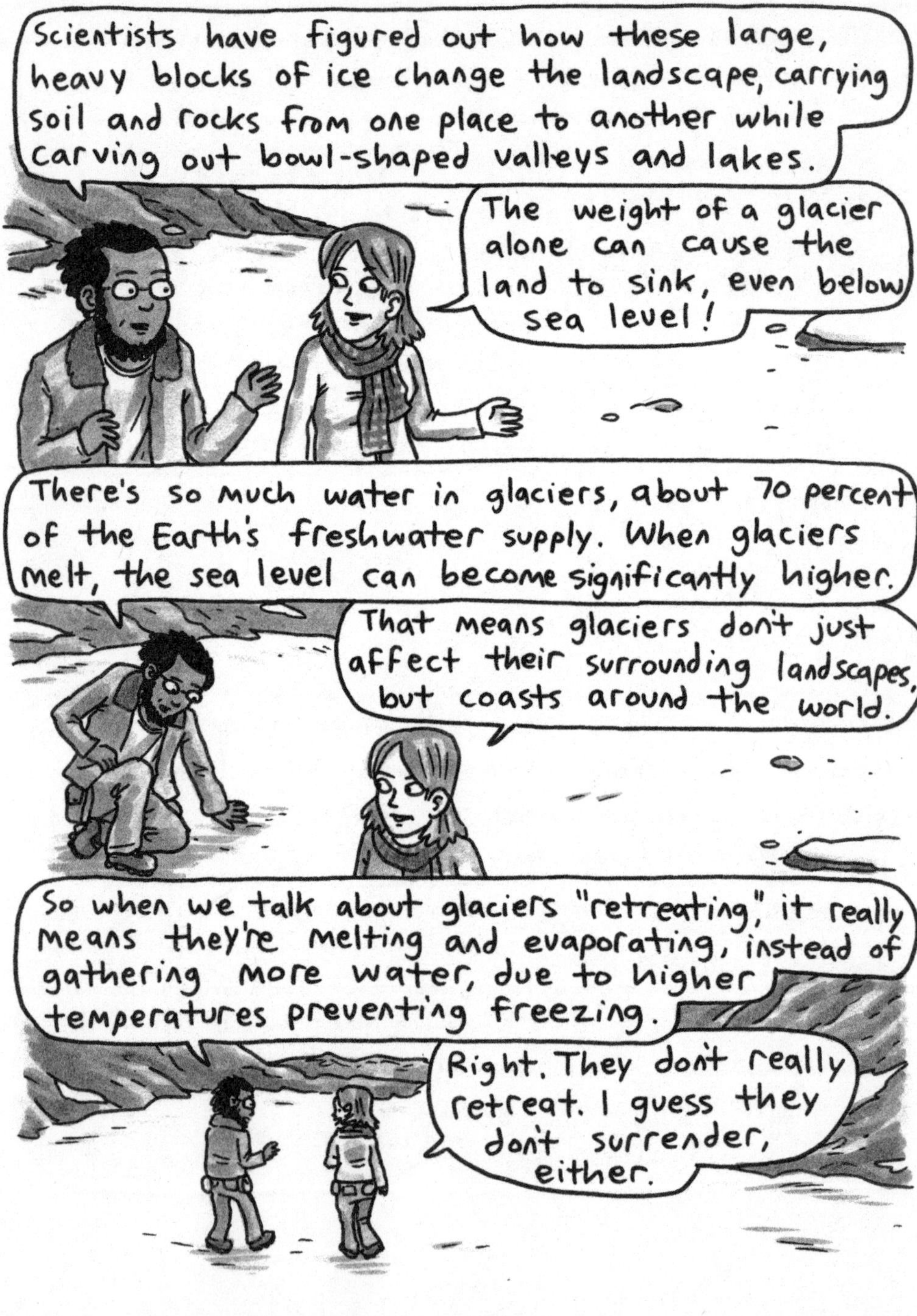
Scientists have figured out how these large, heavy blocks of ice change the landscape, carrying soil and rocks from one place to another while carving out bowl-shaped valleys and lakes.
The weight of a glacier alone can cause the land to sink, even below sea level!
There's so much water in glaciers, about 70 percent of the Earth's freshwater supply. When glaciers melt, the sea level can become significantly higher.
That means glaciers don't just affect their surrounding landscapes, but coasts around the world.
So when we talk about glaciers "retreating," it really means they're melting and evaporating, instead of gathering more water, due to higher temperatures preventing freezing.
Right. They don't really retreat. I guess they don't surrender, either.

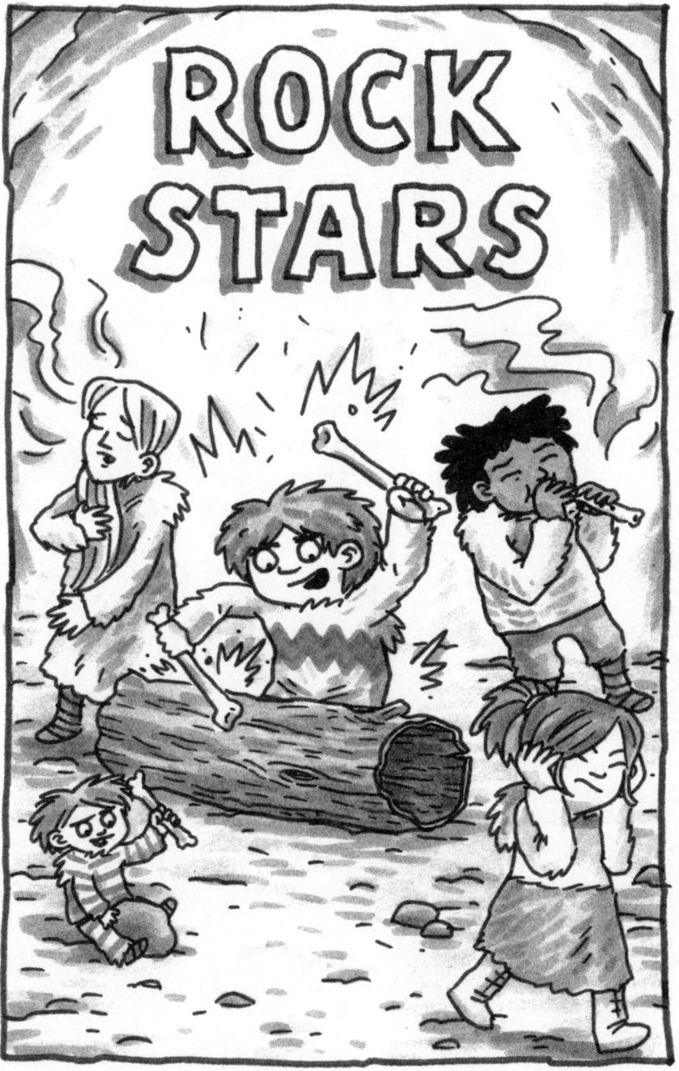
ROCK STARS

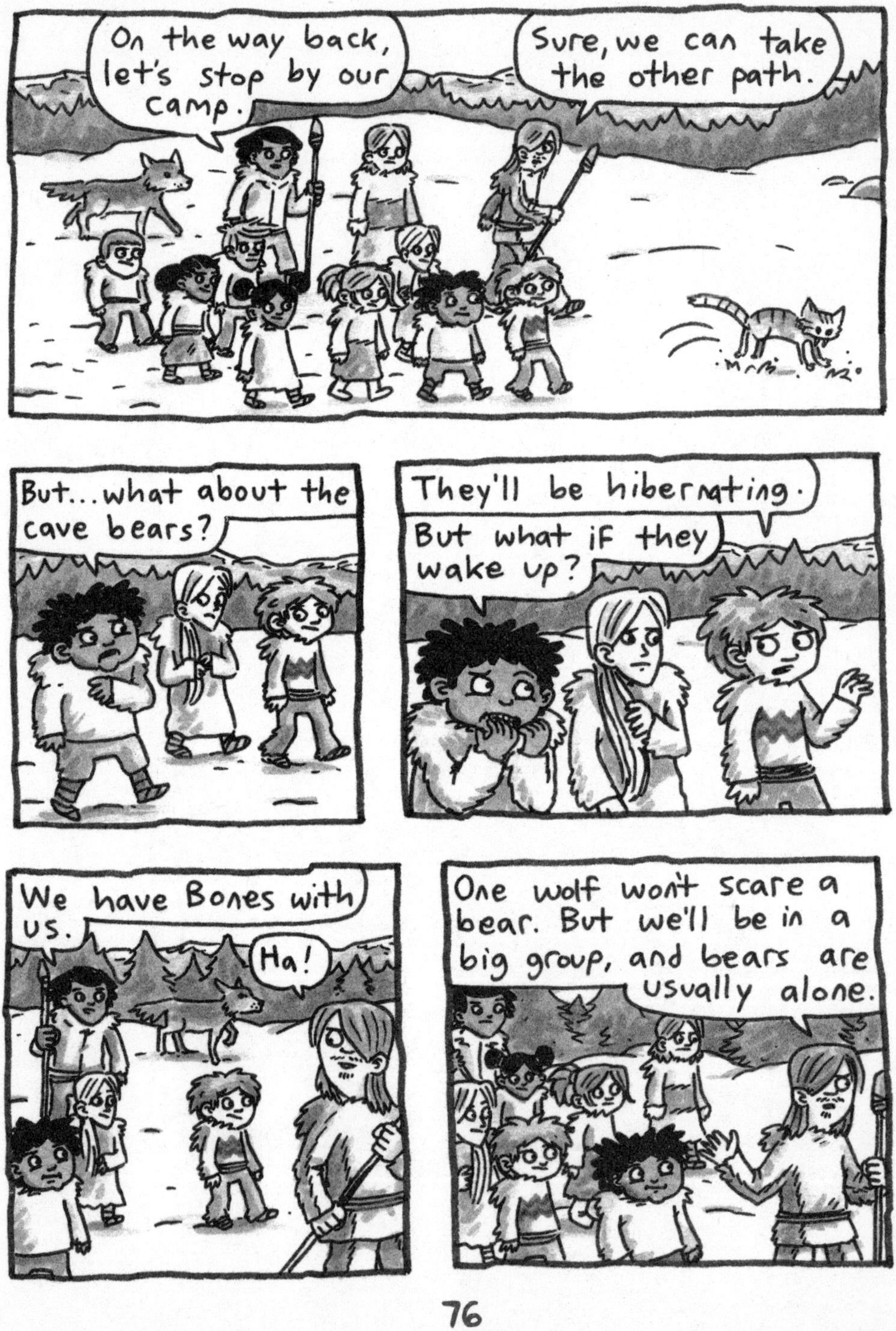

On the way back, let's stop by our camp.
Sure, we can take the other path.
But...what about the cave bears?
They'll be hibernating.
But what if they wake up?
We have Bones with us.
Ha!
One wolf won't scare a bear. But we'll be in a big group, and bears are usually alone.

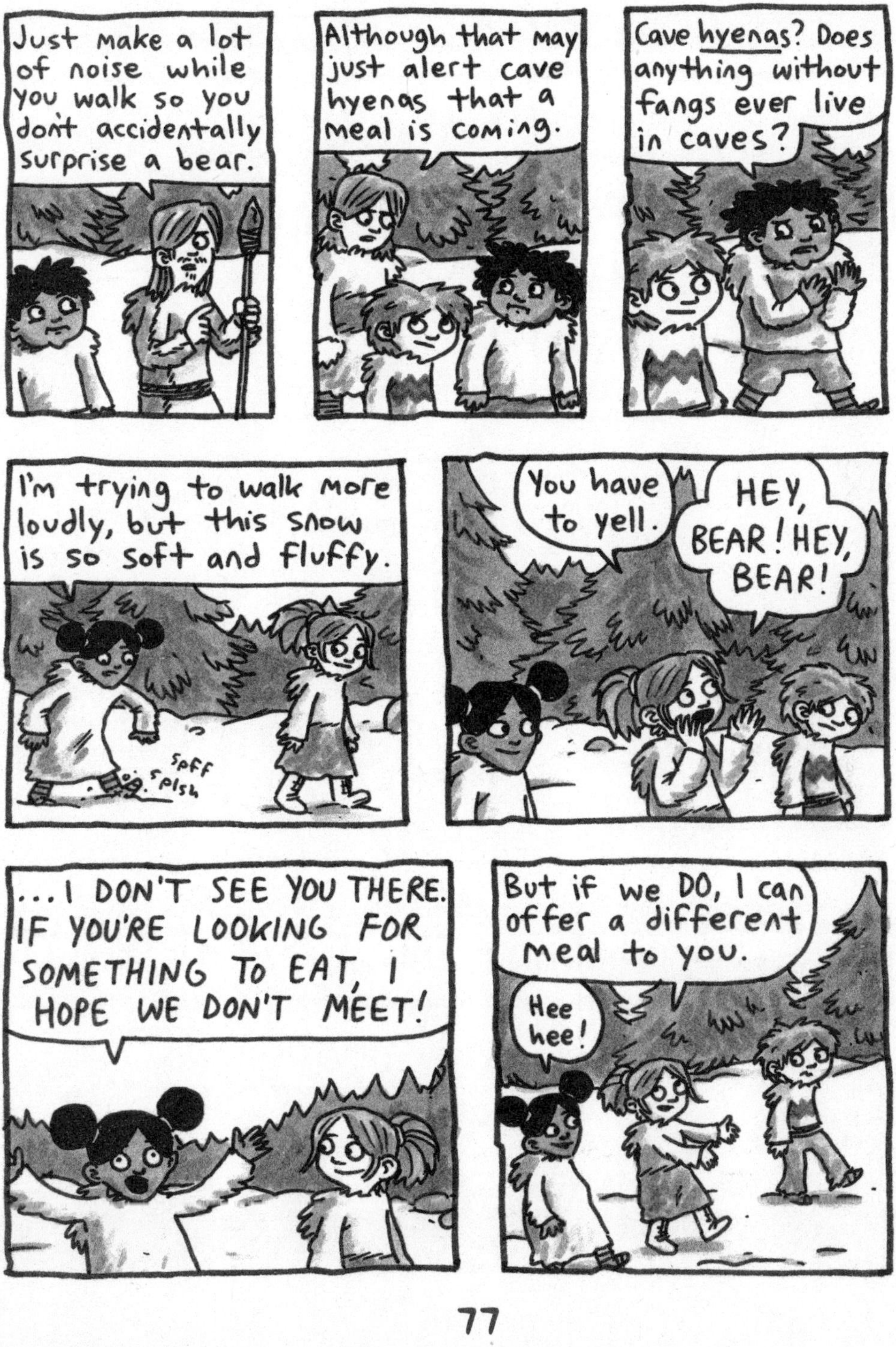
Just make a lot of noise while you walk so you don't accidentally surprise a bear.
Although that may just alert cave hyenas that a meal is coming.
Cave hyenas? Does anything without fangs ever live in caves?
I'm trying to walk more loudly, but this snow is so soft and fluffy.
spff
splsh
You have to yell.
HEY, BEAR! HEY, BEAR!
...I DON'T SEE YOU THERE. IF YOU'RE LOOKING FOR SOMETHING TO EAT, I HOPE WE DON'T MEET!
But if we DO, I can offer a different meal to you.
Hee hee!

78

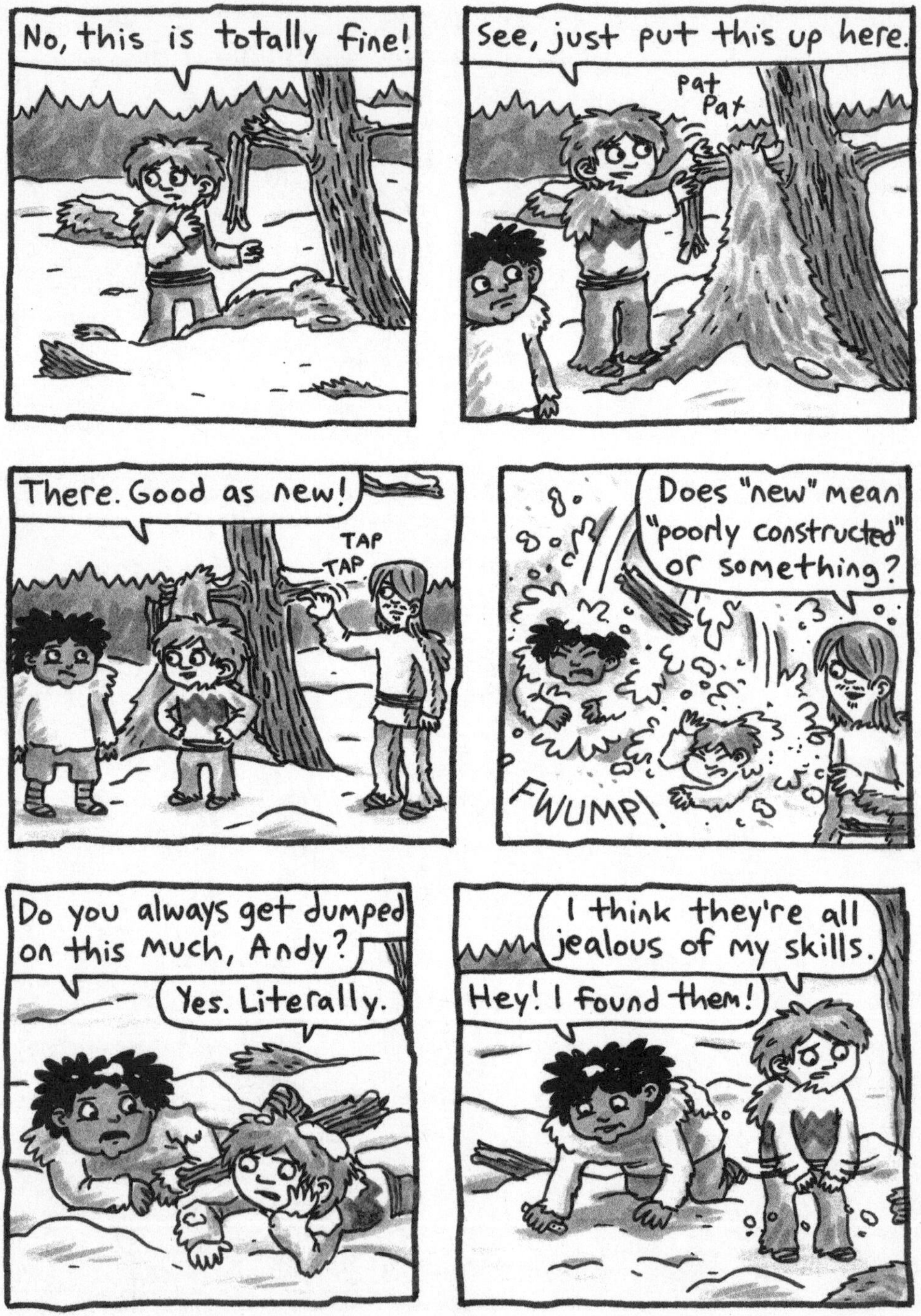

No, this is totally fine!
See, just put this up here.
Pat
Pat
There. Good as new!
TAP
TAP
Does "new" mean "poorly constructed" or something?
FWUMP!
Do you always get dumped on this much, Andy?
Yes. Literally.
I think they're all jealous of my skills.
Hey! I found them!

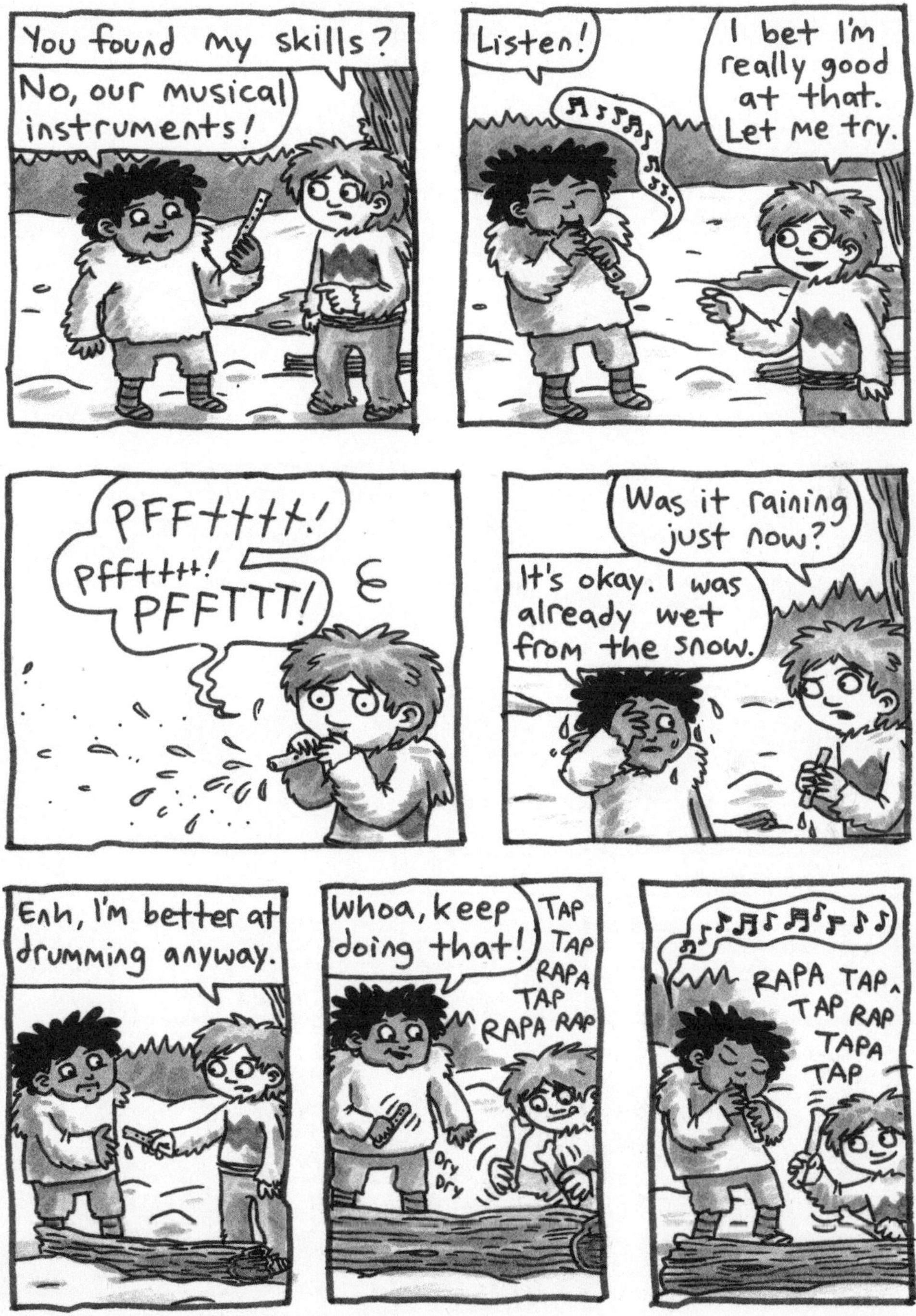
You found my skills?
No, our musical instruments!
Listen!
I bet I'm really good at that. Let me try.
PFFtttt!
pffttt!
PFFTTT!
Was it raining just now?
It's okay. I was already wet from the snow.
Enh, I'm better at drumming anyway.
Whoa, keep doing that!
TAP TAP RAPA TAP RAPA RAP
Dry Dry
RAPA TAP TAP RAP TAPA TAP

85

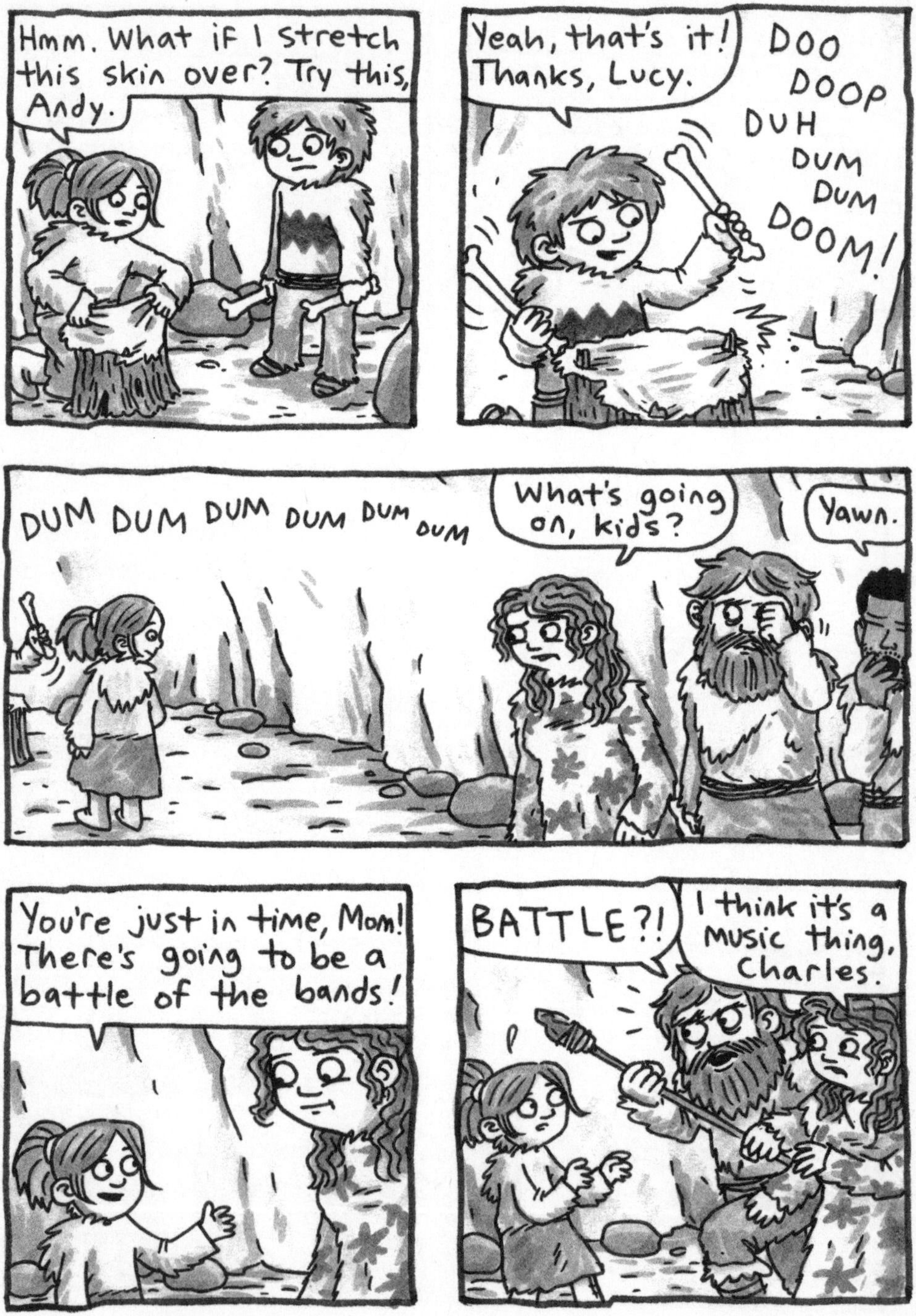
Hmm. What if I stretch this skin over? Try this, Andy.
Yeah, that's it! Thanks, Lucy.
DOO DOOP DUH DUM DUM DOOM!
DUM DUM DUM DUM DUM DUM
What's going on, kids?
Yawn.
You're just in time, Mom! There's going to be a battle of the bands!
BATTLE?!
I think it's a music thing, Charles.

87

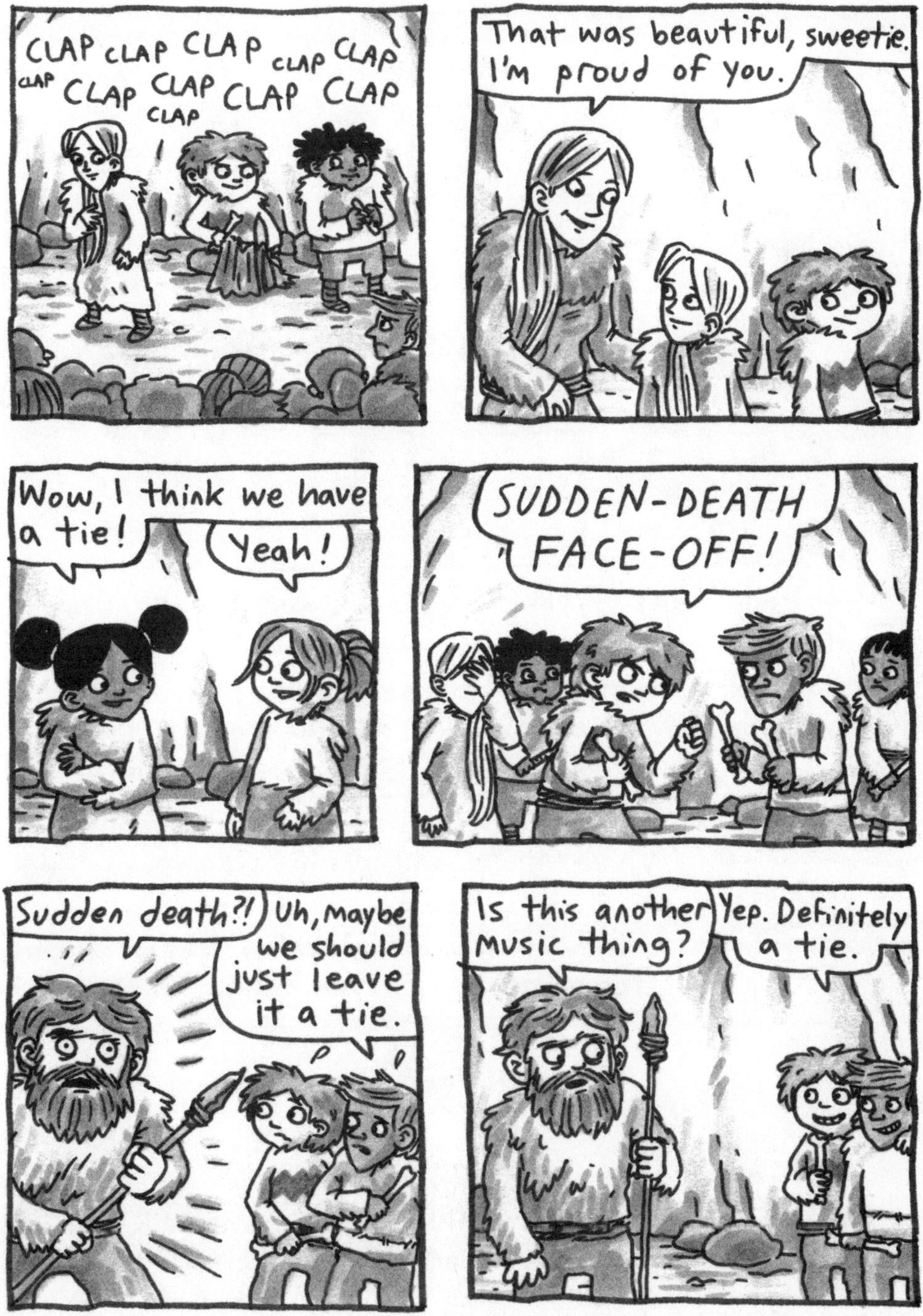
CLAP CLAP CLAP CLAP CLAP
CLAP CLAP CLAP CLAP CLAP CLAP
That was beautiful, sweetie. I'm proud of you.
Wow, I think we have a tie!
Yeah!
SUDDEN-DEATH FACE-OFF!
Sudden death?!
Uh, maybe we should just leave it a tie.
Is this another music thing?
Yep. Definitely a tie.

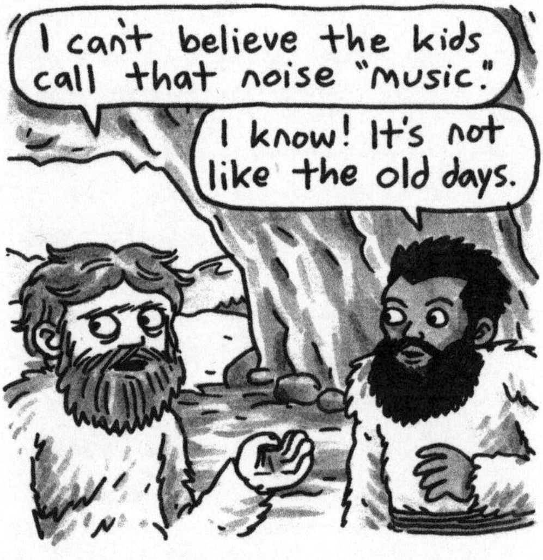
I can't believe the kids call that noise "music."
I know! It's not like the old days.

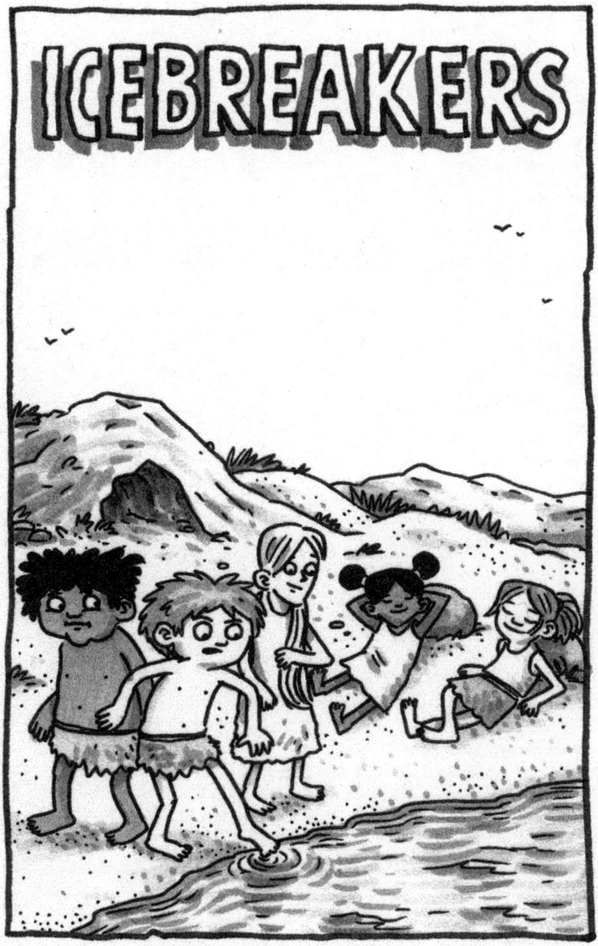
ICEBREAKERS

By studying the bones of the animals
Neanderthals hunted, scientists know they had
a harder time finding food in the cold climate.

Neanderthals broke open
bones to get the nutritious
marrow inside. During
cold times, the bones
were more thoroughly
picked over.

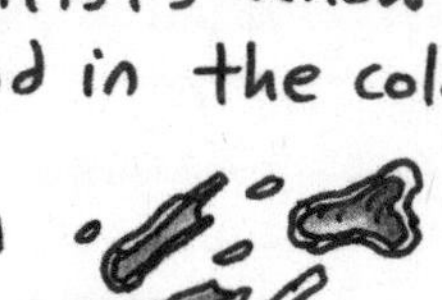

Even tiny
bones with
very little
marrow were
used for food.

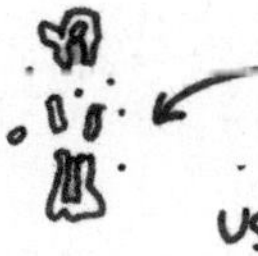

98

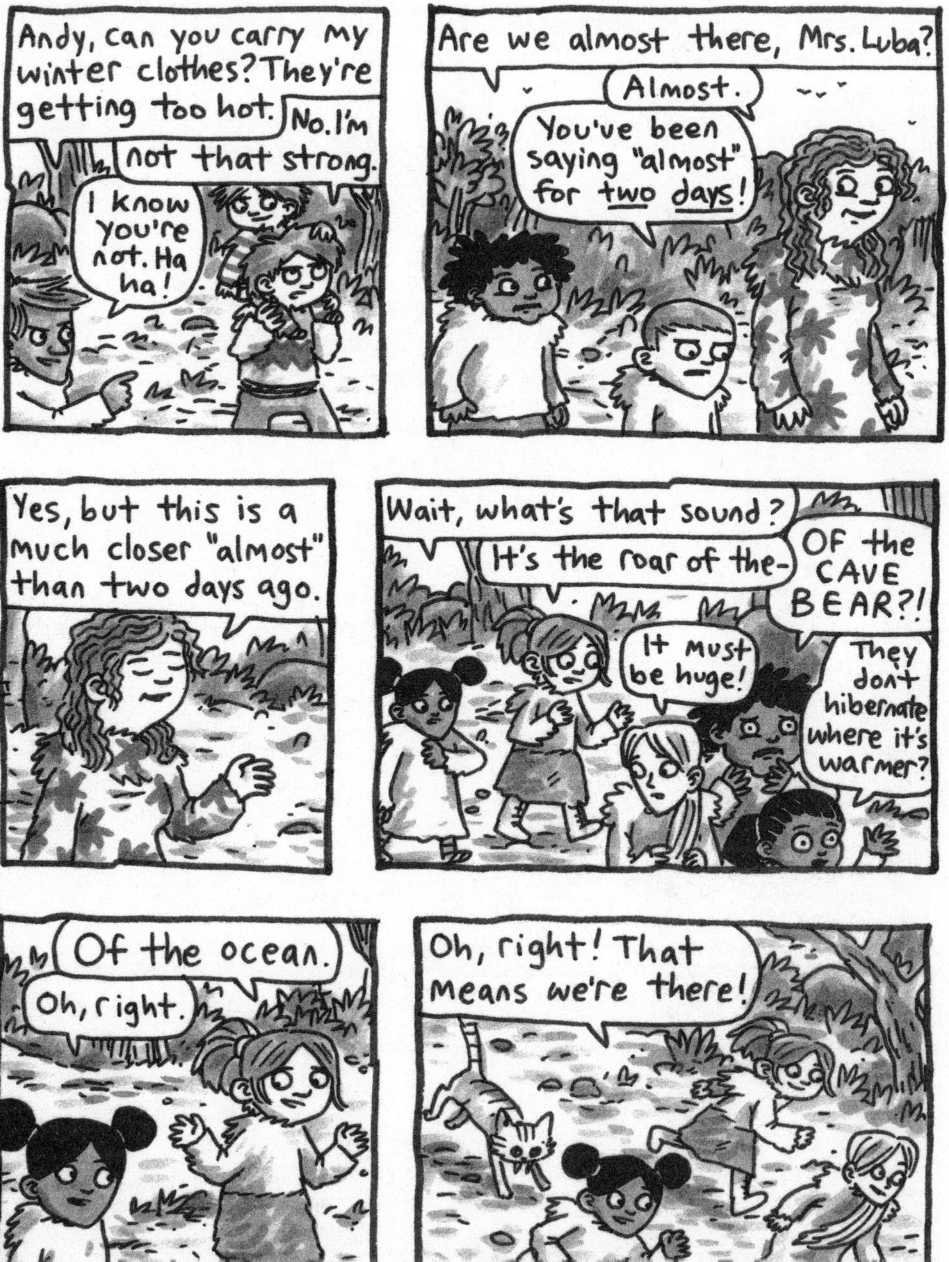
Andy, can you carry my winter clothes? They're getting too hot.
No. I'm not that strong.
I know you're not. Ha ha!
Are we almost there, Mrs. Luba?
Almost.
You've been saying "almost" for two days!
Yes, but this is a much closer "almost" than two days ago.
Wait, what's that sound?
It's the roar of the-
OF the CAVE BEAR?!
It must be huge!
They don't hibernate where it's warmer?
Of the ocean.
Oh, right.
Oh, right! That means we're there!

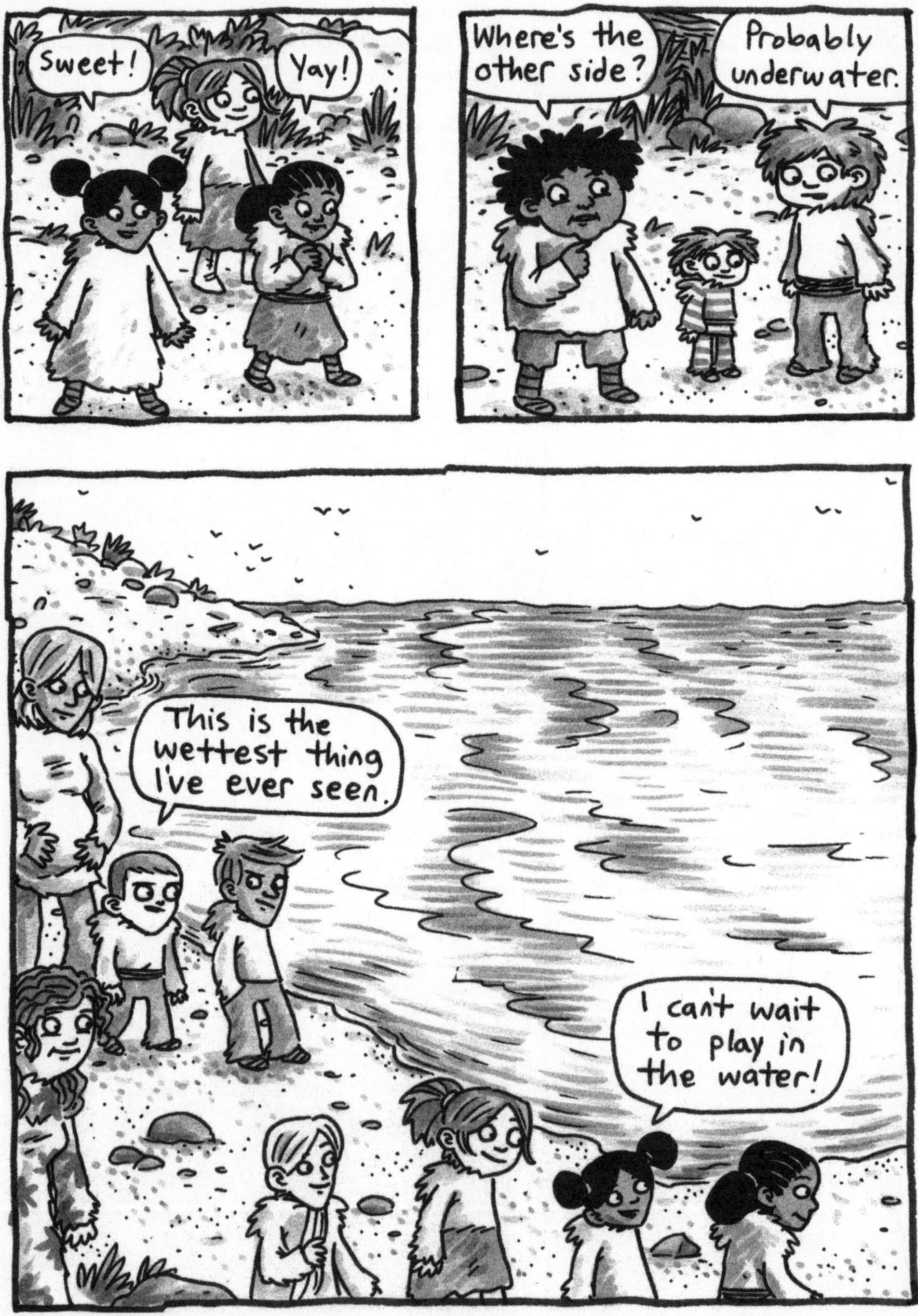
Sweet!
Yay!
Where's the other side?
Probably underwater.
This is the wettest thing I've ever seen.
I can't wait to play in the water!

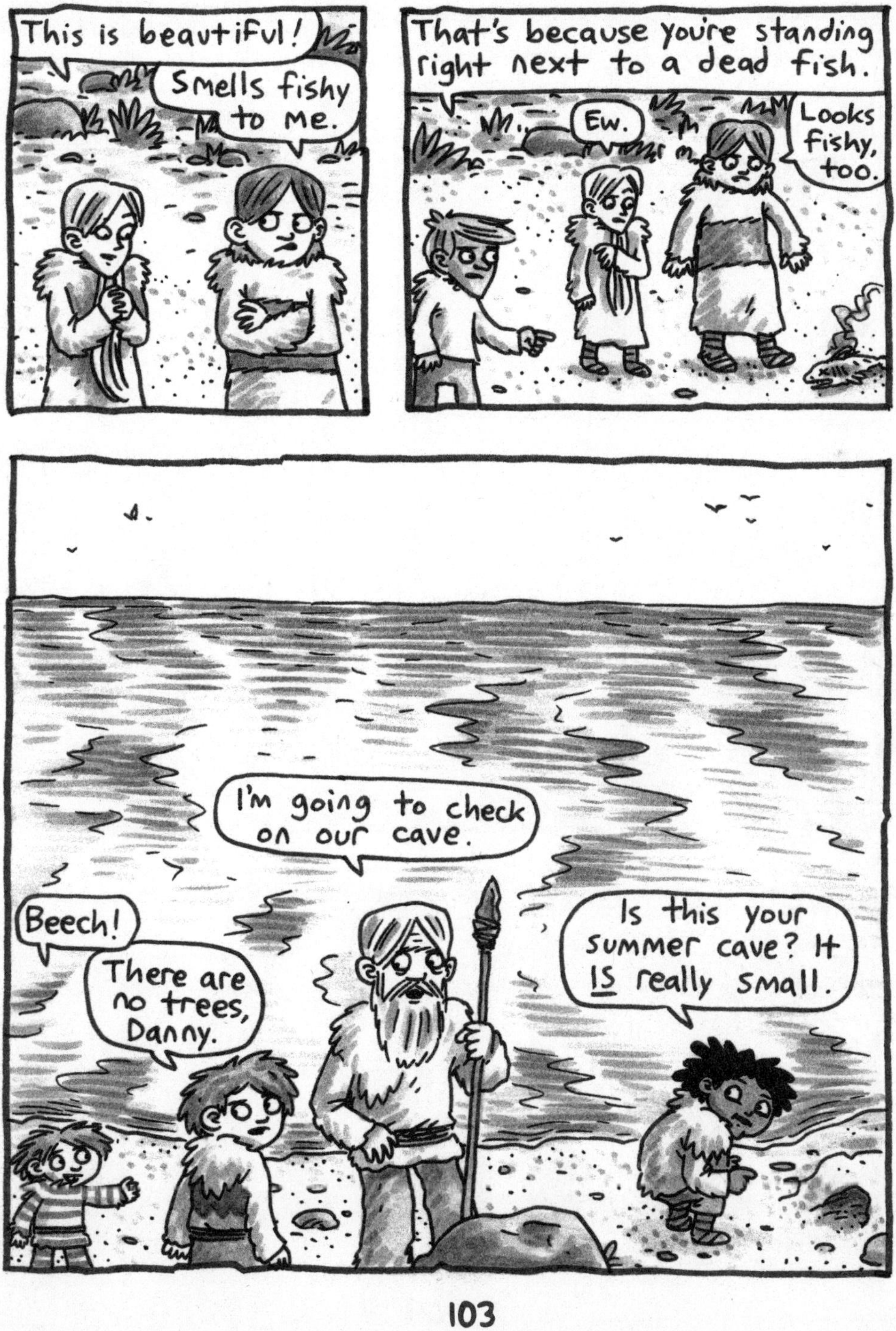
This is beautiful!
Smells fishy to me.
That's because you're standing right next to a dead fish.
Ew.
Looks fishy, too.
I'm going to check on our cave.
Beech!
There are no trees, Danny.
Is this your summer cave? It IS really small.

105

Coins weren't invented until about 2,700 years ago, so early humans and Neanderthals would have had to barter — exchange goods or services for other goods or services.

 A nice stone tool might have been traded for a quality animal skin!

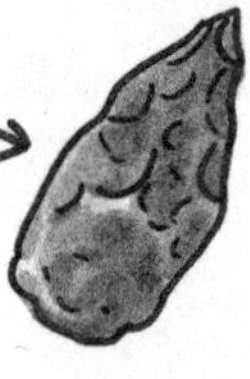

Trading could benefit both sides and lead to the spread of new ideas!

However, the stock market did NOT originate from a prehistoric rock market.

Andy, how do you know what each shell is worth?

Clearly, he judges shape, texture, color, and how intact the structure is...

With additional value for how difficult a shell was to find and collect.

I guess? I don't know, I just figure they're worth whatever people will give for them?

111

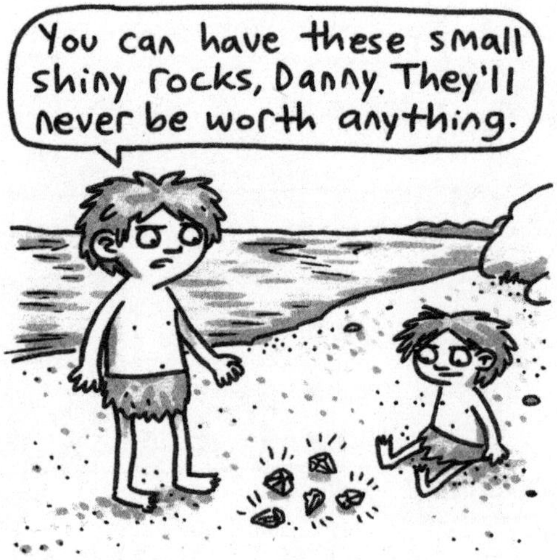
You can have these small shiny rocks, Danny. They'll never be worth anything.

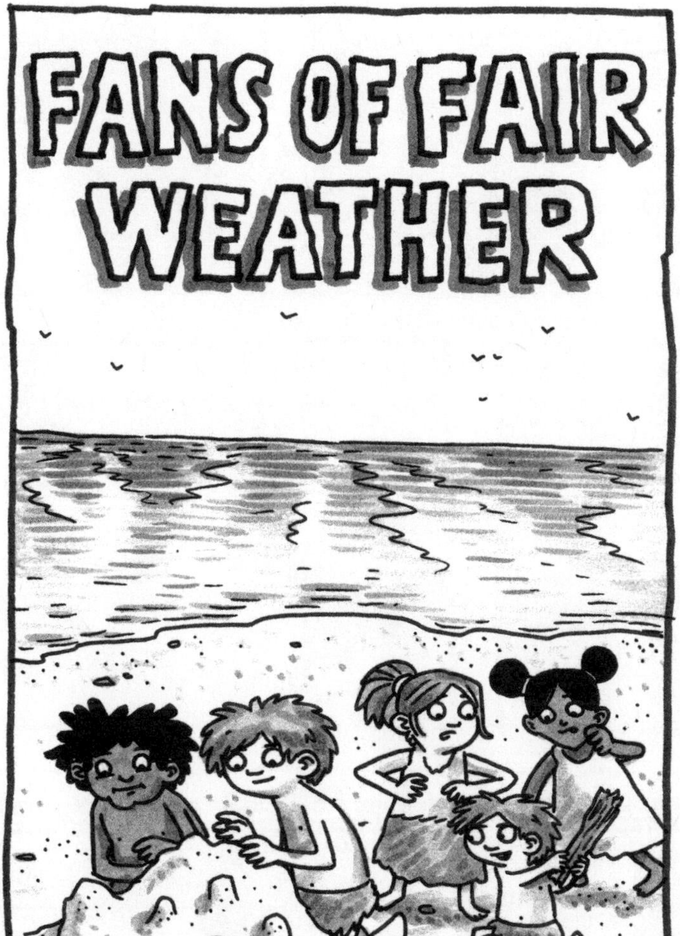
FANS OF FAIR WEATHER

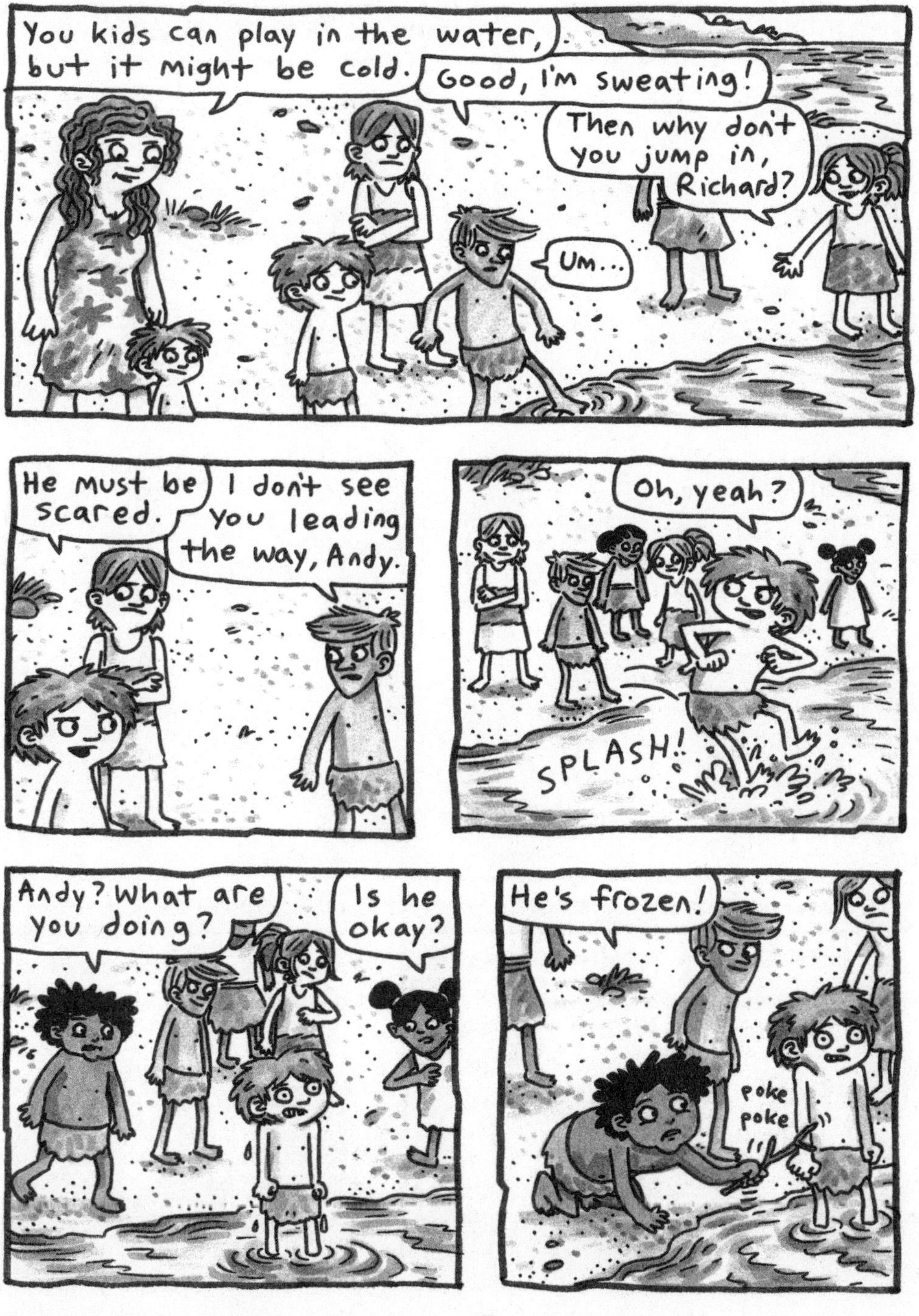
You kids can play in the water, but it might be cold.
Good, I'm sweating!
Then why don't you jump in, Richard?
Um...
He must be scared.
I don't see you leading the way, Andy.
Oh, yeah?
SPLASH!
Andy? What are you doing?
Is he okay?
He's frozen!
poke poke

118

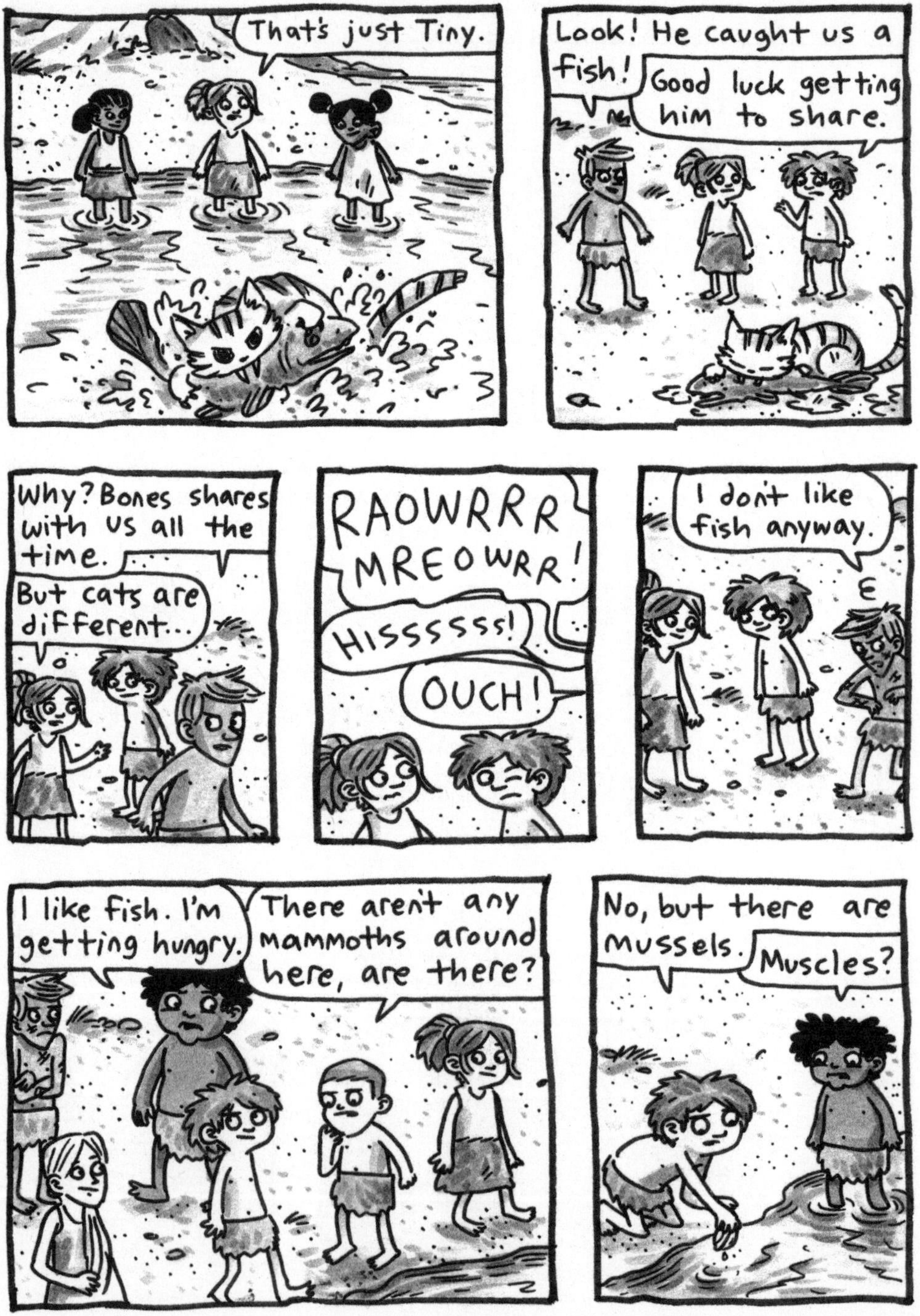
That's just Tiny.
Look! He caught us a fish!
Good luck getting him to share.
Why? Bones shares with us all the time.
But cats are different...
RAOWRRR MREOWRR!
HISSSSSS!
OUCH!
I don't like fish anyway.
I like fish. I'm getting hungry.
There aren't any mammoths around here, are there?
No, but there are mussels.
Muscles?

Mussels are just one type of seafood that Neanderthals ate!

Cooked mussel shells have been found at Neanderthal sites.

Mussels were placed on embers of fires to open them up for eating.

123

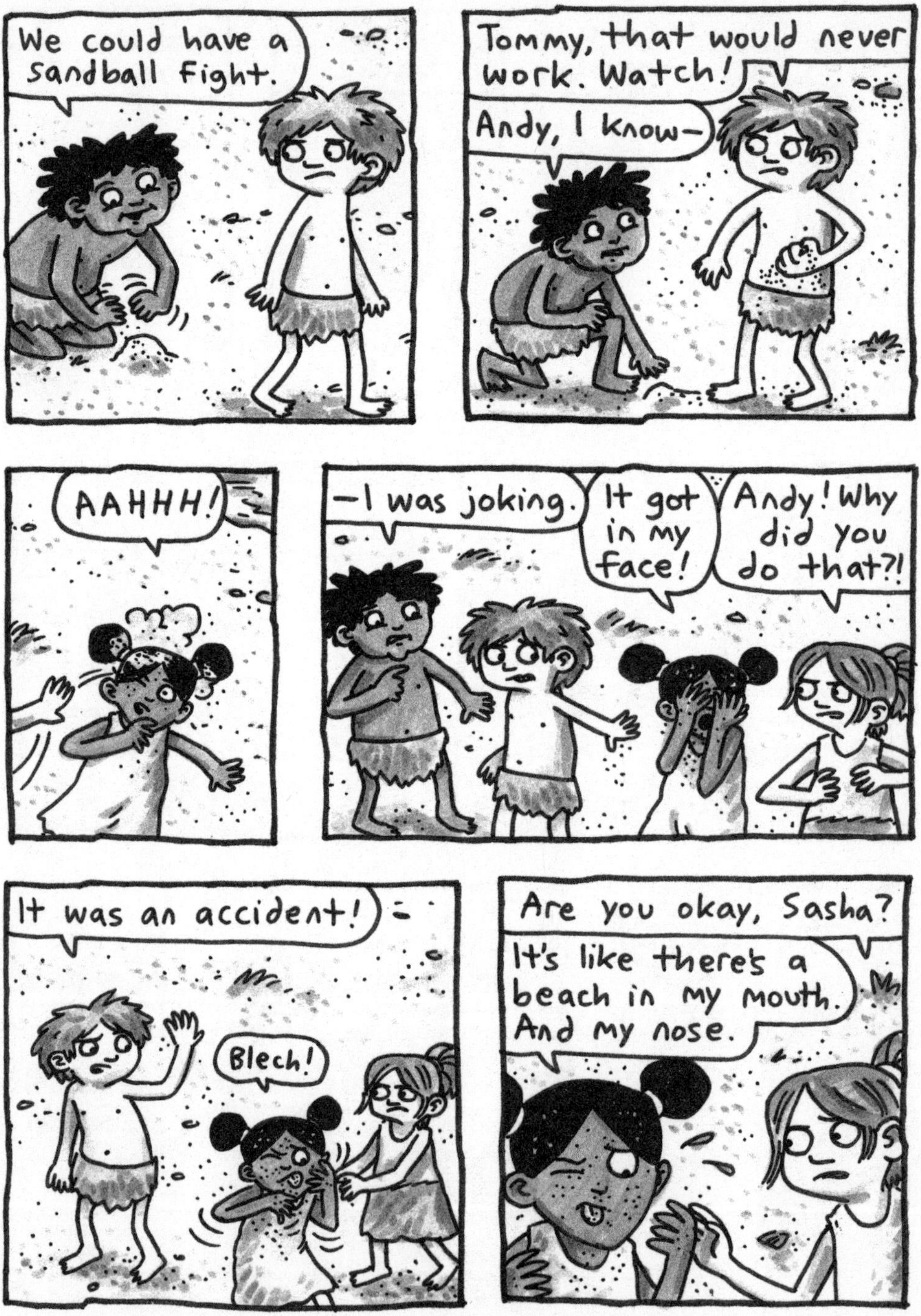
We could have a sandball fight.
Tommy, that would never work. Watch!
Andy, I know—
AAHHH!
—I was joking.
It got in my face!
Andy! Why did you do that?!
It was an accident!
Blech!
Are you okay, Sasha?
It's like there's a beach in my mouth. And my nose.

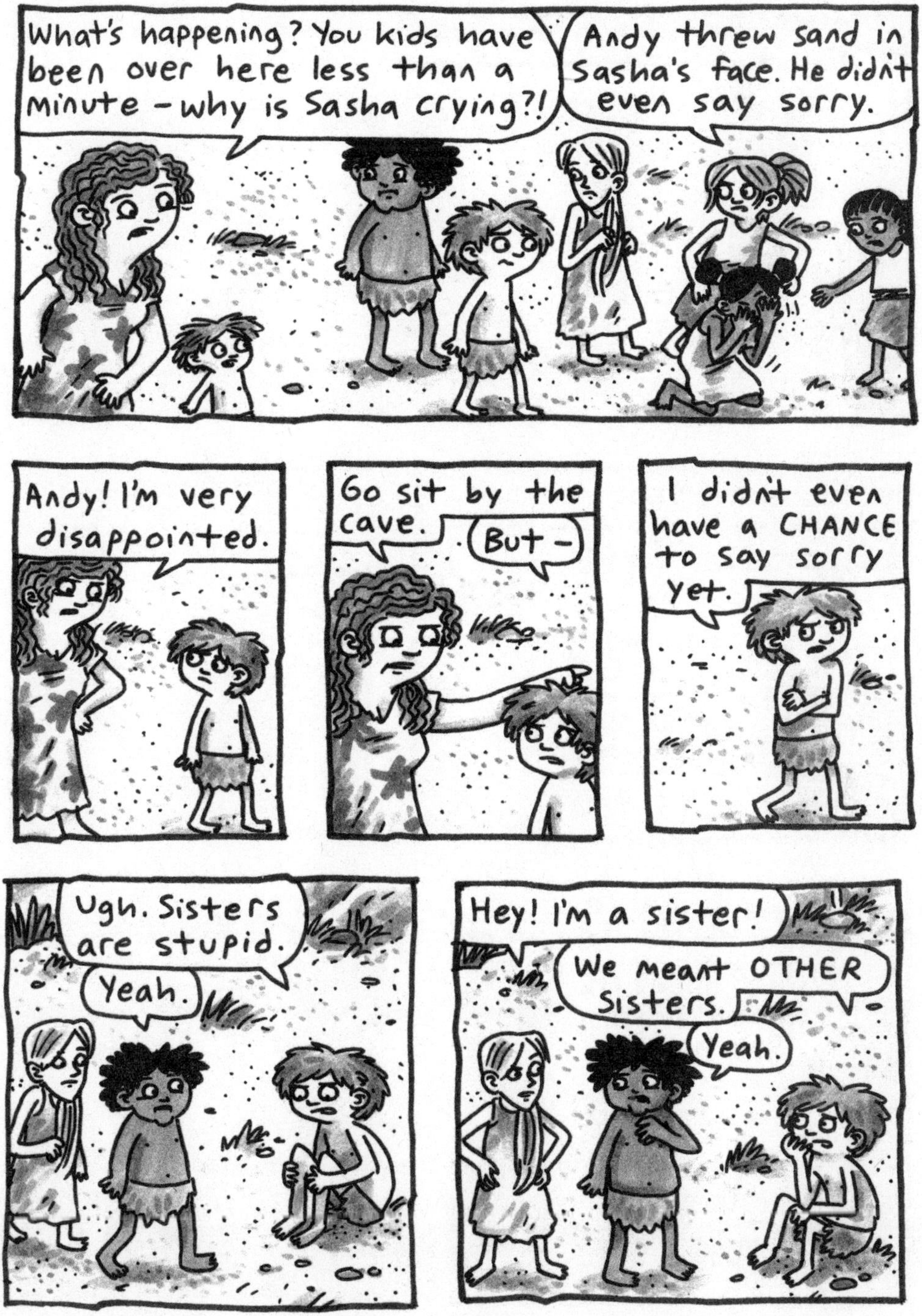
What's happening? You kids have been over here less than a minute - why is Sasha crying?!
Andy threw sand in Sasha's face. He didn't even say sorry.
Andy! I'm very disappointed.
Go sit by the cave.
But -
I didn't even have a CHANCE to say sorry yet.
Ugh. Sisters are stupid.
Yeah.
Hey! I'm a sister!
We meant OTHER sisters.
Yeah.

128

129

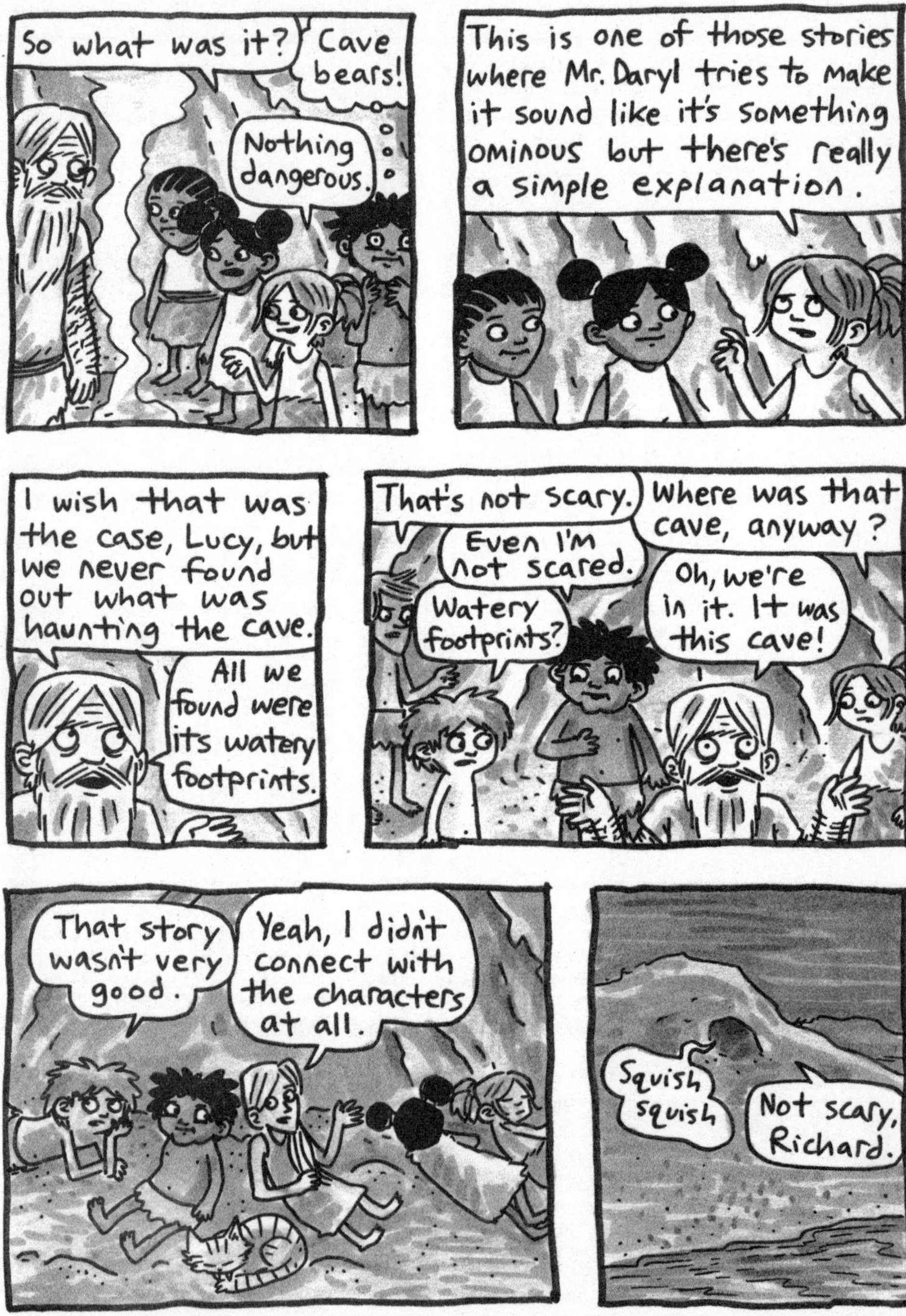

So what was it?
Cave bears!
Nothing dangerous.
This is one of those stories where Mr. Daryl tries to make it sound like it's something ominous but there's really a simple explanation.
I wish that was the case, Lucy, but we never found out what was haunting the cave.
All we found were its watery footprints.
That's not scary.
Even I'm not scared.
Watery footprints?
Where was that cave, anyway?
Oh, we're in it. It was this cave!
That story wasn't very good.
Yeah, I didn't connect with the characters at all.
Squish squish
Not scary, Richard.

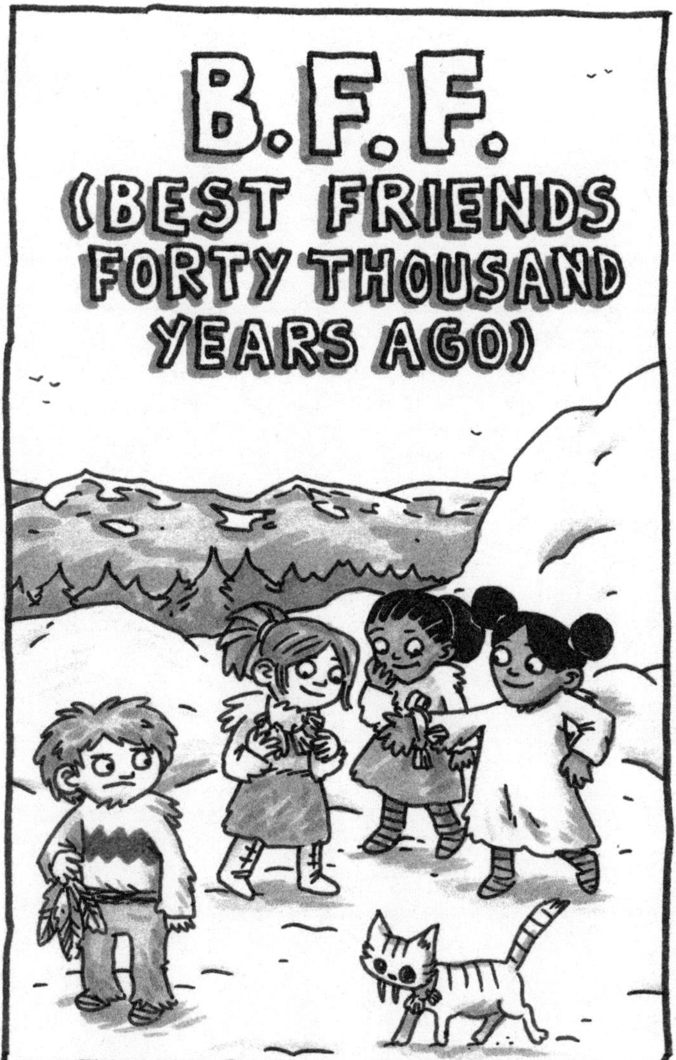
B.F.F.
(BEST FRIENDS
FORTY THOUSAND
YEARS AGO)

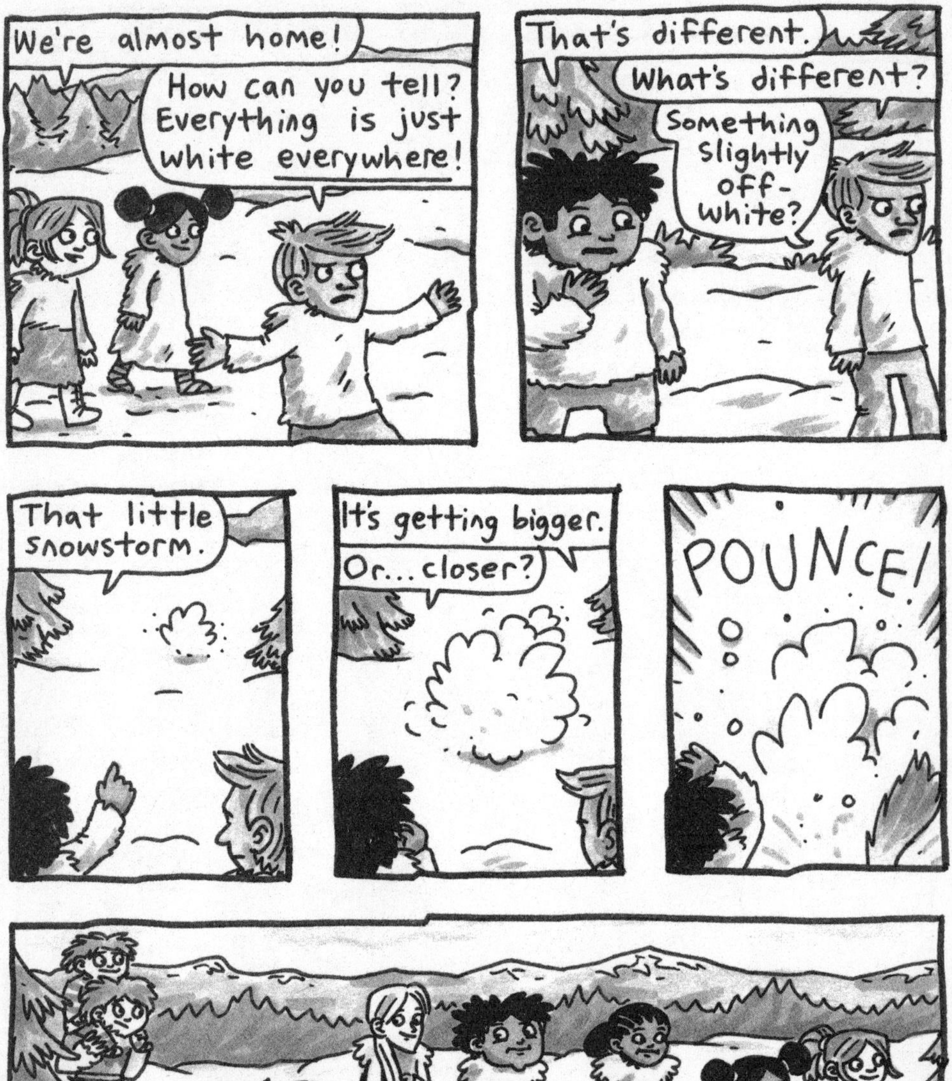
We're almost home!
How can you tell? Everything is just white everywhere!
That's different.
What's different?
Something slightly off-white?
That little snowstorm.
It's getting bigger.
Or... closer?
POUNCE!
Hi, Bones.

139

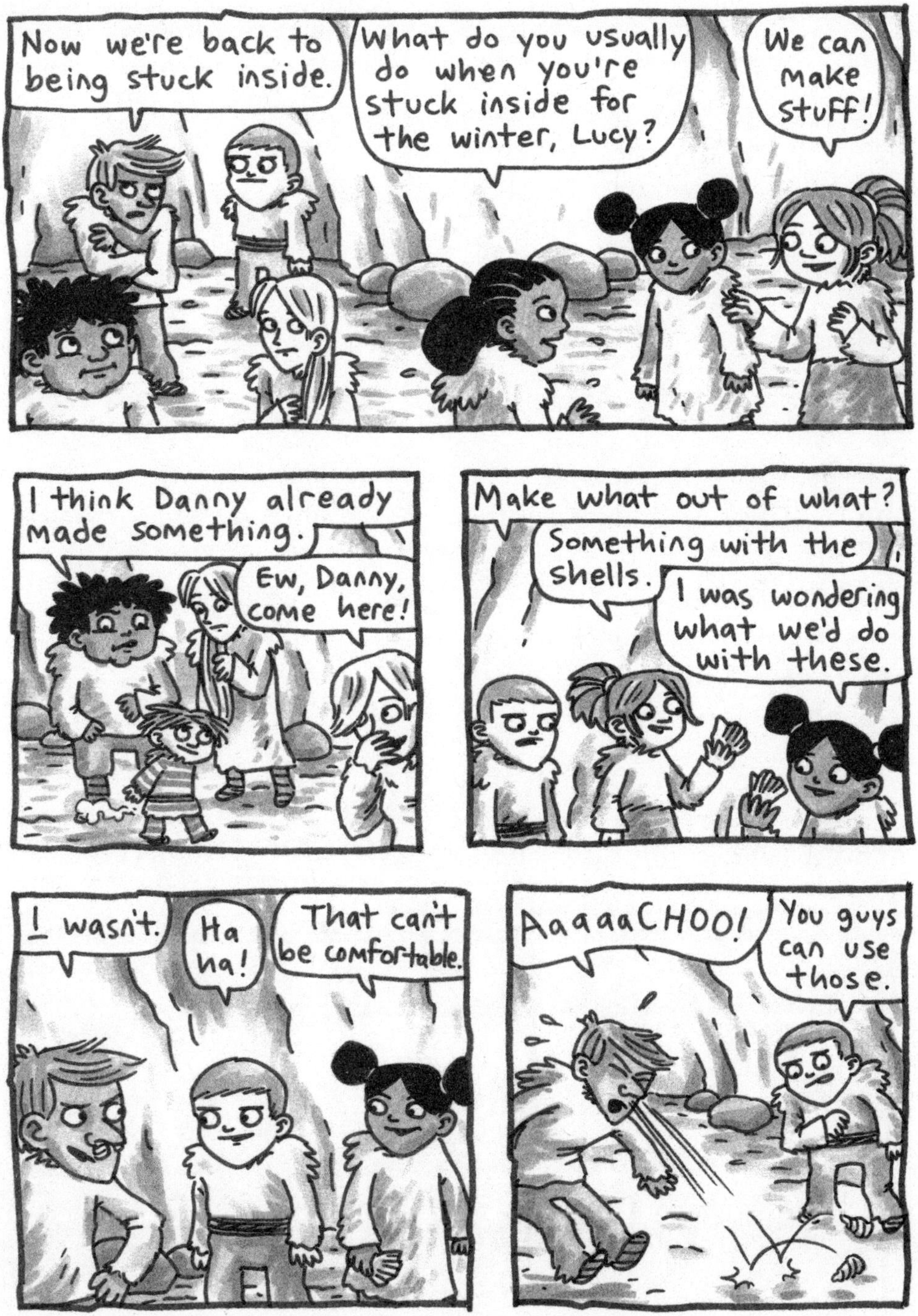
Now we're back to being stuck inside.
What do you usually do when you're stuck inside for the winter, Lucy?
We can make stuff!
I think Danny already made something.
Ew, Danny, come here!
Make what out of what?
Something with the shells.
I was wondering what we'd do with these.
I wasn't.
Ha ha!
That can't be comfortable.
AaaaaCHOO!
You guys can use those.

Shells found in Neanderthal caves have holes that had been drilled by snails. There wasn't anything left in the shells to eat, but the holes were all the same size, making them just right to string on a necklace.

Some shells have colored pigment on them, indicating those were picked specifically for decoration.

143

144

Eagle talons were found at the famous Krapina Neanderthal site! ⟶

Scientists think the talons may have been used to make necklaces or bracelets.

Some of the talons show marks from stone tools.

There are also signs that the talons were polished.

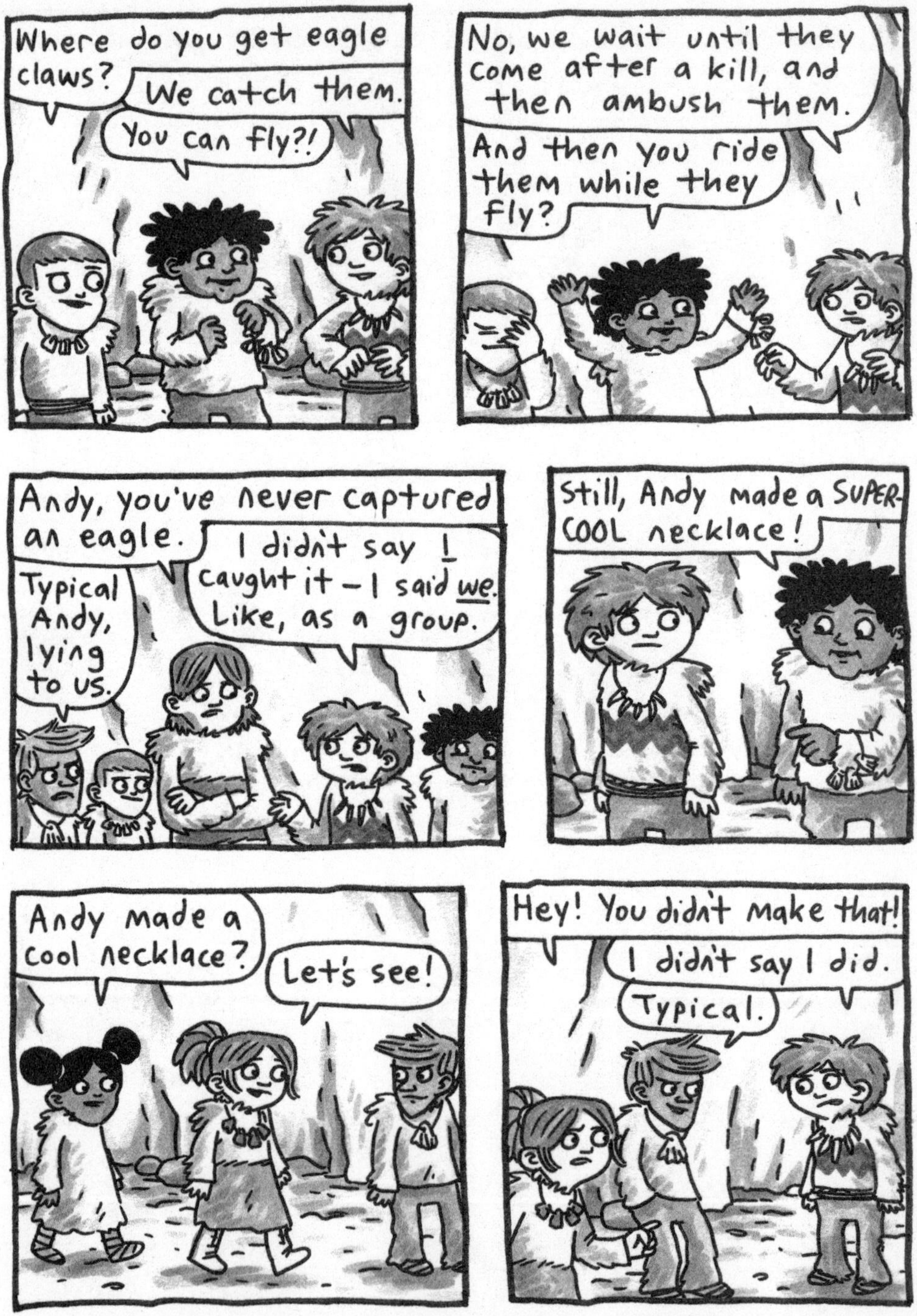
Where do you get eagle claws?
We catch them.
You can fly?!
No, we wait until they come after a kill, and then ambush them.
And then you ride them while they fly?
Andy, you've never captured an eagle.
Typical Andy, lying to us.
I didn't say I caught it – I said we. Like, as a group.
Still, Andy made a SUPER-COOL necklace!
Andy made a cool necklace?
Let's see!
Hey! You didn't make that!
I didn't say I did.
Typical.

147

148

149

150

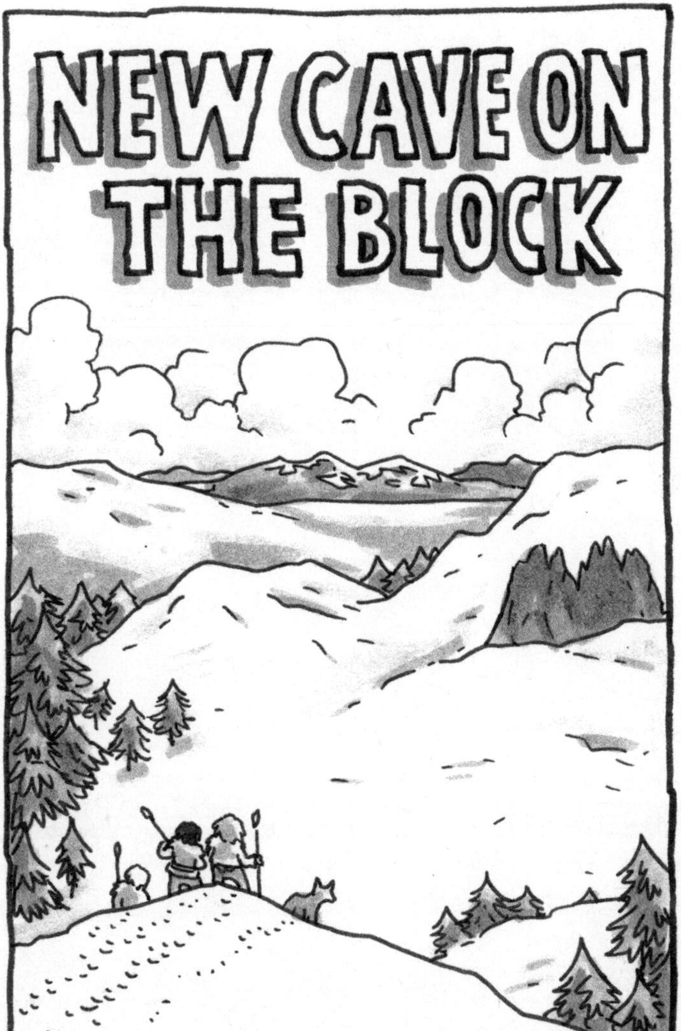
NEW CAVE ON THE BLOCK

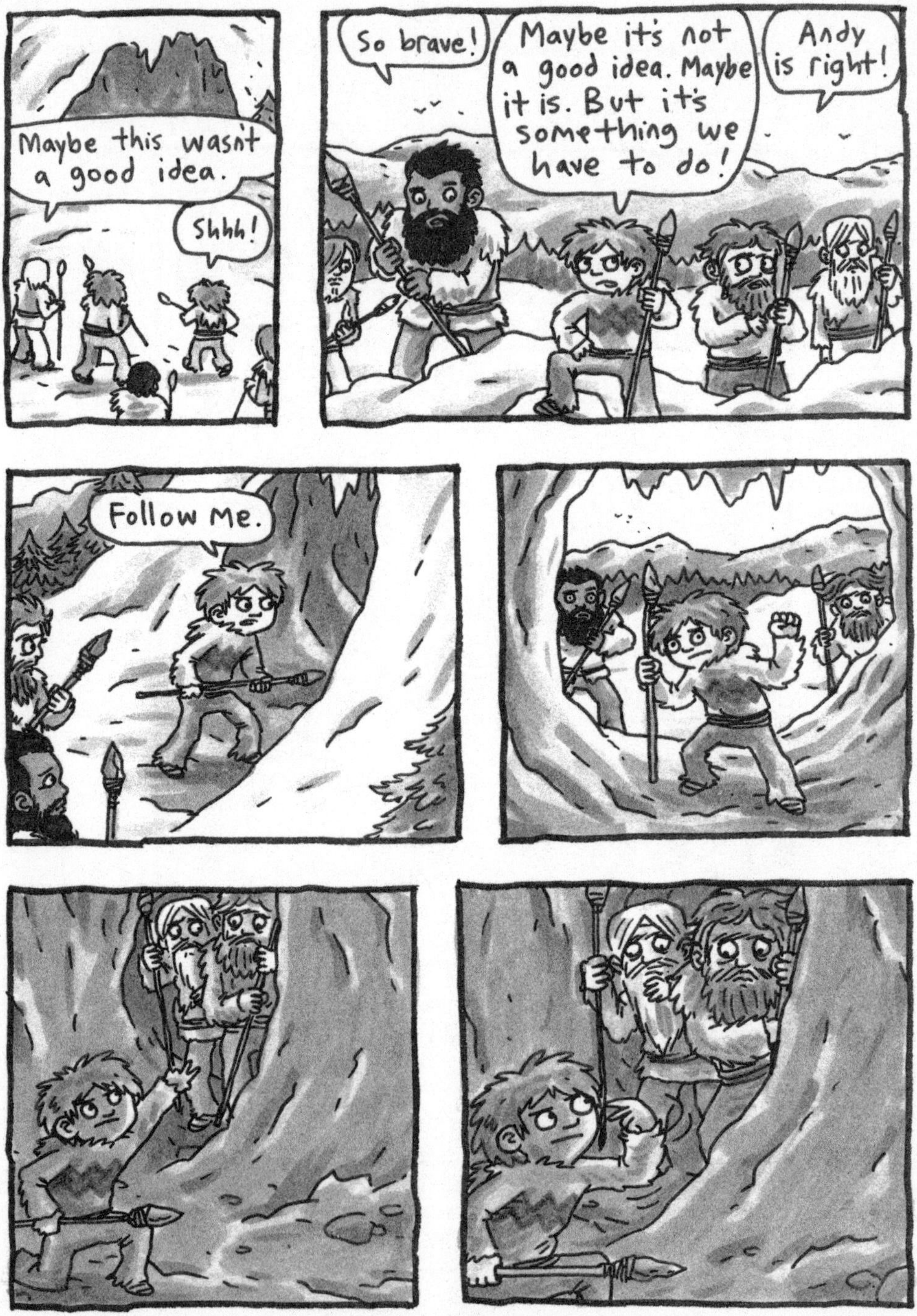
Maybe this wasn't a good idea.
Shhh!
So brave!
Maybe it's not a good idea. Maybe it is. But it's something we have to do!
Andy is right!
Follow me.

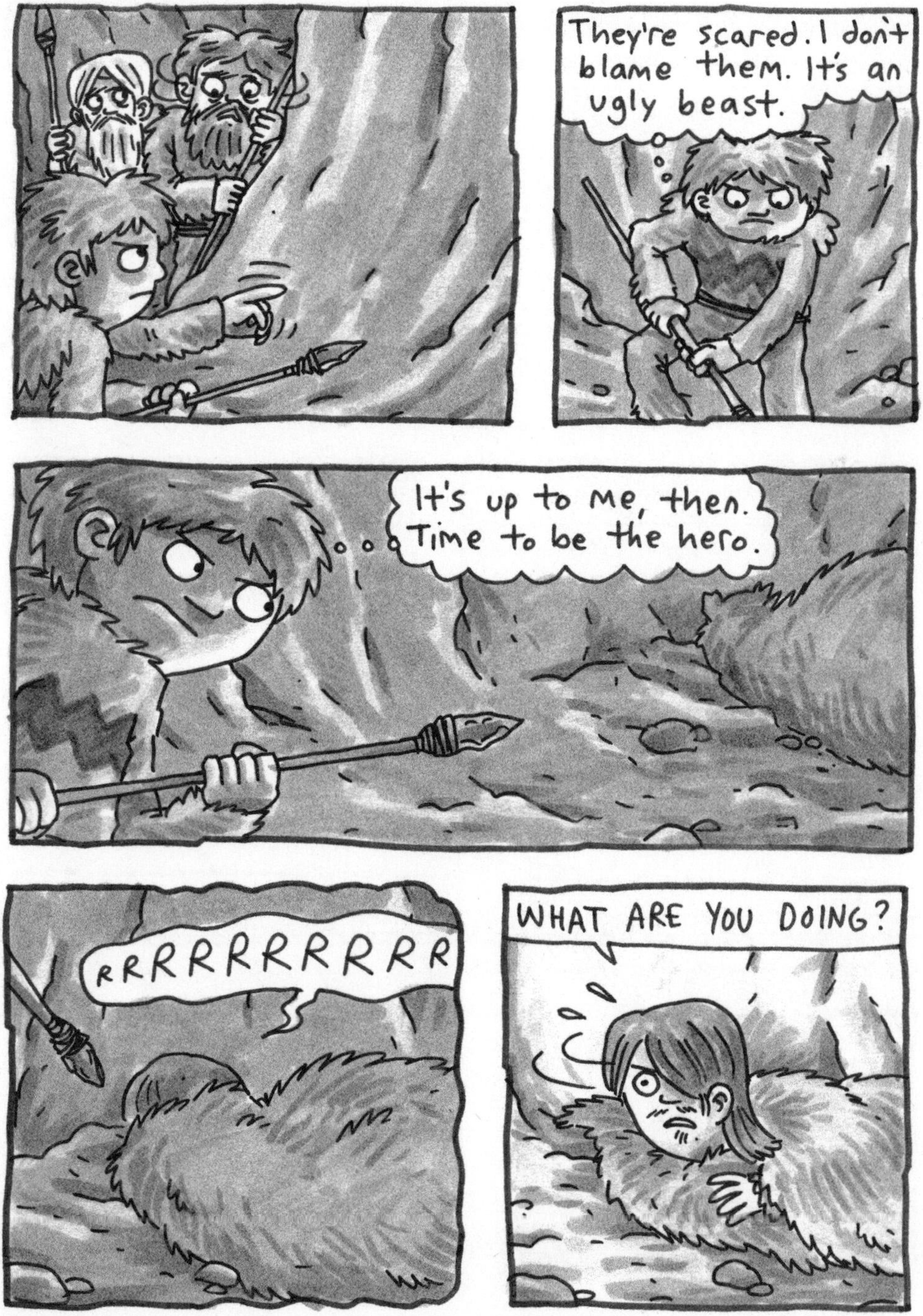
They're scared. I don't blame them. It's an ugly beast.
It's up to me, then. Time to be the hero.
RRRRRRRRRRR
WHAT ARE YOU DOING?

156

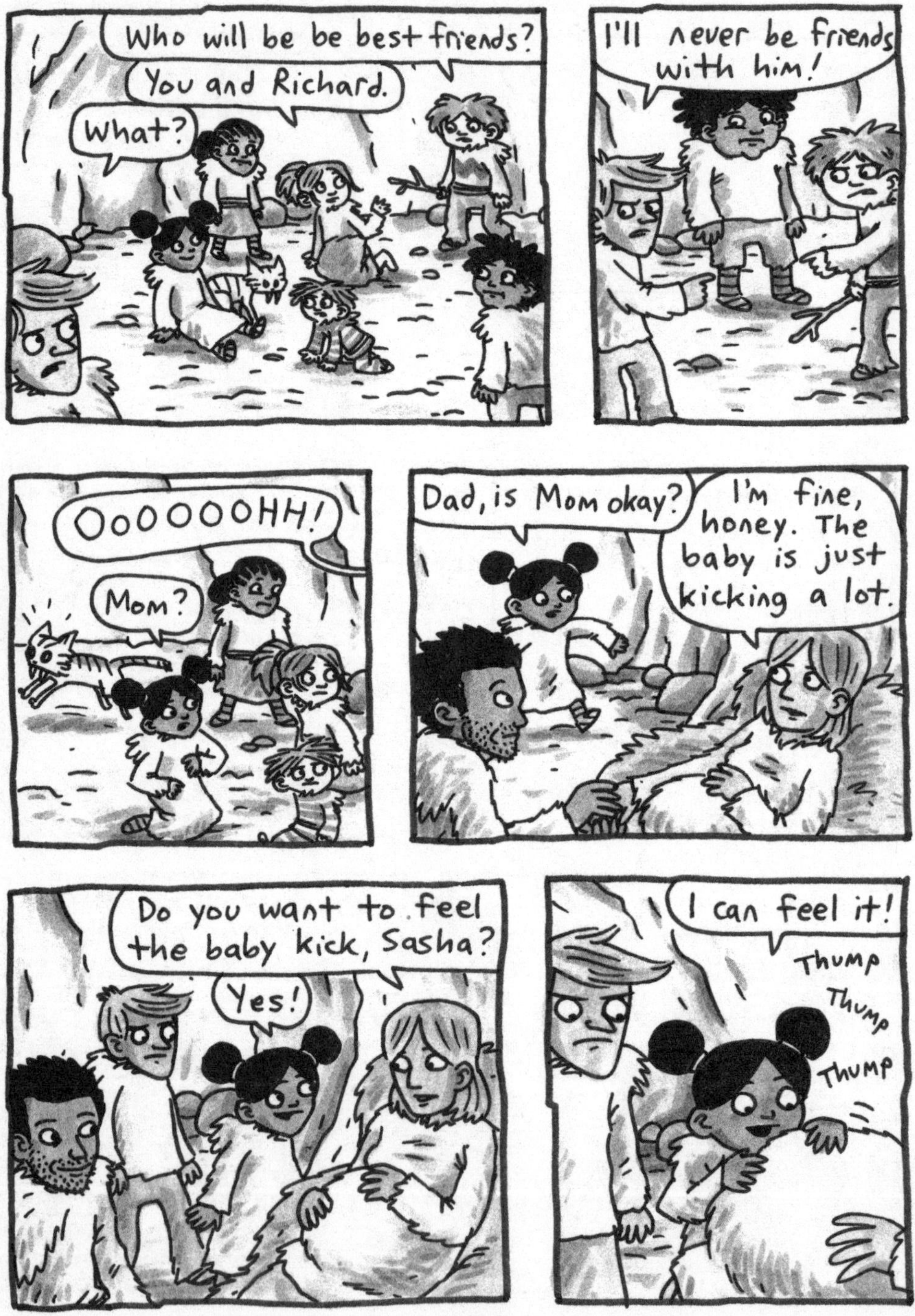
Who will be be best friends?
You and Richard.
What?
I'll never be friends with him!
OOOOOOHH!
Mom?
Dad, is Mom okay?
I'm fine, honey. The baby is just kicking a lot.
Do you want to feel the baby kick, Sasha?
Yes!
I can feel it!
THUMP
THUMP
THUMP

159

162

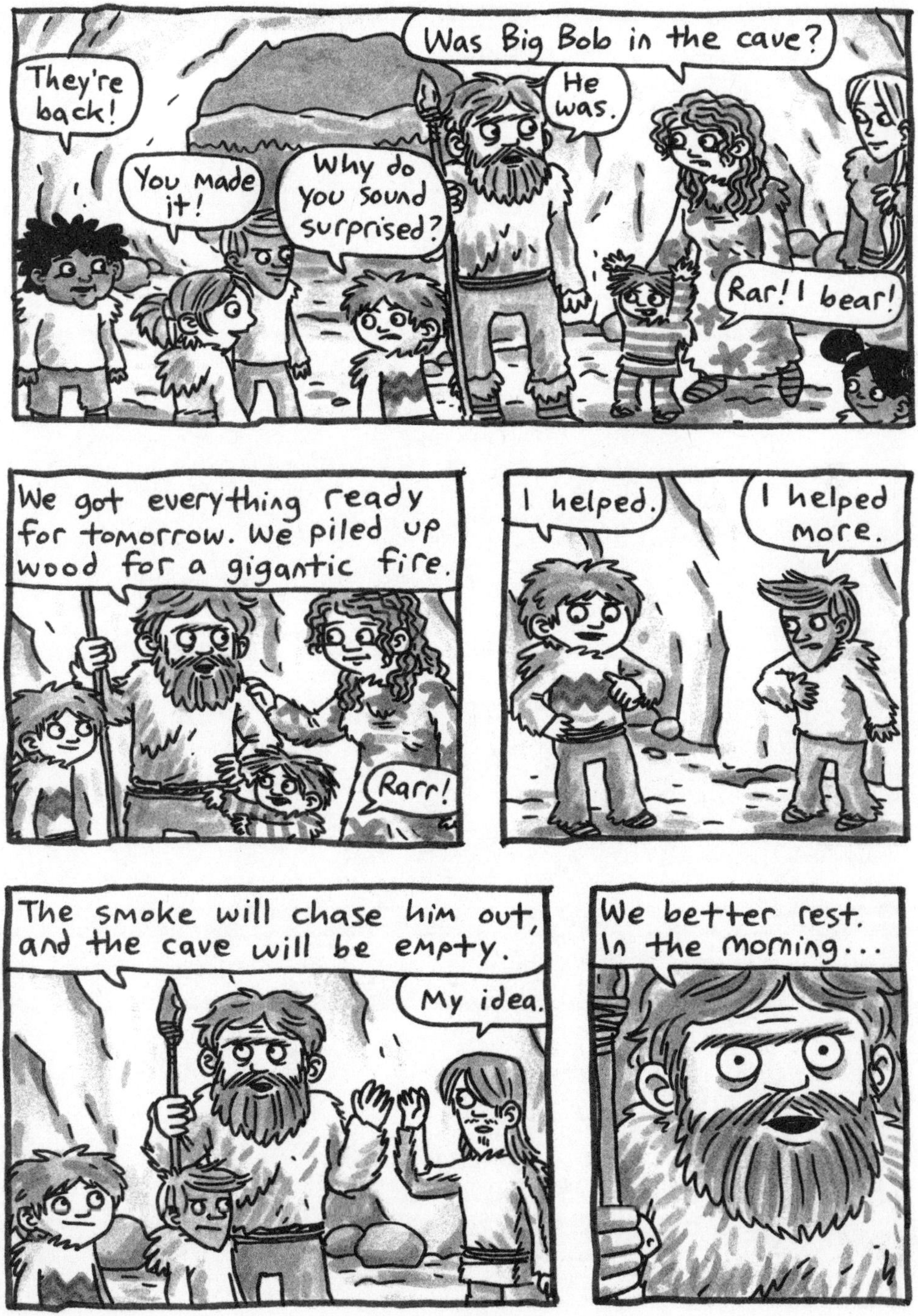
They're back!
Was Big Bob in the cave?
He was.
You made it!
Why do you sound surprised?
Rar! I bear!
We got everything ready for tomorrow. We piled up wood for a gigantic fire.
Rarr!
I helped.
I helped more.
The smoke will chase him out, and the cave will be empty.
My idea.
We better rest. In the morning...

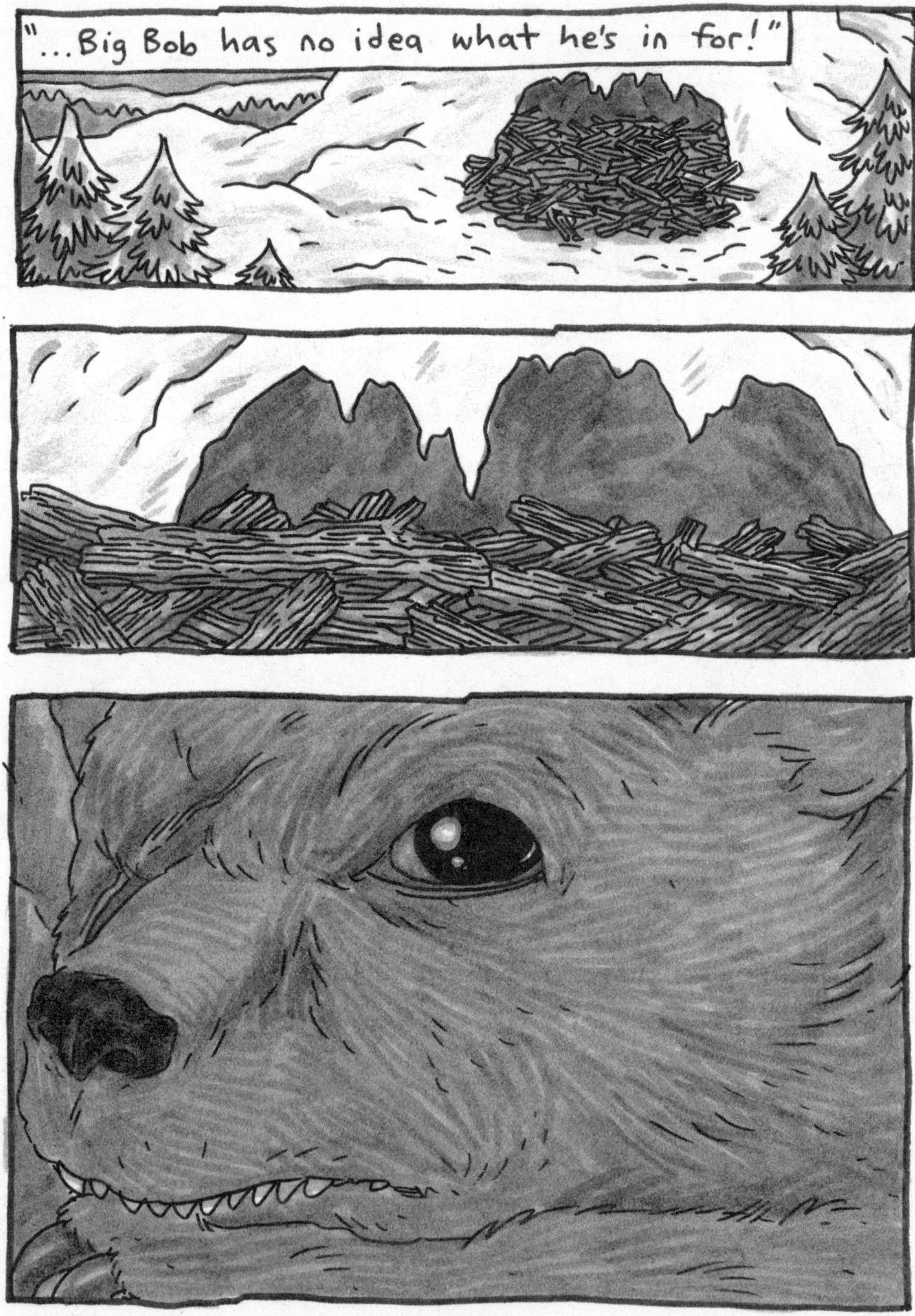
"...Big Bob has no idea what he's in for!"

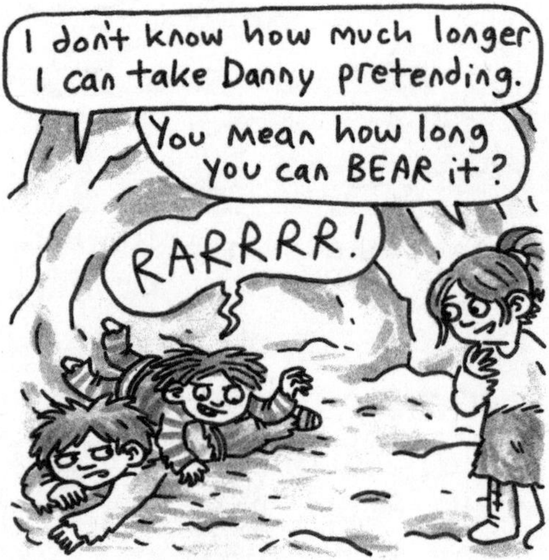
I don't know how much longer I can take Danny pretending.
You mean how long you can BEAR it?
RARRRR!

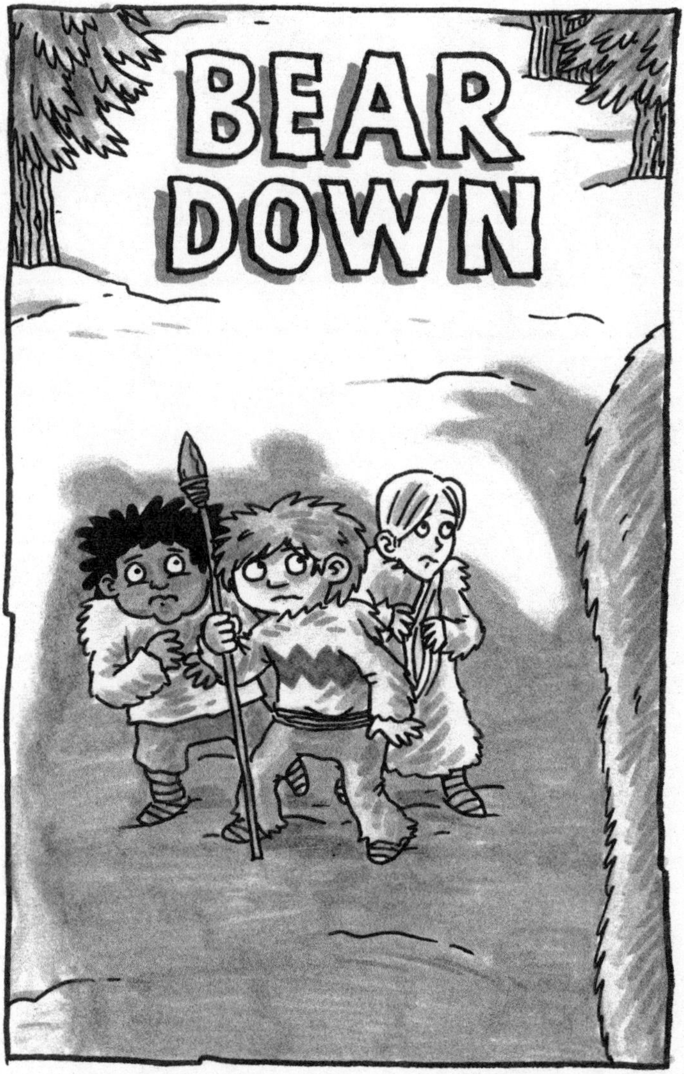
BEAR
DOWN

173

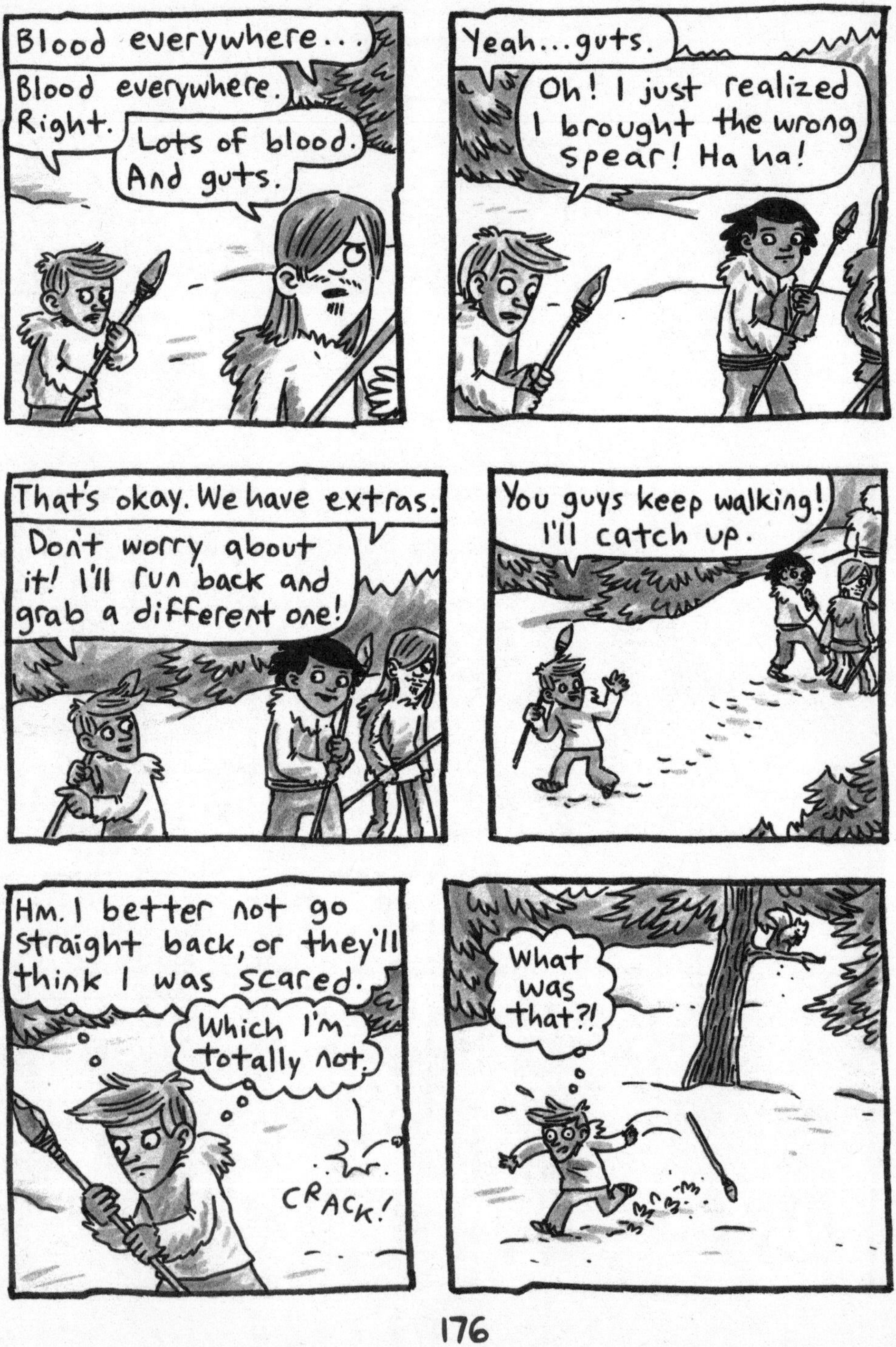
Blood everywhere...
Blood everywhere. Right.
Lots of blood. And guts.
Yeah...guts.
Oh! I just realized I brought the wrong spear! Ha ha!
That's okay. We have extras.
Don't worry about it! I'll run back and grab a different one!
You guys keep walking! I'll catch up.
Hm. I better not go straight back, or they'll think I was scared.
Which I'm totally not.
CRACK!
What was that?!

177

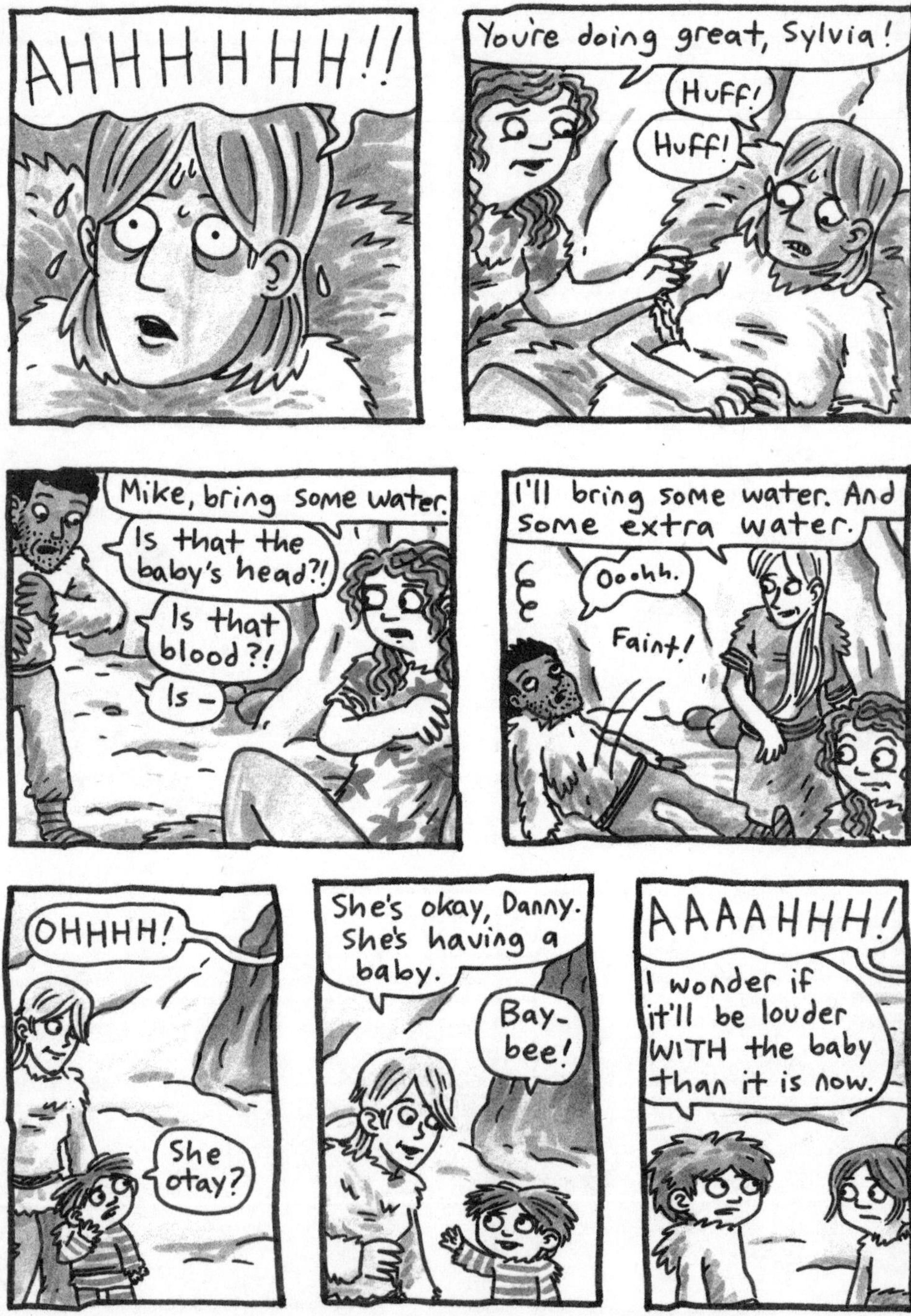
AHHHHHHH!!
You're doing great, Sylvia!
Huff!
Huff!
Mike, bring some water.
Is that the baby's head?!
Is that blood?!
Is –
I'll bring some water. And some extra water.
Ooohh.
Faint!
OHHHH!
She otay?
She's okay, Danny. She's having a baby.
Bay-bee!
AAAAHHH!
I wonder if it'll be louder WITH the baby than it is now.

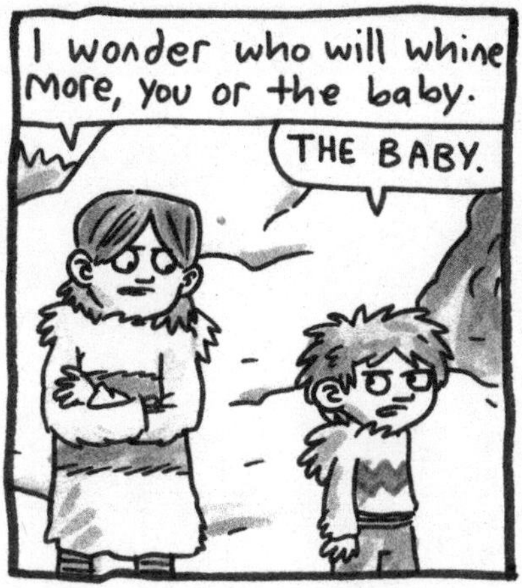
I wonder who will whine more, you or the baby.
THE BABY.

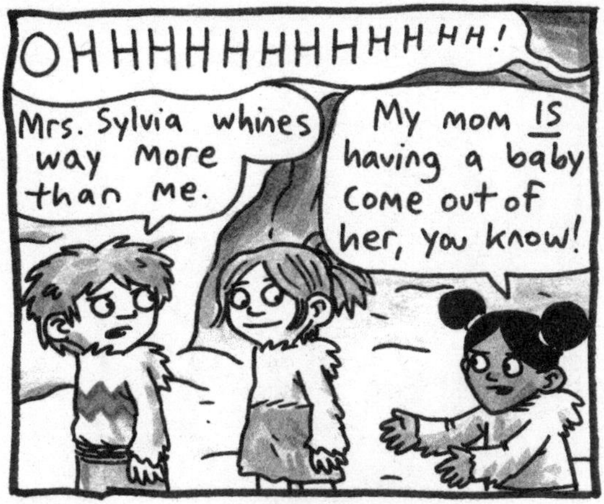
OHHHHHHHHHHHHH!
Mrs. Sylvia whines way more than me.
My mom IS having a baby come out of her, you know!

Neanderthal bones were denser, and scientists think they may have been less flexible at birth!

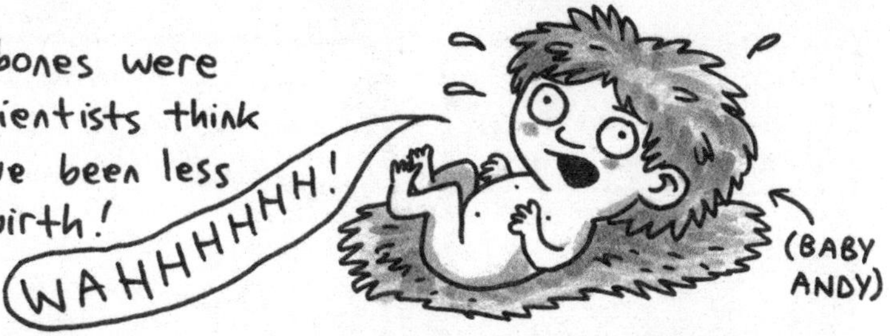
WAHHHHHHH!
(BABY ANDY)

Despite differences in anatomy like the wider hips of Neanderthals, their babies were probably similar in size to early human babies at birth.

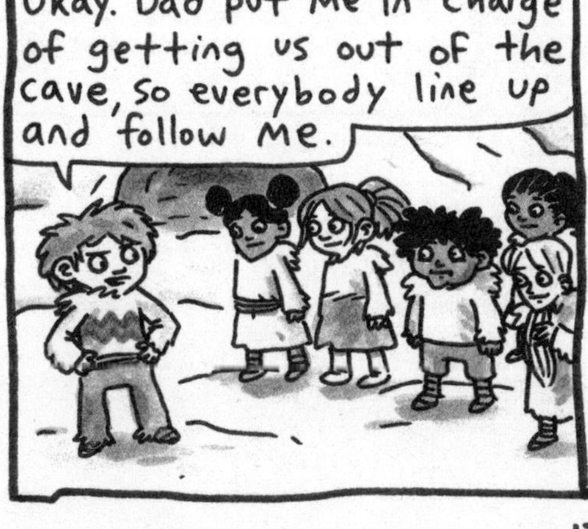
Okay. Dad put me in charge of getting us out of the cave, so everybody line up and follow me.

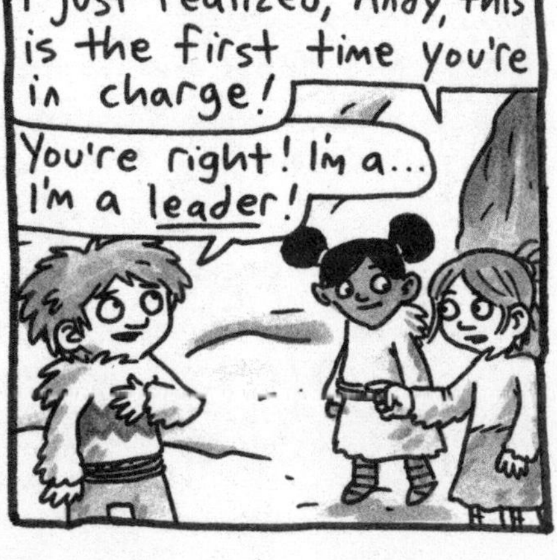
I just realized, Andy, this is the first time you're in charge!
You're right! I'm a... I'm a leader!

181

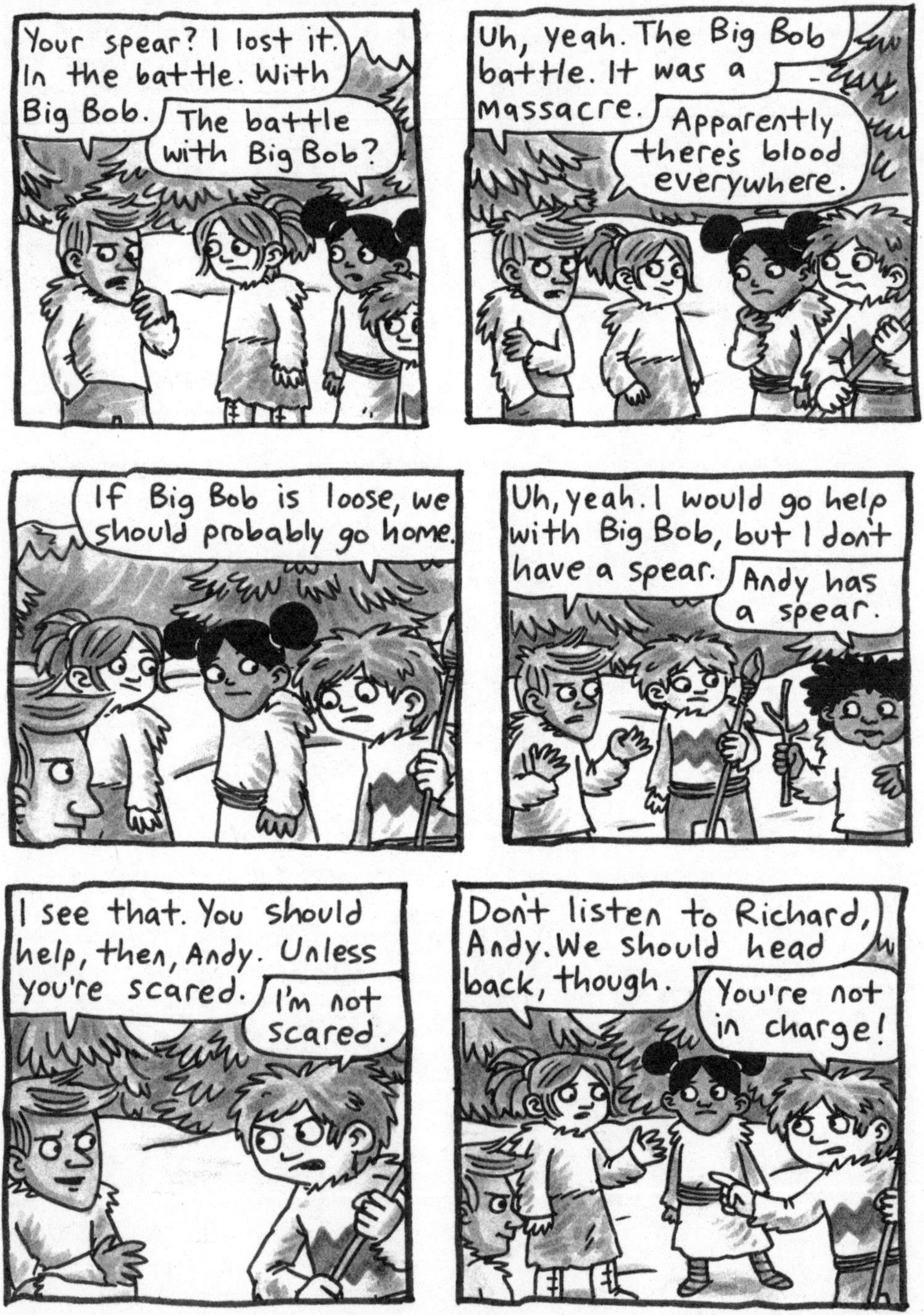
Your spear? I lost it. In the battle. With Big Bob.
The battle with Big Bob?
Uh, yeah. The Big Bob battle. It was a massacre.
Apparently there's blood everywhere.
If Big Bob is loose, we should probably go home.
Uh, yeah. I would go help with Big Bob, but I don't have a spear.
Andy has a spear.
I see that. You should help, then, Andy. Unless you're scared.
I'm not scared.
Don't listen to Richard, Andy. We should head back, though.
You're not in charge!

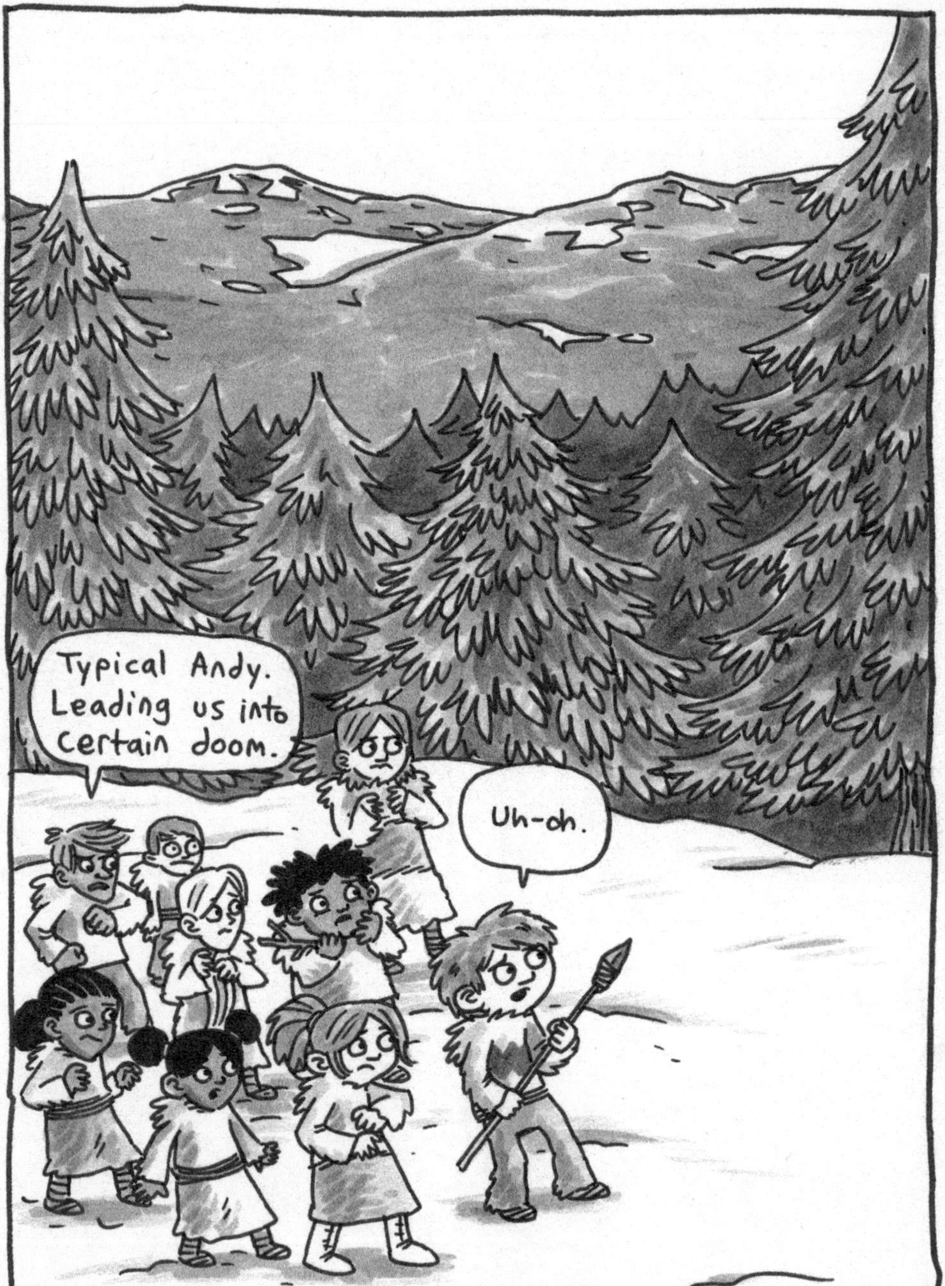
Typical Andy. Leading us into certain doom.
Uh-oh.

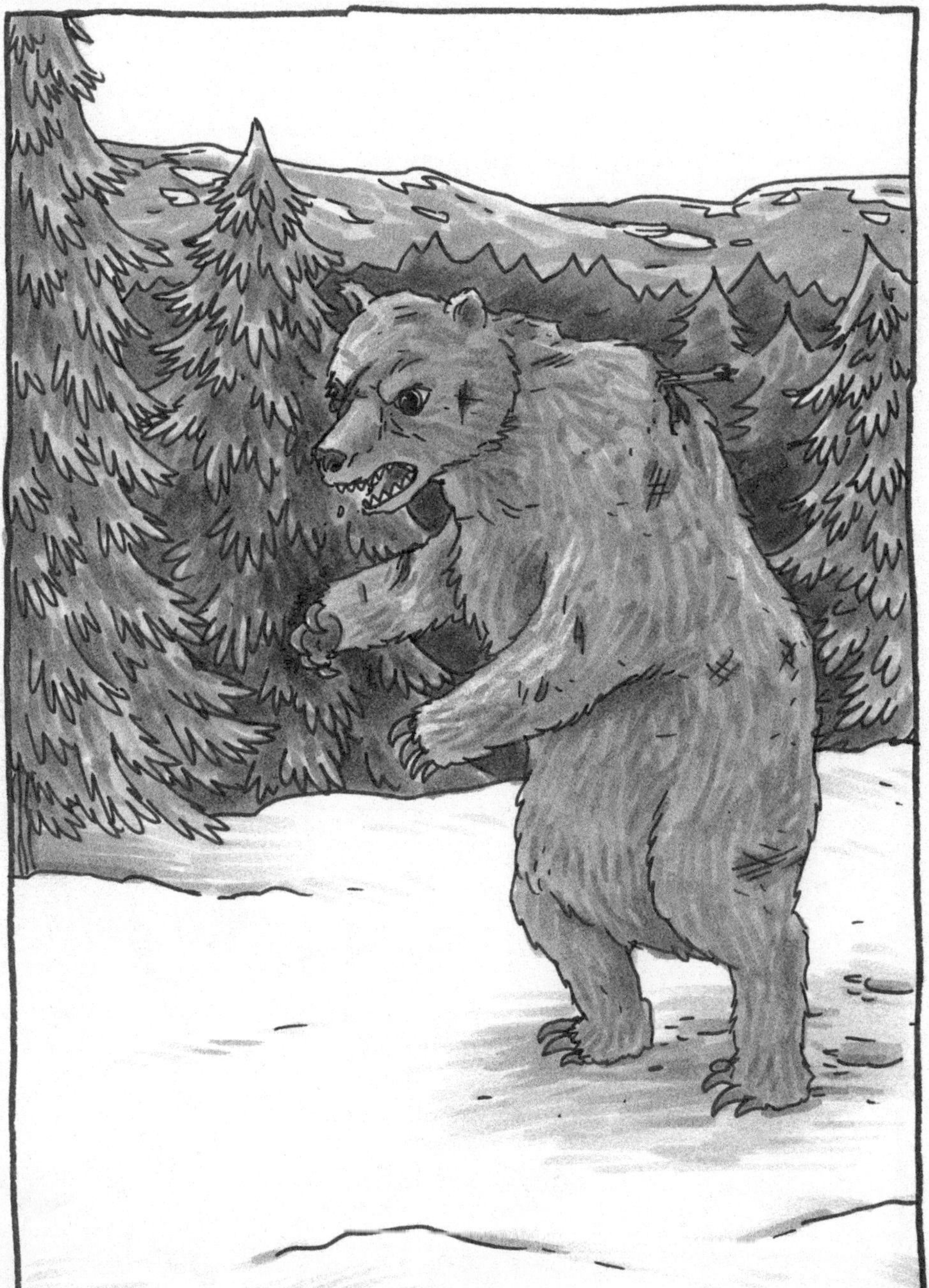

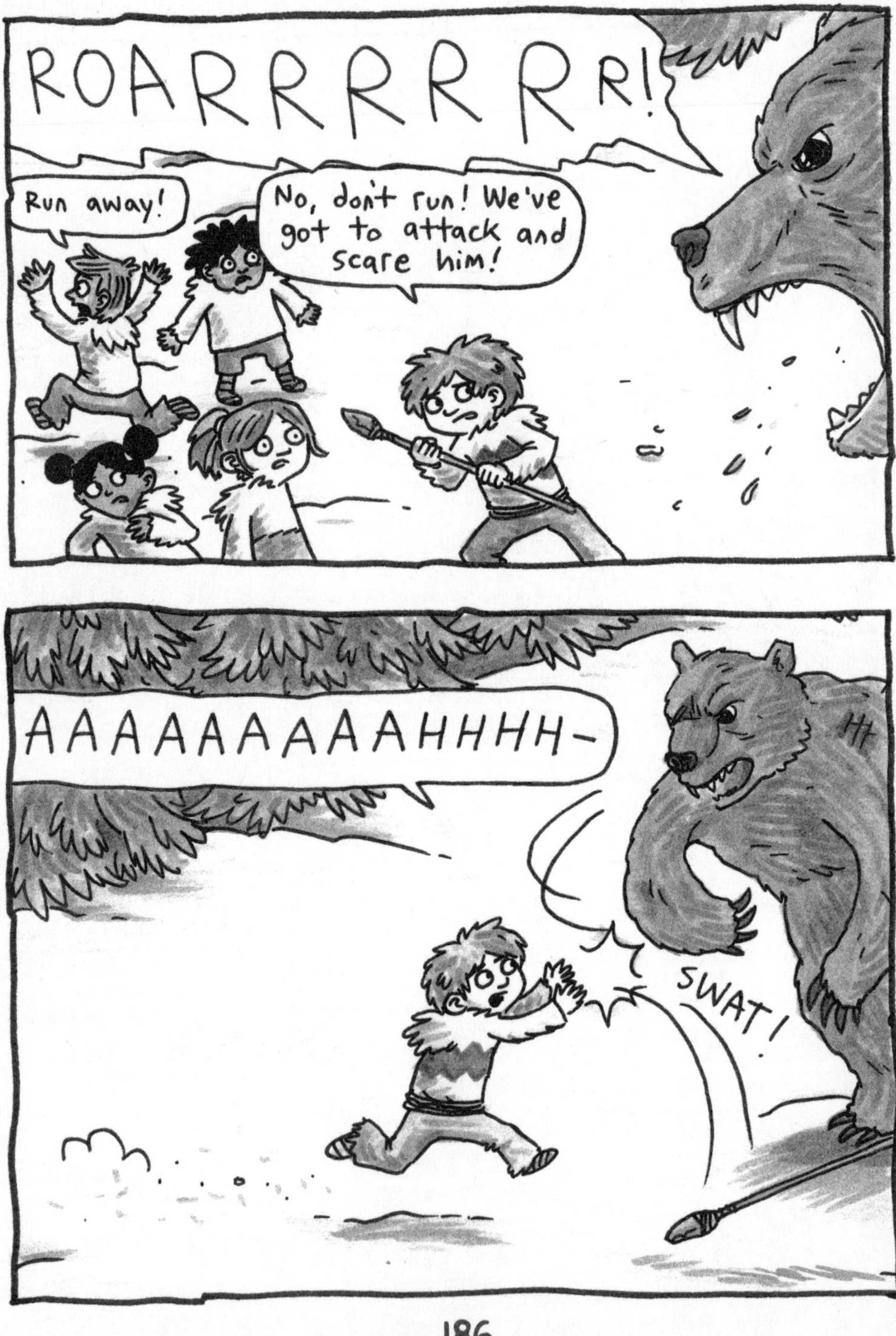
ROARRRRRRR!
Run away!
No, don't run! We've got to attack and scare him!
AAAAAAAAAHHHH-
SWAT!

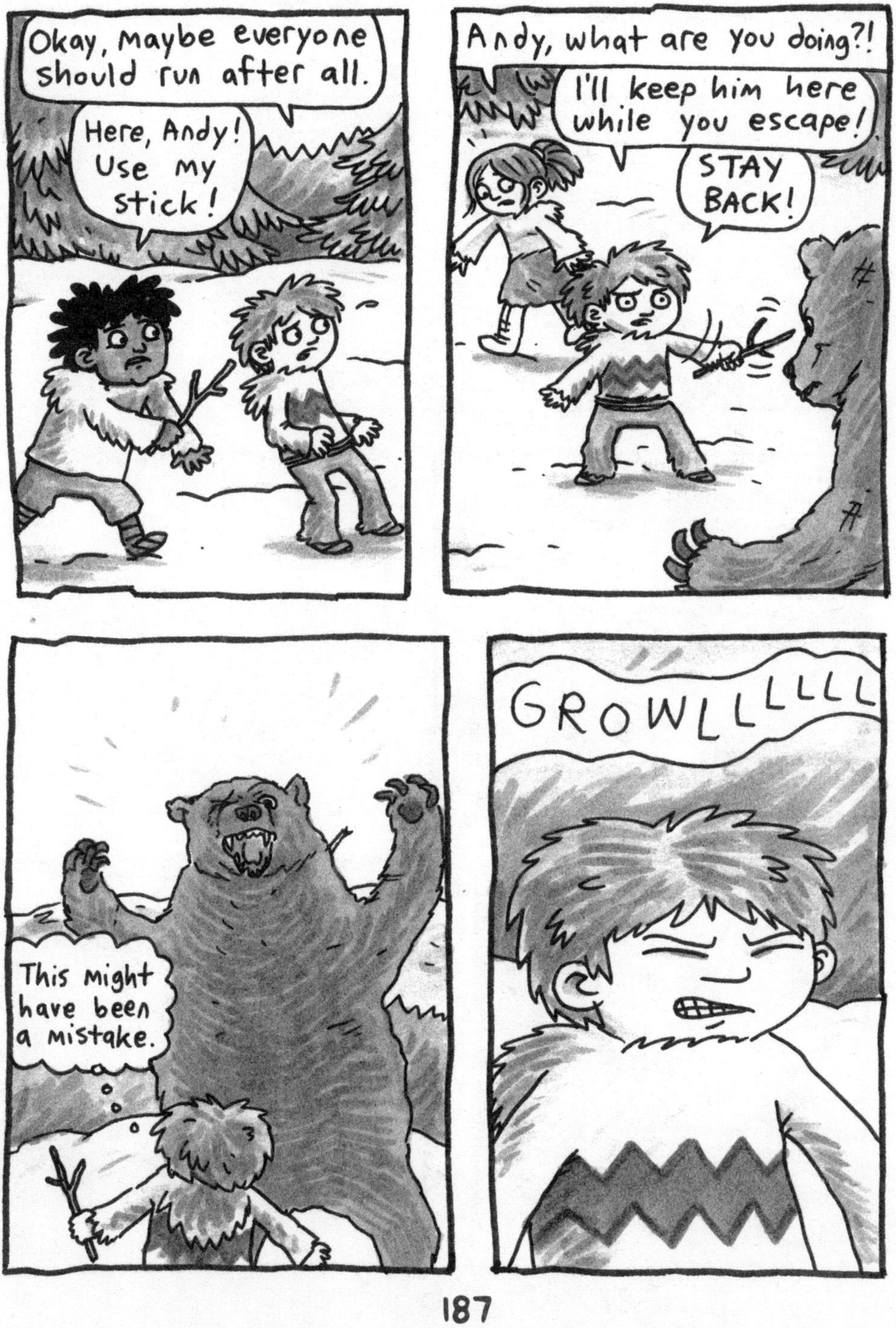
Okay, maybe everyone should run after all.
Here, Andy! Use my stick!
Andy, what are you doing?!
I'll keep him here while you escape!
STAY BACK!
This might have been a mistake.
GROWLLLLLL

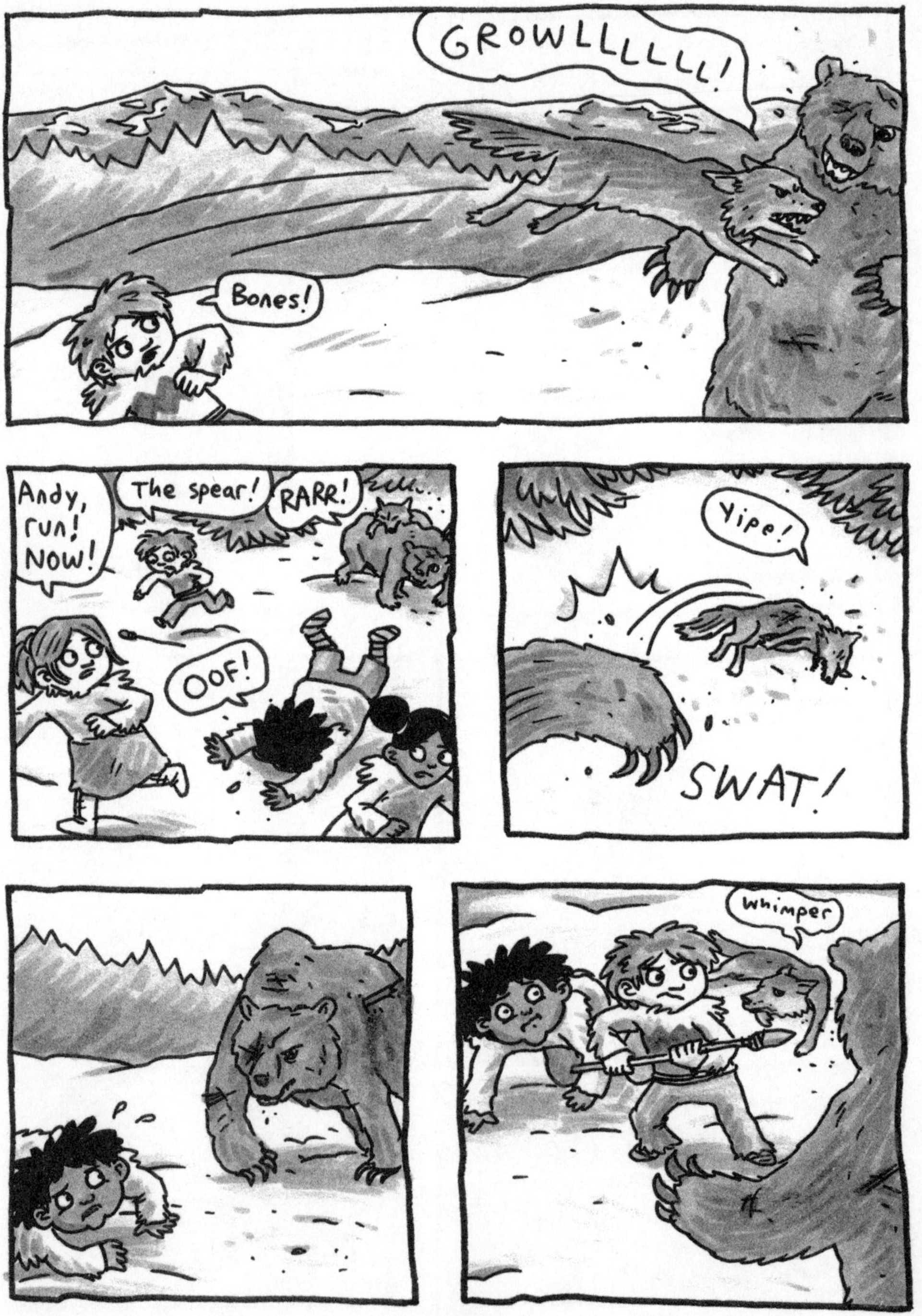
GROWLLLLLLL!
Bones!
Andy, run! NOW!
The spear!
RARR!
OOF!
Yipe!
SWAT!
whimper

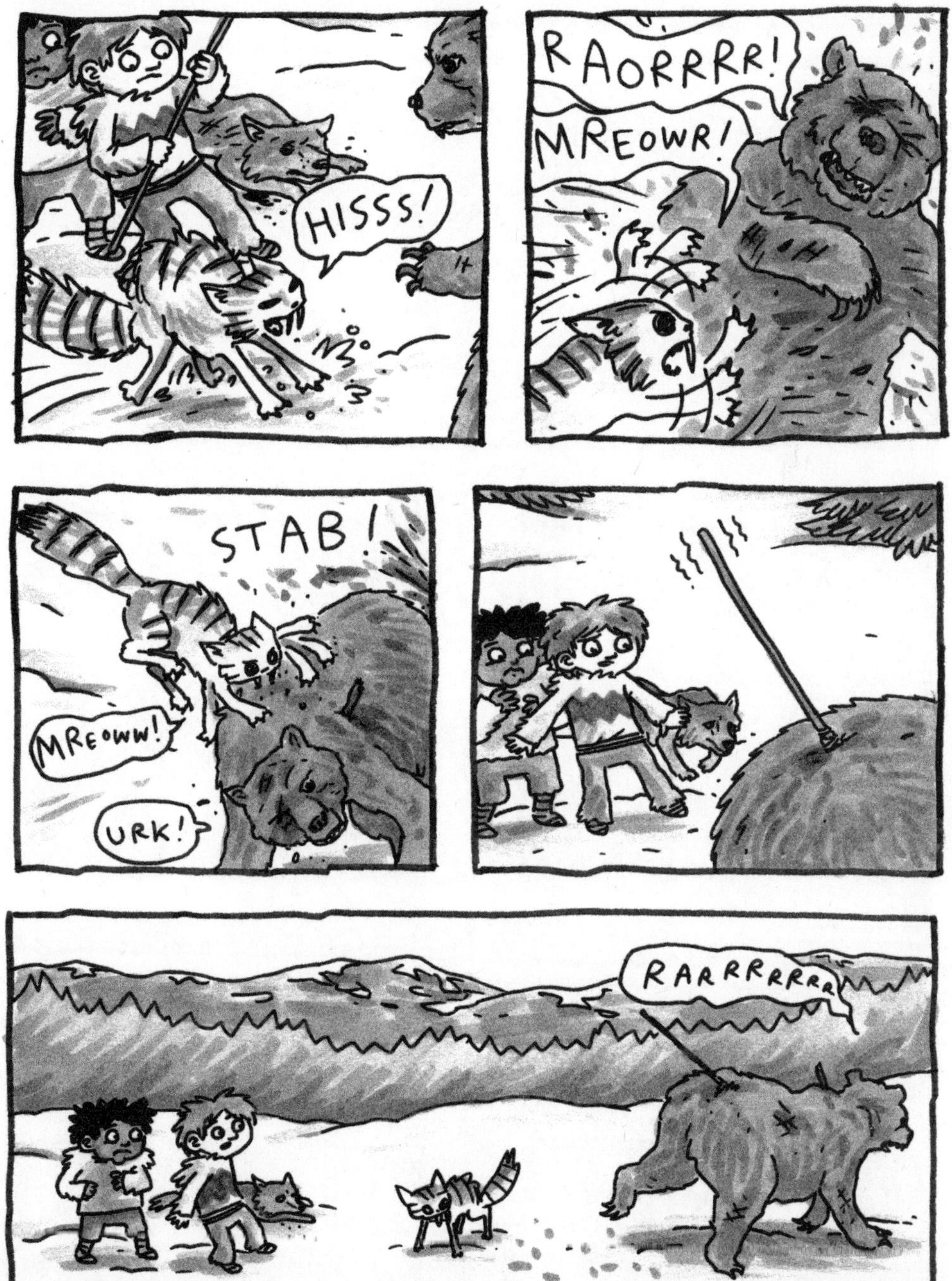
HISSS!
RAORRRR!
MREOWR!
STAB!
MREOWW!
URK!
RARRRRRRR

191

193

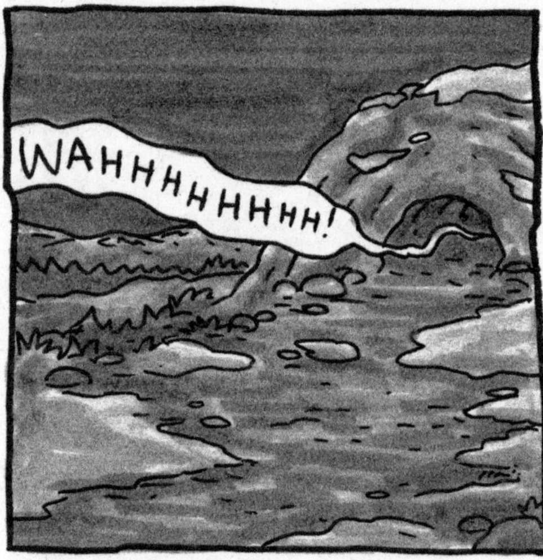
WAHHHHHHHHH!

THE END

...OF WINTER
(AND A GOOD NIGHT'S REST)!

FORTY THOUSAND YEARS LATER... (TODAY)

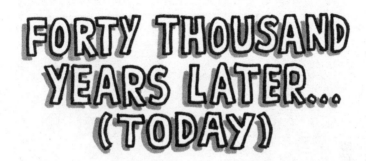

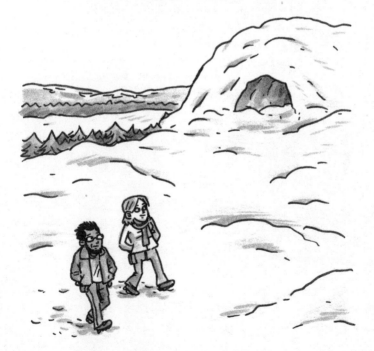

How do we know how cold it was thousands of years ago?

Lots of ways!

The effects of glaciers on the landscape and soil deposits show how much land was covered by ice in the past.

Tree rings show how climate changed over time. Narrow rings can indicate drought or extreme cold.

Microscopic pollen can be found alongside bones and other artifacts. Since different plants thrive in different climates, the type of pollen found can be studied to learn what the climate was like at different times.

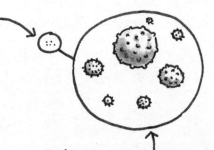

Can't tell how much this pollen made Neanderthals sneeze, though.

Ice core samples contain layers of ice going back thousands of years. The composition of the ice, as well as the dust and debris found in each layer, reflect the conditions on Earth at the time the layer formed.

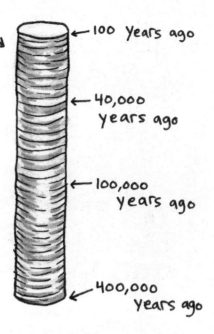

← 100 years ago

← 40,000 years ago

← 100,000 years ago

← 400,000 years ago

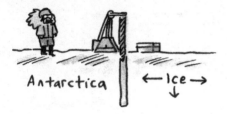

Antarctica   ← Ice →

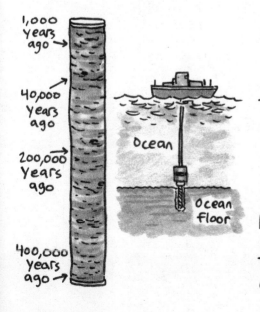

1,000 years ago →

40,000 years ago →

200,000 years ago →

400,000 years ago →

Ocean

Ocean floor

A special drill is used to take ocean core samples from the bottom of the sea. The samples contain thousands of years' worth of sediment deposits that have built up on the ocean floor. Scientists study the remains of plankton and other organisms in each layer to determine the climates of different time periods.

The Milankovitch Cycles involve three key concepts.

ECCENTRICITY

The Earth orbits the sun in an ellipse, not a circle. This orbital ellipse changes slowly over time, so about every 100,000 years, the Earth spends more time farther away from the sun. This cools the Earth.

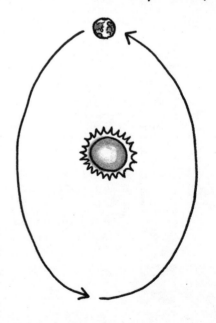

TILT

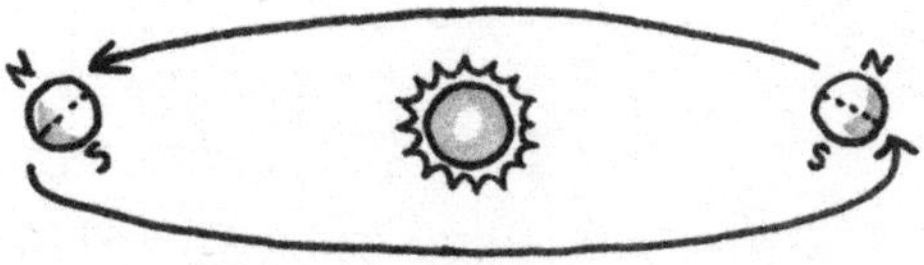
N
S
N
S

The end of the Earth that's tilted toward the sun changes every 40,000 years. When the Northern Hemisphere is tilted away from the sun, our summers are cooler.

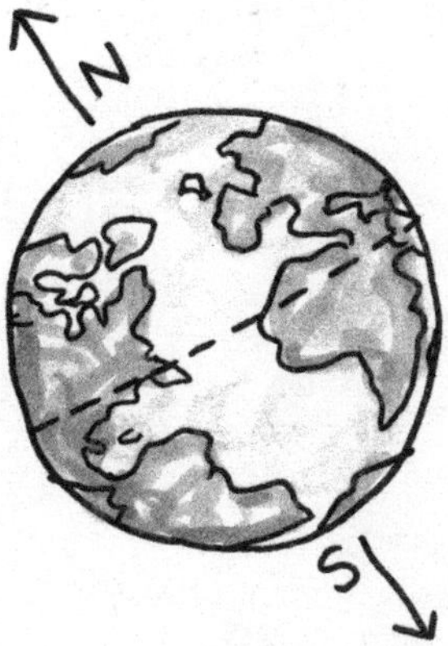
N
S

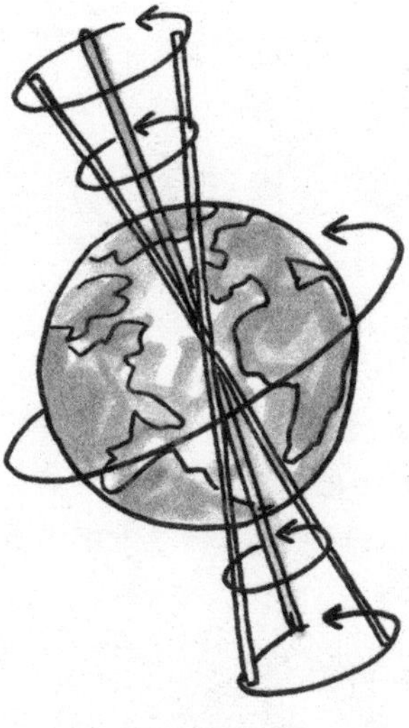

WOBBLE

The Earth's axis – an imaginary line through the center of the Earth – wobbles as the planet spins. Every 26,000 years, this cycle affects the seasons.

The ways these three cycles overlap through time can alter the Earth's climate in significant ways!

Do you want to learn more about Neanderthals, early humans, and cave bears? You can visit these museums to make your own discoveries!

SMITHSONIAN NATIONAL MUSEUM OF NATURAL HISTORY ↘

Washington, D.C., USA

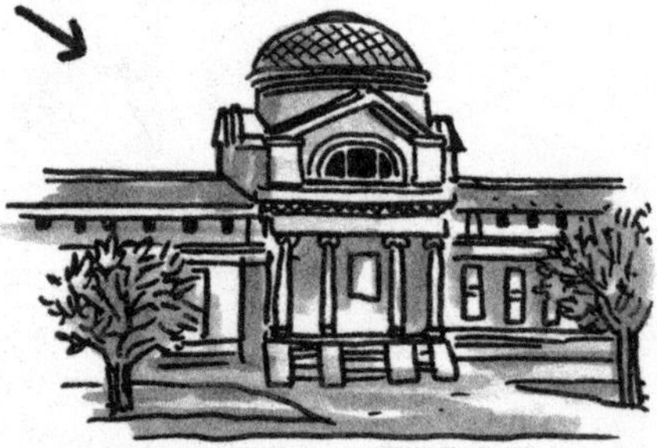

See ancient mammal skeletons and fossils.

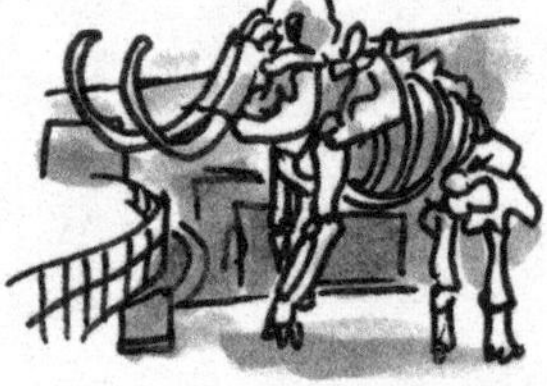

NATURAL HISTORY MUSEUM ↙

London, England

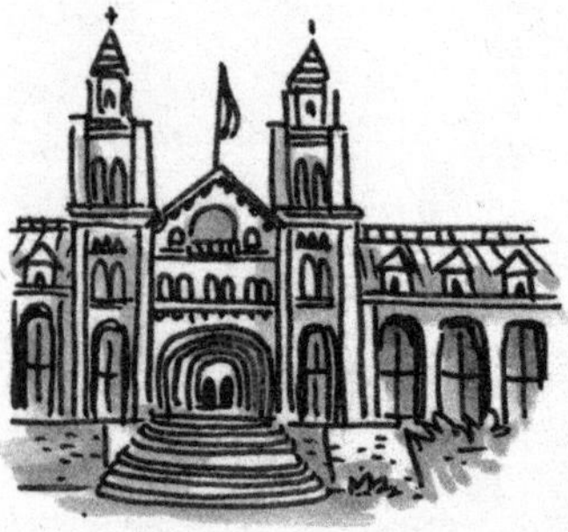

Check museums for special exhibitions like the Natural History Museum's "Britain: One Million Years of the Human Story."

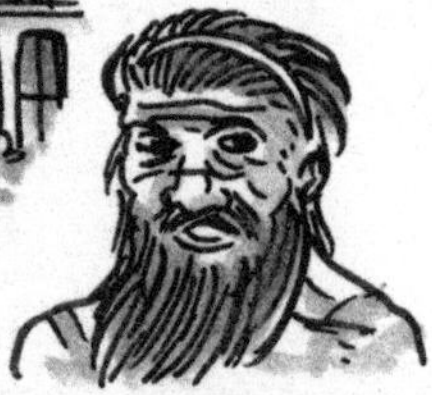

KRAPINA NEANDERTHAL MUSEUM ↘

Krapina, Croatia

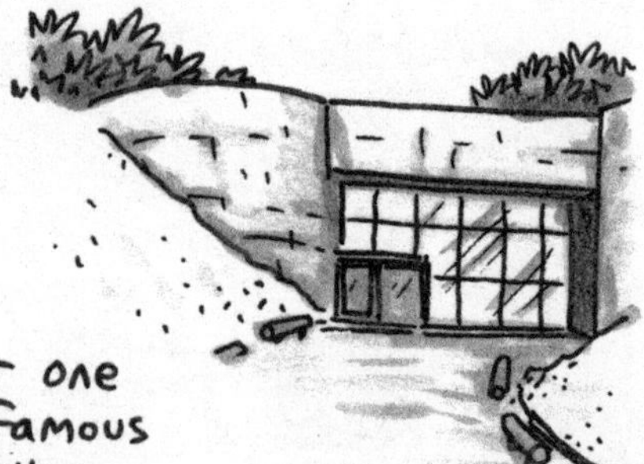

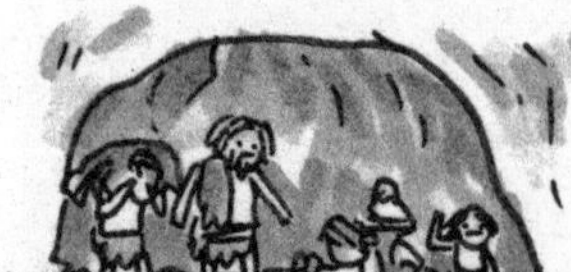

Located near one of the most famous Neanderthal sites.

1899-1905: Excavation in Croatia reveals thousands of Neanderthal bones and artifacts.
Find anything?
Uh...
1953-1957: In Iraq, nine buried Neanderthal skeletons are found.
I wonder if they had a funeral, too.
1991: Dating of bones shows that Neanderthals and early humans lived at the same time.
But how did they feel about each other?
2010: DNA studies show that Neanderthals and early humans had children together.
Marry me!
2014: Dating of Neanderthal bones and tools indicates the species died out around 40,000 years ago.
TODAY: New studies and discoveries continue to reveal how Neanderthals weren't as dumb as once believed.
You're a Neanderthal!
Thanks!

FICTION VS. FACT

What's true in Lucy and Andy's story based on what scientists have learned, and what's stretching the truth? Read on!

WHAT DID NEANDERTHALS KNOW ABOUT BEAR SAFETY?
Neanderthals most likely knew how to deal with cave bears. For bear safety today, check out information from a trusted source like the National Park Service (not Phil!).

COULD NEANDERTHALS OUTRUN EARLY HUMANS?
The body type of Neanderthals wasn't as good for running, so early humans would have been faster. Neither group should have been running on slippery ice, though!

DID NEANDERTHALS HAVE WINTER COATS AND PARKAS?
Because bones of animals like the wolverine have been found in their caves along with bone needles, scientists know early humans made warm garments. No conclusive evidence has been found to show Neanderthal winter clothing was as advanced.

DID NEANDERTHALS TAKE VACATIONS? Neanderthals may have occupied different territories for different seasons, but travel was far more difficult, so they wouldn't have made weekend trips just for fun.

DID NEANDERTHALS GIVE GIFTS? Neanderthals may have given gifts on certain occasions, or to cement relationships. They probably didn't have birthday parties. Especially since they didn't have cake!

WERE THERE PETS 40,000 YEARS AGO? There were no domesticated animals or pets in the time of Neanderthals. Too bad, but at least pets weren't ruining the furniture! Of course, there was no furniture, either.

DID NEANDERTHALS HAVE FIRES INSIDE THEIR CAVES? Evidence of smoke pollution and fires has been found inside Neanderthal caves. They didn't have chimneys, but caves could have high ceilings and extra openings so people wouldn't breathe in too much smoke.

SILLY CAVEMAN MYTHS

CAVEMAN RIDING A T. REX

If a caveman did meet a T. rex, he'd get eaten! Fortunately, dinosaurs died out 65 million years before Neanderthals or humans first lived!

CAVEMAN INVENTING THE WHEEL

The first wheels weren't invented until almost 6,000 years ago.

CAVEMEN BONKED CAVEWOMEN ON THE HEAD AND DRAGGED THEM BY THE HAIR

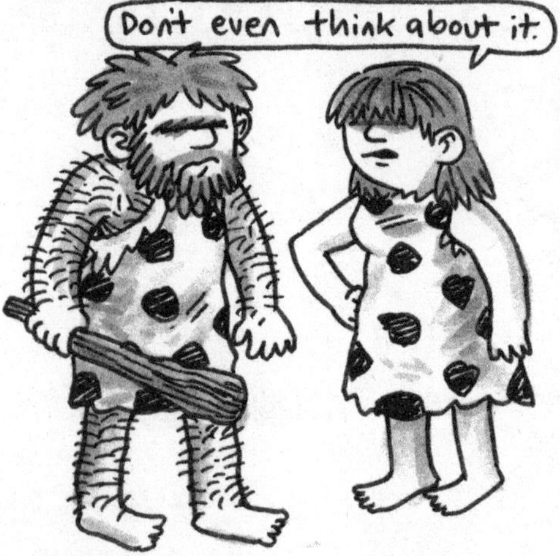
Don't even think about it.

This myth was popularized after appearing in many 1920s comic strips. There is no evidence of this ever happening, and there's no good reason cavemen would have behaved this way. Not only is it dangerous, it's not very attractive!

CAVEMEN HAD HORRIBLE POSTURE

Because one of the first Neanderthal skeletons had a spine curved by disease, people at first depicted all cavemen with an overly hunched back.

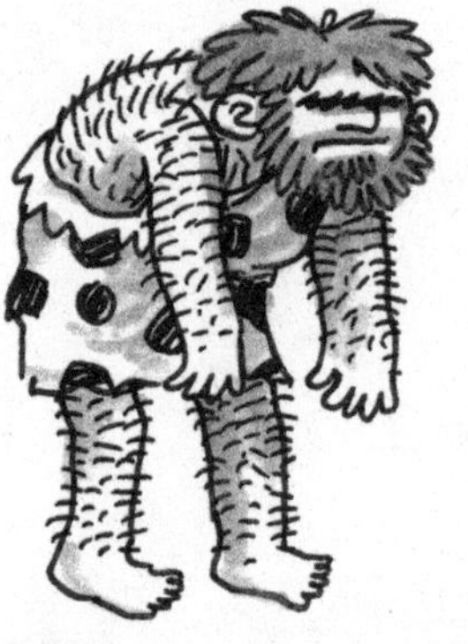

CAVEMEN WERE REALLY, REALLY HAIRY

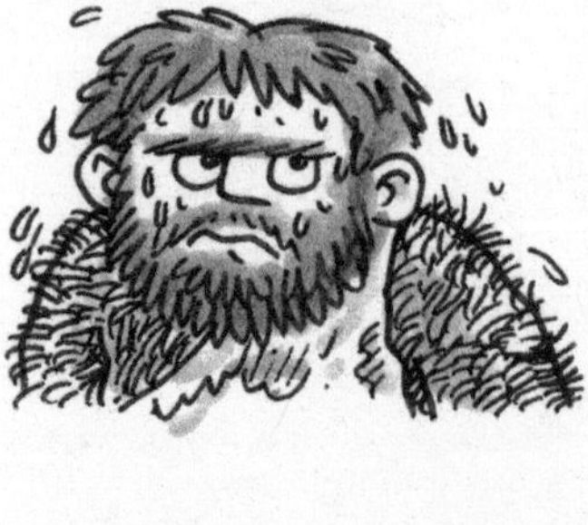

Neanderthals may have been slightly more hairy than humans today, but studies have shown that being too hairy could have caused Neanderthals to overheat— even in a cold climate!

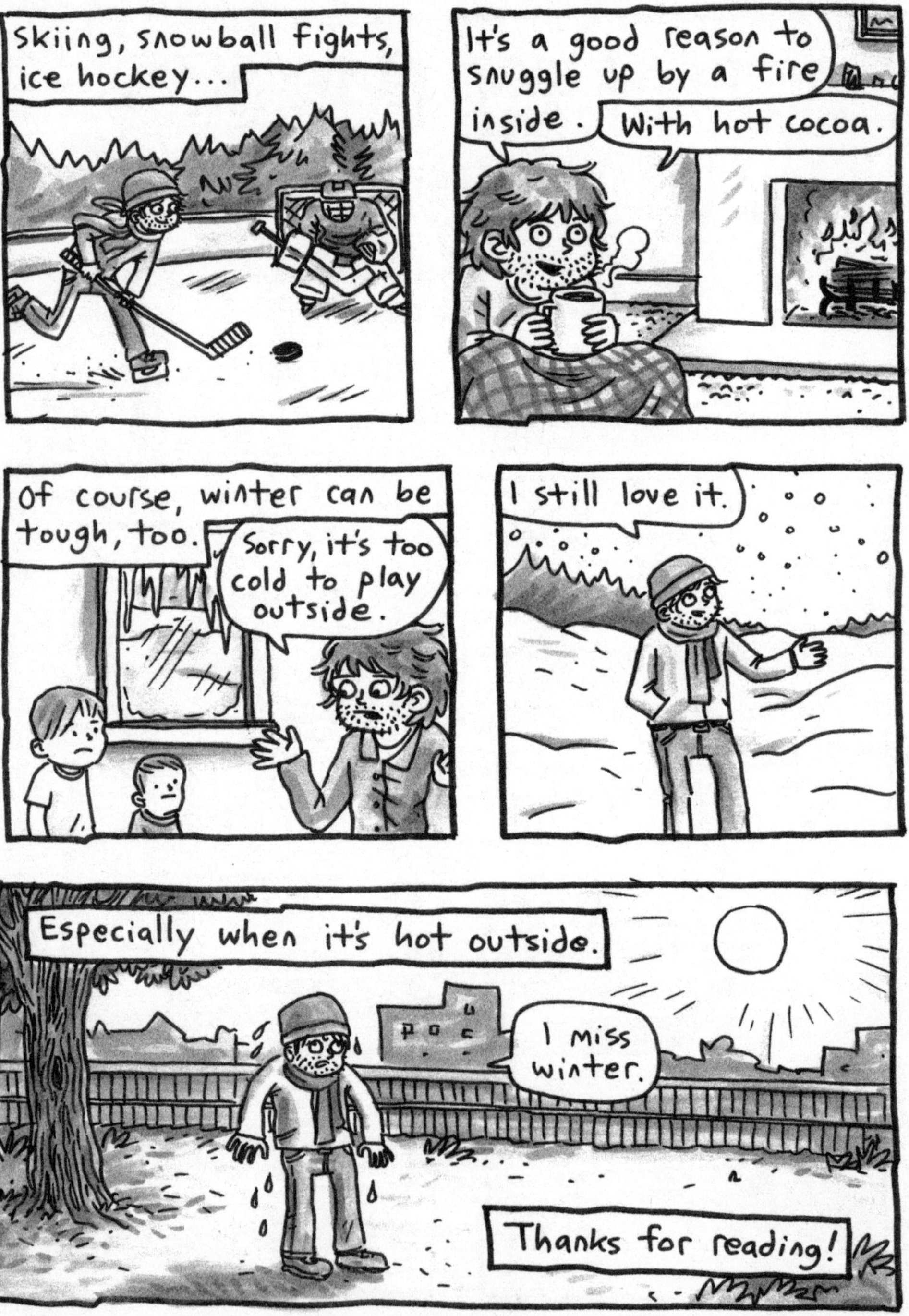
Skiing, snowball fights, ice hockey...
It's a good reason to snuggle up by a fire inside.
With hot cocoa.
Of course, winter can be tough, too.
Sorry, it's too cold to play outside.
I still love it.
Especially when it's hot outside.
I miss winter.
Thanks for reading!

THINGS GET WILD IN THE NEXT LUCY & ANDY ADVENTURE!

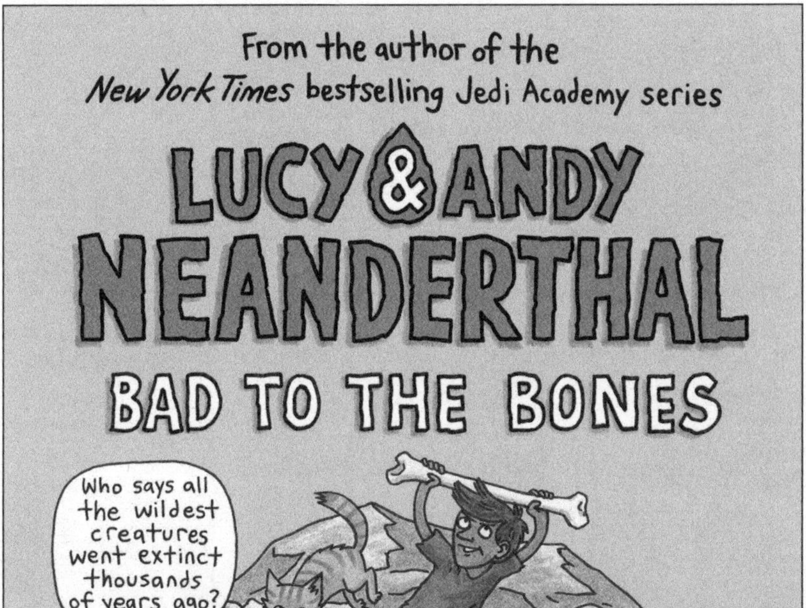
From the author of the
New York Times bestselling Jedi Academy series
LUCY & ANDY
NEANDERTHAL
BAD TO THE BONES
Who says all the wildest creatures went extinct thousands of years ago?
Jeffrey Brown

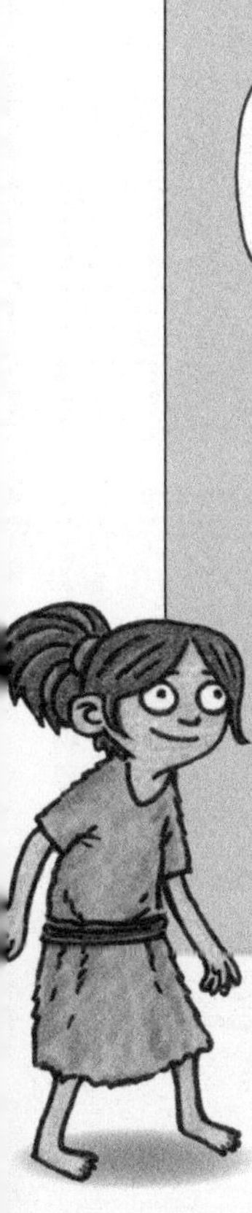

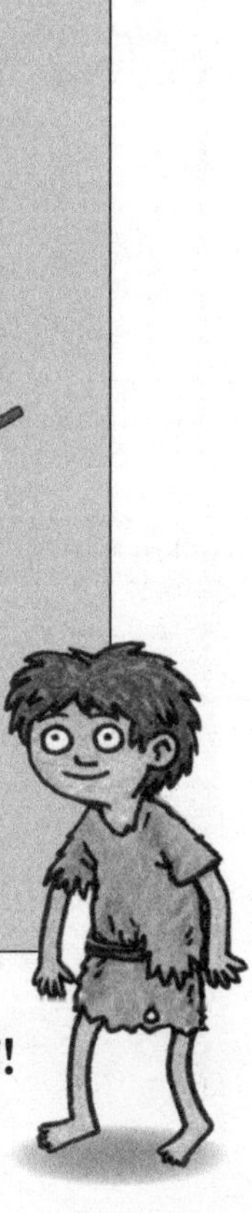

Don't miss *LUCY & ANDY: BAD TO THE BONES*!

COMING SOON!

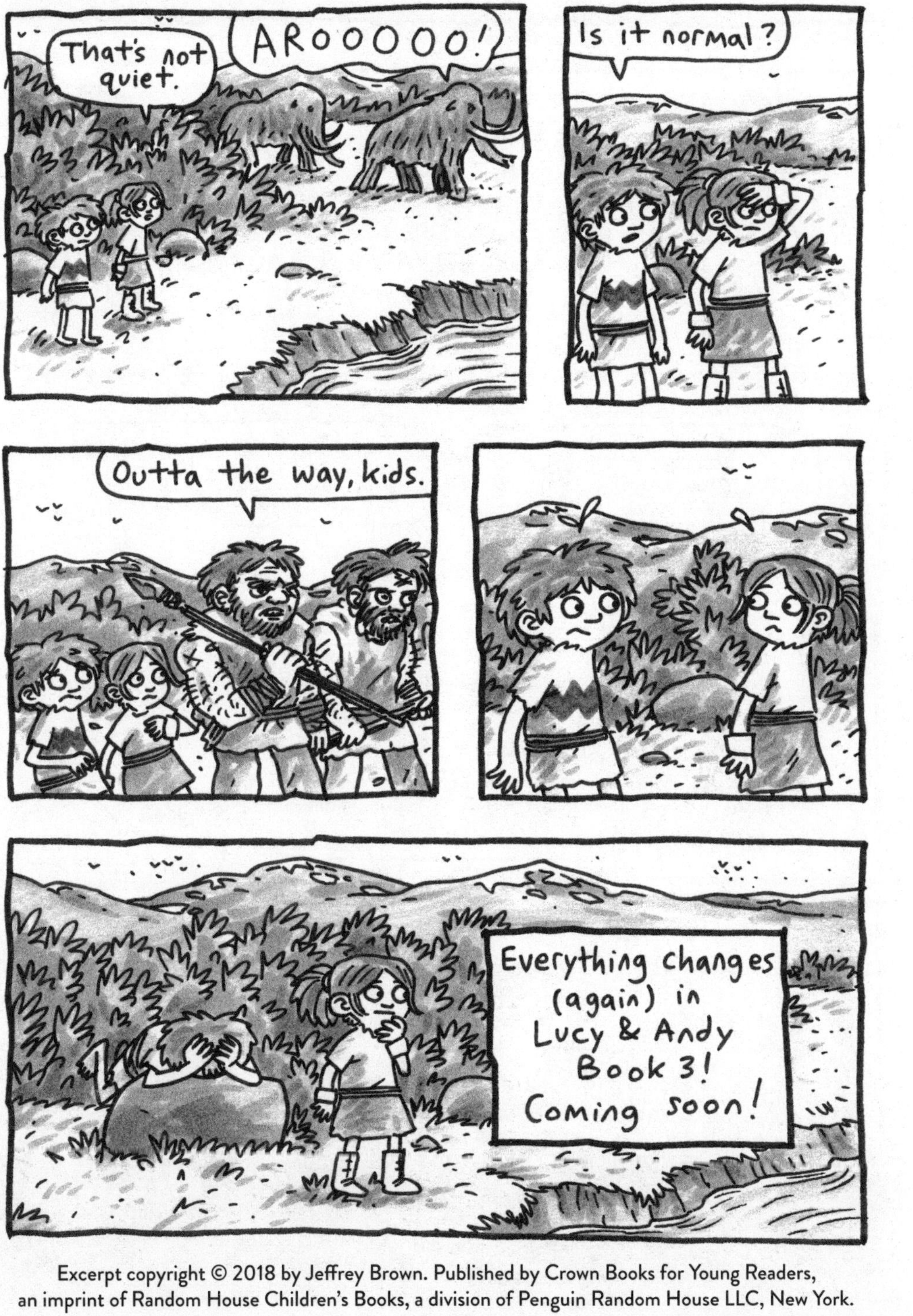
That's not quiet.
AROOOOO!
Is it normal?
Outta the way, kids.
Everything changes (again) in Lucy & Andy Book 3! Coming soon!

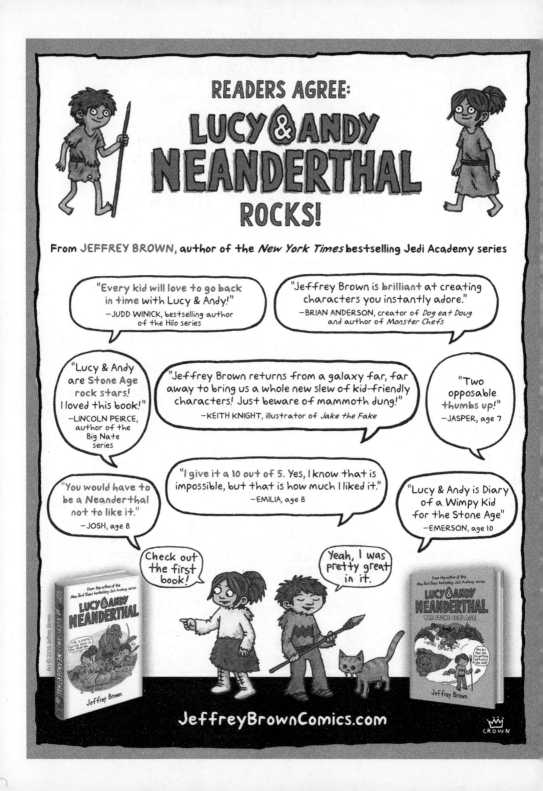